They call her
TAMARA . . .

She's small and dark, free and daring, the daughter of the rich lawyer Charles Armitage, but her love is the son of a carpenter. She's tagged along with Mark Martin, learned to swim with him in the river, to pound nails at his side as he follows his father's trade. And now that the rebels have begun to fight the British, she'll chop off her long hair and wear boy's clothes to serve at the Temptation tavern and spy on the British. She'll put her skill at carpentry to use as the only woman building ships in Boston harbor. She'll sew up a wound to save the life of the man her sister loves.

For Tamara, her sisters,
her brother Ned and the
people they love in Boston,
the battles of the Revolution
change the course of life,
banish the distinctions of
class and mark new beginnings.

Novels by
Lydia Lancaster

Desire and Dreams of Glory
Passion and Proud Hearts
Stolen Rapture
The Temptation

Published by
WARNER BOOKS

The Temptation

by Lydia Lancaster

A Warner Communications Company

WARNER BOOKS EDITION

ISBN 0-446-81771-6

Cover Art by Tom Hall

Warner Books, Inc., 75 Rockefeller Plaza, New York, N.Y. 10019

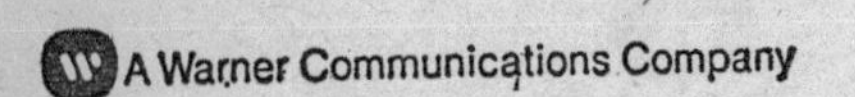

Printed in the United States of America

First Printing: November, 1979

10 9 8 7 6 5 4 3 2 1

The Temptation

One

From his vantage point on the stable roof, Luke Martin had a clear view of the back of Charles Armitage's house and the comings and goings of the servants. Watching the activities was almost as good as seeing a stage play at Drury Lane, back in London, he thought, as he ripped up the old, curled shingles preparatory to replacing them with new ones. Luke had only arrived in Boston yesterday, with just enough money to keep himself until he could find permanent employment. He had carried a duffel bag containing a change of clothing, and his chest of tools, the latter of secondary importance only to his life.

When he'd walked from Widow Greene's boardinghouse at sunup, his first sight of the house itself had brought a whistle of surprise to his lips. It wasn't that it was enormously large or ornate. He'd seen many larger houses in London, particularly the town houses of the nabobs. Built of wood, as were most of the houses in Boston, the clapboards were narrow and the windows many-paned, and it was set on a narrow lot that ran deep in the back, giving ample room for gardens and outbuildings. Still, it spoke of a prosperity that Luke hadn't expected in the quiet-spoken, conservatively dressed gentleman who had so kindly offered him work when they'd met at The Temptation, a workingman's tavern, last evening. Lawyering must be profitable here in the New World.

A movement below him caught his eye as he raised his hand to wipe away the sweat on his forehead. The day was coming on hot, and as it was still a bit before midday he wondered how much hotter this Boston could get. A woman had come to the back door to throw out a bowlful of scraps to the fowl in the chickenyard, and then paused to exchange a few words with a gardener who was weeding the kitchen garden. As she was plainly dressed, with graying hair nearly hidden by an equally plain cap, Luke surmised that she must be a servant, probably the cook. That made four servants that he'd seen so far. Jonas, a black man who had said he was Mr. Armitage's personal servant, had been watching out for him when he'd arrived and had directed him to the stable and pointed out the pile of new shingles and a keg of nails; there was the gardener, and another black man, Abel, who was the coachman, and now the cook. Luke had been pleased to learn that both Jonas and Abel were free. Luke didn't hold with slavery, it went against a man's grain to think of another man being held in bondage, no matter his color.

"You'll be brought a bite to eat at noon, and if there is anything else you need you are to ask Abel, or ask for me at the kitchen," Jonas had told him, his teeth white and smile friendly in his dark face. Then Luke had been left alone, a feeling that brought a great deal of satisfaction to the young carpenter, because it implied trust that he'd give an honest day's work for an honest day's pay.

Now the man Abel led a saddled horse around to the front of the house and Luke surmised that the lawyer was about to travel farther abroad than he could cover on foot. Luke removed his jacket. His shirt was stuck to his back but he didn't slow his pace as he went on ripping up the old shingles. If he was inclined he could manage to make two or even three days' work of the reshingling, but he had no thought to cheat the man who had befriended him without knowing anything about him except that he was a carpenter, newly arrived, that he knew no one in Boston, and that he was in need of employment. He would finish the job as fast as it could be well done, and he knew that Charles Armitage would be able to find no fault with his workmanship.

He paused only long enough to see if Armitage would come around to the back to see how the work was progressing, but a moment later he heard the horse's hoofs on the driveway. In a way he was disappointed. He'd have liked to see the man again, because he'd been favorably impressed with him last night, putting him down as a gentleman who was fair and honest and who did not look down on those of a lesser social standing. Not being looked down on was one of the reasons Luke had decided to shake the centuries-old dust, steeped with social inequities, from his feet to try his luck in this new country where he'd heard that such distinctions were not as clearly defined and that a man could hold his head high and feel inferior to no one, so long as he was honest and industrious.

Even as the hoofbeats faded away, a little girl no more than four years old came around the corner of the house. Her hair was fair and curled around her face from the heat, and she was walking as fast as she could. From what Luke could see of her, she was an extraordinarily beautiful little creature, and he wondered what her mother might look like. The lawyer's wife must be an uncommonly comely lady to have mothered the child, who was too well dressed to be one of the servants' children and who was obviously, from the surreptitious manner in which she kept looking back over her shoulder, trying to avoid adult supervision.

The child headed straight for the stable and to Luke's consternation she began to climb the ladder to the roof. It took him only seconds to scramble down and intercept her.

"Here, now, ladders are no place for a little lady! You'd best come with me." Luke held fast to the tiny hand, damp in his own, after he'd transported her back to the safety of solid ground. "I'll take you to the kitchen, likely they'll know what to do with you."

The child kicked his shin. The attack caught him by surprise and he let go of her to hop up and down on one foot, choking down a word that wasn't fit for the ears of one so young. A small pink tongue stuck out at him as she turned and ran.

Little demon! For her age, she ran very fast. She had rounded the side of the house before Luke caught up with her. He made a grab for her arm, and she opened her mouth and screamed with rage at the same moment that the mistress of the house stepped outside the front door.

"How dare you! Take your hands off my child this instant!"

Although Luke had lived all of his life in London and had seen many famous beauties passing in their sedan chairs and carriages, he had never beheld such a vision of loveliness as the lady who stood in front of him, her face flushed with haughty anger. Like the child's, her hair was a light golden blond, elaborately dressed under a morning cap. Her eyes were a startling blue, so deep that they seemed violet, and lashed with deep brown that was echoed in her delicately arched brows. Her complexion was faultless, unlike that of so many of those London beauties whose faces were marred by the use of cosmetics that contained arsenic or lead, or other destructive ingredients that proved disastrous all too soon.

"He hurt me, Mama! He chased me and he hurt me!" The child ran to take refuge behind her mother's skirts, looking out at him from that haven to stick her tongue out at him again.

"I was only trying to keep her from harm. She started to climb the ladder to the stable roof. No one was with her to watch her." Luke was quick to defend himself against the outrageous charge. "I'm the carpenter Mr. Armitage hired to replace the shingles."

The look the vision gave him was unlike any he had ever been given by a female before. Some of those great ladies he had seen in London had glanced at him but it had been obvious that they hadn't seen him, for a person of his station was beneath their notice. This look was different. It made him feel like a worm, like some white and nauseous creature that had crawled out from under a rock, as if such an abomination had no business inhabiting the same earth that she inhabited. He felt anger rise in him, a thing that seldom happened because by nature he was good-humored and able to shake off life's petty slights as of no consequence.

"Then your place is on the stable roof, not wandering around the grounds molesting children. I'll speak to my husband about this when he returns. In the meantime, get back where you belong and do not presume to trespass where you have no business to be!"

She did not raise her voice, but the icy contempt of her voice made Luke's blood roil. Without looking at him again, Mistress Armitage took her small daughter by the hand and went back into the house. Once inside, she did raise her voice, in a way that boded no good for the person for whom she was calling. "Martha, come here this instant! How dare you let Lillian evade you!"

Another little head poked around the edge of the open door. Also fair, also extraordinarily beautiful although not quite as beautiful as either her mother or her sister, this child was no more than two, but for all that she possessed a remarkable vocabulary. "Lillian is naughty. Martha's nice and now she'll be in trouble. Mama's a bitch."

Luke's mouth fell open. Shaking his head, he returned to the stable and resumed his work. After a moment he began to chuckle in spite of his anger. So Mama was a bitch! He was mightily inclined to agree with the younger child. He wondered where such an infant had picked up such a word.

Then his smile faded and his mouth tightened. Likely he would be discharged before the work was completed, because of the older brat and her mother. He went on working at a steady pace. He'd do the best he could for the lawyer before that beautiful shrew he had married demanded his ejection from the property.

He hoped that the lawyer would be fair enough to recommend him to others, in spite of his wife. If he wasn't, so be it. Luke was young and strong, and he could always get by. If he hadn't been sure of that, he would have stayed in London.

The day grew even hotter, and he was grateful for the shade of the huge maple that dappled the roof where he was working. Absorbed in his work, this time he failed to notice the movement below him until a girl's voice called out to him.

"Hello up there!"

Luke lifted his head and looked down. This was a younger woman than the one who had thrown the scraps to the chickens, a good deal younger, no more than nineteen or twenty. She was carrying something wrapped in a napkin in her right hand, and a wooden mug in the other. From this height, she was foreshortened, but the face that looked up at him was fresh and comely. Her eyes were blue and the hair that showed under her cap was light brown, and she was dressed in a plain gray muslin, enveloped with a large white apron.

"Hello down there!"

"Come down. I've brought your dinner."

Luke lost no time in complying. He was ravenous, having last eaten well before daylight, and that only a piece of bread and cheese because Widow Greene had not yet prepared breakfast for her boarders.

On the ground where he could see the girl better, he discovered that the figure that had appeared plump from the stable was merely well rounded. His eyes lighted up with appreciation when he noted the curves set off a slender waist. At the same time, the girl knew that she liked what she saw, and he liked what he saw, and pleasure surged through him.

"It'll be cool there under the maple tree," the girl told him. She looked at him with unfeigned curiosity, admiring his broad shoulders and more-than-average height, his muscular arms and the way his hair, darker than hers, curled over his forehead from his morning's exertions. "Are you bound or free?"

"Free. And you?"

"Bound. Mistress Armitage's father chose me to accompany her from England when she and Mr. Armitage were married. Mr. Edmonton had been a military man and my father used to be his sergeant. My father liked gaming too well and he was in debt, and Major Edmonton settled his debts in return for seven years of my service. I still have nearly a year to serve."

The cider in the wooden mug was good, and the bread had been baked that morning. The mutton was done to a turn and well seasoned, with no hint of the taint that mutton bought from a London stall was apt to have in hot weather. Luke ate and drank with relish. "Is Mistress Armitage a good mistress to you?"

"I do my work, except when Lillian gets away from me. I'm sorry you got in trouble as well as me this morning when the imp ran off, but you needn't worry overmuch about it. Mr. Armitage never allows any of his servants, or anyone he hires, to be punished without reason."

Luke felt a quick relief. Maybe he wouldn't be sent off before this job was done, after all. "She's a beautiful woman, for all her sharp tongue. Is she always so hard to get along with?"

The girl beside him sat down on the grass to wait for him to finish eating. "She despises this new country and only wants to go back to England and her fine friends there. The marriage was of her father's arranging. Some of the gentry in London have gone stark wild, and her father wanted her married to a sober man and removed from there. You're lucky not to be bound. For all Mr. Armitage is so kind, I'll be glad when my time is up and I'll be free."

"You aren't married?" It didn't hurt to be sure.

"No, nor can I be until my bond is up. That was one of the stipulations, that I would not wed until my term of service is over, unless Mistress Armitage herself gives me permission, and she will not." The girl was perfectly frank. "I've had offers, plenty of them, women aren't as plentiful as men over here, and any woman can find herself a husband if she isn't too choosy."

Looking at her, Luke thought that Martha—that was what Mistress Armitage had called her—could have found a husband any place in the world she abided. Close up, her curves were even more delectable than they'd seemed from a distance. The kerchief that was crossed over her breasts only emphasized what lay beneath it, no matter how modest her garb. Her skin was like peaches and cream, so that he knew, without touching it, that it would be soft and silky, enough to drive a man to distraction. She'd be an armful for any man, and more. And from the warmth in her eyes, a willing one, provided that she liked the man in question.

"You'd be content to stay here in Boston?"

"I like it here. There are five younger than me at home, and I've no mind to return. I'm twenty years old, already a spinster, but in spite of that I'll be able to pick and choose once I'm free."

"If Mr. Armitage is so kind, why doesn't he make his wife allow you to marry?"

"It's not only the contract, but he gave his word to Major Edmonton, and the gentleman is dead now and Mr. Armitage isn't one to break his word to a dead man. He's tried to persuade his wife to let me wed, but she'll have none of it, and his honor won't let him go against her wishes after he'd promised her father. Major Edmonton liked me, he knew I'd be a good maidservant to Mistress Millicent, and so he wanted to make sure that I'd stay with her here in this new country."

Martha stood up and stretched, her breasts swelling under her snug bodice in a way that made the blood rush to Luke's head. "I must get back now. There's no telling what that imp Lillian will be up to. Annabelle's no trouble at all but Lillian must have been spawned in . . ." she broke off, her hand over her mouth but her eyes dancing with merriment. "Never mind. Will you be here again tomorrow?"

"The work will take at least another day. Your name is Martha, isn't it?"

"Martha Simpkins."

"I'm Luke Martin. Maybe we'll see each other tomorrow."

He watched the swish of Martha's skirts as she entered the house through the kitchen doorway, and then he climbed back up the ladder and resumed his work. He began to whistle as he worked. Things were looking up. Martha liked him, and he liked her. She wasn't promised to anyone else, and if he was half the man his erstwhile London companions had thought he was, he could get her for himself if he decided he wanted her. Coming to America had been the smartest thing he'd ever done.

He paid a second visit to The Temptation that evening. Escape seemed essential when Widow Greene cornered him as soon as he returned from his work, disappointed because the lawyer hadn't returned home in time to inspect what he had done so far.

Patience Greene was by no means satisfied with the little she had learned about her new boarder when he'd come to her home on Milk Street and said that Lawyer Armitage had recommended him. She liked to know all there was to know about any boarder she allowed under her roof. A woman couldn't be too careful, especially a widow with no husband to protect both her property and her good name. He had not, she pointed out, divulged the denomination of the church he had attended in London, nor convinced her that he was not a tippler. She was everything that Eli Bates, the proprietor of The Temptation, had told Luke that she was, along with the warning not to tell her that Eli had recommended him to her. Sharp, nosy, self-righteous, she was one of those good women that any man worthy of the name did his best to avoid. But her house was clean, Eli had told him, and she set a good table.

Eli himself looked up and nodded to Luke as he entered The Temptation, and Luke had no sooner found a place for himself on a bench than he came over with a mug of cider and put it down in front of him, waving aside Luke's gesture of finding the pence to pay for it.

"This one's on me. How did you find the widow? As fiesty as ever?"

"She seems a decent woman," Luke said cautiously. He tried not to stare at the middle-aged man's head, completely bald on top and seeming to have been badly mutilated at some time in the past. In other respects, Eli was as thin as a rail, had a lively interest in other people and a humorous twinkle in his eyes.

The sparkle deepened when Eli saw how hard Luke was trying not to stare.

"Injuns," he said. "They lifted my hair. 'Twas in the French and Injun wars, up Canada way. It made me lose my taste for woods runnin'. I've been content to be a tavernkeeper ever since. It's less excitin' but a deal safer. You haven't told me how you found the widow. Is she as mean as ever?"

"She seems to be a good landlady." Luke had learned long since that it was the better part of discretion to say too little rather than too much.

Eli laughed, showing that he still had a good share of his teeth in spite of his age.

"Too blamed decent, that's the rub! Wait right where you are, young feller. I have something I want to show you."

He was back in less than a minute, although it took Luke longer than that to recognize him because he'd removed his apron and put on a wig. The wig was jet black and tied back in a queue and stood out in violent contrast to his weatherbeaten face.

"Do you like it? How do I look?" Eli turned this way and that, preening himself, showing off his adornment from all angles. "Makes me look younger, doesn't it? Makes me look like a respectable man! Patience Greene's eyes'll pop out come Sunday meetin'! I always go to meetin'. It's the only place she can't tell me what she thinks of me. She'll look twice this time, she'll see me as I really am!"

Luke choked on his cider. She'd look twice at him, all right—she'd have to in order to recognize him! Luke only hoped that she wouldn't burst right out laughing. There was one thing, though: As long as the widow was hell-bent on forcing him to accompany her to church, there'd at least be the entertainment of seeing her reaction to this bandy rooster's new coxcomb.

"It looks fine, Eli." The given name came naturally.

"I think so, too. I paid dear for it but it's goin' to be worth every shilling."

The other men in the tavern were hiding their smiles either behind their hands or their mugs, but even so Eli was going to notice their amusement at any moment. To provide a distraction, Luke asked a question.

"Do you think that Mr. Armitage will come in tonight? I got off on the wrong foot with Mistress Armitage and I'm not sure he'll want me back."

Every eye in the room was on him now, as the

other patrons of The Temptation pricked up their ears. Eli forgot his tonsorial ornament and gave a great snort.

"Her! Far's I kin see, anybody in the world'ud get off on the wrong foot with her! Hoity-toity, Queen of the May! It was a sad day for the lawyer when he married that one, for all she brought him a heap of money. Not that he married her for the money, mind you, you needn't think that, because he didn't. No, the unfortunate man loves her. . . ."

Eli broke off and swallowed as if he had a mouthful of something vile, and clamped his mouth shut and glared around at the other men in the room. "Enough of that! It ain't for the likes of us to talk about Mr. Armitage's wife in a tavern. You'll all kindly forget what I said."

Heads nodded, and the faces were serious now. It was apparent that the lawyer was well liked and that not one of the men present would discuss Eli's outburst. Luke breathed a sigh of relief that it had ended when it had, because Mr. Armitage himself chose that moment to enter the tavern.

"Eli, you look magnificent! You'll have half the single ladies in Boston running after you the first time you wear that wig on the streets. Luke, I want a word with you." Charles sat down beside Luke and asked for a glass of punch.

Luke waited. All eyes and ears had turned their way but the lawyer seemed to take no notice. Older than Luke by only a few years, Charles Armitage had a thin, sensitive face and grave eyes that nevertheless held friendliness toward all his fellow men. As he had the night before, Luke once again felt that here was a man who could be trusted.

"I looked at the work you did today, and I'm well

satisfied with it. I'll expect you back tomorrow to finish it."

Luke drew a breath of relief. Martha had been right: Charles Armitage was not an unreasonable man who would take his wife's part no matter how wrong she was.

"I'll be there. And Mr. Armitage, would you have any objection if I asked Martha Simpkins to walk out with me?"

"None at all. You understand that she cannot marry for another several months, of course?"

"She told me that. I'm in no position to think of wedding, anyway, right now."

"There is just one thing. Martha is a fine girl, and she is under my protection." The lawyer looked at Luke steadily, and Luke felt uncomfortable. The implication was plain. There were to be no fun and games with Martha. He would be welcome to court her, with marriage in mind, and that was all.

Well, that wasn't so bad, once he came to think of it. He was twenty-three, he had a whole new life ahead of him in this new country, and a wife, provided that she was the right one, would be more help than hindrance to him. A man liked his comforts, and he hadn't had many of those since his mother had died. There wouldn't be any hurry about deciding, anyway. He and Martha would have to get to know each other better first, and then they'd see if the attraction they'd felt for each other at their first meeting was a permanent one.

Charles Armitage did not stay long. He'd particularly wanted to see the young man he'd met for the first time yesterday evening, to let him know that in spite of the misunderstanding between him and Millicent he was to return to finish his work. He drank his punch, and spoke briefly but warmly with most of the men who were in the tavern, and then he left.

The lawyer was well aware that it was unusual for a man of his wealth and position to frequent a tavern such as The Temptation. Most of his social equals patronized either The Royal Coffee House or The Bunch of Grapes, and never set foot in a lowlier establishment patronized by common workingmen.

But if Charles had been asked who was more important to the growth and prosperity of the colonies, an artisan or a lawyer, he would have replied that lawyers could be dispensed with before any good workman, a man who knew how to build and who wasn't afraid of honest toil. The earliest settlements had proved that, over and over. They'd failed because of a lack of good workmen and a surfeit of gentlemen adventurers. Gentlemen had their place, but the world turned by the efforts of the workingman. The gentlemen of his acquaintance were long on theory and dissertation, but if you wanted to know which way the political wind blew, it was better to listen to the common man.

He'd walked to the tavern, and he walked back. His horse had done a day's work and needed its rest, and he liked the exercise. It gave him a breathing space before he had to face Millicent and her constant complaints about America, where there was little amusement and few friends of her own standing, and those so dull that she was perishing of boredom.

Charles Armitage loved his wife. He'd loved her enough to want to marry her, even knowing the wild companions she had run with in London. He'd hoped that he'd be able to win her love in return and that they could build a rich and satisfying life in Boston, far from the corruption of the Old World.

But it hadn't turned out that way. His own life was rewarding enough. He liked his work, he liked the men he knew, he had a lively interest in people from all walks of life and no feeling of superiority to those less fortunate than himself. But he had failed to win Millicent's love. It was a cause of deep sorrow to him, especially as he went right on loving her in spite of her coldness and discontent.

If he had it to do over, he wouldn't have insisted on the marriage that Millicent so obviously hadn't wanted. She still believed that he had been influenced by the dowry that she'd brought with her. Actually, the money had meant little to him. He'd had enough, from his father, to live on in comfort even without working, and wealth for wealth's sake meant little to him. But it was too late now. Divorce was unthinkable, even if there hadn't been the two children, both of whom he loved dearly even though they were girls.

There was still time to get a son. That was one area where Millicent agreed with him, although for different reasons. Millicent wanted a son to inherit from her uncle, her father's older brother, who held both a title and a fortune and who had never married so that he had no son of his own to inherit. To Millicent, fortune and title were all-important, and as long as there were no other male heirs to inherit, she was willing to suffer Charles' lovemaking often enough to try to produce a son.

Millicent looked up from her chair by the curtained windows when Charles entered his drawing room a few moments later. She was dressed as elaborately as if she'd been expecting guests, her hair piled high on her head, two long, silken curls falling over a creamy shoulder. She was even more beautiful in her young maturity than she had been when they had been married, except for the petulance that habitually marred the perfection of her mouth.

She placed one delicate finger between the pages of the periodical she'd been reading, and frowned. "So you finally deigned to come home! I suppose you've been in that despicable tavern again, consorting with the scum that frequents it."

"I've been at The Temptation, yes." Charles kept the sigh he felt inside him from entering his voice. "But it's still early, Millicent. You have little cause to complain. Most of your friends' husbands remain away much later than this, as a matter of nightly habit."

"And I suppose you've told that despicable workman to return tomorrow, in spite of his inexcusable behavior!"

"His behavior was not inexcusable, my dear. If he'd allowed our daughter to climb the ladder to the stable roof, and perhaps fall and injure herself, that would have been inexcusable."

"Pah! Why can't you remember who you are? Why must you always align yourself with common men, men who aren't fit to wipe the dust from your boots?" Millicent's voice rose, became shrill as it always did when their opinions differed. "Have you given any thought to our visiting London this summer? I'll swear you haven't! It isn't that you can't well afford it, you simply take pleasure in thwarting me!"

"We have no valid reason for making such a long voyage. I have my work, Millicent. And all of our friends are here." There was no point in arguing with her, Charles knew that from past experience. He could only stand firm for what he felt to be right. London, the London Millicent yearned for, was not a fit place for his children, let alone his wife. She must content herself here.

It wasn't that he wanted to deny her anything that would make her happy. But he knew that once he took her back to London, it would be virtually impossible to persuade her to return to Boston. The only thing that kept her with him as it was, was her lack of sufficient funds to live in the manner she demanded, and so he was forced to keep her short of money. He could neither allow her to raise their children in the kind of society she craved, nor to take them from her and raise them himself, motherless. As it were, Lillian already gave fair intimation that given even a modicum of chance, she would turn out exactly like her mother, shallow, selfish, intent only on her own pleasure. He shuddered to think what would become of her if she were to be reared in Millicent's London, to say nothing of what might happen to their gentler younger daughter.

All thoughts of a peaceful, contented hour at home with his wife before they retired left him. Millicent would turn from his embraces again tonight, as she did whenever he displeased her. This time his sigh escaped him.

"I've had a long day. I'll go to bed now, if you will excuse me."

Shrugging, her face cold, Millicent returned to her book of fashions. Charles made his way upstairs, where he looked in on his little daughters. Sleeping, even Lillian looked like a cherub, and Annabelle was one in truth, at least so far. Gazing down at them as they slept, their faces luminous in the moonlight that filtered in through the windows, he hardened his heart to giving in to Millicent to the detriment of his daughters' futures.

As it happened, Luke did not see Martha the next day. It was the cook who brought him out his noonday meal and she did not volunteer any information, but before he had finished eating, the younger of the two little girls came out and, hands behind her back, regarded him solemnly.

"You're Luke Martin," she said. "Mama doesn't like you."

"That's right." Luke took a deep draught of cider. It was taking him a while to get used to it, but cider rather than good English ale or beer seemed to be the rule here in Boston and so he supposed that he'd have to accustom himself to it. "And you're Annabelle."

"Martha likes you."

"Can't she come and tell me so herself?"

"Mama won't let her. But Martha told me to tell you she can't come out. I'd like a piece of cheese, please."

Luke broke off a piece of cheese and gave it to her. She ate it gravely, never taking her eyes from his face.

"I'd like a drink of cider, too."

"No cider." How did he know if the child was allowed cider? He didn't want her mother out here again, charging him with some crime.

But it wasn't Mistress Millicent who appeared, but Lillian, her face screwed up with displeasure at finding her baby sister consorting with an oaf. She cast Luke a look that was meant to wither him and took her sister by the hand, yanking her away.

"I'll tell Mama! You aren't supposed to talk to hired men, you naughty girl! Come away this instant!" She sounded, Luke thought, torn between amusement and pity for this child who had to contend with both Mistress Millicent and her older sister, exactly like a miniature version of her mother.

"I like you!" Annabelle managed to fling over her shoulder before her sister dragged her from sight.

The man Jonas came out just as Luke had nailed

the last shingle in place shortly before five in the afternoon.

"Mr. Armitage instructed me to tell you that you are to apply to a Mr. Peters, a builder, about employment. He said that Eli would tell you where to find him." The black man's face was impassive but there was a glint of humor in his eyes as he added, "Mr. Armitage instructed me to tell you that the family attends services at the Cockerel."

"The servants too, Jonas?"

"That is so." Jonas inclined his head and left him, but Luke had the distinct impression that the servants in this house did not mind seeing their mistress thwarted.

Luke had been brought up as a strict Lutheran but he wasn't averse to trying out another denomination. He had been of a mind to attend the Episcopal Church, to see how he'd like it, here in this new land. He had already heard the bells of Christ Church, and they were the sweetest he'd ever heard. Boston was filled with churches, their bells ringing out at all hours of the day. For all its rowdy element and its stews, which Eli had taken pains to warn him against, this must be a mightily God-fearing town.

Eli, when he asked him that evening, not only knew how the Cockerel had come by its name, but also he was only too glad to pass on his knowledge, being a man who liked a good story.

"Seems that some of the members of New North had a disagreement with other members, and split off from it. They built themselves a church they could run to their own liking, and called it the New Brick. Others called it the Revenge Church. But then Deacon Drowne made a monstrous cock out of some brass kettles, and they stuck it on top of the steeple for a weather vane. I wasn't around at the time but the story is that some man climbed up the spire and got himself astraddle of the cock and crowed at New North, once 'twas in place. And the name the Cockerel just sort of stuck."

Luke looked at him suspiciously, but decided that the older man was telling the truth. The story was good enough to warrant another mug of cider.

The Cockerel was on Middle Street, and Luke would have had no trouble in finding it even if Widow Greene had not accompanied him, it being the church she attended. The copper weather vane stood out like a landmark.

His interview with Mr. Peters, a rotund man with shrewd eyes, had gone well. Mr. Peters was willing to give him a week's trial, with an eye to discharging another workman who liked his cups too well, if Luke's work passed muster. Henry Atkins, the other carpenter, was too apt to show up late for work, or not at all, for Mr. Peters' liking. As Luke had no doubt that he could give satisfaction, things looked good for him.

Eli Bates was there before them, and for a moment the widow's eyes remained blank as he bowed to her. Then they widened with shock and her face went so white, and then so red, that Luke was afraid that she was about to be taken with a seizure. He hoped he would not be forced to escort her home before he had a chance to see Martha and decide whether or not she was as delectable as he'd thought she was, and worth the restrictions imposed on him by Mr. Armitage.

Then, to Luke's consternation, Patience Greene spoke so audibly that the gathering congregation heard every word.

"Look at that old fool! A banty rooster masquerading as a peacock! He was ugly enough before but now he's nothing short of ludicrous!"

Eli's face went redder than the widow's had been

a moment before. He was a stricken man, but even so he recovered himself with remarkable rapidity.

" 'Morning, Luke. If you'll stop by to see me one day, I'll be glad to recommend a good place for you to board now that you'll be able to afford something better. The Widow Clark would be glad to take an upright, steady young man, and her table is the best in Boston."

The two antagonists glared at each other until glances of outrage and a few "Shhh's" forced them to move on into the church. Luke had only a brief glimpse of Martha, sitting well to the back, as was proper for a servant. It was Annabelle, the younger child, who slipped a piece of paper, folded very small, into Luke's hand as she walked sedately down the aisle to one of the favored, reserved pews, with their renters' nameplates on them, with her family.

Luke had no chance to read the note until he was in the privacy of his attic room at Widow Greene's. The handwriting was untutored, and the spelling so bad that he could hardly decipher it.

"Tonit, at the hr of tn, undr the mpl tree. Do not cum to the huse, she wld hev yu snt awa."

Whatever Martha's duties were, Luke thought, serving as the children's governess was decidedly not one of them. He was grateful that his own father had used the birch as regularly as the schoolmaster to insure that he obtain such schooling as they could afford, in spite of his inclination to play hookey. A little book-learning stood a man in good stead and Luke silently apologized to his strict, hard-working father who'd wanted his son to obtain more education than he'd been privileged to come by, having been apprenticed out as a carpenter at the age of ten.

Luke's father was dead now, a full twelve years

after his mother, a gentle woman who had done much to mitigate his father's sternness, had died. His father's passing was what had decided him to try his luck here in America, and he was grateful now that the hard-working man had been careful enough with his money so that there'd been enough left to pay his passage and he could come over as a free man.

And so at the hour of ten, Luke waited under the maple tree that grew beside Mr. Armitage's stable. Martha was so late in coming that he was at the point of leaving in disgust, when she finally slipped out of the house to join him.

She was breathless as she apologized. "She kept me late. I'm sorry you had to wait, but I won't be able to stay long. Lillian can't be trusted to stay in bed, and if she was caught wandering around the house I'd be in for it. Mistress Armitage is in a bad mood tonight."

Tentatively, Luke put his arms around her. Her reaction set him back on his heels and sent the blood racing through his body, hot and pounding. She pressed herself against him, her arms going around his neck, her face lifted to his, barely discernible in the starlight. "Aren't you going to kiss me?"

He kissed her, and that was a mistake. Things were going too fast. He'd kissed a good many girls in his life, but none of them had affected him as this one did. Her skin smelled sweet, it felt like silk, only warm and vibrant, filled with life, to the touch. He felt himself tremble. Lord, but she was an armful!

His voice sounded thick when he finally held her away from him to get himself back under control. "Do you always kiss men like this, after you've just met them?"

"No. Only I have a special feeling about you, and I had to find out if I was right about it. I think maybe

I was. At least I liked it just now. I liked it a lot, more than I ever did with the others. You're a lot of man, Luke Martin. Maybe you're the man I want. Maybe I'm glad that Mistress Armitage never let me walk out, or get married, until you got here."

Her honesty pleased him, and he made to draw her into his arms again. But this time she was the one who pulled away.

"No. Not now. I have to get back. But I'll come out again tomorrow night, if you want to come back."

She'd slipped away from him before the protest rose to his lips, and after his initial disappointment he was just as glad. He'd never known a girl like Martha before, and if she'd stayed he wouldn't have been responsible for his behavior, and then Mr. Armitage would have been severely displeased with him. He had a notion that if Mr. Armitage were to withdraw his friendship, he'd find almost all other doors in Boston closed to him. Just because he'd felt his body turn into a pillar of fire when Martha had kissed him was no reason to ruin his chances here in the New World.

"I'll be damned!" he muttered to himself, as he started back to the boardinghouse.

At the widow's he found himself doubly damned. Patience Greene had locked the door for the night, and he was faced with either pounding on it to rouse her to admit him, rousing the entire neighborhood at the same time, or spending the night outside.

He hoped that it wouldn't rain.

Two

Samuel Peters was not an easy man to work for, but Luke had worked for worse. Mr. Peters was hard to please but he knew good craftsmanship when he saw it, and as long as a man was steady and reliable that man was assured of steady employment. So with his immediate future assured, Luke turned his mind to the next most pressing problem, that of his involvement with Martha.

There were no women to be had at The Temptation, even if Luke had been desperate for feminine companionship. Eli did not hold with serving girls.

"They're nothing but trouble. A woman's got no business in a man's drinking place, it disrupts things. Besides, what would Patience Greene think if I had women in here?"

He looked at Luke curiously. "You ain't hankering after a woman, are you? I reckon Mistress Armitage chased you off the way she did all the others that took a fancy to Martha."

"She hasn't exactly invited me into the house to bundle with Martha, that's a fact." Luke's grin was wry. "But she hasn't chased me off, either. I don't chase that easy."

"Well, there's plenty of women to be had, if a man knows where to look, and I can tell you. Had plenty of 'em in my day, before I decided to get respectable and settle down. Only if you go get yerself one of them, don't let the widow get wind of it or she'll throw you out on yer ear. And I want you to get in her good graces so you can put in a good word for me now and then, after she gets almighty fond of you."

Luke laughed. "You want a lot. What's in it for me?"

"Free cider. And good advice. Like where to find the entertainment young fellers like you have got to have, and have the women reasonably good-lookin' and reasonably clean."

"I might take you up on that sometime. For now, I guess I can wait." Martha had certainly gotten under his skin. Seeing her wasn't all as easy as Luke made out to Eli, but the way he felt about Martha he didn't want any other girl, no matter if she was reasonably clean and reasonably good-looking and more than reasonably willing to compensate for what he couldn't have with Martha.

For Luke, Sunday was the worst day of the week. Not only was it hard to get up and get going after staying late at Eli's on Saturday night, but also on Sundays he had to sit in church and be all too aware of Martha sitting in the pew behind him, as fresh and exciting as a spring morning. As there was no way to more than speak a civil "good morning" to her under Millicent Armitage's watchful eye, Sundays had become a torment.

But there was no way that Luke could get out of going to church. Sunday meeting was the high social point in Patience Greene's life and she looked forward all week to making careful note of what the ladies wore, storing each detail in her mind to discuss with neighbors who attended different churches and who returned the favor. Since Patience Greene had become almighty fond of her clean-living, hard-working newest boarder, she saw to it that he got to services every Sunday to assure the salvation of his soul.

"Of course Samuel Peters let Henry Atkins go and put you on in his place! Henry Atkins hasn't set foot in a church since he learned to drink hard spirits from a bottle, instead of milk!" Patience said sharply. "He's a damned man, and any who associate with him are likely to be damned along with him, and Samuel Peters is smart enough to know it, whereas a righteous young man like you will help grease his way into heaven. Are you ready to go, Luke? We mustn't be late, it isn't seemly."

Being so near to Martha, without being able to hold her and touch her, fair to drove Luke mad. It was enough to tempt him to hunt up some of those women Eli had told him about.

He didn't do that, mainly because he was convinced that if he did, word of it would somehow get back to Martha, and she wouldn't like it. And if word didn't get back to Martha, it was almost certain to get back to Mr. Armitage, and he wouldn't like it and if he didn't like it Luke's path to the winning and wedding of Martha would be filled with obstacles that would prove well-nigh insurmountable.

But there were other means of distraction, and he sought them out to fill in his time after his working hours. He began to frequent the North End, more to satisfy his curiosity than anything else. It was hard for him to believe, at first, that a city so saturated with churches and the pious people who filled them could have such a shady district as the North End.

The North End itself was a contradiction in terms.

There the homes of the wealthy stood side by side with the lowest houses of ill repute, or so nearly as to make no matter. It was a section abounding in dark alleys and noisome dens populated by pimps and prostitutes, by bullyboys and jacktars, by Irish shillalah boys and sundry other less desirable types of humanity.

On the other hand, the Hutchinsons lived in the North End, and the Clarks, as well as a substantial number of solid, middle-class artisans, brewers, shipwrights, cobblers, cordwainers, bakers, silversmiths, all honest, upright citizens who raised their families in decency and comfort.

But as rich in distraction as the North End was, Luke soon tired of it. It was too hard to stay out of fights, and if he allowed himself to be drawn into them because of his own young animal enthusiasm, word of that would get back to Martha, or to Charles Armitage. As tawdry as the women Eli had spoken of were, in the cover of darkness there was an attraction about their painted faces and gawdy clothing that wasn't always as easy to resist as he'd thought it would be. Luke was far from being a prig. He didn't believe that relieving the itch that all males are born with would necessarily condemn him to perdition. But the chances of contracting another kind of itch, not so easily shed, was too great. Evidence of what that kind of itch did to a human body was all too prevalent. The thought of passing it on to Martha, to the children that he hoped they would have, was a greater determent than any moral values that had been ground into him in his boyhood.

Inevitably, he was drawn back to The Temptation and the company of the two men he had come to admire more than any others he had ever known. He liked Eli for his dry, salty wit and his independence of spirit, and he looked up to Charles Armitage as one of the fairest and most intelligent men he had ever had the privilege of calling friend. To his own astonishment, he found that listening as Mr. Armitage explained matters of political importance to the less well informed held more pleasure than all of the riotous and fleshly amusements he could have indulged in if it hadn't been for Martha.

It was a revelation to him that the affairs of the colonies seemed to be run not from the Statehouse but from the taverns. Every man with the wherewithal for a mug of cider or a leather jack of ale thought that he could manage things better than those appointed over them, and gave positive voice to his opinions. In England, some of the loudmouths would be taken and hanged for treason, but in Boston a man seemed able to utter the most outrageous statements with impunity.

"What's the matter, wouldn't any of them women you been huntin' for give you a tumble?" Eli prodded him, his eyes filled with merriment, when Luke had finally abandoned his nightly rovings to come back to the tavern that he'd come to think of as home.

"Never asked them," Luke grinned back at him.

"It's just as well. You'd better keep your nose, and your other parts, clean, if you're determined to wait around unitl Martha Simpkins is free. Besides, I'd hate like tunket for word of your carryings-on to get back to Patience Greene. She sets a lot of store by you. She thinks you're an upstanding, pious young man, exactly the son she'd have liked to have if her husband hadn't been too worthless between the sheets to give her one. Go on, get out of here, no more free cider tonight. So far I haven't seen any return on my investment!"

"It isn't easy to bring your name into the conversation."

"I never thought it would be. But you're a bright

young feller, you'll find a way if you put your mind to it. Only your goings-on had better be downright righteous, or you won't be able to do me any good at all. Just bear in mind that I can always find some other upstandin' young feller to foist off on the widow, for the price of a few mugs of free cider."

It was a week after that conversation with Eli that Luke passed by another tavern on his way from the house that Mr. Peters was putting up, and noticed a great deal of unusual activity.

"What's going on?" Luke asked a prosperous-looking man who was about to enter the establishment. "Isn't it kind of early for a drinking party?" It was only a little past noon, and Luke was in search of some bread and cheese and cider for his dinner, and this tavern nearby had seemed a likely place.

"It's a sale of paupers," the man, red-faced and harried-looking, told him. "Let me pass, if you please. My wife wants me to bid in a likely young'un to help her around the house."

Luke was aware that such sales took place in England, but he had never given it a thought since he had landed in Massachusetts. His curiosity was piqued, as well as his displeasure, but there wasn't time to find another place to eat; Mr. Peters was a stickler about punctuality.

The common room of the tavern was well filled when he entered. At the far end, he saw a small group of miserable-looking humanity, huddled together as if for common comfort in their distress. There was an old woman, so decrepit that Luke wondered if anyone would want her services. And a man with the telltale flush of the consumptive on his thin face, his eyes filled with dejection, and a middle-aged woman whom he took to be a widow whose husband had left her unprovided for.

Likely she would be bid on; she looked strong and healthy. Three children pressed close to her. Hers, Luke wondered? Was there any chance that they would be allowed to stay together? He winced, wishing that he'd gone without his dinner rather than have to witness such a sale of human beings.

Two of the children were girls, around nine or ten, their arms around each other, their eyes wide with apprehension. The man Luke had questioned nodded toward them. "Sisters. Their father died a week gone, and their mother two years ago. I'll try for the older girl; my wife will probably be satisfied with her."

"They're to be separated, then?" The knot that had formed in Luke's stomach tightened.

"Can't be helped. It isn't likely anyone would want the two of them together. But somebody will take the other one, they both look healthy and bright."

Now Luke's eyes were caught by the third child, a little boy of no more than three. His face and hands had been scrubbed clean but the mop of dark hair that hung over his forehead was unkempt and his clothing was ragged and his feet were bare. His face was thin and pinched, his eyes filled with fear and bewilderment. "How about the boy?"

"Offshoot of a whore. Heard tell she died, and without his ma around to pay for his keep the tavern she worked in has to get shut of him. He'll be hard to get rid of, he's too young to be any use working. Maybe some farmer'll take him, some man without a son, and raise him up to help with the chores, but it isn't likely. He'd have to be older."

The boy gave Luke one look from his haunted eyes, and Luke bolted. God! A whore's child, a helpless little bastard, put on the block to be sold off like a piece of beef or a plucked chicken, not up to standard so there'd be no takers. Luke wondered if the boy's father even knew if he had a son, or would care if he did.

The memory of the lad's face haunted Luke all the rest of the day, so much that Mr. Peters shouted at him twice for not watching what he was doing. How did he know, for sure, that he had no son like that boy, one who had been sold as a pauper for whatever work he could do, or put in some workhouse to either survive in abject misery, or to perish simply because no one cared? An unwanted child cast adrift in a world that had no place for him, a world without comfort or love, or even the means to keep breath in his body, simply because some man had wanted his moment of pleasure.

He didn't think that he had any by-blows that he didn't know about. He'd never been all that casual about scattering his seed around, partly because he'd been choosy and partly because his father would have skinned him alive if some girl he'd been with had come up with consequences. Knowing his father, he'd known that he'd have forced him to marry the girl whether he was inclined to or not, and a lifetime spent with a woman you didn't care about was something to think about long and hard.

He had no appetite for Patience's boiled cabbage and baked beans and fresh berry tart with thick cream that evening, in spite of the fact that he'd gone without his dinner. Patience was convinced that he was sickening with something, and forced a concoction of her own brewing down his throat, so bitter that he gagged on it.

"I feel better already. In fact, I feel so much better that I think I'll go out for a breath of air." His smile sickly, Luke escaped before Patience could go to her cupboard and fetch down another concoction that was sure to work if the first one didn't. As always, he made directly for The Temptation.

But it seemed as if his luck had run out. There would be little peace and relaxation even here among his friends tonight, because as soon as he entered he saw Henry Atkins, the man Mr. Peters had discharged for drinking, sounding off at one of the long tables.

There was a four-day stubble of beard on Atkins' face, and his small washed-out eyes were filled with malice as he looked up and saw Luke.

"Well, well, will you look who's favorin' us with his company! I'd of thought that with so much money in his pockets, drawing down them good wages that I used to draw before he done me out of my job, he'd be over to The Royal with his fine friends!"

Luke ignored him and sat down at the opposite end of the table. Atkins had been festering a hatred of him ever since he had been discharged. Whenever they chanced to meet, either here or in the lower sort of dive Luke had so recently haunted, Henry had derogatory remarks ready on his tongue. If Luke hadn't been so much taller and heavier, Henry Atkins would have done him a harm. As it was, he took it out in talk.

"I know why he's here. The Armitage woman run him off when he took a fancy to Martha Simpkins, and now he's got nothing to do but take it out in drowning his sorrows. A girl like that, all big in front and with hips like hers, any man'ud feel bad if he didn't get to use 'em like they're meant to be used!" There was a lascivious leer on Atkins' face as he sought to shame Luke for his failure to snatch Martha away from her watchdogs in front of the other patrons.

Luke half stood, the cords in his neck standing out at the mention of Martha's name by that foul tongue, but Eli's hand on his shoulder pushed him down again.

"Henry, finish your drink and git on home to your wife and young'uns. You got no call to be spending your money on drink, anyways, with those children of yours most likely hungry."

"My money's as good as anybody else's in here!" Henry spluttered, his face mottling.

"No it ain't, leastwise till you sober up and git yourself a job. I ain't going to serve you anymore. Now git."

For a moment it looked as if the man were going to fight it out, but besides Luke and Eli, other unfriendly eyes bored into his. Muttering and glaring, he drained his mug and swaggered out, saving what face he could by throwing back, "Well, Ann's waitin' for me anyways, so I was going soon's I'd finished that one."

"I ought to crack his neck," Luke growled.

"Leave him be. No matter if he's as no good as any man that ever walked, you could still end up in jail and it ain't healthy there. You got more than Atkins eatin' at you, Luke. What's the trouble?"

"I happened to see an auction of paupers today. I didn't know things like that went on in Boston."

"What did you think Boston is, an anteroom to heaven? We're a seaport, man! An' seaports breed misery along with prosperity. Every city has its poor, there ain't no gittin' away from it."

"There was a little boy, a whore's bastard."

"Young'uns' got a way of gittin' born, whether they're wanted or not. Maybe the preachers have a point, insisting that the marriage vows ought to be said before a man takes a chance on bringin' offspring into the world. It'd be a heap more comfortable for the children, anyways."

Even Eli's cider, usually of superior quality, tasted bitter.

"But what happens to them, those children who get sold?"

"It ain't usually as bad as you're thinkin'. Most of them end up with families that take good care of them. Sometimes they're raised up like one of the family, especially if it's a boy taken by a man without sons. It ain't unusual for them to inherit, even, in a case like that. 'Course, they ain't all that lucky. Some of 'em have it mighty rough till they git old enough to make their own way."

"It isn't right. Something ought to be done."

All that week, Luke was unable to get the picture of the little bastard boy out of mind. Luke had never been so miserable in his life. He avoided even Eli's tavern. What was the use of free cider if the cider was sour? And when, come Sunday, little Annabelle Armitage slipped another note into his hand and Martha didn't dare raise her eyes to smile at him, his misery came to a head. She couldn't slip out to meet him under the maple tree that evening, because Lillian wasn't feeling well and she'd have to stay in the children's room all night to watch over her. But Lillian had been at services, and Luke would have sworn that the child wasn't ill at all. Charles Armitage had been absent, he was away to help a friend of his in New York straighten out his legal affairs, and Mistress Armitage was merely taking advantage of his absence to show Martha that she was still the mistress and Martha the bound girl.

He brooded about it all that night and the next day, to such an extent that he mashed his thumb with the hammer and had to exercise more control than he'd thought he had not to howl and curse so that Mr. Peters would know that he'd been careless. Thumb swollen to twice its normal size and throbbing, he did a good day's work anyway, but the pain served to put an even sharper edge on his temper.

Millicent Armitage be damned! He was going to see

Martha, and he was going to see her tonight. He nearly paced a hole through the floor of his attic room waiting until it was full dark, and then he walked to the Armitage place and made his way to the stable where his low whistle brought Abel, the coachman, from his quarters above the stable itself.

"Land o' Goshen! Is that you, Mr. Martin? What you wantin' at this time of night? You'll be in mighty big trouble, happens that Mistress Armitage catches you!"

"Mistress Armitage isn't going to catch me." Luke's voice was grim. "Is the cook to be trusted? If you were to go to the kitchen and ask her to find a way to get word to Martha that I'll be waiting for her under the maple tree no matter how long it takes her to get there, would she do it without letting anyone else know?"

Abel thought it over. "I think she'd do it." It wasn't his place to be disloyal enough to Charles Armitage to point out that none of the servants were fond of his wife.

Luke fumbled in his pocket for a coin, but Abel shook his head. "I don't need a tip for running a message. You wait right here."

He was back within five minutes, although to Luke it seemed longer. And then the real wait began. Abel assured him that Mrs. Gatesby, the cook, would see that Martha was told that he was there, but there was no telling how long it would be before she could slip out of the house without being missed.

It was a long wait, so long that Luke had almost given up in despair, before Martha slipped through the shadows to join him. In the loft room above the stable, Luke had listened to Abel's snoring for nearly three hours, every separate snort and gurgle setting his nerves even more on edge.

"Luke! Oh, Luke, I was afraid that you'd given up

on me and gone on home. That Lillian wouldn't settle down to sleep, I had to put her back to bed three times before she finally dropped off, and then I didn't dare leave her until I was sure that she wasn't shamming. She's full of tricks, that one."

Luke caught her into his arms and pressed his cheek against hers. He was trembling, and so was she. He reached up and took off the cap that covered her hair and buried his face against the fragrant, silken tresses.

"Martha, will you marry me?"

Martha pulled back just enough so that she could look at him in the faint light from the stars. Here in the shadow of the maple tree, it was hard to make out his face at all except as a pale blur against the darkness.

"Why, I thought it was all settled! It never occurred to me that you'd never asked me, not in so many words."

"Well, I'm asking you now! Will you, Marty?"

"You know we'll have to wait."

"I don't want to wait!" His voice was rough, and so were his hands as he drew her close to him again, so that the whole length of her body was pressed against his and he could feel her heart beating through her bodice. "Marty, I'm already half out of my head from waiting! Doesn't that woman have any heart? Is she made of marble instead of flesh and blood? Can't she remember how it was?"

There were tears on Martha's cheeks, tears of frustration as deep as his own. "No, she doesn't. I don't think she's ever loved anyone. I know she's never loved anyone as much as I love you! She doesn't think that anyone beneath her own social status has any right to have feelings, their only purpose in life is to serve her and do exactly what she wants."

Luke's mouth came down over hers, shutting off her anguished words. Her mouth was soft and warm, it parted under his, he could taste her sweetness, as sweet as honey. Every muscle in his body was rigid, he felt as though he were going to burst from the pressure inside of him, and the tremor of Martha's flesh, pressed so tightly against his, showed him that she was feeling an agony that was equal to his own.

It wasn't right! No one on earth should have the power to keep two people who loved each other as much as he and Martha loved each other apart. There ought to be laws to protect people from people like Millicent Armitage. Class, privilege, no wonder the common men who met at The Temptation ranted and raved about the common people's rights!

They'd sunk to their knees in the grass, and the dew on it was cold through the cloth that covered Luke's knees, but not cold enough to cool the fire that raged inside of him.

"I can't wait all that time, Marty. It isn't human. I've got to have you, you belong to me, I need you now. . . ."

"Luke, Abel will hear!" Martha's whisper was torn with something very close to grief.

"No I won't. I'm asleep!" The soft words came down to them from above, only to be choked off as Abel betrayed himself. You big fool, you! Abel raged at himself. Why couldn't you have kept your stupid mouth shut? Now you've gone and spoiled it for those two nice young folks.

Under the maple tree, Martha was crying. "I know, Luke, I know! I feel the same way, as if I can't stand it. If you want me, we can find a place. . . ."

If he wanted her! Luke nearly whooped with exultation. He held her even closer, feeling as if he were soaring up into the clouds. To have her, to actually have her, all the hot, giddy sweetness of her, tonight!

Then, unbidden, unwanted, the face of the little bastard waif who'd been put up at auction came to float in front of his eyes. A bastard, an unwanted child.

But it wasn't the same, he raged at the image that wouldn't go away. If it should happen, between him and Martha, the child would not be unwanted! They'd be married as soon as that bitch in the big house would let them, the child would have a name, both he and Martha would love it with all the love in their hearts.

But people would know. Martha would be shamed in front of all of Boston. And knowing Mistress Armitage, her punishment would be several times greater than her crime. Millicent's rage would know no bounds, even Charles Armitage wouldn't be able to protect Marty from his wife's spiteful revenge for having dared to disobey her.

He cursed, long and fervently. Martha put her hand over his mouth to still the sound. "Luke, Luke!"

She was frightened, she'd never seen him like this before. His arms around her became more gentle, his lips brushing against her cheeks, her eyelids, sought to soothe her.

"We can't," he said. "We'll have to wait. But as soon as Mr. Armitage gets home, I'm going to get after him to at least see that we can walk out together the way other couples do! You aren't a slave, damn it, you're only bound! He'll help us, I know he will."

He had to help them. If he didn't, Luke didn't know how he was going to stand it.

He left her still on her knees, her hands over her face, still crying. He had to leave her, he had to get out of there, before he lost all reason and burst into Charles Armitage's house and laid violent hands on Charles

Armitage's wife, and then everything would be ruined for them, forever. A man who has to spend the rest of his life in prison doesn't make a very satisfactory husband.

Three

"You're stark, raving crazy!" Eli shouted. His face had turned an alarming red and the veins stood out on his forehead, pulsing.

"Whoa up, or you'll have a seizure and never get to bed with the widow!" Luke cautioned him. "Just think about it, Eli. I tell you it might work! If Mr. Armitage could locate the boy and we could get him, it's almost bound to work!"

"I'll have nothing to do with it!" Eli's eyes were baleful as he glared at Luke. But Luke had his mind made up, and when his mind was made up he wasn't an easy man to dissuade. The argument went on, back and forth, with Eli's face growing redder and Luke's more stubborn, until Eli gave in.

"All right, if you're so danged set on it! But I warn you that if it doesn't work, you're never going to set foot in my tavern again! We'll ask Charles Armitage the next time he comes in, he's the one to handle it for us if it can be done at all. Likely he won't be able to locate the little beggar anyway. Somebody else probably bid him in and won't want to give him up."

Luke had thought about it all day Monday, and now it was Monday evening and he was so sure that his plan would work that he had put it to Eli. The tavern-keeper was so determined to win Patience Greene that Luke had been sure he'd accept any scheme that had even a modicum of chance of succeeding. He hadn't expected all this opposition. Maybe it was harebrained, but it was the best chance they had.

"Did I hear my name mentioned?" It was Charles himself, come in to catch up on local events while he'd been away.

"Yes, you did. I'm mighty glad you're back, Mr. Armitage. There was a pauper boy up for bid last week and we were wondering if you could locate him. A little fellow, about three."

"A pauper boy? And so young? In that case I will certainly make inquiries. It might be that I could find a family to take him. These cases are pitiful, especially when the child is so young."

"You won't have to look for a family. Eli wants him." Luke's face was perfectly innocent.

Mr. Armitage had the grace to look startled, a thing that seldom happened. "Eli! You can't be serious!"

"Yes, I am. Eli's heart was touched by the lad's plight, and he's ready to take him if it can be arranged."

"Eli is a good man, but for a child to be brought up in a tavern!" The lawyer's voice was doubtful. "It wasn't what I had in mind for him."

"You'd be sure he was in good hands and wouldn't be mistreated." Luke pressed his point home. "I'd keep an eye on him. Likely most of the men who come in here regular would do the same. He'd grow up with a lot of friends, have a decent chance in life. And Eli'd leave him all he owns, when the time comes."

"Yes, I can follow your reasoning." A smile tugged at the corners of Charles' mouth. "In different circumstances, you'd have made a good advocate yourself, Luke.

I only want to be sure that Eli really wants the boy. Do you, Eli? Have you taken the time to think it through?"

Eli opened his mouth and closed it, opened and closed it again. "I want him," he said.

"Then if you're sure, I'll set things in motion. It shouldn't be too difficult to locate the child."

Eli gave Luke a baleful look laced with vicious reproach. If it didn't work out as Luke planned, he would have lost a friend and gained an enemy.

"Mistress Greene, could I have a word with you?" Tri-cornered hat in hand, Luke waited, a picture of respectful diffidence, until the widow invited him to step across the threshold into her parlor.

"My land, Mr. Martin, you aren't ailing again? You look quite flushed." Patience Greene rose from the chair beside the window where she had been catching the last of the light to finish mending a sheet. She bustled over to Luke and put her hand on his forehead. "You are flushed! You should get yourself to bed this instant! I'll fetch you my fever cure and bring it up to you directly."

Luke repressed a shudder. "Please, Mistress Greene, I'm quite well. It's just that I'm worried. I may confide in you, may I not?" Hobnobbing with Charles Armitage had improved Luke's grammar and he used this new skill to further elevate the widow's esteem of him, already laced with motherly concern for the orphaned young man in a strange land.

"Of course you may! You aren't in any trouble? You haven't lost your employment with Mr. Peters?" The widow's mind raced on to something even worse. "You aren't in difficulties with some young lady?" As soon as she realized what she had just said she became flustered and her face flushed scarlet.

"Indeed I am not!" Luke saw his advantage and

pressed it. "It's something quite different, and most unusual, Mistress Greene."

"Well, come out with it!" The widow did not like being kept in suspense. "Whatever is it, Mr. Martin?"

"Last week, at a tavern where I went for my noon meal, I chanced to see a sale of paupers. Never having witnessed such an event, I paid particular attention." So far it was the honest truth, and that strengthened his position.

"There was a little boy among the unfortunates, a little lad no more than two or three, quite alone in the world. He stuck in my mind, but as a bachelor there was no way for me to offer him my protection. But not being able to forget the lad, I made inquiries and learned where he had been placed." Luke looked perturbed, his forehead creased, his eyes reflecting inner misery. The widow was visibly impressed.

"Well, then, if he had been placed there is nothing further to fret you, is there?" She tried to comfort him.

"But it is where he has been placed, Mistress Greene! He was bid in by a certain Eli Bates, who owns a tavern. A single man at that, with no motherly woman to see to the lad's welfare. I admit that the news left me shaken, and this evening I stopped in at this Mr. Bates' establishment to see for myself how the child is faring. I happen to know that Eli is a good man. As you might know, I stop in at The Temptation quite often, when Mr. Armitage is there. I do like talking with Mr. Armitage; it's an education in itself."

At the mention of Eli's name the widow's nostrils flared, but she subsided at the mention of the well-known and respected lawyer.

"A tavern! For a small boy? I never heard of anything so ungodly!"

"I thought so too, Mistress Greene. But I must admit that Mr. Bates seems to be fond of the lad and wants to do his best for him. I talked with him myself, and the boy seems happy there. But Eli hasn't the least notion of how to care for a small child, what to feed him, or even how often to wash him, as far as that goes! He asked me if I knew of some kind-hearted lady who would advise him in the upraising of the child, and I thought of you immediately."

Patience's face was now so scarlet that Luke was afraid that his scheme was going to fall through.

"That man! That disreputable, dirty old man!"

"If you please, both he and his establishment seem clean to me, even by my dear mother's standards of housekeeping. And there is no doubt that the little lad likes him and that he loves the lad and took him out of the kindness of his heart. But there still remains the problem of nurturing"—that was a good word—"the child, and any advice would be most welcome. If you could but see him, Mistress Greene! Pitifully thin, and he's been mistreated in the past, for certain, and his eyes are so frightened of the world! I was left orphaned myself, although at a much more advanced age, so I know a little of how he feels."

His reference to his own orphaned state touched the widow's heart. Luke had never had occasion to tell her just how old he had been when he had been orphaned.

"You're a fine young man, Luke." For the first time, Patience felt that it wouldn't be unseemly to call him by his given name. Maybe he was grown up, but an orphan is still an orphan! "Your concern does credit to you."

"I'm afraid that coming to you is a most uncalled-for liberty, Mistress Greene." Luke was now the picture of abashed contrition. "I told Mr. Bates that if he would bring the lad here you would surely look at him and give him directions as to his care. I was so agitated with concern for the child that I overlooked the fact that I should have consulted you first. Not that it matters overmuch." He risked an appraising look at his landlady. "Eli told me that he will feel his way by trial and error and that the lad will come to no harm. Only it doesn't seem right to experiment with a child so young, however good at heart Eli feels toward him. What if he were to do something wrong, something that would harm the boy? And I thought, I hoped. . . ." Luke paused, as if he were afraid to go on.

"You hoped?" Patience prompted him, her flush actually deepening as Eli's purely imaginary words took hold of her.

"I hoped that if you would indicate that you would see the lad, I could tell Eli to bring him here at your convenience."

The widow rose to her full height, five feet and one-eighth inch. Her plump body quivered. "Indeed I will see the child! No man in the world is capable of raising a child properly, much less a man like Mr. Bates! You are to bring the child immediately, so I can see what needs to be done.

"What good's that going to do me?" Eli demanded. "Seein' Tod ain't seein' me!"

"You won't let the lad out of your sight, you stupid old goat!" Luke told him, his voice exasperated. "Not even with me. You'll come with us, and she'll have no choice but to let you in. You dote on the lad, you idiot! You're a man tormented by loneliness, a man whose heart was torn to bleeding shreds at the boy's plight, and now that you have him you can't bear to be separated from him even for a moment!"

"And you think she'll swallow that?"

"Certainly she'll swallow that! And on top of being the all-loving father, you are going to be the stupidest man in the colonies. She will give instructions. You will beam and repeat them to make sure that you have them right, but you will have them all wrong. Do you begin to follow me?"

A smile took form on Eli's mouth, spread to his eyes, and made them water. "She'll have to keep mighty close tabs on the lad to make sure I'm doin' right by him."

"Now your brain is working. Make a woman think she's needed, and the battle is half won. Can you leave the tavern? She's waiting for me to bring Tod to her right now."

"I'll close the danged place," Eli said. "Just this once, mind you! After this our visits will have to be after services on Sunday. Just let me get my hair, and I'll be right with you." His voice rose. "Everybody drink up! This tavern is about to be closed for the evening!"

One man was startled into dropping his mug, and Eli refused to refill it.

Luke felt more than a little like a fool as he walked Martha to Patience Greene's house to introduce her to the widow. Anybody'd think that his landlady was his foster mother instead of Tod's, and that he had to have her approval of the girl he was going to marry.

They'd have to wait. That was an established fact. Charles Armitage had once again done his best to prevail on his wife to give her permission for Martha to take a husband, even to set her free of her bondage a few months early, but it had been to no avail. All he had accomplished was to obtain Millicent's reluctant permission for Martha to walk out with Luke two nights a week, provided that she was home again before the clock struck ten. But it was better than nothing, and a great deal better than they had had before they'd been granted that much.

The lad Tod had been living with Patience Greene for over a month now. The battle had been bitter, but she had won it in the end. However, the victory had not been all on her side. Eli had insisted that he should be free to visit the boy at her house whenever he wished, and she had had to give in. And so far, she had no inkling that that was exactly what Luke and Eli had planned.

Luke used the key that Patience had entrusted with him to unlock the front door and called out, "We're here, Mistress Greene!" He expected Tod to come running to greet him, his face alight. The change in the boy was astonishing since he had found the first love and security he had ever known. A frustrated mother all her life, Patience's capitulation at her first sight of the pinched little face and the huge frightened eyes had been complete.

But on this early evening there was no sound of running feet, no excited boy shouting his welcome. Instead, Patience herself appeared from her parlor, her face a brick red, her eyes blazing with a fury that Luke had never seen there before.

"I have found out Tod's origins," the widow said, her words bitten off one by one and cast at Luke's feet like so much offal. "A bastard, the son of a common prostitute! Mr. Martin, you are to go to Eli Bates' tavern immediately and fetch him back here so I can tell him what I think of him for perpetrating this hoax on me, and he can remove the child from my premises."

"Mistress Greene, you don't mean that! You're upset."

"Of course I'm upset! What decent woman wouldn't be upset? A bastard in my house, worse than a bastard! All of Boston laughing at me! Go this instant, Mr. Martin!"

They were in for it now, and in view of the mood the widow was in there was nothing Luke could do but obey. His heart felt like lead as he left Martha to try to calm the furious woman, and fetch Eli, who would skin him alive and boil what was left of him in oil.

Who the devil had told Mistress Greene? Luke would like to get his hands on him, whoever it was. Only it must have been a woman; tattling was a woman's pastime, not a man's, so even if he knew what woman it was Luke would have to bear the frustration of not being able to wring her neck.

"Now, ain't that the devil to pay! I knew something like this would happen when I let you talk me into the damn-fool scheme!" Eli said.

"Maybe she'll have calmed down by the time we get there," Luke said halfheartedly.

"Not her, she won't have! Oh, Lord, how do I get into things like this? What have I done to deserve it, outside of makin' a friend of a worthless scoundrel like you?"

"Well, it almost worked. She was softening up toward you, you know she was. And what about Tod? This isn't going to be easy on him either, you know."

"Tod'll be all right. He's my boy. You didn't think I was going to send him back where he came from, did you? It's my life that's ruined, and it's your dad-blasted fault. I ought to take you apart and feed you to those pigs that wander around the streets, only I'd be afraid I'd end up eatin' some of the pork you went to make up!"

The widow, her rage intensified rather than otherwise by the wait, was ready for them. She held a broom in her hands and the moment Eli entered her house she began belaboring him with it as well as with her tongue.

"You scoundrel! You unmitigated, worthless man! Get out of my house, and take that boy with you, and never let me lay eyes on either of you again!"

Luke's heart felt like the last drop of blood was being wrung out of it when he saw Tod, with Martha's arms around him, huddled in a corner, his eyes huge and bewildered in his white face. God, what was this doing to the boy?

"Take him!" Patience screamed. "Take him this minute!"

Eli took him, by the hand, and Tod went with him, his head hanging. Luke had never struck a woman in his life but he had an overwhelming urge to strike Patience Greene to the ground.

"Come on, Martha, we'd better leave." He'd collect his things in the morning. Tonight he didn't trust himself to stay that long for fear that he would actually lay hands on the woman in front of him.

"Wait," Martha said, laying her hand on his arm to hold him back. "Oh, dear, I was afraid this would happen!"

Standing in the doorway, still brandishing her broom, the widow had crumpled to the floor in a faint.

They brought her around, although Luke would have preferred to leave her where she had fallen. She came out of it sobbing, her face crumpled, her hands picking at the bodice of her gown. "My little boy!" she said. "Oh, God, I've lost my little boy!" Shoulders shaking, she wept against Martha's breast as Martha held her and tried to comfort her.

"Did you see his face? Did you see how his shoulders drooped and his head hung when Eli took him away?" Her sobs were tearing her apart.

"Luke, can you find something for her to drink? Wine, or better yet, brandy?"

In this house? "There isn't a drop. Tea's the strongest thing she allows on her premises."

"Brew her some tea then. Mistress Greene, you must stop crying, you'll do yourself a hurt."

"I don't want tea. I want my little boy! What have I done to him? Luke, did you see his face?"

"You asked me that before." Luke's voice was grim. "Yes, I saw it."

"Bring him back, Luke! Go and bring him back! I don't care if his mother was a whore, it wasn't his fault, I was angry at Eli, I wanted to get back at him for making a fool of me! I can't live without Tod, he's mine, he belongs to me!"

"Eli won't be inclined to give him back."

Patience looked at him with stricken eyes. She took a deep breath and stopped sobbing. "Bring him back, Luke. You can tell Eli I'm sorry, that I didn't mean what I said. You can tell him he can see Tod whenever he wants to, just like before."

Luke looked at Martha. "Marty, fetch me that Bible on the table."

Martha brought the Bible, and Luke took the widow's hand and laid it on top of it. "Now swear that you'll never do anything to hurt either Tod or Eli again as long as you live."

Patience swore, with tears running down her crumpled face.

"You have her right where you want her, Eli. If you can't hogtie her now it's your own fault," Luke told the tavernkeeper. "If she can't get Tod back any other way, she'll marry you to do it."

"Or break that broom over my head."

"Go on. Lay it on the line. Strike while the iron is hot!"

"One more platitude, and I know what I'll strike!" Eli glared at Luke. "All right, you stay here with Tod. She ain't goin' to lay eyes on him agin' till I've got it in writin'!"

They were married three weeks later. It was not a small or a quiet wedding. Never having been married before, Eli wanted it done up brown. If the state of Luke's head was any indication the next morning, he'd done it up a little too brown.

He came down to breakfast, fearing that his head was going to fall off with every jarring step although he took care to place each foot on the treads with the delicacy of a cat. He headed straight for the kitchen in search of something, anything, to quench his raging thirst.

What he saw made him forget both headache and thirst. Patience was already astir, preparing breakfast. She was humming, and there was a look of utter and shining astonishment on her face. Luke backed out of the kitchen before she caught sight of him.

"I'll be damned!" he thought, his face breaking into a grin. He wouldn't have thought that Eli had it in him.

In March of 1754, Luke and Martha were married at the Cockerel. It was a far more elaborate wedding than either of them had dreamed of. Standing in lieu of Martha's father, Charles Armitage insisted on footing the bill. Martha was radiant in a blue satin gown, made for her by the best seamstress in Boston, that exactly matched the color of her eyes. It was trimmed with lace as fine as any that adorned Millicent's finest imported dresses.

Millicent Armitage sat in the family pew, and behaved, here in the public eye, as though this wedding pleased her immensely. Pleased or not, and she was not because she thought that Charles had taken leave of his senses to spend so much on a former servant, and a bond servant at that, but no hint of their raging quarrel over the matter marred her beautiful face.

Eli stood as Luke's best man, and Charles gave Martha away. Lillian and Annabelle acted as Martha's attendants, fairy children in pale pink. Lillian was as aware of her own beauty and importance as her mother. Annabelle slipped her hand into Martha's and held it tight, her sweet face puckered up because she was losing her beloved nursemaid.

There was a celebration at The Temptation after the ceremony. Millicent had flatly refused to have it in her own house, and Patience's house was nowhere near large enough to accommodate all the well-wishers. Luke was popular, and Charles Armitage was a favorite among the common folk, who knew that he had their interests at heart and no contempt for them in spite of his aristocracy and wealth.

Millicent stayed for only five minutes. Then she left, holding each of her daughters by the hand, but Annabelle broke away from her and ran back to her father. Laughing, he lifted her in his arms and said that she could stay.

Millicent never knew that when Charles and her

younger daughter returned home hours later, Annabelle's head, sleeping on her father's shoulder, was slightly tipsy, and filled with ecstatic dreams because she'd been promised that she could visit Martha and Luke often, so she hadn't lost either of her friends after all.

Four

If he hadn't owed Charles Armitage such a debt of gratitude, more than he could ever repay, Luke would have refused to let Martha go to Millicent Armitage on the night of November 20, 1758. It was cold and blowing up a blizzard, and Martha owed her former mistress nothing, and there were their own three youngsters for her to look after, the youngest, Timothy, only three months old in the cradle that Luke had fashioned with his own hands before the eldest, Mark, had been born. Mark was three now, and John was nearly two, but if Mistress Armitage had had her way none of them would have been born at all and Martha would still be in her service.

In all his life, Luke had never come to hate anyone as much as he hated Millicent Armitage. The months of waiting for Martha's bond to be up had been months of pure hell. He'd been terrified more than once that he'd lose control and that Martha would end up pregnant. The fact that the blood flowing in Martha's body had been as flamingly ardent as his own had made it doubly difficult. Martha had ended up crying so often, and Luke shaking as though with an ague, that it had seemed as though they were living in purgatory.

Charles had done everything in his power to make it up to the young couple. He'd made them a wedding present of enough money to make a down payment on a small house with a good parcel of land behind it, some mile and a half from his own home on Beacon Hill. There was room behind the house for a salad garden and a poultry run and raspberry bushes and half a dozen apple trees, and it had been Charles who had suggested that Luke buy a team of oxen and build himself a heavy wagon so that he could do hauling in the winter months and add to his income. He had lent Luke the money for the team and it had paid off handsomely.

When Luke opened the door on that November night, the wind was already blowing a few flakes of snow from lowering clouds.

"It's Mistress Millicent's time," Charles told him, blowing on his chilled fingers. "Dr. Peabody is already at the house, but she's asking for Martha."

Martha's face betrayed none of the emotions she must have felt at being asked to tend the woman who had treated her with such a lack of consideration. She'd go for Charles' sake, not for that of her former mistress. Luke and Charles had become close friends, and Annabelle was in her house almost as often as she was at home. But Millicent and her older daughter, Lillian, still treated them as if they were beneath their notice. They were never invited to Millicent's home, except when Millicent peremptorily summoned her to care for the children if either of them were sick. Then she went for Annabelle's and Charles' sake, just as she would go tonight.

She took her cloak from a peg on the wall and pulled the hood well over her head. "Tim will do all right, he always sleeps straight through now. I'll be back as soon as I can," she told Luke.

The lawyer had come in his enclosed chariot, but

as he handed her in he remarked jocularly, "If this keeps up I'll have to send you home by sled. It's kind of you to come, Martha."

"Pray God it's a boy, this time," Martha said. Personally, she couldn't care less whether Mistress Millicent ever had the boy she so desired. It was Charles she was thinking of, a man needed a son to carry on his name, and besides, Millicent would be in a fury if this one turned out to be another girl unqualified to inherit from her Uncle Basil back in England.

It was no surprise to Martha that Millicent was bearing the pain of this birth with fortitude. For a son, Millicent would have borne any amount of pain. But this birthing was difficult, as both Millicent's pain-racked face and the doctor's concerned manner attested. It looked to be a long night.

The bedchamber was sumptuously furnished. The massive four-poster bed was hung with silk, and the windows were draped with the same material, both in the delicate shade of apple green that was so becoming to its occupant. The furniture had all been imported, at tremendous expense. In this Charles had given in to his wife, although his own tastes ran to less ornate surroundings and he'd have been pleased with the fine cabinetwork now being turned out by a few artisans in the colonies themselves.

Dr. Peabody nodded with satisfaction as he saw how efficiently Martha settled in to help him. A huge fire burned in the fireplace, and the room was stiflingly hot, so that the physician's forehead was beaded and he looked uncomfortable in his skirted coat. In the bed, Millicent's hair was plastered to her face, and the veins in her throat stood out as a contraction seized her, making her sink her teeth into her lower lip while her hands clutched at the bed coverings.

The doctor drew Martha into a far corner of the room and spoke to her in a low tone so that Millicent could not overhear.

"I don't like the looks of it. I warned her against lacing herself so tightly, but she paid no heed to my advice. The infant is lying at an angle, and we have our work cut out for us. I'm glad you're here, Martha. Try to talk to her, to keep her calm. Her struggling only makes it harder."

There were times that night, before it was over, when Martha was afraid that even the doctor would not be able to save the unborn child, even if he managed to save the mother. Even with all of her built-up resentments against Millicent she couldn't help feeling pity for the woman who lay struggling to eject the infant from her body. Her own children had been born easily but even so she remembered the pain, which was hard enough to endure even in a birth that midwives called easy.

"It's a boy," Millicent said over and over each time the pain subsided and she had a moment of respite. "It's coming so hard because it's a boy, and a big one. A son at last! Why doesn't he get born? How much longer?"

"Not long." Martha tried to soothe the tormented woman.

"He must be enormously big!" Millicent gasped, and in spite of her agony her eyes glittered with triumph. "A great, strapping boy after all this time, and thank God, now no need of bearing more children! Never, never will I go through this again!" Her voice rose to a shriek as another contraction arched her body. "Do something, damn you! I can't bear it! Help me!"

Daylight had illuminated a world of blinding white before Millicent gave one long drawn-out animal scream and thrust her baby into the world. Martha received it in the soft clean cloth she had ready at hand and her heart constricted. The child was a girl, tiny, seeming too weak from its own ordeal to survive. Even the doctor, with all his experience, paled when he saw the sex of the child.

"My son! Let me see my son!" Millicent gasped, panting for breath. Her face was as white as the pillow-shams and she was drained of strength but she still tried to lean up on her arms to see the baby.

"It's a girl, Mistress Armitage." Martha got the words out and her arms closed around the infant with instinctive protectiveness.

"You lie! It's a boy! Show me, give him to me!"

She took one look and her eyes blazed with bitter hatred.

"Take it away! Get it out of my sight!"

"Now, Mistress Armitage . . ." Dr. Peabody, exhausted himself, tried to make his voice firm.

"Shut up! You blundering old fool, why did you save it? A girl, a worthless girl!"

"It isn't the child's fault that she's a girl!" Martha said hotly.

Charles chose that moment to enter the room. He had heard the last tortured scream and the small mewling cry of the infant and known that the ordeal was over. Like the others, he was tired from the long vigil, and his face showed the strain of the hours of waiting.

"You!" Millicent screamed at him. Her voice dripped with venom. "What good are you to me, a man who can only inflict daughters on me? Get out of my room, I don't want to look at you! You did this to me, you and my father, that sanctimonious, bigoted old religious maniac! Had I married as I chose, I'd be the mother of boys, a son to inherit! I'd be in London where I belong, taking my place in the society to which I was born!

Take your mewling daughter and leave me! This is the end, do you hear me? No more, no, never again! Why should I bear you more children when you can only father females?"

"Millicent, the child is welcome in this house, no matter her sex. She is ours, and we will love her as we do Lillian and Annabelle." Charles' face was as white as his wife's. "I care not a whit if she's a girl and neither should you."

"Madam, you must control yourself, I beg you!" Dr. Peabody said. "The child will need nourishment and your temper will have an adverse effect on your milk."

"Find a wetnurse, then!" Millicent raged. "I will never nurse her, you can depend on that!" She raised herself on one elbow and looked at her husband, the hate in her eyes so visible that Martha felt it like a blow. "And find yourself a mistress as well, for you will never again share my bed!" With that, she turned her face to the wall and lay in grim silence.

The doctor drew the others from the room. "Her doldrums are the result of her difficult confinement," he told them, but there was little conviction in his voice. "No doubt she will be herself in a day or two."

Martha didn't believe it. The birth had been difficult, and Millicent had suffered more than flesh and blood should have to suffer, but she had meant every word she had said. She had no love for this child whose sex had disappointed her, and even less love for the husband who had inflicted it upon her. In spite of the pity she had felt for Millicent Armitage a short time ago, her old dislike of her returned tenfold as she carried the child down to the kitchen to clean it and dress it in front of the kitchen fireplace. To curse your own child, to wish it had died at birth! Such wickedness was beyond understanding. For all their money and station in life, she would not have traded places with the Armitages, never in a hundred years. She and Luke were richer by far in everything that mattered.

Luke was beginning to worry before the jingling of sleigh bells heralded the return of his wife. The two older boys had waked two hours ago and he had fed them, and they had given him no trouble, but now Tim was awake and crying lustily, his hunger pangs unappeased. Luke laid the child back in his crib, having been pacing the floor with him in an effort to quiet him.

The air that struck his face when he opened the door was frigid. There was Martha, being handed down from the sleigh by Charles himself. Her face was red from the cold, and she was carrying a closely wrapped bundle in her arms. Now, what in tunket! Charles hadn't thought to pay her for her services with a ham, or a side of bacon?

They hurried into the house and Luke closed the door and went over to throw another log on the fire. "How went it?" he asked. "All is well, I trust?"

A mewling sound from the bundle that Martha was already unwrapping in front of the fire made his mouth drop open and put an expression of ludicrous surprise on his face. Charles, his eyes filled with misery, looked at him with appealing abashment, a state that was so foreign to him that it set Luke back on his heels.

"My wife was so weakened by the birth that she can't feed the child. I'm afraid that there was no choice but to bring her here so that Martha can feed her along with your own infant."

Luke picked up the word "she" and whistled under his breath. So it was another girl, and he'd be willing to wager that Mistress Armitage hadn't taken it kindly. He went immediately to draw the lawyer a mug of cider to ease the awkwardness of the moment.

"I have enough milk and to spare," Martha said. "But right now I can see that Tim is the one who is famishing!"

"I have Tamara's cradle in the sleigh. Abel is bringing it in now," Charles told him, taking the cider gratefully. Unlike most other men he had refrained from easing his waiting with spirits while Millicent had been in labor, and now he felt the need of something to relieve his weariness. "I hope that you won't be inconvenienced for long."

There was more here than met the eye, Luke thought. Millicent Armitage would not have fed the infant herself, except for a day or two while a suitable wetnurse was found, even if she had had an easy time of it. He knew that the highborn ladies of Millicent's world had their breasts bound as soon as possible after giving birth so that their figures would not be spoiled, just as they turned their children over to other nurses so that their pleasure-seeking would not be interfered with. But apparently this child was to remain here for an indefinite period of time.

"Pick Tim up for me, Luke, and I'll lay Tamara in his cradle until her own is warmed by the fire," Martha instructed him.

He made the exchange and then drew two more mugs of cider, one for himself and one for Abel. "To the new baby," he said, lifting his mug. "May she thrive and prosper!" If Charles noticed that his wife was not included in the toast, as was customary, he gave no indication, but lifted his own mug and drained it.

"If there is anything you need for Tamara, let me know. I'll stop by every day to see her in any case, until she can return home." Charles shook Luke's hand, his clasp firm and warm, and there was warm appreciation in his eyes.

As soon as the door had closed behind Charles and Abel, Luke turned to Martha, who was already loosening her bodice to feed Timothy. "So the child is another girl. And how did Mistress High and Mighty take it?"

Martha's face flamed with the anger she had kept repressed all this time so as not to further distress Charles.

"You'd not believe how she carried on! She cursed the baby, Luke, she actually cursed it! Yes, and Charles too. She wouldn't even look at the child, much less give it a name, and when Charles said they would call her Tamara, she laughed and said that it sounded heathenish like a gypsy name and that it suited the dark, ugly brat it had been given to. She's wicked, Luke. I don't care how blue her blood is, she's wicked and she'll never go to heaven!"

Mark, their eldest, had crept up to Timothy's cradle and was peering down at the tiny mite who rested there. "She is ugly. Wouldn't you have wanted me, Mama, if I was ugly?"

Luke took an affectionate swipe at him. "You were the ugliest creature ever born into this world when you were that young! It's a thing that passes, son."

Mark reached out with one finger and touched the baby's face. Then he looked at his mother, his blue eyes, as candid as Luke's, filled with sudden worry.

"Mama, you always say that Mistress Armitage gets everything she wants. And she wanted a boy. She's given us Tamara. Does that mean that she's going to take Tim?"

Martha's temper faded and she began to laugh. "Goodness no! Tim's blood is nowhere near blue enough to suit Millicent Armitage."

"My blood isn't blue at all, it's red as anything,

and so is John's because he scraped his knee yesterday and I saw it. But I don't know about Tim, because I never saw his blood."

It was Luke's turn to laugh. "Shall we cut him to see? Or maybe just prick him with a needle?"

"A needle. That won't hurt as much. I'll get one, I know right where it is in Mama's workbox!" Mark was already scuttling across the room to fetch the needle when Luke caught him by the scruff of his neck.

"Hold on, son! It was only a manner of speaking. Timmy's blood is as red as yours. There's no need to stick him to prove it."

Relieved, Mark went back to the cradle. "All the same, she is ugly. Timmy's pretty."

"I'm afraid she'll never be the beauty that Lillian and Annabelle are," Martha conceded. "Tamara's going to be dark, she must be a throwback to some ancestor." And she added in a lower voice for Luke's benefit only, "If the poor little mite survives at all! And even if she does, what kind of a life will she have with a mother who can't abide the sight of her? Mistress Armitage isn't going to get over it, Luke. She meant every word she said. I feel so sorry for Charles and for this poor infant, I could cry."

Five

When Tamara was unhappy, she went away. Not in the sense that other children go away, by withdrawing into themselves. Tamara went away literally, on her own two feet, regardless of the consequences.

There were not many consequences, actually. Millicent cared little where the child was as long as Tamara was out of her sight. Lillian and Annabelle grew lovelier to look at with every passing year, promising to surpass even their mother in beauty. They would make brilliant marriages, provided that Millicent ever managed to get them to London. The blood was there, and the dowries, and with their beauty there would be titles in the family yet.

Tamara, on the other hand, was impossible. Nobody on earth could make a beauty of the pointed-faced little girl with the tangle of dark, straight hair that refused to take a curl no matter how many curling rags or irons were put to it. An hour later and it hung straight and limp again, flying away with every breeze or movement, and Tamara was seldom still.

The child was a skinny little thing with knobby knees, and her eyes, while large and of her father's hazel, were lashed with short, stubby lashes rather than long, curling ones such as her sisters possessed, and they were far too solemn except when her father was at home and kept her at his side as his constant companion.

But Charles had his affairs to look after and there were long hours every day, and sometimes several days together, when he was not at home. Her sisters paid little attention to her. Annabelle was always kind to her and had genuine affection for her, but their mama kept Annabelle and Lillian busy at lessons most of the time.

The older girls had to learn how to read poetry aloud, with expression, to play the piano, to dance. They had lessons in posture and deportment and singing, in French and embroidery and drawing.

As for Lillian, she was someone to be avoided at all costs because her tongue was as barbed as her mother's and she reveled in teasing the ugly duckling of the family whenever Tamara was unfortunate enough to attract her attention.

The place that Tamara loved the best in all the world was the Martins' house. Her father took her there often, in the chariot if the weather was inclement, in the sleigh if snow covered the streets, but most of all Tamara loved it when Papa took her up in front of him on Sheba, his Narragansett pacer. Mama said that the mare was a disgrace for a gentleman to ride but Papa told her that the Narragansett was the best horse the world had ever bred for comfort in riding. Rhode Island bred, these animals were not creatures of great beauty, but they had an easy gait that ate up the miles, and their stamina and sure-footedness made them much favored by men who had distances to cover. Mama, Tamara had noticed, looked down on anything that originated in the colonies. If it didn't come from England, it wasn't worth having.

Of all the people in the world, next to Papa, Tamara loved Mark the most. She loved her sister Annabelle, who was seldom allowed to accompany her and Papa to the Martins now that she was of an age to be schooled in catching a wealthy husband. And she loved Martha and Luke, but it was Mark who made the world go round, and this in spite of the fact that he paid no attention to her except to tell her to get out of the way and stop being a nuisance. John was kinder, and Tim, who was only three months older than Tamara herself, was a great deal jollier, always laughing and teasing and capering, but it was Mark whom Tamara worshiped.

Tamara was three the first time she went away. Papa was out of town on one of his journeys, and Annabelle and Lillian were at their lessons, and Mama had gone in the chariot to visit her friend Grace Gammage, who had also come from England and who was Mama's dearest friend.

Tamara knew the way. She was an observant child and she knew, from going with Papa, every turning and corner of the route, even through Boston's ridiculously winding streets that Papa had told her had originally been cowpaths, taking no notice of straight lines from one point to another but wandering as the cows had pleased. What she hadn't realized was that the distance would be so far for her short legs, rather than perched in front of Papa on Sheba, who made it seem like no distance at all.

The child put one foot in front of the other, over and over and over. It was hot in the midday sun, but she kept on going. She grew thirsty but she kept on going. Her dress became rumpled and the rough cobbles underfoot made her light slippers form blisters on her heels but her feet kept on moving. It never once occurred to her to turn back, and she seemed so sure of herself and her whereabouts that none of the passersby thought to ask her if she were lost.

Mark was nailing a board back in place on the low fence that enclosed the poultry yard. Martha did not care for having chickens and geese wander into her kitchen and dirty her freshly sanded floor. At six Mark was a sturdy boy, big for his age and already thoroughly familiar with saw and hammer and awl. They were more than playthings. Tools were something that could be used, something to fit a boy's hand as if his hand had been expressly made to hold them.

Mark's hand reached toward the keg of nails and a nail was placed in it, the right way around. He pounded the nail in and reached for another, which was also placed in his hand. A third nail was forthcoming in the same miraculous fashion before he thought to look up to see how they were managing to fly out of the keg and into his hand at the exact second he wanted them.

"You again!" Mark said. Tamara handed him another nail and he pounded it in. That ought to hold it. He looked beyond Tamara to the street, but there was no horse tethered there. "Now how in tunket did you get here?"

"I walked." The last nail not being needed, Tamara dropped it back into the keg.

"You know something? You don't have as much sense as a gadfly! Your mother will skin you alive."

Tamara didn't answer that, no answer being called for.

Martha came to the open back door and shaded her eyes with her hand. "Who are you talking to, Mark?" She made out Tamara's diminutive form then and exclaimed, "Mercy! How did you get here?"

"She walked," Mark told his mother, disgust plain in his voice.

"You poor little mite! You must be tired to death, and thirsty too. Come along, let me get you a drink and then I'll clean you up before Mark takes you home."

Tamara submitted uncomplainingly to the cloth that Martha applied to her face and hands. The tea had been good. In the summer, Martha brewed a quantity of it and let it cool, and put in the juice of the limes that were so plentiful because of the trade with the islands, and a little honey or sugar. Like most other Bostonians, Martha did not trust plain water from the town pumps for quenching thirst.

"Aren't you hungry after your long walk, love? I can't think how you ever found your way all alone!" Corn bread and honey appeared on the scrubbed table, and Tamara applied herself to it with the same seriousness that she applied herself to everything. She had a neat way of eating that never failed to please Martha. "Why did you do it?"

"I wanted to help Mark. I like helping Mark."

"She's a pest. Do I have to take her home? She found her way here, she could find her way back."

"Yes, you have to take her home. Anything might happen to her if we sent her by herself. She might get run down by a horse or a cart. But she couldn't walk that great distance back anyway, her poor little feet would fall off at the ankles. You can take her on Daniel." If they were to ride at all it had to be on Daniel, the gentler of the two oxen, because the Martins did not own a horse.

"I'll feel like a fool riding Daniel through the streets with a little girl!" Mark protested.

"Then feel like a fool." Tamara would be safe with Mark, and they owed Charles too much and were too fond of him to take any chances on harm coming to Tamara. Besides, Martha loved the little scrap of humanity for her own sake.

If Mark felt like a fool, Tamara was in seventh heaven as she perched behind him on Daniel's broad back, hanging onto his waist for dear life. The good smell of Mark penetrated her nostrils as she pressed her face against his shoulder blades. Ordinarily Tamara would have preferred to be abroad in Boston during the early hours of the morning, when the street vendors were most prevalent. "Fresh mackerel! Fresh cod and haddock, straight from the ferryways!" "Milk, who wants milk, fresh sweet milk?"

The fish vendors had horns that they blew, to add to the delightful din, and in the colder months oystermen with their wares in sacks on their backs cried "Oys! Oys! Big and juicy, buy my oys!" And little black chimneysweeps would chirp, "Sweep o' sweep, sweep o' sweep!" Some of the children from the more respectable families were afraid of these dirty urchins, but Tamara was not. She was only sorry for them for having to do such dirty work.

And she loved the bells. It seemed that every hour of a Bostonian's life was regulated by the church bells. Tamara could already recognize Christ Church's sweet peals, the sweetest in the world, Papa said, while New North's off-key tone made her wince and King's Chapel made her feel sad. She had learned to count by the "passing" bell, which tolled out the age and the sex of the departed.

She loved the narrow, twisting streets, their names changing every short distance in order to facilitate the finding of an address in a town where few houses were numbered. She loved it when she and Papa were afoot and they had to step into someone's doorway in order to let a horse and cart go by, even if the horses were hitched tandem in order to take up less room. She loved the unfamiliar skin tones and dialects and outlandish clothing of the men who came from the ships in the harbor, and although she had no claim to beauty as

Lillian and Annabelle had, she nearly always drew a smile from them in return for her own.

As they wended their way now, pedestrians smiled to see them because of Tamara's shining eyes and Mark's red, embarrassed face. Mark thought that Tamara deserved a whipping for running off. She was the peskiest child he had ever known and her being a girl made it worse. Mark liked most children. He liked his younger brothers and he had a special liking for Tod Bates, whose parents often brought him to visit, even though Tod was more than three years older than he was. But a baby girl-child was another matter entirely.

All the same, when he slid off Daniel to lift Tamara down in front of her own house he mouthed, half under his breath, "Be careful not to let anybody see you or you'll get a whipping."

As low as his voice was, Tamara heard him, and her smile would have dazzled anyone who had chanced to see her. But there was no one to see; as a matter of fact, she had not even been missed.

As it happened, Millicent Armitage would not have cared a whit if at the moment her youngest daughter had been chasing the town bull on the common. Millicent was seated in her dear friend Grace's drawing room, still feeling shaken because she had so nearly not bothered to call on Grace today because of the heat, which she detested. Her entire attention was focused on Grace's totally unexpected house guest, arrived so recently that her friend had not yet gotten around to sending her word of his arrival.

It was beyond belief! George Hartgrave's presence in Grace's house had been like coming face to face with a ghost from the past. The personable young man had, in fact, been one of the elite clique with whom Millicent had run before her father had so treacherously married her off to Charles and banished her from the only life that was worth living.

Back in that pleasure-filled past, Millicent had never considered George as a candidate for marriage. He had been possessed of neither a title nor a fortune, which had disqualified him. But she had consoled herself with the fact that he would be eminently qualified as a lover, providing the marriage she made was exalted enough to make it worth his while to have his name linked with hers.

George himself would be forced to look for an heiress who could do as much for him as the husband Millicent had hoped to acquire would do for her. Both of them, naturally, George's wife and Millicent's husband, would be sufficiently intelligent to accept extramarital affairs as a matter of course.

And now he was here, as handsome as ever, and still, unbelievably, unmarried! The lady he had aspired to had not been forthcoming, owing to a scandal that George had brought down on his own head by a liaison with another lady whose standing was so high that not even his most influential friends had been able to protect him from the King's displeasure when it had come to his ears. His father had been obliged to banish him to a rundown country estate until the muddy waters had subsided.

Unfortunately for George, getting back into the society of his choice had not been as easy as he had anticipated. His pocket had been most uncomfortably flat, and he had been forced to look for additional funds at the gaming tables. When luck had gone against him he had set himself up as a liaison man between one of the more disreputable gaming houses and certain young men with more money than sense.

"And damme if one of the young fools didn't have a father who knew someone who knew someone who had the ear of the King!" George laughed now, recounting his adventures to his enthralled audience. "And so my newest pursuit of a suitable heiress came to naught, and this time my father decreed that I get entirely out of the country for a while. You see before you a man with no luck whatsoever, Millicent. If Cousin Grace hadn't seen fit to offer me hospitality I don't know what I would have done!"

He smiled at Grace warmly, and Grace purred. George was only a second cousin but he'd be a sensation in this backwater and his glory would reflect on her, his kinswoman. Thank goodness for the actual blood relationship, else her husband, who was as stodgy and conservative a Tory as had ever lived, would never have allowed her to extend the invitation when he had presented himself at her door.

George turned to Millicent, whose lips were parted and whose face was flushed with excitement at his refreshing gossip, so long missing from her life.

"You at least found a measure of prosperity, even if you have to enjoy it in this godforsaken place! I've often thought how wonderful it would have been for us if my ancestors had seen fit to provide for me more handsomely. What a swath we would have cut! Damme, you haven't changed a whit. If you were in London you'd still set society by its ear. Everybody we knew thought it was nothing short of a crime when your father forced you to marry that dull lawyer and packed you away to the colonies. We talked of nothing else for weeks, and they still remember you and wonder when you'll come back."

Millicent's blood pounded against the tight lacing that Dr. Peabody still warned her against at every opportunity. Pompous old fool, what difference could tight lacing make now? She had not shared Charles' bed since Tamara had been born, and it was Peabody's doing as much as her own, because he had believed every word of complaint as to her physical condition that she had made, and warned Charles that another confinement might prove fatal to her.

Three daughters were quite enough, thank you! And Charles, being Charles, had accepted the doctor's verdict and had taken his own way of coping with his frustrations by absenting himself from home for long periods of time. Millicent neither knew nor cared if he found consolation elsewhere. Knowing him so well, she suspected that he didn't, the more fool he! So long as he left her alone, she was satisfied.

She had been lucky in her pregnancies. They had neither aged her nor impaired her figure, but no woman can go on bearing one child after another without suffering the consequences eventually. She had seen too many women who were old at thirty, their skins dull and dry, their teeth rotted and half of them missing, their bodies rendered shapeless. And there was always the chance, however remote, that something might happen to Charles and then she would be free to return to England and take up where she had left off, with no restraint from either husband or father. With her looks and with the considerable fortune that she would take with her, even a titled husband would not be out of reach, a husband, moreover, who could father a boy to inherit from Uncle Basil and further enhance her prestige.

She put down the delicate china teacup and studied the man who had so suddenly emerged from the glittering world across the ocean. What a charming rascal he still was for all that he was so many years older than when she had last seen him! George's were the kind of looks that wore well until past middle age. He was of several inches above average height and his hair was as fair as her own, and there was still that reckless light in his eyes that made her breath catch.

God, but it had been a long time since she had been in contact with any man who could make her blood race through her body and set it to tingling. All these years in this deadly Boston, without even the mildest of flirtations to relieve the tedium! She was a hot-blooded woman, as she had been a hot-blooded girl, and Charles had never satisfied her with his gentle lovemaking, always mindful that she was a lady.

George Hartgrave would never make that mistake, she'd be bound! It was a pity that she had never had an opportunity to test him or any other man except her husband. She had been so young back there in London, and she had been afraid of ruining her chances, so she had always managed to restrain herself at the crucial moment.

Grace Gammage was well aware of the incipient intrigue that was flickering to life before her eyes, and her own general boredom made her not averse to fanning the flame. As George was her cousin she could not have an affair with him herself, even if her husband did not stay at home of nights and keep a watchful eye on her. But watching this affair flourish under her own auspices would add some spice to her otherwise colorless days. Besides, she was genuinely fond of both Millicent and George. Why shouldn't she help them find a measure of distraction from their troubles?

It was growing late. Ordinarily Millicent would have left an hour before this. Her eyes met and clung to George's as she prepared to depart, and there was no mistaking the invitation in them if a man were as worldly-wise as George.

Her chariot was waiting, with Abel on the driver's seat, and her maid Agnes was summoned from the kitchen where she had been waiting on her mistress's pleasure. During the drive home Agnes's sharp eyes did not fail to notice Millicent's agitation.

That Mr. Hartgrave, now, he was a one! Agnes had caught a glimpse of him as he had kissed Millicent's hand as he'd handed her into the chariot, and he'd held her hand a deal longer than necessary. He was a handsome devil, one to put all the other men in Boston to shame with his gentlemanly bearing and the clothes that could only have come from the finest tailors in London.

There's something in the offing, Agnes thought, and she felt the same thrill of vicarious excitement that Grace had felt. She'd wager her next quarter's wages on it, even if wagering was held to be a sin. Looking at her mistress, her cheeks as red as a dairymaid's, her lips moist and half parted as she smiled, Agnes was sure of it. Oh, yes, there was something in the offing, and Agnes was glad that she would be around to see it played through to the end.

If she played her own part properly there would likely be a little something for her in it, as well. A lady couldn't go abroad without her maid accompanying her. Agnes would be obliged to know more than she should, and her mistress would be obliged to make it worth her while to be discreet.

As the chariot turned into the drive, Agnes's sharp nose and small pale eyes took on an avid look as she let her imagination take full rein. If Mr. George Hartgrave stayed in Boston long enough, she might well have a tidy little nest egg put by for her old age before he left!

Six

Ordinarily Millicent drank her morning tea, served to her before she arose, with relish, but on this particular morning a little more than two months since the arrival of George Hartgrave in Boston, the aroma rising from the cup made bile rise in her throat.

Her head ached, and her eyes felt swollen and gritty. She felt feverish as well. For a moment she wondered if she were coming down with some annoying ailment, and then memory flooded over her and she turned her face into her pillow, her hands clenched.

George was returning to England. Even now he would be aboard the ship that had caught the morning tide. And in spite of all his avowals of love for her she knew that he was eager to go. The fact that she had known from the beginning that George would leave her did nothing to mitigate her misery.

She'd fallen in love with him, that was the trouble. What had started out as a casual affair had ended up as a burning passion that threatened to consume her. She had never felt like this in London, when any affair had begun with the frank understanding that it would end as soon as someone more interesting came along. That had been part of the excitement of it, to take what was at hand while keeping an eye out for something better.

But now she felt as if she had been rent in two. Word had come that George's father had died, and whatever estate he had left now belonged to George. It would not be as much as he wanted but it would serve to put him again in society, where he could add to it by his wits and his charm. Scandals die quickly. By now his latest peccadillo would have been replaced by something else, and besides, as a bereaved son he would be accorded a welcome out of common courtesy. Young men had a habit of settling down once the responsibility for their estates had fallen on their own shoulders, no matter how many wild oats they had sown in their carefree days.

She was going to be sick. She'd tossed and turned half of the night, telling herself that she wouldn't cry, but in the end she had sobbed until her whole body had ached. She had actually made herself ill.

"Damn him!" Millicent said.

She had to get up, she felt as if her bladder were about to burst. She threw back the light coverlet and got to her feet but the room whirled around her and she would have fallen if Agnes hadn't been there to steady her.

"Oh, my God, I'm sick!" Millicent had moaned.

"Yes, *madame*." Agnes had picked up such elegant Frenchified expressions since her own future had begun to look brighter.

Millicent caught a glimpse of herself in the mirror that hung over her dressing table. She saw that her face was white, and there were purplish shadows under her eyes. Her hair was disheveled from her night of tossing, and she looked . . .

"Oh, my God!" she said again. She looked as she

had looked during her last pregnancy in its early stages, before the morning nausea and dizziness had passed.

It wasn't true. It couldn't be true. But she knew, with a hollow certainty, that it was.

Ruined. What chance now for the brilliant marriages for Lillian and Annabelle? What chance to contrive and connive to get them to London, and use all her wits to snare titled husbands for them? The daughters of a notorious woman, a woman who had had the bad taste to present her lawful husband with a bastard, would hardly be highly regarded on the marriage market. Even Charles would not overlook this. She sank back onto the bed and stared her ruin in the face.

Agnes bent over her, straightening her silken nightgown, straightening the coverlet.

"Perhaps this time it will be a boy," she said.

The words dragged Millicent back from the last stages of despair. A boy, a son, a male offspring to inherit from Sir Basil! A light, barely discernible, began to show at the end of the tunnel that had been so black that she had had no hope of emerging from it.

The faint glimmer of light brought her back to sanity. Her mind, numbed by the enormity of what had happened to her, began to function again.

It would be a boy, and he would inherit. All of her old dreams came flooding back, and color returned to her face. Charles was only a man, and men were easy to deceive, particularly when they loved a woman. And Charles loved her, even now that she had given up all pretense of being a wife to him.

Agnes had turned to the dressing table, where she picked up Millicent's nutmeg holder and toyed with it. It was a pretty trinket, made of Battersea enamel, and just large enough to hold a single nutmeg. The inside of the cover was pierced so that it formed a grater. Every fashionable person, whether man or woman, carried one so that no matter where they went they could have freshly ground nutmeg to add its delicate savor to wine or dessert. Agnes handled it lovingly, turning it over and over in her fingers. Her eyes were on Millicent. She didn't speak. She didn't have to.

The sour taste intensified in Millicent's mouth. "Would you like to have it, Agnes?"

Agnes put it in her pocket. "Thank you, *madame.*" Her tone gave no evidence of her satisfaction. The nutmeg holder was by far the most valuable of the gifts her mistress had given her since her liaison with Mr. Hartgrave had begun, but it would not be the most valuable before this affair was finished. Mistress and maid understood one another very well.

Charles returned from his latest trip with a sense of futility. Even the satisfaction of having met Mr. Washington, in Virginia, along with his lady, faded as he entered the house that he had built with such hope for the future only to watch that hope crumble into dust with the passing years. His brief glimpse into the home life of Mr. Washington and his Martha had only served to point up the deficiencies of his own. Martha Washington was far from a beautiful woman but her fondness for her husband was so apparent that anyone could see that the two were happy together and would continue to find contentment in each other.

There was a patter of feet on the stairway as Charles entered the hall, and then a shriek of delight as Tamara threw herself into his arms. Her arms encircled his neck, threatening to strangle him, and her tiny body trembled with joy.

"Papa! You're home!" Tamara fastened her fingers in his hair, innocent of powder, and plastered his face with kisses, and Charles' mood lightened. Here, in this miniscule, far-from-beautiful child, was the fulfillment of his life.

He was fond of Annabelle, who was a tractable child and returned his love, but there was something about this waiflike little creature that tore at his heart-strings every time he saw her. He loved Lillian as a matter of course, but his eldest daughter had a hard, selfish core that so exactly corresponded with her mother's that it was hard to feel toward her as he did toward his younger children.

"And what have you been doing with yourself while I was away?" he asked as he set Tamara back on her feet.

"I went to see Mark." Tamara's eyes sparkled with mischief, and she held her fingers to her lips. "But it's a secret. Mama doesn't know."

"I wouldn't dream of telling her. Secrets are always to be kept." Charles' voice was as grave as the situation called for. "And how did you find the Martins? Well, I hope."

"I only saw Mark and Martha. John was playing with someone else and Tim was taking a nap. Mark brought me home on Daniel. He smells delicious. Daniel, I mean, not Mark, but Mark smells nice too. Like dirt and fresh-sawed wood."

Tamara's face glowed, and Charles felt again that tug at his heart. When Tamara smiled it was almost possible to believe that she would grow up with a beauty of her own that would last infinitely longer than the superficial beauty of her mother and her oldest sister. He could picture her as an old lady, her face wrinkled with years but with the fine bone-structure still there, and that dauntlessness of character that could not be quelled.

He felt the familiar stiffening of his back as Millicent appeared at the head of the staircase. Lord, how lovely she was! When he had been away for several weeks he nearly forgot the perfection of her features, the magnificence of her slender but ripe figure, and on returning it never failed to strike him again full force, as if it were the first time he had ever seen her.

Today Millicent was dressed in pale green, the color that most became her, and her fichu of imported lace set off her perfect complexion and the brilliance of her violet eyes. Her morocco slippers were dyed to match the gown, her ankles were slender and perfectly turned as she lifted her skirt to descend the staircase.

"Charles! You're back at last!" Her voice gave no hint of the relief she felt. If he had delayed much longer, all of her plans would have gone for naught. Incredibly, she lifted her cheek for his kiss. Feeling like a fool, Charles complied, briefly, perfunctorily, as had become his habit since Tamara's birth.

Millicent's laugh tinkled out, filled with amusement. "Is that all the warmth you can conjure up after so long a separation?" But there was no trace of either anger or petulance as she linked her arm through his and drew him into the library that was his own special sanctuary. There she left him to pull the bellcord by the fireplace. "Sit down, you must be tired after your journey."

Jonas entered the room, and his usually impassive face lighted up as he saw that his master had returned. "Welcome home, Mr. Armitage!" The tone of his voice conveyed far more than his words. Charles seldom took him with him when he traveled abroad, not only because he felt that traveling with a servant was ostentatious, but also because he needed Jonas here to keep the household running smoothly. Jonas could be trusted. Charles knew that even in an emergency the black man would cope with it as efficiently as he would be able to himself.

"Jonas, help your master off with his boots and bring his slippers, and then fetch him a rum flip. And I'll have a sherry to keep him company." Millicent sat down in a smaller chair and regarded Charles with a touch of her ordinary disapproval. "Your coat is rumpled, and I swear you didn't put on a clean shirt this morning! I knew you should have taken Jonas with you to look after you."

Jonas knelt to pull off Charles' boots, giving no indication of his resentment at Millicent's assumption that he didn't know how to make his master comfortable without her instructions. As his back was to his mistress, she didn't see the grin on his face, which sobered again almost instantly when Charles winked at him.

"You know I like to travel fast, with no frills. And my shirt was clean this morning, it's simply dusty because of the dryness of the roads."

"And did you meet Mr. Washington and his lady? Tell me, what are they like? Is Martha Washington as plain as everyone says she is?"

"She's a fine-looking woman. She is so naturally kind that her looks scarcely matter after making her acquaintance."

"And wealthy, too! Grace says that Mr. Washington benefited by twenty-five thousand pounds through his marriage!"

"I have no idea as to that, and it didn't occur to me to ask him." Charles' voice was dry.

"Charles! But he did benefit, all the same. Mistress Custis brought him two hundred slaves of her own, as well as her estates near Williamsburg."

"Not so many as that. I believe it was only one hundred and fifty slaves." A smile twitched at the corner of Charles' mouth. As much as he disliked petty gossip, it was pleasant sitting here in his favorite chair with Millicent questioning him much as any other wife would have plied her husband with questions after he had returned from a journey. Tamara had carried a cushion and placed it on the floor as close to his feet as she could get without actually sitting on them, and Millicent's face showed genuine interest. Such scenes of contented domesticity were so rare in his life that he allowed himself to relish it even though he knew that its promise was false.

The first sip of the flip deepened his sense of contentment. Mr. Washington kept a good cellar, but nobody could make a flip as Jonas did, not even Eli Bates, who was no mean hand at them. He'd be glad to get over to The Temptation this evening and share his experiences with Eli and the other men who would be there. He'd stop and take Luke along with him. Their interest would be avid, and they would make everything he told them the subject of discussion for days afterward.

"Actually, we talked politics most of the time. That was the purpose of my visit, you know."

"Politics! I expect you never noticed what Mistress Washington was wearing."

Charles looked bewildered. He'd made the journey particularly to learn Mr. Washington's opinion on the Indian situation, whether or not he thought that continued trouble with France could bring them swooping down in their hundreds on Boston and the other seaboard towns. Boston, and all of the colonies, needed more troops for protection, but these colonists, particularly those in Massachusetts, had an aversion to paying taxes even for something so essential.

"Something sprigged," he said, in answer to his wife's question. He racked his brain. "There might have been lace on her apron." This last in a doubtful tone.

Millicent's eyes fell on her daughter, and Charles felt a prickling along his spine. But Millicent only patted Tamara's disheveled hair and said, "Run upstairs and change into something more presentable. And tell Mistress Witherspoon that Lillian and Annabelle may be excused from their lessons early because this is your father's first night at home, and you may all take supper with us."

The spinster sister of a local schoolmaster was only too grateful to be permitted to return home early. Annabelle was a joy to instruct, but Lillian, with her air of superiority, invariably made the poor lady's head ache before the day's lessons were over.

Clean and shining, Tamara sat at the table that evening as straight as a die, and never stirred or even spoke, too afraid that her mother would dismiss her if she attracted her notice by daring to as much as wriggle.

How pretty the red wine looked in the glass goblets, with the candlelight shining through them whenever the glasses were lifted! How beautiful Mama looked, in the violet gown she had changed into, exactly the same deep shade as her eyes. It was enough just to sit there as quiet as a mouse when Mrs. Gatesby, the cook, entered the larder before it had a chance to scuttle back into its hole, and absorb the joy of having Papa home again.

Millicent motioned to Jonas to refill Charles' glass, but this time Charles shook his head. He had drunk more than usual tonight. There was something about returning from any journey that led to heavier-than-usual consumption. And tonight, with Millicent being so cordial toward him, and his daughters on their best behavior, his sense of contentment had gotten the better of his judgment.

"No more, thank you, Jonas. If we've all finished, I'd enjoy hearing Lillian and Annabelle play the piano. Weren't they working on a duet when I left for Virginia?" Having them perform would give him a respite from thinking of things to say, and he enjoyed the instrument when it was well played.

Tamara virtually held her breath during the performance, so as not to disturb the perfection of this hour by as much as a ripple. Somehow there was another glass of wine in Papa's hand, although he had said he didn't want any more, and its color along with the tinkling notes of the music made the moment even more perfect. Her sigh went all the way down to her soul when the performance was over.

"That was lovely. Thank you both very much. I'll say good night to you now, as I'll be going out for a little while."

"Must you go out tonight, Charles?" He was surprised to see that Millicent's mouth drooped not from petulance as much as from disappointment.

"It isn't absolutely essential, if you'd rather I stayed at home. Was there any particular reason you wanted me to stay in?"

"It's just that I'm bored to distraction with nothing but feminine companionship. Since you've been gone I've seen no one but our daughters and a few other women. Ladies do not get invited out in the evening when their husbands are not at home, or entertain either, for that matter."

"In that case, I'd just as soon stay at home and make an early night of it. Lillian, Annabelle, would you like to play something else for us?"

"No. Annabelle keeps making mistakes," Lillian

said. "She doesn't practice as much as I do. But I'll play something for you by myself, so that you won't have to listen to all those jarring discords."

"Annabelle does not either make mistakes!" Tamara forgot her determination to remain quiet so that her mother wouldn't notice that she was up far beyond her bedtime. "She plays pretty!"

"Mama, why hasn't Tamara been sent to bed? It's almost nine o'clock! She's only a baby, she shouldn't be up this late."

"It's because Papa's home, Lillian." Annabelle's sweet face looked troubled, but she moved to put her arm around her little sister. "She has as much right to stay up to see him as we do."

"She does not. We're a good deal older than she is."

"Girls, girls! No bickering!" Millicent demanded. Her voice nearly turned sharp, but she caught herself and turned the sharpness into an amused laugh. "Your Papa will think that you're savages. You've all been up too late as it is. Run along, so that your father can relax."

Tamara went to lift her arms to her father and receive his kiss. Annabelle, shy but determined not to be left out, followed suit. But Lillian, determined to outshine both of them, swept him a deep, graceful curtsey.

"Good evening, Father. I'll be sure and keep my little sisters quiet, so that you won't be disturbed."

Charles and Millicent did not stay up very much longer themselves. After another hour of desultory conversation, with Charles endeavoring to dredge up from his memory details of his journey that might amuse her, he decided that it was time for him to follow his daughters' example and seek his bed. It was disconcerting that he, who could be so eloquent when he was pleading a client's case or discussing colonial affairs with his more affluent friends or the men who frequented The Temptation, should find it so hard to carry on an ordinary evening's small talk with his wife.

Jonas had turned down his bed and laid out his nightshirt and left one candle burning. The house was quiet and the bed looked inviting. He undressed quickly and was just about to put himself between the crisp, clean sheets when Millicent entered the room.

She had disrobed preparatory to retiring, and she was wearing nothing except a filmy dressing robe with ruffles from neckline to hem. Her hair was loose and cascaded down her back and over her shoulders, and her hands were behind her neck.

"Charles, Agnes has gone downstairs and I can't get this necklace clasp loosened. Do help me, it's caught in my hair."

She was wearing a scent that seemed to envelop him as he worked at the clasp. As he attempted to loosen it, she turned her head. Her lips were parted and her eyes were soft. Her hand, as she reached up to touch his face, was as delicate as the brush of a butterfly's wing.

"I missed you. I'm glad you've come home."

Her mouth was only inches from his, pink, moist, enticing. "Millicent, don't. . . ."

"Charles, I missed you." She had turned all the way around now so that she was in his arms. "I know I've been a bad wife to you, but I was so young when we were married! I'm older now, and I've done a lot of thinking since you've been gone. I'm lonesome, Charles. I'm only a woman, I'm human, I need someone."

"Millicent, you mustn't. We mustn't. You know what Peabody said. It isn't safe for you. . . ."

"That was more than three years ago. I've never felt better in my life. I'm completely recovered,

Charles." Her mouth trembled, and her eyes were filled with appeal. "We can't go on like this, it isn't natural, it isn't human! I know better about myself than Dr. Peabody."

Three years, Charles thought, his head swimming. Three years, and every night of those three years he'd been frantic with wanting her, needing her. And she had never come to him like this, of her own accord. Any enjoyment she had ever had of him had been against her will, a response of her body rather than her heart. She looked well, she must be well, or she wouldn't be here now, like this. Could she really want him, after all these years, want him for himself? Had she matured enough to realize that they could be happy together, if only she would allow it?

His thoughts were jerky, chaotic, hardly coherent. The touch of her satiny skin, her warmth, her fragrance, drove even those thoughts from his mind as his senses burgeoned. God help him, he loved her, he'd loved her to distraction ever since the first time he'd seen her and despaired of ever having her. This might be the only time in his life when he'd possess her completely, wanting him as much as he wanted her.

"Now, Charles!" Her voice was urgent, her hands a siren's hands. All thought was gone now, and there was nothing but the woman in his arms, the woman he had loved for so long and so frustratingly. He held her close, his mouth sought hers, found it, drove all other considerations from his mind. Her slender waist, her swelling hips, her soft, firm breasts under his seeking hands closed around him like a mist, shutting out all the rest of the world.

He didn't blow out the candle. He wanted to see as well as touch, to savor every inch of her, to drink in each last second of this incredible thing that was happening. If she despised him again in the morning, it would still have been worth it.

Luke looked at Eli with his eyebrows raised as the two friends watched Charles take his leave from The Temptation. "The lawyer is in fine fettle these days. I don't recollect ever seeing him so contented."

"He has reason to be." Eli glanced at the other patrons who were still enjoying their cider or grog, and lowered his voice. "Patience heard it from Mistress Vaughn who had it from Mistress Witherspoon herself that Mistress Armitage is in the family way. Looks like the lady has finally come to her senses about Mr. Armitage and decided she has a durned good thing in him."

"You mean he had a good thing in her!" a voice from behind them sneered. Both of them turned, and both of them glowered when they saw that the man who had uttered the lewd remark was Henry Atkins, Luke's deadly enemy as far as Henry, not Luke, was concerned.

"You keep your filthy tongue in your mouth where it belongs!" Luke said angrily. "Nobody invited you to join in our conversation in the first place!"

"I've as much right to talk as any man in this room!" The slighter man had had enough to drink to make him belligerent. "Who's going to make me keep my tongue in my mouth, I'd like to know?"

Luke half rose, but Eli's hand on his shoulder pushed him down again. "Get out of my tavern," he said. "And don't come back until you've learned some respect for your betters!"

"My betters? Just because the lawyer's rich doesn't make him any better'n me!" Atkins spat on the floor, and the spittle splattered on Luke's shoe. Luke took his kerchief from his pocket and tossed it at the drunken man.

"Wipe it off."

"You go to hell!"

"Blasphemy, in my tavern!" Eli was outraged. "All right, Luke, you have my permission to teach him some manners."

Luke wiped the spittle from his shoe with his kerchief, and then, deliberately, stood up and crammed the kerchief into Atkins' mouth. While Atkins was still spluttering and gagging he picked him up by the back of his shirt and threw him out through the open door.

Atkins landed on his hands and knees and yelped with pain as the cobbles skinned his hands. His language was enough to make even Luke blanch. Atkins scrambled to his feet and tried to re-enter the tavern, intent on revenge, but Luke's massive form filling the doorway and the hostile eyes of every man inside made him change his mind. Mr. Armitage was well liked and none of Eli's patrons meant to stand by and hear his wife, or the lawyer himself, maligned by a no-good rumpot.

Cursing, but under his breath this time, Atkins lurched down the street in search of a more friendly atmosphere. It seemed that he never could get the better of Luke, or of Eli, who was Luke's friend, or of the lawyer who was a friend to both of them and who had been instrumental in getting him thrown out of the best job he had ever had. Even when he'd made his wife tell one of the Widow Greene's close neighbors that the boy the widow had taken into her house was the bastard son of a whore, it had rebounded in their favor, with Eli marrying the widow, and Luke and Charles Armitage as pleased as punch. But someday, someday!

Back at The Temptation, Luke raised his mug. "Eli,

it makes me feel good all over to hear about Mr. Armitage. If any man deserves to be happy, he's the one!"

Half a dozen men raised their mugs to drink to that; the only ones abstaining were those whose mugs or glasses were empty.

At three o'clock in the morning of February 4, 1762, Martha stepped out of Mistress Millicent's bedchamber with a flannel-wrapped bundle in her arms. She almost stumbled over Tamara, who was huddled on the floor just outside her mother's room, wide awake in spite of the hour and looking half frozen in spite of the blanket she had wrapped around herself.

"My goodness, what are you doing here?" Martha asked, startled half out of her wits.

"Waiting for my little brother." Tamara's voice was hushed, her eyes pools of patient hopefulness.

"Well, he's here. Come along downstairs and we'll show him to your father together." Martha couldn't find it in her heart to scold the child, who had kept the long hours of lonely vigil when she should have been asleep in her bed as her sisters were.

Charles stood up from his chair beside the fire as Martha and Tamara entered. Tamara tugged at Martha's skirt.

"Let me," she said, her face glowing.

Martha nodded.

"Papa, I have a baby brother."

Charles swooped her off her feet and lifted her so that her face was on a level with his own. "Is that a fact? You're not just funning me?"

"No, no, Papa!" Tamara was shouting now, her voice loud and shrill with unbearable excitement. "He's right here, Martha has him! Show us, Martha, show us my little brother!"

They looked at him together, close by the fire, when Martha turned back the blanket to expose his face. The infant was large, and even now, moments after his birth, his face had none of the redness nor wrinkles associated with a newborn child. There was a fuzz of fair hair, as soft as down, on his head.

Charles looked at Martha, a mute question in his eyes. "Millicent?"

"Dr. Peabody is still with her." Martha's mouth was firm. She would not tell Charles of his wife's travail in any case, that was the doctor's job, and especially not in front of Tamara. Millicent's pain had been so tormenting that she had not even had the strength to scream. More than once, Martha had despaired that they could save her or the child either. And she had torn so badly that she was hemorrhaging. As soon as Martha had the infant tucked in his cradle with a warm brick, she had to get back upstairs to see if there was anything she could do to help.

"You can't see her for a while yet. I'll let you know when you can. Tamara, you go to bed. Your brother is here now, there's no need for you to lose any more sleep."

Tamara touched her brother's cheek, her eyes melting with love. "He's beautiful. He's the most beautiful baby in the whole world." Her voice had sunk to a whisper again, filled with love and awe and a loyalty that was going to last all of her life.

Millicent's eyes were open when Martha re-entered her room. They were dull and glazed, but she was coherent.

"I'm not going to die. I won't die, not now that I have my son. I'll fool all of you, wait and see."

No power on earth could make her die now that Sir Basil's heir had been born. She'd have to take the boy to London. When the old man died, Edmonton would inherit and as his mother she would be obliged to make her home in London with him. Sir Basil couldn't last much longer, he had been a great deal older than her father. She must make sure that the old man, who might be senile for all she knew, didn't pass Edmonton over. At his age, Sir Basil might even neglect to tell his solicitors that he had a male heir in America.

A little frown etched her forehead, and she stirred again.

"Tell my husband that he must write to Sir Basil at once. At once, Martha, do you understand? He is to write to him tonight and see that the letter goes out on the first ship, and apprise him of the birth of my son."

She slept then, and Dr. Peabody risked going downstairs for a rum toddy. Just thinking of how Jonas would make it, rich with butter and sprinkled with nutmeg, made his mouth water. He needed its stimulation not only to combat his fatigue, but also to give him the courage to tell Charles what he must know.

"Mistress Armitage will never bear another child. She was irreparably damaged by this birth. Be happy that we managed to save her, Charles. And you already have a fine family, three lovely girls and now this boy. Edmonton is as strong and healthy a child as I have ever brought into the world. Most men would consider themselves fortunate even knowing that there could never be any more."

Charles considered himself fortunate. He was so filled with gratitude that there were no words to express it. Millicent was going to live, and he had a son. What man would dare to ask his merciful God for more?

Seven

Mark floated on his back near the shore of the Charles, his eyes closed against the beating of the sun on his face. This respite from his chores was one he looked forward to on such scorching days as this. His father believed that every boy should learn to work, and Mark had his own particular duties, but Luke also believed that every boy has an inborn right to a little time to himself to pursue whatever amusements he chose. Mark's chief amusement in the summer was swimming, not from any of the wharfs crowded with shipping and teeming with other boys with the same idea, but where he could have the place to himself.

A faint sound infringed on his ears, and he opened his eyes and turned his head to see what had made it. He let out a yelp and sank down into the water until only his head was showing. That pest again, that pesky Tamara who dogged his footsteps until he hardly dared to turn around for fear that she would be there.

If Mark happened to be pulling weeds, a small hand would appear beside his, also pulling weeds. If he was carrying water, a small hand would reach out and fasten itself around the bail of the bucket to help him carry it. It was as if he had two shadows, one that disappeared when the sun went behind a cloud, but the other one made of flesh and blood. But up until this moment she had never dared to infringe on his swimming time. How in tunket had she got herself way out here, anyway? It was a long walk even for a boy.

"Go away!" Mark commanded, his voice a shout. "Don't you have any sense? I don't have any clothes on!"

Tamara squatted down on the bank and considered his statement. At eight, she still retained the elfin appearance she had had at three and four. She was still skinny, her chin was still pointed, and the devotion in her remarkable hazel eyes, fringed with incredibly thick lashes, had never changed.

"I don't mind," she told him, having pondered on it. "But why don't you?"

"Boys don't go swimming with their clothes on, that's why, you ninny!" Mark informed her.

In answer, Tamara stood up and took off her dress and her shoes and stockings, stepped out of her petticoats, and began to shed her underdrawers.

"Hey, you cut that out! What do you think you're doing, anyway?"

"I want to swim too."

"Girls don't swim. Honest to . . ." Mark broke off before he said the word that he wasn't even allowed to think, much less utter aloud. ". . . Sometimes I think you're as crazy as a looney bird!"

"If you can swim, so can I."

"You can't swim at all! You don't know how!" Never since Eve had eaten the apple and gotten herself and Adam kicked out of Eden had there been a girl so perverse.

"You can show me. You showed me how to hammer nails and how to use a saw, and how to milk a cow and how to . . ."

"You keep those drawers on!"

Tamara pulled her pantalets back up and walked into the water. In another minute the stupid girl would drown herself and Mark would get the blame for it and a lot more than for her drowning, too, all undressed like she was and him without a stitch.

"Stop! Stop right there!" Mark swam toward her until his feet touched the bottom. "All right, then, I'll show you! But if you get water in your mouth and strangle don't go blaming me!"

Tamara clamped her mouth shut to show him that she would not get water in it. That at least was a blessing, although Mark had to admit that she didn't chatter the way most girls do, enough to drive a boy insane.

"Back up a little. No, more." Mark backed her up until the water was only a little above her waist, or where her waist would have been if she had had one. "Now, watch me."

He squatted down a little, his arms stretched straight out in front of him. "You do like this, see, and then just lay forward on the water and push your arms down hard, one at a time. Try just pushing your arms down first. That's what keeps you up, see? You push the water down away from you and it keeps you up." He did not add "with practice" because any ninny ought to know that.

Tamara tried pushing the water down. It worked. She watched with undivided attention as Mark lay forward on the water and pushed the water down with his arms to keep himself up. When she tried it, it almost worked, she could tell that it almost had.

Mark waited for her to get tired of it and go away. It never entered Tamara's head to get tired of it and go away. She tried again, and again, and again, and then Mark whooped because she stayed up for three floundering strokes, and then four, and then five, and even if half an hour ago he'd have sworn that no girl could learn to swim he felt proud because he was the one who had taught her. Not good, of course, but she was getting the hang of it, her face set and determined with never a whimper even when she got water in her eyes and it smarted like anything.

A shout from the bank brought Mark's head around.

"Young lad, you there, young Mark, isn't it?" Lord Almighty, it was Parson Eldridge, dressed in sober black but carrying a string of fish he had caught farther down the river. "I thought I saw someone swimming. I have a message for your father. Two of the rungs on my ladderback chair have been broken and I would like him, at his convenience, to mend them. . . ."

The parson of the church that Luke and his family had attended since his marriage, broke off, his face acquiring an expression that filled Mark with awe.

"A girl!" Mr. Eldridge said. "It's a girl there with you!"

Tamara stood up, water streaming from her long hair. "Yes, sir, Parson Eldridge," she said.

The parson covered his eyes with his hands. He trembled. "Come out of there at once! It's Tamara Armitage, isn't it?"

"Yes, sir, Parson Eldridge." Tamara walked out of the water, having been trained to obey her elders. Her drawers had filled with water and they slipped halfway down over her nonexistent hips, threatening to come the rest of the way off with every step she took. Parson Eldridge made a strangling noise and turned his head.

"Mark, cover your eyes! Mistress Armitage, get dressed this instant! Quckly, do you hear me?"

Tamara heard him, but getting dressed quickly when she was dripping wet was easier said than done. Even when she had struggled into her petticoats and dress, which stuck to her skin with a perversity of their own, she was unable to button the buttons on the back with the buttonholes all soggy and limp. She tugged at the parson's coat and then turned her back to him. "If you please, will you button me up?"

Caught between the devil and the deep, the parson attempted to oblige, but his indignant rage caused his hands to tremble and he was unable.

"Never mind, sir. Mark will do it," Tamara said. "He knows how, he's done it before." Which was quite true. During Tamara's visits to the Martins, her buttons had come loose more than once and he had made her decent again without a conscious thought. "Mark, I need you. We can't get my dress buttoned."

Mark stood where he was, waist deep in the river, his face as red as the parson's.

"Can't."

"And why not, young man?" the parson demanded irately. "The child can scarcely return to her home in this condition! Her back will be turned to you."

"No drawers," Mark said.

Parson Eldridge's face went from red to white. There were Mark's clothes, hanging from a bush, his drawers conspicuously on top. He was mother naked!

The parson grasped Tamara's hand in a grip that made her wince although she set her chin stubbornly against crying out. "Come along with me. As for you, Master Mark, get you home and stay there until I have had some words with your parents!"

It was a long, hot, dusty walk back to the Armitage house. The dampness engendered by her wet body's contact with her dry clothing evaporated all too soon, and to make it worse, Parson Eldridge's anger made him stride so fast that Tamara had to take two running steps to his every walking one. Her dress flapped open in the back and her dripping feet, thrust into stockings and shoes, caused blisters to raise on her heels.

Furthermore, she was thoroughly confused. Nowhere in the Bible, as far as she knew, was there any commandment against learning how to swim. Out of all the interminable sermons she had sat through she had never heard one on this particular subject. Her Bible lessons had never mentioned swimming. Moses had been hidden in the bulrushes but he had not, so far as she knew, actually been in the water. Noah had built an ark but he had not swum out to it to get aboard, or if he had, the Bible didn't say so. It was hard to understand. Was the very omission of its mention proof that swimming was a sin?

By the time they reached her home her stockings were stained with blood from the broken blisters on her heels, and her eyes were screwed tight to keep from crying with the pain. There was only one consolation for her confused misery. Papa would explain it to her, and then maybe she would understand.

The two culprits sat side by side in the Armitage library that evening, their backs stiff and their faces tense with apprehension. On the opposite side of the room Charles and Luke faced Parson Eldridge. Luke's face was set and he looked at the parson steadily, with no sign of flinching.

"No, Parson Eldridge, I will not whip Mark," he said.

Charles' face was just as grave, although there was the barest hint of a twinkle in his eyes. "I agree with Luke. They are children, Parson. I can see no slightest hint of intended sin in their escapade. If Mark had not already been in the river when Tamara arrived, he certainly would not have disrobed, and you can't blame him for allowing Tamara to go into the water wearing only her underdrawers. She could scarcely have stayed afloat wearing a full-skirted dress and several petticoats."

"No age is too young to know sin!" The parson fairly spat out the words. "Do you mean to tell me that you are not going to punish these miscreants at all, to the detriment of their souls?"

"We are not," Charles said shortly.

"I'll have you read out of the Church!" Parson Eldridge said, his face black. "Our community will not stand by and see such iniquities go unpunished!"

"May I remind you that the Armitages are not members of your congregation?"

"That may be so, but I can bring pressure to bear to have you read out of the Cockerel. And the Martins are members of my congregation. I will give you one more chance to reconsider before you suffer the consequences."

There was no trace of humor on Luke's face. "Then you will have us read out. I will not whip Mark for a childish prank that meant no harm. If he had done anything evil deliberately he would be punished, but I am his father, and the decision is mine to make."

Charles stood up, indicating that the interview was at an end. "Will you take a glass of wine before you leave?" he asked.

"Sir, I will not!" His back straight, his face thunderous, Parson Eldridge left the house. Charles and Luke looked at each other.

"I guess we're in for it," Luke said.

"I guess we are. But what other stand could we have taken? Injustice is an abominable thing under any circumstances, but when it is directed against children it is intolerable."

He turned to Mark then, whose face was flushed

with relief. "Son, I have just one thing to say. If Tamara insists on learning to swim, make sure that you teach her well! I'd not like to have her drowned."

By morning the story had reached every corner of Boston, and the controversy raged. People took sides. Both Charles and Luke were well known and well liked, and Charles himself was a man of a good deal of importance.

On Sunday morning Luke and Martha and their three sons sat stolidly in their pew while Parson Eldridge read them out of his Church, against the wishes of nearly half of the congregation. On Monday morning, Samuel Peters told Luke that he was discharged.

"You're a good workman, but I have my business to think of. I can't have people saying that I employ a godless man. There's high feeling over this matter, Luke."

On Monday evening, Luke and Charles, with Eli an interested participant, discussed the dilemma over their spirits at The Temptation. Luke's back had been slapped until it was sore, with assurances of men's goodwill, but goodwill does not put bread on the table.

"I'll not back down and crawl begging for readmittance." Luke banged his fist down on the table. "Not even if he'd let me back in without Mark being whipped."

"I didn't think you would." The smile was twitching at the corners of Charles' mouth again. "But I have been thinking." He leaned forward, serious now. "It's time that you set up on your own in any case. You're too good a craftsman to go on working for someone else all your life. We'll have some handbills printed, and advertise in the newspapers, and let people know that you are available for contracts to build. Until you're established, I'll undertake to pay the expenses. You'll need to find a few good workmen to work under you. It will be strictly a business deal. I'll expect repayment with interest when you get on your feet." He would have been glad to make the loan with no interest asked but there was Luke's self-respect to consider.

Eli nodded. "That's the way to handle it! Don't let them get the better of you, boy!" He began to laugh, scratching at his bald scalp. Sometimes the old scars got to itching and fair drove him crazy, especially if the weather was going to change. "I wish I could have seen the parson's face when he found those two youn'uns in the river! It'd be worth being read out of the Church myself to have seen it. Patience was a mite upset, though. She sets a heap of store by you and Martha."

"She isn't going to turn her back on Martha?" For the first time, Luke betrayed anxiety. It would hurt Marty to the quick if Patience withdrew her friendship, and it would hurt the boys as well because they all looked up to Tod with a kind of hero worship, Tod being older and as smart as a whip.

"You'd ought to know better than that. Patience ain't one to turn her back on her friends, no matter how much disgrace they're in. You go to it, Luke! Take Mr. Armitage's offer and set up for yourself. It's time somebody showed these sanctimonious parsons they can't run the whole danged world to suit themselves!"

A week later, the hot spell still continuing, Tamara had another swimming lesson from Mark. This time Mark also took the precaution of wearing his under-drawers in the water, and as a double precaution John perched high in a tree to act as a lookout. At the approach of an enemy he would give a whistle in plenty of time for them to get out and disappear into the nearest clump of bushes.

Tamara learned rapidly, and she had never been happier. Papa had told her that swimming was not a sin, and he had not told her not to do it again. The blisters on her heels still smarted but that was a small price to pay for Papa having stood up for her even against a parson.

As for Mark, he reasoned that if his father had refused to let Parson Eldridge boss him around the least he could do was follow suit even if Tamara was a pest.

Millicent noticed Tamara's sunburn that evening, but only in passing. "You must take better care to keep out of the sun. You'll ruin your complexion, and that and your eyes are your only decent features," she remarked, and turned her attention immediately to Ned.

Tamara knew that her mother loved Ned more than anyone else in the world, but Tamara took it for granted and felt no jealousy. Anybody would love Ned more than anyone else in the world, Tamara did herself, with the exception of Papa and Mark. And she had double reason to love her little brother even though she would have loved him in any case.

Since Ned's birth, Millicent had been softer, less distant, her temper had so improved that it was as if Ned's birthing had been a rebirth for her as well. Mama and Papa never quarreled anymore, and although Papa still traveled a good deal, his absences were of shorter duration. All in all, the world was a smiling place these days, and Tamara had no reason to think that it would ever change.

Eight

"What do you think, Mr. Armitage? Can they do that to us? Do we have to stand for it?"

The question was put to Charles as he sat in his accustomed place at The Temptation. On this particular occasion the tavern was crowded as men gathered to give vent to their indignation at this latest iniquity of Parliament.

"Tax stamps on newspapers, calendars, books, pamphlets, on every legal paper we might have need of! Isn't there anything those fools over there aren't slapping a tax on? How're we to pay it, I'd like to know? Even almanacs. How's a man supposed to get along without an almanac? How's a farmer supposed to know when to plant, and when to expect rain or dry, how're even our wives to know the best time to put down preserves or make butter and cheese?" The voice was filled with indignation that bordered on fury.

"It ain't only that!" another voice broke in before Charles had a chance to answer. "Why, this act'll take all the specie out of the colonies and put it in British pockets! How're we going to do business then, I ask you? What'll we use for money when it's all sent over to England? It can't all be done by barter, not these days it can't!"

The man who had just spoken had a point. There was a genuine shortage of specie in Boston, in all of the colonies. As the people prospered, particularly in the towns, they had acquired the habit of saving their silver coins until they had enough to be melted down and made into cups, mugs, candlesticks, porringers, anything that took their fancy. These silver artifacts were considered a sound investment, as well as being objects of beauty. Silversmiths such as Mr. Revere did a brisk business in melting down coins and fashioning articles to tickle people's egos. The result was that there was scarcely enough specie left in the colonies to go around.

"I don't think it will come to that. I agree that there is a shortage of specie, but the military defense of the colonies has to be defrayed in some way. It has cost England a great deal to maintain troops here to protect us from the French and Indians, and the danger is still present. Most of the common people in England are no better off than we are, some of them worse off, and I can understand why they object to paying extra taxes out of their own pockets to protect us over here."

"But it ain't right! It's nothing short of a crime to just slap these taxes on us without a by-your-leave! They didn't ask if we wanted the damned taxes, did they, no, they just slapped them on!"

"What's Ben Franklin doing over there anyways? Why didn't he stop it? For all the good he's doing us he might as well have stayed to home! Why should we have to pay for a flock of French and Indian wars? It was the gov'ment that started 'em, let the gov'ment pay for 'em!"

"That's right. Some of us fought in 'em! When Gov'ner Shirley beat the drums for volunteers back in

'56 I done joined up. Dick Gridley's outfit I was in, alongside of Paul Revere. Had my own gun, too, all's they give me was a powder horn an' a bullet pouch an' a knapsack an' a wooden bottle to carry my rum and there was plenty of times it was empty! Most froze to death too, 'fore we ever got home. We done our part, now let them do theirs by payin' for the troops!"

Luke, who these days never drank more than he needed to quench his thirst, disregarded the angry man and leaned toward Charles. "When is this so-called Stamp Act going to take effect? I didn't have a chance to look at a newspaper."

"On November 1, not so long from now," Charles told him. There was a worried frown on the lawyer's face. Not since he had come to the colonies had he seen the common men so angry. Indignation was running rampant. Everywhere he went he heard tirades against taxation without representation. If the tide continued in its present trend, violence could easily erupt as tempers ran higher and higher.

"As for Dr. Franklin, I expect he has his own reasons for not giving the bill more opposition. I heard that he had the gout at the time it was debated and didn't take as much interest in it as he might have done. I'd like a chance to talk with him personally, but as that's out of the question we can only wait for developments."

Luke's jaw was set. "Does that mean I'll have to buy their legal paper every time I get a man's name on a contract for a house?"

"I expect it does. It's going to affect everyone, directly or indirectly."

"Are we going to stand for it, like a herd of sheep?"

"I don't know. I wish I did." There were lines furrowing Charles' forehead. "I don't like the temper of these men, Luke. Although I sympathize with their predicament, some of us must keep cool heads. Don't you go running off and aligning yourself with any half-cocked scheme of reprisal! Violence isn't likely to solve the problem, but only to compound it."

Millicent was seated at the piano when Charles let himself into the house later that evening. Ned, who should have been in bed long ago, sat on a cushion at her feet, his face rapt as she made magic come from the instrument, while Tamara occupied herself with a piece of needlework, plying the needle expertly in spite of the roughness of her hands.

It never failed to amuse Charles when he noticed Tamara's hands, hardened and calloused from wielding hammer and saw at the Martins', and digging in their garden, and helping Martha with the heaviest household chores. Charles had only last week seen her at the reins of Luke's ox team, delivering a load of wood! It was as well that Millicent knew little of Tamara's activities and only complained at the state of her hands, which in no way resembled those of a lady except in their delicate construction.

Now Millicent looked up, and the tinkling music stopped. "That's all for this evening, children. Ned, run upstairs and I'll be up directly to hear your prayers."

"I'll see to it, Mother." Tamara put aside her embroidery and rose to her feet, her face eager, and for once Millicent nodded and allowed her to put Ned to bed and hear his prayers.

"You look disturbed, Charles. Is anything in particular troubling you?"

Charles smiled at her. It was surprising how contented he had been these past years, in spite of the fact that Millicent had stopped sharing his bed before she'd been four months pregnant with Ned. His content hinged on the fact that this time it had not been Millicent's revulsion toward him that had kept her from him, but the state of her health. The fact that she'd wanted him enough to risk pregnancy in spite of Dr. Peabody's warnings made him feel that nothing in the world that he could do for her would make up to her for all she had suffered. Everything, that is, except taking her back to England, and they had had few arguments even about that, as Millicent thought that Ned was far too young to expose to the rigors of such an arduous journey.

"It's this Stamp Act," he told her. "The people are up in arms about it."

Realizing what he'd said he smiled, a smile touched with wryness. "I didn't intend that to be a pun, but it is almost literally true. It wouldn't surprise me if some of them considered resorting to firearms before feeling dies down."

"What right do they have to grumble against the law of the land?" Millicent's tone was sharper than it usually was of late. "Rabble! They know perfectly well that Massachusetts is governed by the Crown, so why do they rail against it?"

"They talk of being taxed without representation. And they're worried about the loss of specie from the colonies. They have some right on their side, Millicent. I'm afraid that this coming Pope's Day will be more violent than usual."

"Pope's Day!" Millicent's voice held a world of contempt. "These provincial clods can't even call it by its right name, Guy Fawkes Day! The way the rabble carry on is nothing short of disgusting, a stop should be put to it, I can't see what the governor is thinking of to let the disgraceful demonstrations continue!"

There was no use getting into a political argument with her. Millicent had neither interest nor understanding for the problems of the colonial people. Sighing,

Charles summoned Jonas and asked for a flip, and changed the subject by remarking on how well Ned was developing. That never failed to please her, and so he was insured of peace at least at home for the rest of the evening.

Mark grinned as he saw the portly Tory cross the street in order to avoid having to pass the sign that depicted Oliver Cromwell. Most Bostonians thought as Mark did, that it was a rare jest for the protruding sign to be hung so low that passersby had to duck to pass under it, as though they were bowing to the man who had dared to behead a King.

Mark himself still had no trouble passing under the sign, although it would not be long before he too would have to duck as though he were bowing. All around him the streets were filled with other boys of his age, and younger and older, as they ranged from one end of Boston to the other carrying their miniature Popes on boards or pulling them behind them in carts. There was no doubt about it, Pope's Day was the best day of the year. Unlike Millicent Armitage, Mark had no idea that across the ocean in England, Pope's Day was called by another name, Guy Fawkes Day. All Mark was interested in was the celebration.

November 5 was a day to make the more sedate citizens keep to their houses and wait with what patience they could muster for it to pass. From first light, the boys of the town took over, whooping and cat-calling and generally bent on mischief, but that was only the beginning, a mild prelude to what would come later.

At night, as soon as darkness fell, the serious business of the day got under way. This was when the adults came to the fore, the Boston gangs that the more solid citizens deplored.

In most towns in the colonies, one Pope sufficed. Boston had two. These huge effigies were pulled through the streets on carts by their rival factions, those from the North End and those from the South. The platforms held, besides the Popes, various effigies of priests and friars and the devil himself, and were lighted by numerous lanterns.

The mobs were incredible. Thousands of people thronged the streets, accompanied by fiddlers and drummers who advanced in front of the floats, adding their noise to the din.

The North End gang, comprised in large of Irish cudgel boys and other toughs, started from their part of town and the South End gang from theirs. When they met, a battle ensued. Not a mock battle, but a battle real enough so that heads were broken as the two rival factions fought for the possession of the other side's Pope. It was nothing unusual for a man to be maimed for life, and occasionally someone was killed.

Anything that came to hand was used as a weapon. Cudgels, bricks, stones. The noise was enough to wake the dead and deafen those with good hearing. The North End gang invariably had the better of it; as far as Mark knew their Pope had been taken only once.

After the battle had been fought to its conclusion the two sides joined forces, leaving their wounded and maimed where they lay on the cobbles, and made their way through the town gates to the Neck, where a huge bonfire was built and they burned both of the Popes close to where the gallows stood.

Boston had no police force to keep things under control. There were only a handful of town constables and they knew better than to try to interfere. The celebration of Pope's Day was always carried out, from first light until long after midnight.

There were some in Boston who held that Sam Adams was already organizing these rival gangs into a formidable force to be used at his discretion when real trouble with England finally erupted. Certainly the man was wily enough to realize the potential of such a force, and he possessed the eloquence to bend them to his will. Anything that promised action against those in authority was dear to their hearts.

Mark didn't know whether or not that was true. His father thought that it was, and his father had got it from Mr. Armitage, so there must be some truth in it. His father said that the lawyer was worried about it, that Mr. Armitage said that with the right man at its head, these mobs would make an army formidable enough to make even King George take notice. But on this Pope's Day he couldn't have cared less.

He was a big boy now, almost grown, he was big for his age and strong, and this time he was not going to go home when darkness fell, he was going to remain on the streets. He had not decided which gang to ally himself with. The North End, he supposed, because they were almost always the winners and it was always nice to be on the winning side.

He decided on the North End. There was no way for him, even as agile as he was, to force himself to the forefront of the mob; he had to be content to trail along with the thousands who jostled and pushed and shouted and cursed farther back in the procession.

When the untidy parade stopped in front of the houses of prominent men and demanded refreshment, which was provided from fear of reprisal, Mark got no crumb of it, and his bread and apple, all he'd brought, had long since been consumed. But still he stayed with them, his heart on fire. He was a part of this wondrous spectacle, he was a man in his own right, and he felt a heady power that he had never experienced before.

His feet were dragging now, hours after he had set out that morning, and hunger gnawed at his insides, but he perked back to life when a great shout heralded the approach of the South End procession. The light from the torches made the scene lurid, something that hardly seemed real but more like a dream of Hades.

The battle was joined with no preliminaries; such niceties had no part in the proceedings of Guy Fawkes Day. Fists lashed out, cudgels rose and fell, men screamed in agony as they fell and were trampled. Mark was frightened now. There was no way in the world that he could work his way out of the mob that seemed intent on annihilating itself to the last man. Hearing tell of these battles was a far cry from being in one; all of a sudden it didn't seem as glamorous as it had when daylight, and sanity, had still prevailed.

He felt a blow on his shoulder and staggered, and in pure reflex action he struck out and had the satisfaction of hearing a man yelp. But the fighting was harder now and he didn't know how much longer he could keep on his feet. He felt as if he were being suffocated by the milling bodies that pressed against him, and he knew that if he went down there would be little hope for him. His mother wasn't going to like it when his dead and trampled body was carried home to her on a shutter tomorrow.

A hand clamped down on his shoulder, and then he was literally lifted off his feet. This is it, he thought, and for the life of him he couldn't remember a single prayer that would smooth his path into heaven.

"Make way! Move aside!" For a few seconds Mark didn't dare let himself believe that the voice that was roaring the commands belonged to his father. Then he was set back on his feet with a force that jolted him.

"Hang onto my coattail and don't let go. I need both of my hands to get us out of this."

He was mad, Luke was. He was angrier than Mark had ever seen him. Even through his terror and exhaustion Mark knew that he was going to be in for it when he got home, but he didn't care. His father was here, his huge bulk battering their way out of the mob.

"Don't you dare whip him," Martha said. "Look at him, he's half dead already!"

"I ought to take every inch of skin off his back!" Luke's voice was furious, as well it might be. His coat was ripped off his back, his breeches were torn, there was a cut on his forehead, and one of his eyes was swollen shut and the area around it was rapidly turning black. His knuckles were skinned and one of his front teeth was loosened from its socket. "I thought I'd never find him in that mob! He deserves to be punished!"

"But not tonight. Luke, he's only a boy."

Mark closed his eyes and let himself sink into the abyss of despair. He was still only a boy.

Nine

Instead of wearing its habitual smile, Eli's face was set in a sour scowl as he thumped a glass of flip down in front of the stranger. Luke looked at the tavern owner with surprise. What in tunket was eating at Eli now? It wasn't like him to act in such a surly manner to any patron, even one who wasn't one of his valued regulars.

The Temptation was crowded on that hot August night. The heat and the high humidity had worked together to stir up men's thirsts, and besides, the tavern had been unusually filled every night during these past weeks.

Luke had more than a suspicion that some of Eli's patrons had joined the Sons of Liberty, that secret organization that Sam Adams was behind, but so far at least he didn't believe that Eli had joined it. For one thing, how could he leave his business to attend the meetings and join in the other mischief that the Sons of Liberty were suspected of doing?

"What's up, Eli? You got something against the gentleman?" Luke asked. His own mug of cider was half emptied, and he was debating whether the weather justified having another before he returned home.

"Gentleman!" Eli snorted. "Where've you been

lately? Don't you know a Stamp Act agent when you see one?"

Luke looked at the stranger more closely. He seemed an ordinary sort of man, his clothes conservative and his manner pleasant. "You sure? He looks all right to me."

Thus far Luke had managed not to become involved in the disputes that raged throughout Boston. Like every other man who could read or who had ears to hear with, he knew about the Virginia Resolves and about that lawyer, Patrick Henry's, speech in the Virginia House of Burgesses that had set all of the colonies to talking. He himself had read and reread the accounts in the Boston *Gazette*. "Caesar had his Brutus, Charles I had his Cromwell, and George III . . . may profit by their example!"

Even Luke, who had tried to keep a level head on his shoulders, had been stirred by Henry's reply to the shouts of "treason!" that had risen from the floor. "If this be treason, make the most of it!" A man couldn't help but be stirred by it, but he had his work to tend to, his family to support, and his sons' futures to provide for as best he could.

Now he tried to conceal his displeasure as Henry Atkins insinuated himself at the table, squeezing between two other men. As usual, Atkins had already drunk too much although the evening was young, and now he was eager to put forth his own opinions.

"Ain't you got some poison you could put in his drink, Eli? Rat poison'ud be the best."

"Shut up, Atkins. Nobody asked you fer advice," Eli said.

Henry did not choose to shut up. Instead, he approached the hapless collector, stepping on Luke's foot as he squeezed his way between the seated men again.

"And what's your opinion of the Stamp Act, if I may be so bold as to ask?" Henry asked with mock courtesy.

"It's a legal act, as far as I can see, so it doesn't call for an opinion." The answer was cautious. Harassment of tax agents was the Bostonians' newest sport and one they engaged in with relish.

"Legal, you say? Be damned to legal! You been havin' yourself a real good time pickin' men's pockets?"

"I only do my work, the same as any of you!" The man was not without courage even in these circumstances. "We all have to do our work."

"Happen mine ain't robbing people! Not only of their money, but of the work they got to have to keep from starvin'!"

"Now see here, that's no way to talk." The stranger licked his lips nervously but nevertheless felt compelled to reprimand the speaker. "You'll get in trouble talking that way. I only came in here for a glass of cider, not to get involved in an argument!"

In answer, Henry picked up the man's mug and poured what was left of its contents over the tax collector's head. "There, that oughta quench you good enough!"

Luke stood up. "Here, now, Atkins. . . ."

"You keep outa this, Martin! You ain't one of us, so you got no say. We say we've had enough of this man's company, he's smellin' up the place, and it's time he left!"

"This is a public house. I have as much right here as anyone. I'll report your action!" The hapless Stamp Act man mopped at his head, still endeavoring to maintain a modicum of dignity in spite of the ludicrous appearance he knew he must be presenting to a roomful of men who were no friends of his.

"We'll help you on your way so's you can report it faster! Let's help him out, men, let's show him where the door's at in case he's forgot!"

Luke turned to Eli as Atkins and two other men grasped the agent by his arms and shoved him toward the door. "Eli, do you think we should allow this?"

"I don't see a thing," Eli said. "Sit down, Luke. You don't see anythin' either."

Undecided, Luke let Eli urge him back onto the bench. Maybe he didn't see anything, but what he didn't see told him that the agent, sacrificing caution to outraged dignity, was making the mistake of fighting back as he was forcibly ejected onto the cobbles.

That was all the excuse his baiters needed. The first blow was struck, and another. Two more men followed Atkins and his first supporters out to join in teaching the agent a lesson. The agent's cries of indignant protest gave way to cries of pain as fists landed with telling effect, as his clothing was torn, as one of his teeth was knocked from his mouth, followed by a spurt of blood.

From the sound of it, they had him down and were kicking him. Luke could stand no more. He had no more brief for King's agents than the next man, but five men against one was unfair odds, and besides, they might kill him if they didn't leave off, and that would bring repercussions down on Eli. The recent goings-on seemed to have sent men's reason flying to the winds. He threw Eli's restraining hand from his shoulder and plunged into the melee outside the tavern door.

The odds were against him, and he knew that he was acting with a lack of common sense, but Luke was a solid man and he'd been in more than one free-for-all before he'd decided to settle down and mend his ways.

Before he was quelled by sheer force of numbers, his interference managed to give the agent a chance to scramble out from under and run for his life.

"Hold up, you fools!" Luke howled as a solid fist jarred the side of his head. "He's gone, and you've no cause to kill me just because I kept you from killing him so's you wouldn't end up stretching a rope! Damn it, leave off now!"

"You ain't with us, you're agin' us!" Henry Atkins panted. His rancor toward Luke was raging in him and now that he had allies on his side he had no intention of throwing away his advantage.

Luke knew that he was in for a fight now, and as strong as he was he wasn't sure that he was going to escape with his own life. That Atkins would like to kill him, he knew, or at least leave him so maimed that he would never again be able to follow his trade.

"Let him have it! Show him he can't interfere with honest men!" Atkins yelled, and Luke found himself backed up against the tavern wall with five angry men intent on mayhem hemming him in. A blow to the side of his head made his brains rattle, and then an attack from the other side nearly knocked him off his feet. Teeth bared, nostrils flaring, Atkins was urging his cronies on to the kill.

Eli's intervention with a cudgel that he kept for emergencies brought the uneven battle to a halt.

"Luke's right. The bastard's gone and you gave him something to think about, so now leave off! My wife'll have what's left of my scalp if anythin' happens to Luke. Come on back inside and hev a drink to cool yerselves off. As far as I can recollect, none of you was in The Temptation tonight. I didn't lay eyes on a one of you."

"How about Luke?" The glances directed his way were still far from friendly as Luke staggered to a bench and sat down to nurse his throbbing head. "Took that bastard's side, didn't he? How can we trust him?"

"You know better'n that! You see any of these men tonight, Luke?"

"How could I have? I wasn't here myself!" Luke mumbled. He wobbled his jaw with tender fingers. It wasn't broken, although it felt as though it were.

"And that agent made a mistake about what tavern he was at. We never laid eyes on him, neither." Eli glared at the men who hadn't taken part in the fracas. "We didn't, did we?"

Heads shook. Grins attested to the fact that each and every one of them who had not been involved would swear that neither Luke nor any of the men who had attacked the King's agent had been present at The Temptation this evening.

Outnumbered now, when the men who had so recently been his allies agreed that what Eli said made sense, Henry Atkins left, grumbling in his throat, his rancor against Luke burning the more fiercely for having been thwarted. Eli drew a round of cider all around, waving away motions to pay.

"One thing's certain, things ain't dull in Boston these days! Gives a man an interest in wakin' up in the mornin' just to see what's goin' to happen next!" He drained his own mug and eyed Luke judiciously. "Go on home afore that agent sends a constable nosin' around here. The way you look, you couldn't rightly claim you haven't been in a fight."

It was after midnight when Mark awoke and had to go outside to the privy. He slipped from his cot quietly so as not to disturb his younger brothers, and made his way barefooted and as silently as a woods creature down the steep, narrow staircase.

His father had come in late for supper. It was so seldom that Luke missed being home for supper that Martha had waited for him until the food had begun to turn cold, and had fed the boys before he came in so that their meal at least wouldn't be spoiled.

And what a sight he'd been when he'd come in! His eye was blackened and his shirt rent half off his back, and the smile on his face, intended to reassure Martha that all was well, was so lopsided that Tim had begun to caterwaul with fright.

Even half asleep, Mark remembered, marveling, that his father had been in a brawl over a tax agent at Eli's tavern. Five against one it had been until he'd mixed into it and then it had been two against five, only the agent had run the first chance he'd got. Even so, Henry Atkins hadn't inflicted any damage on his father to speak of, outside the eye and a swollen jaw. Mark reckoned that his father was about the strongest man in the colonies.

Only one thing bothered Mark. Victor or not, Luke had been on the wrong side of the fight, and that was the truth of it. Mark himself had done his share of stone and manure throwing at tax agents, and he'd learned a few words that he dassn't say in front of his mother in the process. Those North End boys knew words that Mark would bet weren't even in the Bible!

The door creaked when he removed the bar and let himself out, but Luke went right on snoring, all tuckered out from the fight. It made Mark grin to hear him.

The grass was soft and cool, damp with dew on Mark's bare feet, and he wriggled his toes as he moved toward the outhouse. He paused for a moment to sniff, because the air at this time of night always smelled nice no matter how hot it had been before the sun went down, almost as nice as it smelled right before dawn.

Only something was wrong with the air tonight. There was a distinct smell of woodsmoke in it, more than there should have been from the banked cooking fires of the town.

Mark forgot the need that had brought him outside and turned his face to locate the source of the smoke, and his feet moved in the direction his nose pointed. Then he broke into a run, at the same time as his voice rose in a shout.

"Wake up! Wake up! The shed's afire!"

The shed burned to the ground. Only the help of their neighbors, who turned out to form a bucket brigade from the nearest town pump kept the sparks from spreading to the house and taking that too. Boston lived in such constant dread of fire that in the advent of an alarm every citizen who wasn't bedridden turned out to help fight it. They remembered all too well that once the entire town had burned, and it could happen again at any time.

Mark's tears weren't all from the smoke, although he would rather have died than admit it. All those shingles he'd spent so many hours riving out, all those hoops he'd cut for the making of water and syrup buckets, gone in a few minutes between midnight and one o'clock of the morning. The riving out of shingles and the making of bucket hoops was work that could be done by a boy on a rainy day, under the shelter of the shed. Tamara was going to have a fit. She was almost as good by now at fashioning the keyhole and arrowhead locks for the hoops as he was, and she'd done her share of work on the buckets that were waiting to be sold.

Luke put his hand on Mark's shoulder. "What's

done is done. And it can all be replaced with hard work. I just thank the good Lord that you got up, else the house might have caught too and burned us all in our beds."

"If I were you I'd get a good watchdog," Charles told Luke the next night at the tavern. "I'm inclined to agree with you that Atkins must have set the fire, with or without the help of the Liberty Boys. Their harassment of anyone they suspect of being a Tory is getting entirely out of hand. A dog would go a long way toward protecting your property, Luke."

"How could it? Isn't there an ordinance that nobody can own a dog more than ten inches high? What protection would a dog that size be?"

"It could bark. Besides, that ordinance isn't enforced. As long as a dog behaves itself and doesn't go around tearing meat from the butchers' hooks no one bothers it. I'll look out for a good-sized animal for you. Just train it to stay at home and you won't get in any trouble. If you do, I can recommend a good lawyer!" There was a twinkle in Charles' eyes. "And I can guarantee that his fee won't be exorbitant."

"Make it a big one then. I can train it all right."

"I'll send Tamara over in the morning. She can give Mark a hand in cleaning up the mess and rebuilding the shed."

"She's a good hand with hammer and nails and that's a fact. If you think she'd like to help we'd be mighty grateful."

For Tamara, the rest of that month was the happiest period of her life. Hands blistered and blackened, she worked side by side with Mark to clean up the debris and rebuild the shed. Annabelle came and tried to help too, because she was still fond of Martha. She'd have come more often if Millicent hadn't kept her so close to her lessons, determined that she and Lillian were to make brilliant marriages. But Annabelle wasn't much good at such rough work, and after a while Tamara and Mark sent her into the house to help Martha.

Left alone, Tamara and Mark didn't talk much except for Mark to give Tamara orders, but that didn't matter. She was with Mark, and so she already had one foot in heaven.

Ten

Tamara always liked to visit Patience Bates. She liked the woman for all she was sharp-tongued, and she liked Tod too. Not as much as she liked Mark and not half as much as Annabelle liked him. Annabelle loved Tod with a devotion that matched Tamara's for Mark.

On this cold October day Millicent had taken Lillian and Ned to visit the Fluckers. As substantial Tories, the Fluckers were one of the few families that Millicent socialized with. She hadn't objected when Tamara and Annabelle had begged off. Tamara was not a daughter to be shown off with pride, and Annabelle had a habit of retreating into her own thoughts to such an extent that she appeared not to be quite bright. Millicent had a good suspicion that the girl did it on purpose, out of perverseness, when she was forced to go somewhere she didn't want to go, but on occasion she didn't make an issue of it. With Annabelle's beauty, she was bound to make a good marriage, and Lillian had to come first in any case. There would be time to deal with Annabelle after Lillian was settled. Now that Millicent had Ned, the girls were of secondary importance anyway.

The former widow's house smelled of gingerbread and beeswax, and the moment Tamara and Annabelle arrived, Tamara's spirits soared because to her absolute surprise Mark was there before them. Tod was staying at home from his classes at Harvard because he had a cold, and Luke had decided that Mark deserved a day off to keep the older boy company.

Patience's face was wreathed in smiles as she made the two young ladies welcome. Being always concerned for Tod's future, she was well aware that counting Charles Armitage's daughters among his friends would be an asset to him. Not that she discounted the friendship of the Martins, either. Martha was her dearest friend and Luke was by way of being a successful businessman since he had set up for himself, and she still looked on him as a son. But the Armitages were society and it gave her great satisfaction to tell her other friends whenever Annabelle and Tamara had been to visit.

Tod had acquired a new book, some dull tome of history. Patience and Eli saw to it that he had plenty of reading matter. Even the poorest boys of Boston were required to learn to read and write at the infant schools, but for them the greatest part of their reading was in the Bible and the newspapers, in whichever order their personal interests dictated. Like the Bible, the newspapers were held to be filled with gospel truth. If it was down in black print on white paper like the Bible, it had to be true. Other reading matter was at a premium and largely for the wealthy, although some poorer families strained themselves to acquire copies of Increase Mather's sermons.

Annabelle lost no time in immersing herself in Tod's book of history, sitting as close beside him as she could get, her fair head bent close to his dark. At sixteen Tod was an extraordinarily handsome young man, his blue eyes in contrast to his dark hair, and his even, intelligent features gave proof that somewhere in his ancestry there had been people of quality. Tamara thought that Annabelle and Tod were the most beautiful couple in all of Boston.

The trouble was, Tod was ridiculously stubborn in his diffidence toward Annabelle. It didn't matter that he had a keen mind and that their father had already bespoken him to be his clerk in his law office while Tod read law. The Armitages were quality, and what Tod was was a bastard, his father unknown and his natural mother too well known. In a town the size of Boston, with only around eighteen thousand people, there would have been no way to keep the truth from him, and Eli and Patience had been wise enough not to try. It was better that he should know from the beginning so that it wouldn't come as a shock to him later in life. And in every way but blood he was their son, and loved more than most.

Patience returned to her kitchen in order to leave the young people alone. In spite of the tartness of her speech, she was an incurable romantic at heart and she could remember only too well the restrictions of her own youth, when she'd almost never had an opportunity to be alone with one young man or another of whom she had been more than a little fond. And she had her dreams about these young people. Tod and Annabelle, Tamara and Mark. Granted that they were overyoung as yet, but how could anything develop between them if they were never granted the opportunity?

Tamara soon began to fidget. The story about the Magna Carta bored her because she was already familiar with it, although both Tod and Annabelle read aloud beautifully. Mark too was bored, more bored than Tam because for her just being in the same room with him was enough.

The two readers looked up from their book when

Mark arose and said that he was going out for a little while. He left so abruptly, the freedom of the streets calling to him, that he wasn't aware that Tamara had jumped up and reached for her cloak to follow him.

Annabelle blessed both her younger sister and Mark, although she did it silently. The times she had ever spent a few minutes alone with Tod were so few that she could count them on the fingers of her right hand. She smiled at Tod, not failing to notice, because there was nothing about him that she didn't notice, that a frown of consternation had appeared between his dark brows. She had an almost uncontrollable impulse to reach out and brush it away.

Imagining his reaction to the touch of her fingers in what would have amounted to a caress, she felt almost as much like crying as she felt like giggling. Tod was as uneasy as a cat with new kittens every time they were alone together. Anyone would think that he didn't know how to comport himself around girls, but that was impossible. He was so handsome, so perfect, that all sorts of girls must be after him. The thought made Annabelle flinch. If some other girl got him, she wouldn't be able to bear it. Why did he always have to act as though she were as hot as one of the pokers used to plunge into a flip, afraid that if he got too near her she would burn him?

"Imagine being so young that you'd rather go chasing off into the streets than stay in a cozy house with a wonderful book like this!" she said. "Can you remember ever being that young, Tod?"

"Yes, I can," Tod said unhelpfully.

Annabelle bit at her lower lip. Still, she was determined. "But aren't you glad that you aren't anymore? We're grown up. Why, in no time at all we'll be old enough to be married. I like being grown up, don't you?"

"It's all right." Tod looked around wildly, seeking escape. Afraid that she'd gone too far, Annabelle took the book from him. "I'll read this time," she said. "Just imagine what it must have been like at Runnymede, when King John refused to sign the Magna Carta and all those knights and barons had to stay for several more days when they'd only come for one day! It must have been a madhouse. But they wore him down and made him sign in the end. Does it tell how they did it?"

Tod relaxed. This was a safe subject, and either his mother, or the children, would surely come back soon. He'd been mistaken in thinking that Annabelle was interested in him. How could she be? He wasn't going to be such a fool as to dream things that could never come true.

"Of course it does. Just see here. . . ." He turned a page, and when Patience risked a peep into her parlor, the dark head and the fair one were close together. Patience tiptoed back to her kitchen. Where in tunket could those younger children have gone? But she wasn't worried. Mark would take care of Tamara, wherever they'd got to. And if he didn't, that one was capable of taking care of herself.

Mark was walking fast, and Tamara had to run to catch up with him. "Where are we going?"

He stopped abruptly at the sound of her voice and kicked an unoffending pebble with his toe. "To the docks. Go back to the house, Tam."

"But I love to go to the docks! Papa wouldn't care as long as I'm with you."

Mark considered that and decided that it was true. It wasn't Mr. Armitage who would mind, it was Mistress High and Mighty. That in itself helped Mark to make up his mind. He did not care for Mistress Armitage, who looked down her nose at him and acted in general as if he were not there at all, on the few occasions when he came into contact with her. These occasions were very infrequent, as Millicent never came to Mark's house the way Charles did, out of friendship. The Martins were so far beneath her socially that visiting them was as out of the question as visiting the lowest orders in the North End, in their ramshackle dwellings that crawled with living vermin.

Martha and Luke said that Mistress High and Mighty was easier to get along with now than she used to be, but Mark couldn't remember her then, so that meant little to him. But he knew how she was now, and he thought it would serve her right if he let Tamara go with him. Besides, Tam wouldn't bother him much. She wasn't like most girls, who talked all the time, she knew how to be quiet and not distract a man from the business at hand.

They walked rapidly, the brisk wind whipping color into their faces. Tamara's eyes were shining. This afternoon was almost as good as those days when she had helped Mark rebuild the burned shed. It wouldn't last as long, of course, but being an entirely unexpected gift of fate it was doubly precious. Besides, Mark was avidly interested in ships and when he was interested in something his enthusiasm made him talk to her more than he ordinarily did.

Papa had brought Tamara to the docks on several occasions, and she loved the noise and the bustle and the exotic smells and sights that could be found nowhere else. Someday she was going to get on a ship and go way across the ocean to England, when her mother and father decided that Ned was old enough to withstand the journey. It probably wouldn't be long now because Ned was already seven and Mama talked about it all the time, with her face so aglow that it made her so beautiful it made Tamara's breath catch. She herself was of two minds about the journey. It would be adventure beyond compare to sail the ocean, and to see London and maybe even the King, but on the other hand, Mark would have to be left behind, and to face months without his companionship was something she preferred not to dwell on.

Her slipper had come loose and she stopped to kneel and secure it. Mark looked back over his shoulder, his impatience on his face. "I'm sorry. There, it's done!" Tamara stood up again, and then she cocked her head, listening. "Mark, did you hear something?"

Mark listened, and shook his head. It wasn't like Tam to indulge in foolish fancies and it annoyed him.

"There! Now do you hear it?"

Mark also cocked his head. "It's a cat, I think. It sounds like a cat."

"Then it's sick, or hurt." Before he could reach out to stop her Tamara darted past him and down a narrow alleyway between the warehouses. When Mark caught up with her she was scrambling over some bales in search of whatever creature had made the mewling noise.

"Oh, my gracious!"

The face that looked up at them from its hiding place seemed that of a child at first glance, its hair bedraggled around its shoulders and the features pinched with cold. "Go away!" the girl said. "Go away and leave me be, and don't go telling that you saw me here either!"

"You're crying," Tamara said. "Why are you hiding like this?"

"Because I don't want to be found, that's why. Now go away."

Instead of going away Tamara ignored both the command and Mark's tugging at her arm to squat cross-legged on top of a bale and look down at the creature who was doing such an extraordinary thing as to hide in an alley.

"Who don't you want to find you?"

"Jake B . . ." The girl broke off before she finished the name. "The man who owns me, that's who. I'm not going back there, it isn't a fit place, I'd liefer starve." To Tamara's and Mark's astonishment she laughed, a laugh not without humor in spite of its bitterness. "Which I'm in a fair way to be doing right now."

"You're hungry?" Being hungry, actually hungry enough so that you were in a fair way to starving, was such a startling idea to Tamara that it took her a little time to assimilate it. She, and everyone she knew, always had enough food that outside of coming ravenous to the table after an afternoon of vigorous exercise in the open air, being hungry enough so that it hurt was almost inconceivable to her. Her eyes were doubtful as she looked at Mark. It was unlikely that Mark would have any money, any more than she did herself. "Mark, have you a penny, or anything at all?"

"No, I haven't. You'd better come along away." Mark had a feeling that Tamara's nosing into this girl's business was going to cause trouble. He was sorry for the bedraggled creature himself but lacking money in his pocket there was nothing he could do about it, and besides, aiding and abetting runaway bondspeople was a felony.

"But she's hungry, and she's cold!" Without a second thought, Tamara removed her own warm cloak and leaned down to wrap it around the shaking shoulders. "We're going to fetch you something to eat, and you can wear this until we get back." Mistress Bates would have some money in the house, and she would lend it to Tamara because Papa would pay it back.

She jumped down off the bale and began to run back

the way they had come, with Mark belting after her trying to reason with her.

"Where're we going to get her anything to eat?"

"Patience will give us some gingerbread and probably an apple or some cheese. She just baked this morning, don't you remember?"

"You'll catch cold. The wind's blowing like anything."

"No I won't. I'll run fast enough to keep warm."

Mark sighed. Tamara was as troublesome as she had always been. He wondered what malevolent fate had decreed that he should always be saddled with her.

They had reached a busier intersection by now and stood facing each other, both their faces red with stubbornness as well as the cold wind. Tamara seldom argued with Mark, but even if he was so much wiser than she it wasn't right to let someone be cold and hungry if there was any way you could help. A little food and a little money would help the poor cold and hungry girl and so she had to get it for her.

Running footsteps on the cobbles behind them made them turn, and they broke off their argument to see the girl Tamara was determined to succor coming toward them, the cloak in her hand.

"See, I told you she didn't want our help!" Mark said. "Here, I'll take it." He reached out to snatch at the cloak to get this business over with as quickly as possible and get Tam back to the Bates' house where she couldn't cause him any more trouble.

"Here, here, what's all this? You there, what do you mean snatching a cloak from a child? You're a thief, that's what you are!"

All three figures turned to discover the owner of the angry voice and Mark groaned, his mouth falling open. Of all the people in the world he'd rather not have seen at this particular moment it was Parson Eldridge.

"She didn't steal it, I lent it to her! You leave her alone!" Tamara said, her voice clear in the cold air.

"What do you mean you lent it to her? How could that be possible, anyone can see that it's much too small for her, and why would you lend your cloak when it's so cold, leaving yourself without one? Oh, it's you, Mistress Tamara! And that Martin boy again, I should have known. And consorting with the lowest sort of creature, a beggar or worse!"

People were gathering now, interested spectators to the little drama being played out. The girl Tamara had tried to befriend thought it expedient to take to her heels, and left Mark with Tamara's cloak in his hands. The parson was as quick on his feet as the girl and he caught up with her in a matter of seconds, holding her fast and shouting "Thief!"

"She is not!" Tamara threw herself into the struggle that was now taking place, the parson intent on holding his prisoner and the prisoner just as intent on getting away. "You leave her alone! I told you she didn't steal my cloak, I lent it to her!"

"Here, help me, some of you! Hold that child off! Her father shall hear of this, and Mark's father as well, and this time we shall see what shall happen!"

Parson Eldridge broke off to give a yelp as startled as it was pained as the toe of Tamara's slipper connected with his shin. "Little demon! Hold her back, there! Consorting with thieves in broad daylight, and attacking a man of the cloth!"

The parson was so shaken that he spat as he talked, to the amusement of some of the spectators, although other, more willing hands reached out to assist him.

This would be food for talk for many an evening. One or two among them still remembered the time when Parson Eldridge had had the Martin family read out of his Church because this lad and this girl had been caught swimming together without a stitch between them.

"I'm sorry! I never meant to get you in more trouble!" Tamara told the bedraggled girl, her voice filled with regret.

"It wasn't your fault, I guess. I shouldn't have let you leave me your cloak in the first place. You just ran away so fast I couldn't stop you." The girl looked so hopeless that Tamara began to cry in sympathy, and to his consternation Mark found his arm around her as he tried to comfort her.

"I told you it was none of our business!" he said, more miserable than reproachful. "Now see what you've done!"

Charles Armitage had seldom been confronted with such a dilemma as this. For two children to be caught swimming in their skins was one thing, but for his daughter to have taken up with a tavern girl of doubtful reputation, and physically attacked Parson Eldridge in her defense was quite another. Millicent was so angry that she had taken to her bed, sick with humiliation at the laughter that was ringing throughout Boston at her expense. The Armitages had many friends, and for them to know about this was bad enough, but for the common people, the rabble, to have the story to roll on their tongues, savoring it as they built it up out of all proportion, was unbearable! Tamara had not only disgraced them, she had also made them a laughingstock.

"The child had no idea of the kind of person she was defending, and Mark could scarcely have told her even if he knew himself. He did try to stop her, I believe; both children were definite on that point."

"A whore!" Millicent spat out, her face ashen in her fury. "A woman from one of those dreadful taverns that should be burned to the ground!"

"I agree that the traffic at some of those places is deplorable, but a port city with sailors newly off ships is bound to have them. And the young woman doesn't seem to be quite as bad as you make out. It seems that she was there against her will. She was bound out to the tavernkeeper's wife to help with the housewife's chores. But the man lost one of his serving wenches last month, and he decided that she must take the wench's place. Only it seems that he had ulterior motives in removing her from his wife's protection, and that was why she ran away."

Charles did not tell his wife that the checking he had done had been done on Tamara's behalf, because Tamara had cried so hard to think of the poor creature locked up as a thief, or returned to Jake Bartlett, who owned a notorious place called The Tar.

"I had the charges of stealing against her dropped, as it is quite clear that she did not steal Tamara's cloak. Tamara thrust it on her because she was cold," Charles said.

"It grows worse and worse then!" Millicent cried. "For our daughter, *our daughter,* to be on the streets in the company of a low boy like Mark Martin was fully bad enough, but if people could have been made to understand that that creature had snatched her cloak rather than having it given to her it would be a little better. It would have been easy enough for you to explain that the child was overwrought by what had happened and been mistaken in her original statements.

Her kicking of the parson could have been an accident, you could have claimed that she had directed the kick at the thief. That boy would have borne her out, he could scarcely do less seeing how you've befriended his father all these years!"

"You'd have had them lie? Tamara, and Mark as well?"

"Charles, have you no thought for Lillian, of marriageable age already? She'll not be able to show her face in Boston for very shame! Any chance she had here is gone. Even our best friends are aghast!"

What friends? Charles would have liked to ask. Grace Gammage and her stuffy husband, and the Fluckers? His own friends, gentlemen as well as common men, were not so quick to condemn a child for an innocent gesture of mercy. How could anyone expect that a gently reared girl of Tamara's age would realize the background of the woman she had tried to befriend?

"Lillian is overyoung for marriage, and the talk will soon die down."

"Nevertheless, it is time we took our children to London, where they can have advantages they cannot have here. Tamara is running wild, and has ever since she could walk. A season in London would smooth even her rough edges. And Ned is old enough now, more than old enough, even you must admit that. It's unthinkable that they should all grow up without being exposed to the culture that is a part of their heritage!"

Millicent held her breath while she waited for her husband's reaction. Her instinct told her that now was the time to strike, while she had a valid reason. The years were passing all too rapidly. Soon she would be old, Lillian might lose her heart to some colonial bumpkin instead of making the alliance that Millicent wanted for her, and there was always Sir Basil, who was growing more impatient to see his great-nephew with every passing year.

"You'd have us turn tail and run because of this fiasco?"

"It would scarcely be running! It will be taken as a matter of course that we should visit my uncle, who is growing so old." Millicent allowed her voice to quiver. "Charles, I have waited for so long, and I've been patient. Even you must admit that I've been patient. You promised me, faithfully, that when Ned was old enough we would go."

Charles regarded his wife and his heart melted. It was true that he had promised, when Millicent had lain between life and death after Ned's birth. He'd have promised her the moon if he had thought it would bring her back from the brink of the grave. His delay at keeping his promise was due to his own dislike of London in particular, and all of England in general, with its stilted social codes and its degenerating element among the aristocracy that Millicent was so fond of.

Sighing, he admitted defeat. He had promised, and although a winter voyage was far from being desirable, it was time to keep his promise. If they made haste, they would be able to spend a good deal of the winter season, the only one that counted, in London. Hopefully, Millicent would be willing to return to Massachusetts once the season was over, and to compensate for the winter voyage, their stay would not be as long as if they waited until next summer.

Millicent was so thrown into preparations for their departure that she gave no thought at all to Charles' unusual activities during the next several days. Even if any of her friends had known what he was about she was so busy telling them about the forthcoming London season that it was doubtful that they could have found the opportunity to tell her. Also, Charles' activities were so discreet that it was doubtful that any of Millicent's friends could have stumbled on them.

Because of Tamara's frantic concern for the woman she had tried to defend, he set about seeing if there was any way he could help the woman. A talk with her convinced him that she was telling him the truth about her mistreatment at the hands of Jake Bartlett. A burly, mean-eyed man, Mr. Bartlett resented Charles' questions and went as far as to tell him that how he treated his bondswomen was none of Charles' concern.

There was no doubt that left where she was, Charity Babcock would end up pregnant, as well as being initiated into general duties with the unsavory characters who frequented The Tar, as soon as Jake himself had had his fill of her. The bruises on her body that Charity showed him attested that she had tried to defend herself against the man's advances and been beaten for her pains, and those bruises were only on her arms and her shoulders. Charles took her word for it that there were other bruises that she could not show him. He was sure that she was telling him the truth.

Charity was not a beautiful young woman. Her face was even-featured but lacked the doll-like prettiness that was so much favored at that time, and her body was painfully thin because the tavernkeeper's wife had been parsimonious with food, as well as overworking her. Still, once she was clean, and Charles had presented her with a decent dress to wear, she was not unattractive. But finding other employment for her after he had convinced Bartlett, by means of an amount over and above what he had paid for her, to release her from her bond, presented an obstacle. No decent housewife would take her after she had been bound to Jake Bartlett.

So what to do with her after he had dug into his own pocket to buy her freedom? There was no question of bringing her home and giving her employment in his own house. Millicent would have known who she was and never have allowed it, and all of Boston would have frowned, even the common men whose friendship he valued.

It was Luke who came up with the improbable suggestion that Eli might be persuaded to give Charity employment at The Temptation. It had taken days to persuade him. Eli had never allowed a woman to set foot in his establishment, except on the occasions of his own, and Luke and Martha's weddings. To Eli, all women were troublemakers, with the exception of Patience and Martha.

In the end Martha was drafted to talk to Patience, with a tale of woe about Charity that would have melted an iceberg. An innocent young woman, who had sought a better life for herself by coming to Boston after her father had died and his farm been sold out from under her for debt, only to be reduced to being sold as a pauper, and whose luck had run completely out when it was Jake Bartlett who had bought her!

Patience bristled. Patience said that she would never allow Eli to employ a young woman, especially one who was only twenty-four years old and who was attractive enough so that no decent woman in Boston had bought her for fear that her husband's eye might stray.

"It's a hard world on paupers, Patience," Martha told her. "I'd take her myself, but it would have to be in my house and we've no room for her, and you can imagine what the scandal would do to Luke's business. We're just beginning to prosper and it wouldn't take much talk to ruin things for us. You can imagine what people would say about our allowing one of Jake Bartlett's girls in the same house with our three boys! But Charity could live at the tavern and never come in contact with your Tod."

In the end, Patience gave in, her heart touched by Charity's plight. If things would have been hard for Tod, if she and Eli hadn't taken him, how much harder they would be for an attractive young woman who had worked for Jake Bartlett, no matter how much against her will!

So Patience instructed Eli to give the young woman work, with the assurance that if anything out of the way went on in his tavern because of it Eli would answer to her. Patience still had a good hand with a broom.

Only Patience could have compelled Eli to take Charity in, but it was now an accomplished fact and even Eli admitted that Charity did her work with a will. Charity's gratitude toward her benefactors was such that even Eli was impressed. No amount of money in the world could have bought the willing hands and the loyalty that Charity gave to her employer. And Tamara was satisfied. She had known all along that her father could fix anything. Now her only sadness came from the fact that she must soon leave Boston, and Mark.

Eleven

Tamara was delighted when Annabelle's cheeks resumed their normal pink and white of health, replacing the greenish pallor of the seasickness that had never left her during the entire voyage. Annabelle had been so ill from the tossing of the ship that it was over a week after their arrival at their Great-uncle Basil's town house that she was able to rise from her bed and walk across the room with anything resembling a normal gait.

Tamara herself was of two minds about London. There was a great deal that she was anxious to see but until Annabelle was able to accompany her she felt compelled by loyalty to remain indoors and take over the nursing chores. Agnes's time was entirely taken up in attending to the needs of Millicent and Lillian, and the other servants in the house were strangers who spoke with such an odd accent that the sick girl could scarcely understand them. And on top of being sick from the voyage Annabelle was homesick, and was only content when Tamara was with her so that they could talk about Boston and Tod.

As to Great-uncle Basil, Tamara was also of two minds. He certainly lived in a fine house, although it was too high and narrow for Tamara's taste, and its brick exterior was so begrimed with the soot of London's coal fires that it was hard to tell its original color.

There was a footman to answer the door, a small army of liveried servants to keep the ornately furnished rooms in order, a cook and several scullery maids, a coachman, a groom, and a gardener, and not one of them friendly or even possible to talk to as Tam had talked to the servants back home.

The entrance hall was floored with marble, the other rooms had Turkey rugs, coal fires smoldered in every grate, and Tamara thought little of them even if they did dissipate the chill that seemed to have settled in the old house so that no amount of warmth could dispel it. How much nicer wood fires were than this coal, which made her sneeze and her eyes water, indoors as well as out!

Mama and Lillian, ecstatic at being in London at last, had no time for her at all, and Papa spent hours away every day at Lincoln's Inn Fields, talking to other lawyers he had used to know or of whom he had heard, or presenting letters of introduction to men with whom he could discuss current affairs both here and back at home. Politics again! As long as he had been forced to make this journey, Charles was determined to put his time to good use and take back with him every scrap of information that he could garner. The interview he managed to secure with Dr. Franklin gave him a great deal of satisfaction, although he did not agree with the man on every detail.

Tamara, who was confined to the house during these earliest days, was using her time trying to make up her mind about her great-uncle. As a man of venerable years she knew that she was required to accord him the greatest respect, but it was hard to respect a man who spilled snuff down the front of his waistcoats that were none too immaculate in the first place, whose chin stubble scratched her face whenever he insisted on kissing her, and whose breath reeked from overspiced food and spirits at every hour of the day.

Not that her great-uncle paid much attention to her, as she was too young and too lacking in feminine pulchritude to interest him, even if his interests hadn't been inclined in another direction. Tamara could only be grateful for his ignoring of her. She couldn't understand how Lillian could bear to let the old man fondle and kiss her, and simper as if she thought he was the handsomest of men and the greatest wit in the world when in fact he was wrinkled and ugly and usually half flown with wine so that his attempts at humor were either pointless or had a point that made Tamara's ears burn, when she understood them, at the same time that they made Lillian laugh with delight and clap her hands and look at him with admiration that tinged on worship.

And Mama was just as bad. She positively fawned on the old man. Papa kept his feelings toward Sir Basil so well concealed that Tamara couldn't tell what he thought, but Ned at least shared her dislike of him although he knew better than to let Mama or Lillian or Sir Basil suspect it.

"He stinks!" Ned told Tamara, his nose wrinkled. "And he's silly. I don't think he's quite right in the head. I expect it comes of being so old and drinking so much wine."

Tamara agreed with him. Great-uncle was a disappointment. The way Mama had talked all these years, he should have been something like an archangel, instead of half senile and prone to let his hands wander over any young person within his reach, even his own great-nieces.

But he was still influential, there was no doubt about that. Invitations were already coming in, bidding Mama and Lillian to social functions that sent them into raptures, and invitations were going out that sent them into equal raptures and the household into a chaos of preparation. Tamara was glad to keep to the great, drafty, overfurnished chamber that she shared with Annabelle until such time as her sister recovered enough to help her explore the real London with Papa.

That day came at last. Annabelle, although still homesick and what Tamara privately called Tod-sick, was still flushed with enthusiasm to see everything so that she could relate it all to Tod when they returned home. Her fingertips touched the dank stones of the Tower with reverence, her eyes filled with awe as she trod London Bridge, her voice was hushed as she explored the shops on Regent Street, and her expression was tragic as she walked at Smithfield, where the smoke and stench of bonfires and burning flesh had once filled the air.

Papa took them to Covent Gardens, and the Haymarket, and driving on Rotton Row. They saw Charles House and Whitehall and Westminster. It was hard to keep track of Ned during these expeditions. The boy darted here and there so that Papa laughingly said they'd have to put a rope on him so they could haul him back when he got out of sight. But he still summed up London with two succinct words, the same he used to describe his great-uncle: "It stinks." And every time, the words were followed by a question: "Papa, when are we going home?"

Tamara and Annabelle would have echoed Ned's question except that they were old enough to realize the answer. Not for a long time, not until spring. Papa had promised Mama, and Papa couldn't break his promise no matter how much he would have liked to.

When Millicent saw the fair head standing taller

than those around it, her heart rose up into her throat and her breath caught. She began to tremble even though she told herself that it wasn't possible. She herself had supervised the invitations to this ball and George Hartgrave's name had not been on the list.

He turned, and her legs began to tremble. It was he, and he had seen her and was making his way toward her through the crowd. "Mistress Armitage? How delightful to see you again, after so many years! Boston seems long ago to me, but seeing you brings back my delightful visit to my dear cousin Mistress Gammage. How is Grace, may I ask? I trust that you left her well?"

How handsome he still was, in spite of the passage of so many years! A few lines around his eyes, but they only served to enhance his distinguished features. As far as she could see, he had not aged a whit.

"And you, madam, have not changed by so much as a degree!" George went on, covering up her momentary lack of response.

"I had not thought to find you here." Millicent found her voice at last.

"I was not invited; formally, that is. I am here under the auspices of a friend. She had the kindness to inquire of your uncle if she might bring me as her escort, as her husband is ill and could not attend. His misfortune is my good fortune, as you can see."

"Then you have no wife of your own? I should have thought you would have been wed years gone!" Millicent couldn't resist that barb. The way he had left her, without a second thought, leaving her to face the consequences of their affair as best she could! She'd be willing to wager that he hadn't given her another thought at all in all these years until he had heard of her arrival in London, and wrangled this invitation in order to see if the years had left their mark on her!

"I have not been so fortunate. I'm afraid the ladies see through me, and so they turn their backs on me." Likely story! It wasn't their backs they turned to him, even if they weren't fools enough to marry him and let him run through their fortunes! He was still hanging onto the edges of society by the skin of his teeth if she was any judge, although he was dressed in the height of fashion, and the Melchin lace at his throat and wrists had cost a pretty penny. She wondered how far in arrears he was to his tailor.

She was being spiteful in pure self-defense, and she knew it. Her knees were still trembling under the satin of her ball gown, and her hand was shaking although she tightened it around her fan to still it.

George's eyes were riveted on Lillian now, who was surrounded by men who had been invited for her benefit and who had been most astonishingly surprised when they had seen her beauty and grace. How such a vision of perfection could have come out of the colonies was beyond them, but now that they had seen her, the competition for her favors was intense.

"My word, but she's lovely! It's hard to believe that you're the mother of a girl of that age."

"And you keep away from her! She isn't for you, and you might as well understand that from the beginning!" Millicent tapped George's arm with her fan, her voice light as though she were bantering, but she was in deadly earnest and George got the message and looked both shocked and pained.

"Madam, I do not make a habit of robbing cradles! Besides, I'm not in the running. I'll wager I'm the only unattached man here who hasn't a fortune. You would have seen to that."

"Just so you understand it."

There was a stir at the entrance to the ballroom.

Jonas, who had accompanied them to look after Charles just as Agnes had been brought along to look after Millicent and Lillian, was bringing Ned in to be presented, briefly, to his great-uncle's guests so that they could admire Sir Basil's heir.

They stood in the archway for a moment getting their bearings while Jonas located Sir Basil, and several ladies exclaimed "What a beautiful boy! How handsome he is!" and more than one masculine voice rose with statements such as "I wouldn't have thought it. It's no wonder that Sir Basil is so proud of the lad."

Jonas had found Sir Basil now, and he led Ned to him. A little space cleared around them as Sir Basil held up his hand for attention.

"Ladies and gentlemen, it is my great pleasure, the greatest pleasure I've enjoyed for many a year, to present my great-nephew, Edmonton Basil Armitage. As you can see, my name and my estates will be in good hands when I must regretfully leave you, but not, we hope, for many years to come!"

There was a burst of applause much more enthusiastic than the trite remarks had called for, but George was staring first at Ned and then at Millicent. His face had paled and his eyes were penetrating as they probed into hers.

"Your son? I had thought he would be younger. How old is the lad, madam?"

Millicent had a dreadful certainty that she was going to be sick. Should she lie, try to dissemble? But he'd know. Indeed, he already knew, for as Sir Basil rambled on, fondling Ned's shoulder and patting his cheeks, he added, "Isn't he a great lad for his age? I swear there must be something in the air of the colonies that promotes physical perfection in children. You've outdone yourself, Millicent! And Grace gave me to understand that you would never have any more children! What a surprise Ned must have been to your husband, and to all of your friends!"

Ned was wriggling, none of this being stared at and fondled to his liking. He cast an appealing look at Jonas, who stood with his face impassive, waiting for Sir Basil to release the boy into his charge. But Sir Basil did no such thing.

"I believe that we'll just keep Edmonton for a while, so that you can all see at closer range my great good fortune in possessing such an heir, of my own flesh and blood!" The old man was high flown with wine although the evening was still young, and he went rambling on.

Ned's face fell as Jonas bowed and left the room. Ned wouldn't have minded mingling with the guests and snatching sips of wine from discarded glasses, and any tidbit that he could find to stuff his stomach, but it was clear that he was to be petted and made over until he'd feel sick to his stomach. He hated being the focus of all eyes, the center of attention, and he wished, for the dozenth time, that he was back in Boston.

Damn him, Millicent thought. Oh, damn him! How could he help but know? Grace, that incurable gossip, would have told him that she and Charles no longer slept together because of the danger of bearing another child. Maybe she had told him herself, she couldn't remember, the room was suffocating. What if he tried to take advantage of his knowledge, to blackmail her? She'd never dreamed that she would meet him again under these circumstances. She'd thought that he would be settled by now, married to an heiress so that he'd be no threat to her even if they did chance to meet. He hadn't written to Grace, not even once, since he'd left Boston, so she'd had no way of knowing that he was still single and a potential threat.

"Like your two older daughters, Ned resembles your side of the family. I believe it was your father who was fair, and you took after him and now your son, as well as Lillian and Annabelle, are carrying on those exceptional looks. I can see no trace of Armitage in him, from this distance at least."

"If you will excuse me." Millicent left him, willing her legs to stop trembling, her back to remain straight, the smile to remain fixed on her face. Part of her mind registered that Lillian was a sensation, that there was no doubt that she would be the most sought-after young lady of the season. Her future was already assured, she'd have her pick of half a dozen acceptable fortunes, perhaps even a title.

But all that could be negated by George's discovery that Ned was his son. An abyss seemed to yawn beneath her feet. One word, one hint, and where would Ned's inheritance be, what would happen to Lillian's chances? They'd all be ruined, herself, Lillian, Annabelle, even Tamara, who hardly mattered. What would Charles do if he found out the truth? He wouldn't abandon his own children, but what of her, and of Ned?

She came back to herself with a start. That was Charles' hand on her arm, his voice asking solicitously, "Don't you feel well, Millicent? You look pale. Not that I blame you. What a crush! The perfume alone is enough to make anyone feel faint for lack of a breath of clean air."

"I'm fine. We mustn't let Sir Basil keep Ned down here too long, Charles. He should be in bed."

"With that I wholeheartedly agree! I'm afraid that your uncle is a bit intoxicated. We'll give him half an hour, and then I'll see what I can do."

When Millicent looked around the ballroom again, George was dancing with a lady of uncertain age, too heavily painted, undoubtedly the one whom he had escorted. He did not approach her again that evening, but it did nothing to lift the dread from her heart. The abyss yawned ever wider and deeper at her feet.

Twelve

George stepped out of the shadows and put his hand on Millicent's arm. In the darkness, she could barely make out his face, indeed she had been ready to hurry past him if it had proved to be someone else.

"I was afraid you weren't coming. You're more than an hour late."

"It wasn't easy to get away. Charles is visiting one of his friends but my uncle kept me with him until he finally dozed off in his chair. Why did you send me that message? You and I can have nothing to do with each other. Can't you understand that?"

"That is the misstatement of the year!" George drew her down a dark alley and then, when they were deeper in the shadows, drew her into his arms. His face came down over hers, his mouth searched for and found hers. His body was hard against her body, strong, virile, and she felt her knees go weak.

Sanity struggled against the tide of pure physical desire that engulfed her. All these years, and she still went wild at his touch. Even knowing him as she did, she wanted him, as strongly now as she had in Boston. Knowing the threat he was to everything she had ever hoped for did nothing to mitigate her desire for him.

There was something about him that drove all reason from her mind.

She pushed against his chest with her hands, but he caught them in his own and held them, stripping off her gloves so that he could kiss the palms. "God, how I've missed you! There was never another woman to compare with you, Millicent!"

"Liar! You've had dozens of women since me!"

"I don't deny it. I said there were none to compare with you. If there were any use in railing against fate I'd curse it for arranging that we should be kept apart when we were made for each other!"

"I don't believe you. It's Ned you're interested in." She couldn't afford to let her senses betray her, there was too much at stake. "What do you want, George? There's no point in ruining me, and ruining Ned's chances. If you did that, I'd never have a shilling to give you!"

George's laugh rang out, echoing against the walls of the narrow alley. "Millicent, you're incredible! Isn't there a grain of sense in that beautiful head of yours? I don't begrudge you Ned. I admit I'm mightily pleased that he's mine. I've been singularly lucky in not begetting children, but at my age I begin to regret having no sons to give me a measure of immortality. I'd begun to think that I was incapable of fathering a child. Ruin you, and Ned along with you? You said it yourself. What advantage would there be in it for me to do that?"

"Then what do you want?" She shouldn't be here. If she were missed there would be questions asked. Not that she was likely to be missed. Charles would be late in returning from his friend's house and she would be back before then. Sir Basil was sound in a drunken sleep, worn out from last night's ball and the amount he had drunk today to counteract the amount he had drunk last night. Agnes was waiting around the corner in the hired carriage that Millicent had sent her to fetch so that no one at her uncle's house would be aware that she had gone out through the request of one of her uncle's carriages.

"You," George said. He kissed her again. "How could it be anything else?"

"You seek some advantage." She knew him too well to believe him even though she knew that the fire that was consuming her was consuming him as well. Some things couldn't be feigned. They had had that effect on each other from the beginning and it hadn't changed. She was still beautiful, her figure was that of a woman of half her age. They were drawn together like steel filings to a magnet. But he still sought some advantage.

"Darling, can you begrudge me your friendship, your patronage? You, the mother of Sir Basil's heir? It would mean a great deal to me, open doors to me that have been closed of late. We can't belong to each other as we should, but as long as you remain in London we can see each other, be together, take what we can from life while it's still offered us. We'd be fools to throw it away and you know it!"

"That, and my patronage." Millicent tried to cling to her last remnants of common sense but he was kissing her again, his hands caressing her in that way that he knew, only too well, drove her mad. It was little to ask. It was all he could possibly ask, for there was nothing else she could give.

Her breath was still coming fast when she rejoined Agnes in the carriage. She had been given the address of one of George's friends, where she could send a message when she could meet George, and where they could be together while the friend absented himself. A mask would conceal her identity going and coming. George was still a master of intrigue.

How long had she been absent from the house? She couldn't think properly, George's presence was still with her, her body still throbbing from it.

"*Madame,* we must make haste," Agnes warned her. The maid leaned forward and gave terse directions to the driver. Leaning back again she dared to ask, "Did all go well? He made no demands?"

"All went well." Millicent's voice was dreamy. In the darkness, Agnes smiled. As long as all went well, then things would go well for her. She already had a neat nest egg laid away, gathered bit by bit over the years from her mistress. How much more she would receive now that there was a renewed liaison to be kept secret, for her to help Millicent accomplish without discovery!

Beside her, Millicent sighed. It was a sound of pure contentment, but not so contented as the sigh George was giving at the same moment.

All had gone well indeed, George thought. If he played his cards right, he would soon own the world, or all of it that he would need. Millicent still loved him, she was like putty in his hands. He had no doubt that he would be able to maintain complete control over her, once he had found the means to remove Charles from the scene. He'd marry her, of course. That was the only way he could be sure of having absolute control over her and her money. After all the lean years he'd endured, he couldn't risk the chance that she might break with him just when his fortunes had changed.

But marrying Millicent would be no hardship. She was still a beautiful woman, with all the fire and ardor he demanded in the women he took to his bed. Ned was young, and from the looks of Sir Basil, Ned would still be young when he inherited. There would be both Armitage's fortune and Sir Basil's at his disposal. The Armitage fortune would be his by right, and as stepfather and legal guardian to Ned, there would be ample time to transfer most of his to his own pocket before the lad came of age.

Nothing must be allowed to stand in his way. This time he meant to make very sure that he was going to have what should have been his by the right of simply being George Hartgrave, who stood head and shoulders above every other man by means of his handsomeness and charm and wit. He'd known, the moment he'd heard that Millicent was in London, that the tide of his fortune had changed.

It was all so easy, after all. Sir Basil was old and had periods when he understood nothing. Besides, being a rake himself, even at his age insofar as he was able, he had no brief against younger men who also sowed their wild oats.

All it took was a word. Millicent had been pleased to renew her acquaintance with a young man who was the cousin of her dearest friend in Boston. Certainly he should be procured invitations to whatever affairs were given by Sir Basil or his friends. Charles himself took no notice of guest lists and invariably managed to closet himself with some sober man whose opinions he wanted to explore. And when there were no galas, no social affairs in the evening, he just as invariably went to visit someone to probe still more deeply into the political situation.

Millicent was living in a dream. Lillian had already received three offers of marriage, two from heirs to considerable fortunes and one from young Frederic Walton, who would inherit his father's title. His fortune was not as great as those of the other two prospects but they need have no concern about that. Charles would make a generous marriage settlement, and when Ned came into Sir Basil's fortune there would be more if it were needed.

Charles did not have a high opinion of Freddie, but that was of little account. Lillian would be Lady Lillian and if her husband was something of a wastrel that was only to be expected in the society in which she would move.

George, too, was content. His plans were going well, and as long as he was contented he found it easy to keep Millicent so avid for him that she would fall into any plans he made. She knew that George was a scoundrel but it mattered not at all to her. Their being together was all that mattered. How had she survived those dreary years in Boston? The thought of returning there was a little like dying, but now, with things going so well, during all these beautiful months that still remained, every day was a delight. Intrigue only added the spice to life that made it worth living.

They had stayed out longer than they had intended, and Tamara sighed to think that they must return to Sir Basil's narrow house. She and Annabelle had been exploring London's byways, some of them less than savory, but Papa thought that as long as they were here they might as well learn about the seamy side of the city as well as the haunts of the aristocracy. Young ladies as well as boys needed to know the more distasteful facts of life, else how could they protect themselves when they grew older?

They'd seen beggars, covered with sores, and dropped coins into their hands. They'd feasted on roasted chestnuts bought from a street vendor. They had explored dark and twisting alleyways where the tenements leaned against each other in varying states of ruin, while Papa had expounded on the possibilities of bettering conditions for the impoverished.

But that had been in the daylight. Now it was dark, and although they had left the more squalid streets before darkness had become absolute, they had not yet seen a cab to take them home. Annabelle was still so filled with the miseries she had seen and wanted to relate to Tod via letter to take notice, but Tamara saw that her father's hand kept a tight grip on his walking stick, and his eyes were watchful. London after dark was not a healthy place for gentle people without armed escort. Even in the more respectable parts of the city prudent folk hired linkboys to light their way.

The man came out of the shadows, dressed in dark clothing, a hat pulled low over his face. Even though she could barely make him out, Tamara had an uneasy impression that she had seen him at various times during this outing, always a little behind them. She had taken no notice at the time; now a sense of alarm flowed over her.

"Papa, that man . . ."

She spoke too late. Charles had been trying to pierce the shadows of an alley to discover whether a footpad might be lurking there, and he did not turn until it was too late to defend himself. The knife found its way between his ribs before he realized that he was being assaulted. Even then, after he fell, he tried to raise himself, but the man's foot struck out and caught him in the temple with such force that his head struck against the cobbles with a sickening thud.

To Tamara, it was like a nightmare. Beside her, Annabelle's mouth was opened wide as screams poured forth, verging on madness. The attacker knelt and tore the gold ring from Papa's finger and searched for and found his purse in his pocket and then he was gone, racing away into the darkness.

Tamara dropped to her knees beside her father. He was unconscious and for a moment she thought that he was dead. But his waistcoat was soaked with blood that was still flowing freely. Her hands frantic, she tore at his clothing to lay the wound bare. The buttons of his coat and waistcoat ripped off as she yanked at them and his shirt tore under her wrenching fingers.

Sickened, gagging, she wasted no time in screaming. She tore at the shirt again to make a wad to press against the wound. She pressed with all her strength. Papa's life, along with his blood, was pouring out of him and she had to stop it. She hardly heard Annabelle's screams; they were of no importance. Even the running footsteps failed to register on her ears until her shoulder was grasped and a man's gruff, startled voice demanded, "Here, what's all this? Begad, he'd been stabbed!"

"Help him! You must help him!"

"Look to the other young lady. Here's my friend, he'll fetch a cab." Tamara's hands were removed from the improvised pad and the man's larger, stronger hands took over.

Annabelle was still screaming mindlessly, her face blank with shock. "Stop it, stop it, I say!" Tamara demanded. "Annabelle, stop that screaming!" When her command had no effect she put her hands on her sister's shoulders and shook her.

It was Tamara who gave directions to her great-uncle's house, Tamara who held Annabelle close during the endless journey over the rough cobbles, every jolt of the carriage setting her teeth on edge because it made the blood from her father's wound run faster. His hand felt cold when she touched it.

"Is he dead yet?" one of their rescuers asked.

"Can't tell. It's a near thing, anyway." Then, realizing that the two girls were listening, he said no more.

Annabelle was rigid beside her, staring at nothing but not crying or screaming anymore. When they reached the house Tamara left her sister sitting there while she leaped from the carriage before it came to a full stop and raced up the steps to pound on the door and scream for admittance.

George opened the door of his friend's flat and caught Millicent in his arms. "I thought you were never coming! Why are you so late?"

"It isn't easy to get away these days. Even Uncle Basil has some sense of propriety, and our social life has been curtailed drastically since Charles was set upon." Millicent was breathless from hurrying and her voice was sharp. Charles noted that her face was thinner and there were shadows under her eyes when she removed her mask.

"Is there no change?"

"He hasn't even regained consciousness, and it's been a full week! The physicians can tell us nothing. His loss of blood alone was enough to kill him, and the injury to his head may have damaged his brain. He opens his eyes on occasion and is able to drink a few mouthfuls of broth, but then he sinks back again."

Not dead. George cursed to himself. That fool he'd hired to do away with Armitage and make it appear that it was the work of a footpad had botched the job. He should have dug deeper into his pocket and hired two men, but the state of his finances was appallingly low. His father, damn him, had gone through most of the estate before he'd inherited, and what remained was not enough to keep him in any sort of comfort. And besides, the fewer people, even of the low order that he had sought out for this task, who knew about it, the safer he would be.

Even with only one man hired to dispatch Armitage to a better world, he should have been dead. What irony of fate that the knife had missed its mark by the narrowest of margins instead of striking to the heart or lungs, as had been intended! The man led a charmed life.

George was in a black mood. He'd gambled nearly everything he could lay his hands on to make an end to Charles Armitage, the only stumbling block between him and two fortunes, and he had lost.

But it might not be too late even now. It was by no means sure that Charles would not still succumb to his injuries. He was hanging onto life by a thread that would take little effort to snap. The trouble was in finding an opportunity. A pillow held over his face for a moment, and who would be the wiser? Not the doctors, certainly, although they stood ready to take all the credit if he should live. Not senile old Sir Basil, to whom it would mean nothing one way or the other. Not Millicent, who even if she suspected, certainly desired her husband's death as much as he did, a death that would release her from a bondage she had hated since the day she had been forced to marry the man.

George called at Sir Basil's house early in the following week to inquire after Charles and to offer his sympathy. But when George managed to make his way to the bedchamber where Charles lay he found the man Jonas with him.

Three days later George called again. This time it was Tamara who was with her father. It was clear that Charles was never left alone, not even for a few seconds. If Jonas had to give in to the need for an hour or two of sleep Tamara took over. Annabelle and Ned also wandered in and out. It was as if there were a conspiracy between them never to leave Charles unattended.

"The strain is killing me!" Millicent said, when she managed to slip away to George's friend's flat. As he caught her hands in his, George felt their trembling, and he held them close to try to still it. "It's the uncertainty that is so devastating! Lillian is beside herself. We have had to relax the rules of propriety to allow her a bit of freedom, lest Frederic Walton lose interest. Agnes accompanies her whenever she goes out, of course. If this goes on much longer I swear I shall lose my mind!"

"It can't possibly go on much longer, darling," George tried to assure her.

Millicent stirred uneasily in his embrace. There was a nagging suspicion in her mind that she had tried and failed to put away from her. Had George done it, or ordered it done? She didn't want to know! If she didn't know then no blame could be attached to her. But still the suspicion kept coming back, especially in the gray hour of dawn when sleep eluded her.

Murder! The thought made her shudder. Yet, if Charles were dead, what a life would beckon to her, hers for the taking! George would be the most handsome and dashing husband in London even if he was virtually penniless. That would not matter at all in view of her inheritance from Charles, and with Sir Basil's money behind her. Lady Lillian for a daughter, Sir Edmonton for a son, the possibilities were unlimited. Even Annabelle would be procured a title, and for all her unprepossessiveness, Tamara would be married to advantage.

But Charles was not dead, and she shuddered again, pushing the thought away from her. If he lived she'd make shrift to accept what she had planned in the first place, several months of every winter season spent in London. It was a deal better than nothing, if nothing like what might have been.

"Is young Freddie as eager for Lillian as ever?" Sensing the trend of Millicent's thoughts, George thought it expedient to change the subject. As alike as they were, it suited him not to have Millicent know that he had been the instigator of the attack on Charles. It was never wise to give someone else a lever to manipulate you, not even Millicent herself.

"Even more so. I swear I don't know what to do. Both he and Lillian have made up their minds for the earliest possible wedding, and now this! It could be delayed for weeks, months, and if Charles were to die there'd have to be a full year of mourning, and with a boy as light-minded as Freddie, who knows what might happen? Some other girl with equal fortune and beauty might come along, one who would be more immediately available!"

"Under the circumstances, it might be possible to go ahead with the wedding plans." Lillian's marriage to the heir of a title was very much in George's own scheme of things, and especially essential if Charles should live. Lillian liked him, and Freddie would be able to draw him higher into the strata of society he desired. "Sir Basil is in favor of the alliance, isn't he?"

"Of course he is! He had his heart set on the wedding this spring so it could be under his auspices. You know he likes nothing better than to make a splash, it tickles his vanity and makes him feel important."

"Then I'd discuss it with him if I were you. People would understand. As long as Charles is incapacitated you have the right to arrange the marriage contract. Perhaps Charles' hand could be guided while he signed it, before witnesses, of course. Sir Basil could be one and I'd be happy to serve as the other."

Millicent broke free of him to pace up and down, her thoughts racing. George was right. There might never be another opportunity as good as this. She knew that Charles was against Lillian marrying Freddie, and to bring matters to a conclusion before he could throw obstacles in the way was eminently sensible. Once the marriage was an accomplished fact there would be nothing Charles could do about it.

Ned wriggled in the embrace of one of his great-uncle's friends. The man, his breath reeking of whiskey, had caught him in a dark passageway. His hand strayed to where it had no business being, feeling and probing, and Ned's face turned bright red and his temper flared. He kicked out with all his might and the man yelped but his grip on Ned didn't slacken.

"Now, now, my pretty young feller, you don't want to act like that! You want to learn to get along in the world, don't you? Be nice to me, and I promise you'll like it!"

"Get away from me, you piece of filth!" Ned hissed. He began struggling again, his face redder than ever.

Tamara chose that moment to come down the passageway, and Ned was quick to take advantage of it. "Tam, make him leave go of me! He's nasty."

Although Tamara was young, she had a habit of keeping her eyes open and her ears as well, and she had some idea of what was going on.

"My brother is needed in my father's room, sir. Be pleased to unloose him." Her eyes, their hazel turning green with anger, bored into the aging rake's, and he let go.

"No harm meant, and no harm done," the man muttered. "I only stopped to pass the time of day, on my way to Sir Basil's study."

"Then you're going the wrong way. It's in the other direction." Tamara kept her eyes on him until he had rounded a corner in the passageway, and then she took Ned's hand.

"You have to be careful around these men, they aren't like Papa's friends back in Boston."

"They certainly aren't!" Ned's voice was hot with indignation. "They're always trying to pet me and kiss me and I don't like it. I'm glad I kicked him."

"You go ahead and kick any of them who act like that," Tamara told him. "But try to keep out of their way as much as you can." If Papa wasn't still so ill he'd know what to do about it. Mama wouldn't be any help at all, she'd only laugh and say that it was time Ned learned how to get along with gentlemen of quality, she wouldn't believe that any harm had been intended.

Lillian wouldn't even be interested, all she thought about was Freddie, and although Annabelle would understand, she was of such a soft and gentle disposition that Tamara hesitated to shock her. She would just have to keep Ned with her all she could, so she could look out for him herself.

They entered their father's room, and Tamara leaned over the bed to brush a kiss on his forehead. His eyes opened, blank and unknowing, and then a faint gleam of recognition came into them. His lips tried to form a word. Tamara bent close but she couldn't make it out. She thought, her heart constricting, that he was trying to say her name.

The moment passed and his eyes closed again as he sank back into the darkness from which Tamara was terrified he would never emerge. All the same, he had known her!

"He looked at you," Ned whispered. "He did, Tam, I saw him!"

Tamara put her arms around Ned and they clung together for comfort. "When he gets well, we'll go home again," she said. Ned nodded, swallowing against the lump in his throat. When Papa got well . . .

Thirteen

Although it was the fifth of March, there was a foot of snow underfoot, and Charles found the going rough when he left The Temptation to make his way home. It was a Monday, and you would think that at this time of night most of the inhabitants of Boston would be in their homes, but the streets were crowded. The citizens were in a state of agitation. Only this Friday past, heads had been broken at Gray's ropewalks, on Hutchinson Street, because one of the ill-paid privates of the 29th had applied there for work to help eke out his salary.

The work had been offered in such four-letter words that the private had gone to bring a number of his friends to help teach Mr. Gray a lesson in how to treat members of the King's regiments. In the battle that had ensued, the soldiers had been trounced by the regular workmen wielding tarpots and wouldering sticks and had had to retreat to their barracks nursing bloody noses and counting their teeth.

Although the British had promised to keep their men under better restraint, both sides had been watching for an opportunity to renew the hostilities. Boys who should have known better ran the streets, shouting

"Bloody-back!" and "Lobsters for sale!" at every redcoat they saw. Civilians made remarks, intended to be overheard, that were hard to ignore.

Now on this night of March 5, 1770, both civilians and regulars were out in full force. Among them was a certain Captain Goldfinch of the 14th, who had run up a considerable bill at the establishment of the barber Piemont. Unable to collect, Piemont had told one of his apprentices that if he could collect, he could keep the money. It was undoubtedly not from generosity, but because the barber couldn't stand to see a redcoat get away without paying. As such an amount of money would be an unprecedented windfall for him, the apprentice determined to collect if it were the last thing he ever did.

A young boy had been knocked down and a crowd was gathering. Some of the soldiers tried to get back to their barracks, but the citizens blocked their way. Ensign Hall, the ranking officer with them, decided that they would have to make a way for themselves with their bayonets, and so they did, but before they gained the barrack's sanctuary a few heads had been broken.

With the crowd in such an ugly mood, it was hardly time for the apprentice boy to spot Captain Goldfinch on King Street and tag along after him shouting about the bill he had neglected to pay. Goldfinch ignored the lad, but the sentry outside the custom house did not. Having endured the hurling of insults and the throwing of offal at himself for days, the sentry forgot his duty insofar as to strike the apprentice.

That was all the crowd needed. They rushed the sentry, whose name was Montgomery, and the cry of "Murder!" went up. The bell of Old Meeting began to clang, and those people who were at home as they had ought to be rushed out of their houses demanding to know where the fire was. Instead of being informed as to the whereabouts of a fire, they were greeted with the news that the regulars were slashing innocent people with their bayonets. Another cry went up, this time much more ominous. It sounded from the Neck to Copp's Hill. "Town-born turn out!"

By now the sentry was thoroughly frightened. Believing that he was protecting his own life, he threatened to shoot the first man who came near him. The answer was to fire and be damned.

Montgomery, seeing a huge mulatto loom up over him threatening to have his claws, shouted for the main guard to turn out and help him.

The guard had to fight its way across King Street to reach the sentry. Charles, who was caught in the middle of a confrontation that threatened to dissolve into bloodshed, laid his hand on the mulatto's arm. "For the love of God, man, leave off! Do you want to see someone killed?"

"Ain't nobody going to be killed. Them guns ain't loaded," the mulatto informed him, his teeth gleaming white in his dark face. A crowd of sailors backed him up, egging him on.

The guard who had responded to Montgomery's appeal for help consisted of only seven men headed by Captain Preston, who was generally better thought of than the run-of-the-mill soldiers. Charles didn't like the way the situation was shaping up. He saw Henry Knox, the plump, affable bookseller, in the crowd, and started to edge his way toward him. But Knox reached Preston first, and Charles heard him beg the captain to withdraw his men, or else Preston himself might be among those slain.

Captain Goldfinch in the meantime was entreating the citizens to go home. Instead, the crowd surged forward and the mulatto, Crispus Attucks, struck Preston with a piece of cordwood that only grazed him but knocked Montgomery flat instead.

Charles did not see who gave the order to fire. He only knew that it could not have been Preston, who was in no condition at the moment to give an order. What he did see was Montgomery get to his feet and fire directly at Crispus Attucks, and Attucks go down with two balls in his chest.

Other men went down under the fire, and the crowd disintegrated into roiling retreat. Charles saw that Captain Preston was pushing the soldiers' guns up and ordering them not to fire.

There was the sound of drums beating the alarm. Half-dressed soldiers rushed into the streets and formed platoons. Lieutenant Governor Hutchinson was there, fighting his way to the State House, his face like a thundercloud. When he spoke from its balcony, people who had come to despise him and everything he stood for regained a measure of confidence in him. He promised them justice, and somehow he got the mobs off the streets and the soldiers locked up in their barracks. Before the sun rose, Captain Preston and his eight men were under lock and key, charged with murder.

The citizens of Boston were mollified. Hutchinson had kept his promise, and justice would be done. Where in Boston could be found a lawyer who would defend them, and where a jury that would not convict? No lawyer, no jury, would dare to go against the demands of the people.

Charles was still sickened when he arrived at home to bathe and change his blood-spattered clothing. Millicent's face turned white when she saw him.

"Charles, is it true? Has there really been fighting?

There are all sorts of rumors flying. And you were there, just look at you!"

"It's true. The latest I was able to find out, three men were killed and seven more wounded. I helped to carry one of the wounded to a doctor, but he's in a bad way, I doubt he'll survive. An Irishman, someone told me, a man by the name of Patrick Carr."

"Lawlessness, utter lawlessness!" Color had returned to Millicent's face, and now it flamed with indignation. "The rabble should be restrained if it means clapping every one of them in prison!"

"I'll not have that kind of talk in my house!" Charles' mouth clamped in a firm line. "That's the kind of thing that keeps this trouble brewing. High-handedness on one side, resentment and fighting back on the other! I'm going to bathe and change and then I'll be going out again. I want to check on Patrick Carr's condition."

"You have no business getting involved in this at all!" Millicent's temper was also up. "If we lived in England where we belong we'd be well out of it, living normal lives instead of being caught in the middle of riots and worse! How can we rear our children in such a barbarous place? I hope that now you'll realize your mistake and make plans to return to London as soon as possible!"

"We've been over that before." Charles' voice was short, his own temper barely held in check. "Do you think I'll allow my son to be subjected to the advances of those degenerates who frequent your uncle's house, or allow Annabelle to be bartered off to one of the fops you set such store by, just as you bartered off Lillian when I was helpless to prevent it? I think I need not mention that London is not the safest place in the world, either, if you remember how I was set upon and almost killed."

"You should have had better sense than to be abroad dark, and afoot, in such a section of town! It's a mercy that you didn't get Annabelle and Tamara killed as well!"

"I grant you that. I showed poor judgment. Nevertheless, such a thing would be unlikely to happen in Boston. Even our rabble does not make a practice of setting upon unarmed men escorting their young daughters! And if there are degenerates among the gentry of Boston, I have not heard of it."

Millicent's face flamed brighter. "Ned exaggerated his tale, you may be sure. He simply does not understand the ways of polite society."

"That, madam, is an untruth. He knows perfectly well the indignities he suffered in your uncle's house until Tamara had to take it upon herself to protect him, a task that should have been your own had you not been so preoccupied with selling Lillian to that young lordling who will ruin her life!"

"You signed the marriage contract yourself," Millicent fought for calmness.

"Without the faintest idea of what was about, and with you guiding my hand! You needn't bother to deny it. I had it from both Tamara and Ned, who were both in the room at the time. There will be no more talk of London. If Ned must be Sir Basil's heir then he must wait until he has gained his majority before I will permit him to return to that evil city, and that of his own free will, which I misdoubt will ever happen, as he no more wants to return there than does Annabelle or Tamara or I!"

"Ned is still only a child. He'll feel differently when he is older!"

"He is an exceptionally intelligent child, intelligent

enough to know filth and corruption when he sees it even if he doesn't know what name to put to it." Charles turned and left her.

Even thinking about the things that had gone on while he had lain helpless and unknowing sent him into a rage that made the blood pound at his temples. This was no night to engage in another full-fledged battle with his wife. Other, more important matters were at hand. He wanted to see Sam Adams, to learn if he could what that firebrand was going to make of tonight's sorry business.

There was no doubt that he would make all he could of it. Charles knew that one of the main reasons that Adams so hated Hutchinson was that Hutchinson had been instrumental in the downfall of the Land Bank, which had tried to ease the currency situation by putting out paper money of its own. Deacon Adams, Samuel's father, had lost his fortune in it, as he had been its director.

Samuel Adams had been a young man at the time, kinging it at Harvard. The collapse of the Land Bank, which ruined his father, had set the lad to waiting on tables, serving boys he had held to be far beneath him, in order to finish his education.

It didn't matter to Adams that Hutchinson had put Massachusetts currency on a sound basis for the first time in the colony's history. He hated the Hutchinsons as the instruments of his humiliation, and he would go on hating them and everything they stood for for as long as he lived. If he could use the rabble of Boston to bring about Hutchinson's downfall, he would do it without a single qualm.

It was, in the end, a confrontation between Samuel Adams and Hutchinson, almost single-handed. Charles attended the sessions and followed them carefully, and although he often found himself in disagreement with the unkempt, fire-breathing man who had failed at everything he had turned his hand to until he had turned to politics, he could not help but be impressed with Adams' eloquence. Onetime law student, merchant, counting-house clerk, brewer, he was still a power to be reckoned with and his single-mindedness of purpose was to be admired.

"The troops must be withdrawn to the castle!" Adams shouted.

"One regiment, perhaps, should be withdrawn to Castle Island," Hutchinson tried to argue. "That should be enough to quell the unrest."

"Both!" Sam Adams bellowed, and he could bellow louder and make himself heard by more people than the governor himself. Both regiments were removed from Boston proper.

"And what do you think of that?" Eli demanded, rubbing his hands together as he and Luke and Charles discussed it at The Temptation. "When Sam Adams talks, folks listen, and that's the truth of it! Leave it to old Sam, he'll get his way every time, and it's a good thing, too. It's high time somebody made those fools who think they've the right to order us around find out that we ain't goin' to stand for any more nonsense!"

"Five men dead," Luke said a good deal more quietly. "Five men, even if they were causing a riot. I can't get over John Adams and Josiah Quincy defending those nine soldiers and getting them off so lightly. Two light sentences for manslaughter, not murder, and the rest went scot-free."

"Someone had to defend them. And it was largely Patrick Carr's insistence that the troops were badgered beyond endurance, and that they were convinced that the mob was going to kill them, that swung the verdict. It took the man three days to die, and he never wavered from his story. I know, I was one of those who questioned him. A man's deathbed statement carries a lot of weight, especially when he was shot in the riot."

Eli snorted. "Massacre, you mean! That's what folks are callin' it and that's what it was!"

"Eli, I was there. You weren't. The soldiers were provoked into defending themselves."

"You keep on like that the Liberty Boys will be payin' you a visit. They don't like talk like that."

"And if honest men knuckle under to a group of men who hide their faces behind soot and stockings and go around frightening and harassing people, there'll be nothing but anarchy. At least the men were tried. I'd call that a moral victory, if nothing else."

"Moral victory!" Eli slammed down his mug in disgust. He beckoned to Charity Babcock, who still worked at his tavern, and she came to carry away the mug and replace it with a full one.

Charity looked a great deal better than she had when Eli had been prevailed upon to give her employment. She had developed into a comely young woman. She wore her reddish-sandy hair, hinting at Scotch ancestry, pulled back smoothly from her temples and knotted at the nape of her neck, and there was serenity in her light hazel eyes. Her hands were roughened from hard work but immaculate. Her plain calico dresses were threadbare but Charity took great care to keep them starched and clean. She had a pleasant word and a smile for everyone, but she was intimate with no one. As far as anyone could see, she was happy.

Charity smiled now as she asked whether Charles and Luke wanted their mugs refilled.

"I believe not, Charity," Charles said absently, but Luke decided that he could use another. When she had brought it, Charity smiled again, diffidently but with such interest that Charles looked up to smile back.

"I'm glad you weren't hurt except for a few scrapes in that affair." Charity flushed at her own boldness in addressing Charles Armitage so intimately, but her eyes were steady.

"I scarcely noticed them." Charles' voice was pleasant, and Charity nodded and turned back to her duties. Only Luke noticed that the pulse at the base of her throat was throbbing, and he sighed inwardly because he had a soft spot for those who can never hope to realize their deepest desires. He himself had been fortunate, with Martha and his three fine sons, and with his business prospering until shipping had gotten so bad that every second businessman suffered. He had a strong suspicion that Charity was in love with Charles in spite of the difference in their ages and stations. It was not a thing that Luke would mention even to Martha. Feelings such as that were not a subject for gossip, however well intended.

"They ought to have been hung, all of 'em!" Eli brought the subject back on track. "And there ain't a man jack of the Sons of Liberty who don't agree with me, I'll lay any odds you want to name on it!"

Charles' smile was tolerant. "For myself, I believe that we should let sleeping dogs lie. It's over, Eli. There's no use in stirring things up again. I have a great deal of faith that some good will come of it even if every man jack of them wasn't hung. I have no doubt that the Townshend Acts will be repealed. At least they will if Samuel Adams has anything to do with it."

Eli lifted his mug. "I'll drink to that!"

Luke's mug and Charles' glass followed suit, and all three were drained dry before they were set down again, an act that was repeated, with overwhelming relish, when Charles' prediction came true.

On that night, both Charles and Luke returned home late and walking none too steadily, Luke to be greeted by Martha with amused compassion for the head he'd have the next day, Charles by Millicent with icy coldness engendered by her anger because the colonists had had their way. When Eli himself finally returned home he was greeted by Patience with her arms akimbo and indignation on her face.

"You needn't try to tell me you haven't been drinking your own spirits, Eli Bates!"

"Don't intend to. Matter of fact, I'll go back and fetch you some if you're of a mind to celebrate along with me. Don't you understand, wife? We won! We showed 'em they couldn't get away with it! Made 'em take the taxes and restrictions plumb off!"

"Not on tea. There'll still be a tax on tea," Patience reminded him.

"Oh, that. Don't much like the stuff myself. Give me a good mug of cider any day. You want your tea, we can afford the tax, but I'd ruther you drank cider. The Liberty Boys don't hold with drinkin' tea, and it might get back to them."

There was no point in belaboring him with her broom, Patience decided. He was in a condition to think that it was amusing.

Fourteen

On the afternoon of December 24, 1773, Tamara slipped the wide wooden paddle under the pies in Martha's oven and lifted them, one by one, from the baking chamber. Martha's kitchen was redolent with the scent of pumpkin and spices, and from the pudding simmering over the fire. Her mother had been furious when she had refused to remain at home for the Christmas Eve festivities planned for that evening, and Tamara's ears still burned from the caustic remarks that Millicent had thrown at her.

"You are sixteen years old, a young lady, and I made sure to invite half a dozen reasonably eligible young men along with their families. You have a new dress and a new head to wear."

The elaborate headdresses of the day, usually of gauze, which was spelled a variety of ways according to the education of the speller—gauz, gauzze—were commonly called heads. Tamara had little or no interest in heads. Her plain caps suited her well enough. This exasperated her mother beyond all endurance.

"Would you make me a laughingstock, with your preference for the company of common working people, especially on such an important occasion when all of our guests will expect to see you here?"

"I doubt they'll notice my absence, Mother. They'll be so busy talking about the fracas at the harbor that nothing else will be on their minds. And Annabelle will be here." Tamara refrained from adding, "As against her will as I would be!"

Tamara had gone, leaving Millicent so angry that she had drunk two glasses of Madeira to gird herself for words with Charles when he returned, hoping that he would return early enough so that she could make him understand the enormity of the permission he had given Tamara to spend the evening with the Martins.

Tamara was wearing a pink chintz dress with a snowy fichu, and a simple cap. The satin and gauze and Morocco slippers would have been out of place in the Martins' kitchen.

"Mark was there, wasn't he? I haven't had a chance to ask him, but I know he was there. And Tod was too. I know about Tod because he told Annabelle, and if Tod was there, Mark was there."

Martha's face was grave as she cast an expert eye on the pudding. "He was there. I don't know what will come of it, I'm sure. Luke says there are bound to be repercussions, and heavy ones, and he got it from your father himself. I thought that after Sam Adams made the governor back down and remove the soldiers from the common, after the massacre, that things would settle down and ways be found to avoid trouble. And then those men had to destroy that British schooner, what was its name again? back last year, June it was, and bring more reprisals down on us. Luke was beside himself at the idea of our Massachusetts men being taken to other colonies or to England itself for trial, and Mark was even worse. It seems that the younger they are, the more hot-headed they are."

"It was the *Gaspee,*" Tamara said absently. "Mother and Father had a terrible quarrel about it. Papa admitted that the men were operating entirely outside the law, both in running contraband and in destroying the schooner, but he would not concede that our colonists should be removed from being tried right here. It seems that they're forever at each other's throats these days. I'm sorry for Papa. He's always been a stickler for the letter of the law, and he's being torn apart by this controversy. Only in the end, he sticks with the colonies, and that's what drives Mother half mad with fury."

A little smile twitched at the corners of Martha's mouth. She had grown plumper and more comfortable-looking over the years but she was still an extremely pretty woman. There were only a few strands of gray at her temples, and her face retained the country freshness that had first attracted Luke.

She still attracted Luke, Martha thought with even deeper amusement. Tonight, Christmas Eve, after their guests had left and her own boys had either left with them to seek additional amusement elsewhere, or gone to bed, she knew that Luke would turn to her, as avid for her as he had been when they were first married.

Her cheeks turned a shade pinker as she thought about it. It wasn't only Luke, she admitted to herself. She'd be glad when they were alone and she could go into his arms, and feel as young as she had when she'd first seen this husband of hers on the stable roof at the Armitages', and known before she'd ever gotten a closer look at him that he was for her and that no other man would ever suit her. The memory of their frustration, which had nearly driven them mad, during all those months when Mistress High and Mighty had refused to let them marry, could still set her to trembling with fury.

Well, she'd gotten the best of it, in the end. She and Luke were happy. They had their differences, two such fiery people couldn't help but have differences during the course of the years, but they always made up again, and their reconciliations were all the sweeter for the quarrels. They loved each other, their love deep and abiding and strong enough to last a lifetime. But Millicent Armitage was a cold and discontented woman, for all her wealth and prestige. Thinking of how her former mistress had cheated Charles out of the love and comfort he deserved for all these years, Martha had to draw herself up short lest she let the thought spoil this most important of occasions.

"This dumping of all that tea into the harbor must have sent your mother into fits," she remarked, knowing that Tamara wouldn't take it amiss.

In spite of the seriousness of the situation Tamara couldn't help laughing. "Oh, it was a sight to see! She thinks that every one of those rascals should be taken and hung. She's convinced that Papa knows who at least a few of them are and she demanded that he turn them in. Of course he refused. Lucky for us, when you come to think of it, with both Mark and Tod right there in the thick of it. Only where is it all going to end?"

"I haven't the least idea. Mark thinks that things have gone too far to be turned back now. Luke is still for keeping cool heads, but that's your father's influence talking. He sets great store by your father's opinions, and rightly so."

"It's maddening to have to stay at home and not be in on any of it!" Tamara had a childlike impulse to stick her finger into one of the pies to test it, but she managed not to give in to it. As her mother had said, she was sixteen now. "I'd have given anything to dress up in rags and blacken my face and help dump that tea! The way those British are acting, I'd as soon never drink tea again as long as I live, but Mama still has it in the house although Papa disapproves. He won't drink it himself but he lets her. I expect he thinks that if he objected he'd start a full-scale war right in our house."

Martha's mouth firmed. She was more worried than she wanted Tamara to see. She loved her sons equally but Mark was her first-born and she had no desire to see him imprisoned or hung. He was seldom home at night anymore, but hung around with those Liberty Boys, and who knew what deviltry they'd hatch up next?

The King wouldn't stand for it forever. Some of them at least were bound to be taken and tried. The thought of Mark being bundled aboard a ship and taken to England and imprisoned there, where there would be no chance of a fair trial, was one that kept her awake on more nights than she had let Luke know. He himself was worried enough without her adding to his burden by voicing her own fears.

"I hope the men won't be too late. Tim at least ought to come in soon. He and John are too young to spend their evenings at Eli's tavern. Not that they can't think up enough mischief to get into without making themselves sodden with drink!"

"The house looks beautiful." There was pride in Tamara's voice. She herself had brought in the green branches that decorated mantel and windows and that added their piney scent to the good odors of cooking. "Shall we put the silver candlesticks on the table?"

Martha nodded and Tamara hurried to fetch the candlesticks from the parlor. She handled them lovingly, delighted with their clean lines. Luke had had Mr.

Revere make them from coins he had saved, and they were Martha's proudest possession.

There were a few pieces by Mr. Revere in Tamara's own home, but her mother looked down her nose on them. They were nowhere ornate enough to suit her taste. Her own choice was the Queen Anne pieces that had been imported from England, fit to grace any of London's greatest mansions. But Tamara, like her father, thought that Mr. Revere's workmanship would never go out of fashion no matter how unadorned it was.

She placed the candlesticks in the center of the table that Martha had spread with a white cloth, and added a few sprigs of greenery. Watching her, with her face so rapt, Martha thought that she had never seen such a change between childhood and young womanhood.

Tamara's chin was still pointed but it was nowhere near as sharp as it had been as a child's. Her dark brows swept in perfect, graceful lines above eyes that were startling in their beauty. The short, stubby lashes that had been the bane of Millicent's life when she had regarded this ugly-duckling daughter of hers were even thicker now, so thick that they enhanced rather than detracted from the eyes they framed. Martha supposed that there were some who would still call Tamara plain, but to her way of thinking Tamara had a beauty that even her sisters and her mother lacked.

They both stopped what they were doing to listen when they heard hoofbeats directly in front of the house. Then the soft clopping stopped, and they looked at each other with apprehension on their faces. Martha's face paled, and Tamara caught her breath. Soldiers, sent to arrest Mark? Tamara's heart pounded under her fichu, and her hands clenched under her embroidered silk apron. There was only the sound now of the fire crackling on the hearth as they waited for footsteps to approach the door, and a pounding that would demand admittance in the name of the law.

The footsteps approached, and both their breaths were stilled, and then there was one light tap on the door and the sound of tinkling, delighted laughter. At the same second the door opened, and there was Charles with Annabelle wrapped in her cloak against the chill, her face rosy with excitement and her eyes so sparkling that Tamara's breath came again in a gasp of pleasure.

"I've brought you another guest, Martha, and you can expect one more," Charles was laughing. "I left The Temptation only a short time ago, and Eli had already decreed that Tod should come here with Luke and Mark to share your festive board. And thinking of the gathering at my own-house tonight I took pity on this daughter of mine and so I kidnaped her right out from her mother's nose and fetched her along. I'm afraid she'll smell a little of horse. There was no way to have the carriage brought around without a delay that might have undone us, so I put her up behind me on Sheba. Poor old creature, the double weight was almost too much for her. Come spring I'll put her out to pasture and replace her with a younger horse. Now I must be off home again to face the music, and I don't mean the trio that Millicent has brought in to furnish us with entertainment."

He stopped only long enough to kiss Annabelle's cheek, and then Tamara's in turn. Tamara saw the sadness in his eyes because he, too, could not stay here where the friendship was as warm as the leaping fire in the fireplace, where the food would be simpler but set much more easily on the stomach because it was partaken with the people he loved the best.

"Mama can scarcely make a scene in front of her guests, so you should be safe until they leave." Sympathy softened Tamara's eyes. "And then you'll either have to come to fetch us home, or send after us, and we'll both be there to help you bear the brunt of her fury." Divided among three it should not be so hard to bear, she thought.

"I don't care how angry she is, it will be worth it!" Annabelle said. She threw off her cloak and turned to Martha. "Is there anything I can do to help? How long will they be, do you think?"

"Not long." It was her father who answered her. "And I wish I were fortunate enough to be one of your company this evening. Unfortunately, I shall be obliged to listen to my wife's Tory friends expound on the criminality of this latest scandal for the entire evening, and bear with their censure because I will not be able to agree with them. I shall have to remind them that I shall also have to bear the censure of the more religious-minded of Boston for allowing such a gathering on Christmas Eve, which they will be sure to construe as un-Christian. It seems that I'm caught between two fires no matter which way I turn."

His voice was rueful but there was no indication of contrition in his expression. Charles was a man who would always do as he saw fit regardless of the censure of others. For himself, he saw no sin in marking Christmas with festivity, although many in Boston disagreed with him and tried to force their opinions on others. It seemed that all Englishmen were pigheaded, Tory or Whig.

Young Tim and John were the first to come in, after having prowled the streets for any rumor or bit of fact they could pick up. The others were close on their heels.

Tod's face flushed crimson when he saw Annabelle standing by the table, still dressed in the party gown that had been made for her by Millicent's mauntamaker. All of Boston's best dressmakers were Irish. The rich blue satin picked up the color of her eyes, and her face under the elaborate headdress of gauze was as lovely as an angel's.

Annabelle made no pretense that she was not in love with Tod. Tod, on his part, tried to keep his love for Annabelle concealed and within strict bounds. The education that Eli had managed for him, and his position as Mr. Armitage's law clerk, could not compensate for his lack of gentle blood. If Annabelle refused to recognize the gap between them he himself was always acutely aware of it.

But there was no time for brooding now. Though he knew he was a fool, he was eager to grasp what little was offered him. This night, for instance, in the company of all his friends, he was with the ones who meant the most to him—especially this entirely unexpected delight of having Annabelle here as well. He'd contrive to sit beside her at the table, even to touch her hand if the opportunity presented itself. The thought made the blood rush to his face. Thankfully, he was dark enough so that no one noticed.

He accepted the mug of cider that was thrust into his hand. Laughter rang around the table in spite of the contretemps he and Mark had been mixed up in a few evenings before. Here, with no alien ears to overhear, they could relate their experiences, the danger, the excitement, the actual scuffling and fighting that had taken place.

"We were on the *Beaver,* but the *Eleanor* and the *Dartmouth* had their full share too. I know for a fact that half of the Masons in town were in on it; they hatched the whole thing at the Green Dragon over on Union Street. And I recognized William Molineaux and Dr. Young and Paul Revere. And I'm pretty sure I saw John Hancock."

Mark stopped to guffaw. "John's ruffles were peeking out from under his blanket! In fact, not a one of us could have been mistaken for genuine Indians unless a man was blind, and drunk to boot. We were in good company, Mother, whether you think so or not."

"Three hundred and forty-two chests of tea, valued at eighteen thousand pounds!" Tod said. "But it was their own fault. We told Hutchinson to send those ships back where they came from, and instead he and Colonel Leslie over there on Castle Island ordered to fire on the ships unless they could show a passport that he'd signed. I have it on good authority that Mr. Rotch, who owns the *Dartmouth,* begged for leave to return to England. Josiah Quincy gave a rousing good speech at Old South while we were all waiting for Mr. Rotch to come back from Milton where he had to go to ask the governor's leave to sail."

"There must have been seven thousand of us at Old South," Mark put in, grinning. "That will give you some idea of how many people are determined not to let Parliament walk all over us! The meeting started at Faneuil Hall but 'twasn't anywhere big enough to hold us all. Do you recollect how dull and rainy it was, Tod? I felt sorry for the ones who couldn't crowd inside. But all of Sam Adams' men, even from other towns, got in, you can count on that! The North Caucas and St. Andrew's Lodge had a hand in it, too, there were plenty of them there. Women, too, and a scattering of youngsters. But only about a hundred and fifty of us actually went aboard the ships."

"I saw one man trying to save a little for his own use," Tod said. "It was taken away from him and he was laid flat. But the thing that impressed me was that the British fleet didn't make a move to stop us. There it was, only a quarter of a mile away from us. I expected to be blown into the harbor at any moment!

"Then it turned out that Admiral Montague had been visiting a friend of his near Griffin's Wharf and he'd seen the whole thing and didn't lift a hand. We never knew he was there until we were marching back to the Statehouse and he popped a window open and told us that we'd had a fine tea party but that we'd have to pay the piper!"

"Mistress Andrew's two youngsters were frightened half out of their wits when their father came home still wrapped in a blanket and carrying a tomahawk, his face all blackened with soot," Tamara put in eagerly. "She said she had an awful time getting them quiet again. I went myself the next morning to see the tea washed up by the tide. There was tea all the way from Boston to Dorchester, free for the taking by anybody who cared to pick it up! I was tempted to take some myself and dry it out to see how it would taste. I expect it would have been salty. Mark, I'll never forgive you for not telling me what was going to happen, so I could go and watch the fun!"

"If I had, you'd have been in the thick of it and got yourself trampled! Knowing you, you'd have contrived a way to get yourself up in a blanket and go with us to the ships. And what would your father have thought of that? To say nothing of your mother!"

"I'd not!" Tamara leaned forward. "Got trampled, I mean. But I certainly would have contrived to go along! It isn't right that men should have all the fun just because they're the ones who wear the trousers! We women are just as patriotic as you are, for all we're compelled to wear skirts. I could have passed for a boy without too much trouble, don't you think? I'd have borrowed some of Ned's clothes, they should be a reasonable fit."

Luke bellowed with laughter. "You know, I believe that you'd have done just that! You always were half boy, the way you grew up with a hammer in one hand and a handful of nails in the other, and went swimming in your skin with Mark here."

"Luke, there's no need to bring that up," Martha said, but if she thought that Tamara was embarrassed she was mistaken. Tamara was so filled with excitement about the dumping of the tea that she hardly noticed the reference to her learning to swim in only her under-drawers.

"You needn't look so crestfallen, lass. Mark didn't tell me what was in the wind, either," Luke said.

Martha fixed him with a cold eye. "You were there at Old South. I know you were. You were seen. Patience told me."

It was Luke's turn to look crestfallen. "But I didn't get myself up like a red Indian and go to help dump the tea!"

"No, and you didn't stop Mark and Tim from going, either!"

"Stop them! How could I have stopped them, even if I'd had any notion they'd obey me, with Eli standing right beside me? He'd have throttled me!"

"Luke, you aren't telling me that Eli was mixed up in this?"

"Mixed up in it?" All three, Luke and Mark and Tod, roared with laughter. "Wife, when Eli opened up his tavern after it was over, to help us celebrate, he served us with soot still on his face!"

"Father, are you sure that you didn't go?" Mark asked him.

"That I did not." Luke was suddenly serious. "I leave that sort of thing to the Liberty Boys. I have my own affairs to attend, and no time for schoolboy pranks!"

Mark flung down his napkin and flared at Luke. "Pranks! You call it a prank to show those Englishmen that they can't force their tea on us whether we want it or not?"

"And what are you if not an Englishman?" Luke retorted. "That's one of the things Charles Armitage deplores, the way we here in the colonies are setting ourselves apart from other Englishmen who happen to live in England, as though we were two alien races, bound to be at each other's throats! I grant you that as Englishmen ourselves, those over there have no right to force their will on us, who are also Englishmen! But as Englishmen, we have no right to take matters into our own hands and use force to right our wrongs when we have leaders who can effect it by debate and decree, given a chance!"

"This is Christmas Eve and I'll not have a war flare up at my own table in my own house! Luke, Mark, this isn't a tavern. And we have guests." Martha spoke sharply, a thing she so seldom did that when that tone was heard in her voice her menfolk stopped and listened.

Both Luke and Mark were subdued, giving her apologetic glances. To help ease the strained silence that threatened to mar the joy of this evening, Annabelle sought for some piece of gossip to throw into the conversation.

"What do you hear of the romance between Henry Knox and Lucy Flucker? Mama is terribly upset about it. She says she wouldn't blame the Fluckers at all if they locked Lucy in her room until she comes to her senses. I can hardly wait to see how it comes out. Lucy is absolutely recalcitrant, and she told me herself the last time I saw her that she'll have Henry whether her parents or the devil himself says that she can't!"

"Henry Knox is a fine young man even if he wasn't born with a silver spoon in his mouth. He's done well for himself. I doubt there are many men in Boston as well educated for all he had to get his education from the shelves of the bookseller he worked for before he opened his own shop. His manners are on a par with any of the bluebloods from Harvard College that make his shop their gathering place. Lucy may be from a fine aristocratic family but she's no beauty with all that weight she carries. In the Fluckers' place, I'd settle for Henry for her. They still have their son, that fine officer in the British Army, to pin their higher hopes on, so they might as well let young Lucy be happy."

Having said his say, Luke went back to eating. Annabelle kept the subject going, it being one that was of current interest to everyone in Boston. "She is terribly heavy. It just seems natural to her. But Henry's heavy, too. They'd make a good match, I think."

"She'll wear them down in the end. I never saw anyone as determined to get what she wants," Tamara remarked. The romance between Henry and Lucy was second only to politics as a matter of discussion these days.

The meal over, Tamara and Martha washed up the dishes while John and Tim hulled popcorn and fetched in apples from the root cellar to roast, and Annabelle and Tod drifted to the parlor, where Martha had struck flint to the fire when she'd known that they'd be here. Annabelle and Tod counted as guests, and Martha wanted to give them a little privacy so that Annabelle would have the chance to try to wear Tod down. Tamara, on the other hand, was family, and Martha didn't give letting Tam help with the dishes a second thought.

Alone in the parlor, because the others knew better

than to risk Martha's ire by bothering them, Annabelle sounded Tod out.

"Don't you think it's romantic, Tod? About Henry Knox and Lucy Flucker, I mean. How could anything be more ridiculous than for her parents to think that just because she's a Flucker, she's too good for Henry?"

"I'm afraid that most people think that way," Tod said stiffly. "Blood counts a great deal in the world, Annabelle."

"Well, I think it's silly! What's the difference between one person's blood and another? This is America, not England, and things are different here. If I loved someone and wanted to marry him, I wouldn't let any such a stupid thing as blood keep us apart!"

"You'd have to do as your parents wanted. America isn't that much different." Tod poked at the fire, which didn't need poking, his face serious and withdrawn. "Any man who'd take advantage of a young girl's foolish feelings toward him is a cur and deserves to be horsewhipped."

Annabelle sighed. Instead of drawing Tod closer to her, she seemed to be driving him farther away. He was as skittish around her as a colt when it sees its master approaching with a bridle in his hand for the first time. A little more, and he'd take to his heels.

"I know!" she said. "It's Christmas Eve, so let's make up poetry. Let's see who can come up with the silliest thing, to make the others laugh."

The popcorn was popped and the apples making a delectable aroma as they roasted in the ashes when Annabelle and Tod reappeared. Luke felt a momentary disappointment that they'd rejoined them so soon. He, too, hoped that Tod would get up the gumption, one of these days, to take what he wanted, just as he'd taken Martha, even if the circumstances were a little different. Still, he'd lay his money on Annabelle. She wasn't Charles Armitage's daughter and Tamara's sister for nothing.

"Tod's a real poet!" Annabelle informed them, her eyes dancing. "Just listen to this doggerel he made up about Henry Knox and Lucy!

For whoever heard
Of a case so absurd
As a marriage deterred
Or even deferred
By scolding the boy
And caging the bird.

A grin spread across Luke's face. That was rich, that was, and fitting, too. Tod was clever with his pen. Even Martha was laughing when Abel came to fetch Annabelle and Tamara home. In the confusion of leave-taking the piece of doggerel was forgotten, thrust carelessly into Mark's pocket. None of those present knew that within a week it would be repeated from one end of Boston to the other, as a result of Mark's finding it again and reading it aloud at The Temptation for the amusement of Eli's patrons.

Tamara and Annabelle had other things on their minds, such as the coming storm when they arrived at home and had to help their father stand up against their mother's rage. Their hands clasped together tightly during the ride home in the sleigh, but it was Tamara who summed it up.

"We must only try to divert as much of Mother's anger as possible, from Papa to us. It isn't going to be pleasant, but it can't take anything away from what we've had."

Fifteen

It was the utmost contingency that had forced George Hartgrave to undertake this second journey to Boston. His affairs in London had so far deteriorated that he was left with no alternative than to attempt to finish that which had failed when Charles and Millicent had visited Sir Basil.

It was the luck of the devil that Charles had not succumbed to his wounds at the hands of the hired assailant, but once Lillian's marriage to young Walton had been accomplished he had been almost content. It was as well then to leave well enough alone, and depend on their patronage to fill his needs.

But things had been going less well of late, and even worse in the weeks just past. The elder Walton was still very much alive, and Freddie had overextended his credit and could not extract another sovereign from his father, and as Lillian's waspish tongue had gained her enemies among the ladies of quality, their patronage had worn thin and George had found his own situation little short of desperate.

There was only one sure way to improve his fortunes, an improvement that would be permanent. Charles Armitage must die, and he and Millicent must marry.

George was little short of amazed at the state of affairs he found in Boston. Back in London, he had heard talk of it, but he had paid little attention, as the antics of a mob of rowdies held little interest to him.

His cousin and her husband lost no time in apprising him of the facts. The whole colony was agog over Parliament's swift reaction to the affair at Boston Harbor. King George's fury at the dumping of the tea had been so choleric that the repercussions fell nothing short of disaster. The Boston Port Bill had been signed by the King in March of this year, 1774, closing the Port of Boston and naming Salem as the capital of the colony and Plymouth as the seat of customs. Boston was to be starved into submission.

An indignation meeting had been held early in May and committees drawn up, and Paul Revere had taken his horse for a long, hard ride to New York and Philadelphia. He had carried broadsides with him of the Boston Port Bill, bordered with black and with a crowned skull and crossbones depicted under a cap of Liberty, and handed them out along his way. He himself had designed the broadsides, or so people said. According to Mr. Gammage, Revere was the second man in the colony who ought to be hung, following only Samuel Adams.

His Majesty's Ship the *Lively* had arrived on the tenth of May to insure that the port was closed to all traffic. Governor Hutchinson was recalled to England to report on Massachusetts matters at firsthand, and General Gage had been appointed to take his place. The larger part of Boston cheered when Hutchinson's ship sailed, glad to see the last of him although much less glad to see General Gage in his place.

The King's own regiment, the 4th, and the 43rd from Ireland landed on the day the Port Bill went into effect. The 38th and the 5th landed on their heels, along with the Royal Welsh Fusiliers. A train of artillery took up its residence on the common, and the marines arrived. Gage brought eleven regiments in that summer. This time he intended to have enough troops to keep order.

When George arrived, much put out because he had had to land at Plymouth and make his way to Boston from there, he found business in ruins. Outside of the British Navy, there was not a sailing vessel in the harbor. The wharfs, usually the scene of bustling activity that spelled prosperity for the town, were deserted. Soldiers drilled and marched, almost five thousand of them, very nearly a third of Boston's entire population.

Five thousand troops or not, provisions for the beleaguered town began to pour in from the other colonies. Far from taking advantage of Boston's lack of trade to further their own fortunes, as King George had hoped, they stood behind Boston to the hilt. If it could happen to Boston, it could happen to them. Farmers feared that their farms would be confiscated or that taxes would be levied on them to support the Episcopal Church, that offshoot of papism. It was within the realm of possibility that the colonies would be reduced to the same status as Ireland. Everything they had worked for was in jeopardy.

Wagons carried loads of codfish from Marblehead. The South sent rice. Meal and flour came from Maryland. Philadelphia sent money. And London itself sent money —not all of the citizens in England agreed with their King. Rye and bread came from Baltimore, and flour and more money from Virginia.

The towns in Massachusetts itself did not lag behind. There was rye and sheep and cattle from Chelmsford Groton, Wrentham, and Pepperell. So many provisions poured in over the Neck that no one went hungry. Colonel Putnam himself drove a flock of sheep all the way from Connecticut and was lionized by the citizens of Boston.

Because work was virtually unobtainable, the selectmen started projects so that men could be kept busy. Crews were made up to clean the docks and repair them, to pave the streets with cobblestones. Most of the out-of-work men were glad to give their time and effort to earn the rations they were given from the largess that had come in, but some of them, Henry Atkins included, were not.

Then Tories from outlying districts began to pour in, refugees from the rough treatment they received in their own Boston-sympathizing towns. There were hundreds of them. Some were simple workingmen or farmers, but there were doctors and lawyers among them, merchants and large landowners.

The town meeting had been abolished. General Gage had been instructed to lay his hands on Sam Adams and John Hancock and send them to England for trial. But although the town meeting had been outlawed, England did not think of county meetings. Joseph Warren drew up a paper that was debated and passed on in Milton, the Suffolk Resolves, which amounted to what came near a declaration of war.

General Gage got busy and fortified the Neck to keep the avenge-minded countryside from pouring into Boston to take it away from him. Bostonians slapped their thighs and said that the fortifications were little more than "beaver dams" that could be kicked down by well-booted feet. No one at all believed Gage's story that the fortifications were to keep his own men from deserting.

The general had his own troubles. The boats that carried bricks for the fortifications unaccountably managed to sink, wagonloads of provisions for his troops tipped over, and laborers he recruited refused to work, so that he had to send all the way to Nova Scotia for workmen. Boston sniggered behind its hands. It wasn't licked yet.

This was the situation that George Hartgrave found when he presented himself once again at his Cousin Grace Gammage's house. To make it worse, he learned that Charles Armitage was at present in New York, keeping his finger in the general pie. How the devil was he to find an excuse to leave his cousin's house and make the journey to New York to seek out and destroy the man who stood in the way of everything he must have?

"Indeed, things are so desperate that Millicent was determined to pack them all up and return to England but Charles wouldn't hear of it. He actually forbade her to bring the subject up again, can you imagine that? The temerity of the man is beyond belief!"

"I couldn't agree more. How is Millicent, dear cousin?"

"She's distraught, as you can well imagine, but seeing you again will raise her spirits, I'll be bound!" Grace rose to pull the needlepoint bellpull, determined to set things in motion. "But if you mean how does she look, the woman is phenomenal. I swear she doesn't age one year in ten, while the rest of us poor females have to suffer the consequences of the years."

George was so deep in his own thoughts that he almost failed to rise to the bait, but fortunately he recovered in time. "My dear sweet cousin, of what consequences do you speak? If I wasn't well aware that you have no daughter, I'd have sworn that you were she when I cast eyes on you a few moments gone!"

Grace preened. George had changed, although not overmuch. He was a little heavier, a few more lines had appeared around his eyes. He didn't take proper care of himself, that was obvious, but she would see to his health now that she had him under her thumb. In times like these they needed a distraction most desperately, and with George again as her house guest she would be the most sought-after woman in Boston. He must stay for a long time. Every hostess in town would vie to entertain him. She clasped her hands together, her eyes shining with anticipation of the triumphs to come.

Millicent propped herself up on the pillows and pulled the sheet up to cover her breasts. George was glad that it was dark enough in the room so that he could see only the outlines of her face. In spite of Grace's assurances, his first sight of Millicent had shocked him. There were lines of strain around her eyes and across her forehead, and her complexion had finally begun to suffer from the cosmetics that she used so lavishly.

But if her face had aged, her body had not. It was still magnificent, her breasts high and firm, her waist still nearly as slender as it had been before she had borne four children, her thighs only slightly thickened. And the passion that had just spent itself had been as great as it had been those other times, culminating in shuddering spasms of glory that had carried both of them to the heights.

But now George could sense, rather than see, that Millicent was frowning again, the lines of strain that had been eased by their lovemaking back on her face.

"The slut is trying to blackmail me, George! She knows that Ned is your son, and even though I have bribed her heavily for her silence all these years, now she hints, more than hints, that if I do not come up with a large lump sum to insure her continued loyalty, she might feel compelled by conscience to tell Charles what she knows! It would be ruin! Charles would cast me off, and one word to Sir Basil would lose Ned his inheritance!"

Damnation! Would that ancient, tottering old ruin in London never die? In spite of the steel nerves that George had had to develop in order to pursue his particular mode of existence, he was shaken. This was of immediate danger to him as well as to Millicent. Even if he managed to dispatch Charles to his Maker promptly, Agnes would still have a hold over them. Half of Boston knew that Charles and Millicent had not lived together as man and wife for years before Ned's conception. There would be counting on fingers, were such a rumor to be started, and who would believe in Millicent's innocence? Certainly not Charles, once Agnes whispered her poison into his ear! Something would have to be done about the woman, and done quickly.

"I don't know where to turn. What am I to do? I don't suppose that you could raise some money, a hundred pounds at least, to keep the creature quiet?"

"For God's sake, don't go to pieces! I'll think of something." He tried to make his voice sound confident, but to his consternation Millicent began to cry.

"I've been so alone! Thank God you've come, because I can't cope with it any longer! Her demands grow bolder every day. I've had to lie to Charles about two or three pieces of jewelry that I gave her, I told him that I lost them, but that can't go on without arousing his suspicions. He knows that I'm not that careless. And lately her demands grow bolder every day. Threaten her with prosecution, with prison, you're a man, she'll believe you where she wouldn't believe me. Do anything, but her silence must be insured!"

George pulled her back into his arms again, muzzling her breasts. His hands sought all the secret places of her body, until the tenseness gradually left it and she relaxed again, warm and eager. She must be calmed and reassured lest her desperation drive her to some act that would ruin them both.

Her thighs separated and she drew him down on her, her arms around his neck, moaning softly. "I've wanted you so, needed you so! You've had other women, but I've had nothing! George, love me, love me now!"

Thank the powers that he was still virile enough to perform more than once in a night. Millicent had always been insatiable where he was concerned, and the years that had separated them had done nothing to lessen it. But even as he satisfied her, his mind was busy with the problem that faced him. The removal of two people from the face of the earth entailed more problems than the removal of one, and more danger.

Still, it must be done. London, and a fortune in hand and another in the offing, and Millicent; nothing on earth must keep him from attaining them.

He left soon after. It was nearing dawn and even though Charles was away, others in the household would soon be stirring and it would not do to be caught in Millicent's bedchamber. Millicent had let him in well after midnight; even Agnes didn't know that he was here.

He stiffened as he caught a glimpse of a white nightgown around a bend in the hallway. Agnes, he'd be bound! Her room was close by Millicent's in case her mistress should want her during the night; she must have been wakened by that soft scream of delight Millicent had uttered only moments ago, and come to spy. The figure disappeared, but his resolve was strengthened. Too much was at stake for him to play a waiting game.

It was well after dark that same day when George let himself into the Armitage house again through a kitchen window. On this Wednesday evening, Millicent and Annabelle had taken the chariot, along with Ned, to attend a musical evening at the Fluckers'. Grace and her husband had also been invited, but that had been easy to get around. He had explained that he had to see a recent arrival from London about his affairs there, and this man had asked him to meet him at the Royal, as his business was pressing him for time. George would present himself at the Fluckers' as soon as his business had been completed.

Tamara, he knew, invariably visited the Martins every Wednesday, to help Martha during the afternoon and to stay for supper, and Mark walked her home later in the evening. Mrs. Gatesby, the cook, retired to her quarters at the top and back of the house immediately after the supper was cleared away and the kitchen set in order, and furthermore the woman suffered from a swelling of the legs that kept her in her room once she had retired. The young housemaid, Louise, lived at home with her family, Charles being so lax with his servants that he allowed her to come in by the day instead of living in as she should have done.

Although the lower rooms were in pitch darkness except for the faint glow of the hearth in the library, George moved through the house as silently as a cat. Agnes would be in her mistress's room, waiting up to help Millicent get to bed when she returned.

Agnes was sitting close beside a small table with a petticoat in her hands, securing a ruffle that had come loose. The candle on the table flickered in the draft as George opened the door and she looked up from her work, her face registering an almost comical surprise.

"You are to come at once. Your mistress has been taken with a sudden indisposition and needs you to accompany her home." One brief glance had shown

George a pair of scissors that rested on the table, and he restrained a smile as he re-evaluated his original plan. They would make doubly sure that Agnes's "accident" would be fatal.

Agnes laid the petticoat aside and went ahead of him as he stood aside for her to leave the room. She did not see him pick up the long, sharp scissors before he followed her.

Agnes was a tall woman, but George was a strong man, and his breathing did not as much as quicken as he lifted her off her feet at the head of the staircase and hurled her down.

He was down the stairs and kneeling beside her in an instant. A quick thrust with the scissors, to imbed them deep in her chest, and it was done. An afterthought made him take the front hem of her skirt in his hands and rip it, so that it would appear that she had caught her foot in it while descending the stairs.

He raised his head and listened. There was no sound from above. He'd counted on its taking Mrs. Gatesby a little time to rouse herself and light a candle and make her way from the servants' quarters if she heard anything at all, but it was possible that she had slept through the crash of Agnes's fall. No longer young and with her bad legs, getting safely away before she could investigate had seemed no problem. It was a stroke of luck that Charles' stay in New York was so lengthy that this time he'd taken Jonas with him. If the black man had been in the house George wouldn't have dared to do what he had done tonight.

There was a satisfied smile on George's face as he leaned over Agnes again, taking care to get no drop of blood on his clothing. He could detect no breathing. There wasn't a shadow of a doubt that she was dead.

Then he stiffened, cursing under his breath as he

heard light footsteps approach the front door, the grating of a key in the lock, and then Tamara's voice.

"It's only me, Agnes. You needn't come down."

Still cursing silently, George melted from the hallway and a few seconds later he was outside the house, pulling the kitchen window down behind him before he disappeared into the shadows.

Tamara paused for an instant after she entered the house, listening for Agnes to answer her, but the only sound she heard was a rasping, gurgling noise that she could not identify. There were no animals in the house, because her mother would not allow pets, despising pawprints on her carpets and dog or cat fur on her furniture. Tamara felt an unidentifiable alarm rise in her breast to replace her earlier annoyance with Mark who, along with his father and John, had not appeared for supper. No doubt they were at The Temptation, embroiled in another of those political debates that were taking place in every tavern in Boston, indeed throughout the colonies, ever since the Intolerable Acts had been passed and the Congress had convened in New York. Anyone would think that all the affairs of the colonies were to be settled in the taverns, as debates raged until closing hours and men's voices raised in loud demands as to why this or that or something else wasn't done to teach Parliament and King George a lesson.

Or maybe the Liberty Boys were meeting at Old South Church, where they gathered regularly, and Mark had gone along there to keep himself in the thick of things. In that case John and Luke would be with him. Things had degenerated so much since General Gage and his troops had inflicted themselves on the town that even Luke was mixing into politics, where he had always kept clear of them before, believing that they were best left to men of Charles' and John Hancock's caliber.

So Martha and Tamara had eaten their supper alone. Not even Tim was at home, much to Martha's annoyance. Her youngest, at least, she wanted to keep free of this political uproar. When they had put the men's portions away to keep for them Tamara had decided to go home.

"But you mustn't walk home alone, Tam! It's full dark, and the streets are filled with soldiers. It isn't safe."

"I almost wish that one would accost me! I'd raise such a fuss that he'd be mobbed, and I'm just in the mood to cause trouble! But General Gage keeps his troops under control, Martha. He won't stand for them molesting decent women. As bad as things are to have them here at all, Papa says that we're fortunate in the general who was sent to overlord us."

"At least take Tige, then." But Tamara had looked at the dog that Luke had acquired after the firing of his shed all those years ago, and shaken her head.

"No, the poor thing can hardly walk. In case of trouble, I'd have to protect him! And I want Mark to be shaken when he comes home and finds that I set out alone. Maybe it'll teach him to come home to supper!"

In spite of her confidence, she had taken to alleys that the soldiers were not apt to know about, dark twistings that she could lose herself in if one dared to follow her. The roundabout way had not improved her temper, although she knew every turning as well as she knew the palm of her hand from the days when she and Mark had used to explore the alleys of Boston together when they had been children.

Why she and Annabelle had to have so much trouble with their men she couldn't fathom. Annabelle because Tod thought he wasn't good enough for her, the silly ass, and Mark because it had never entered his thick head that Tamara was grown up now and of marriageable age and that if he didn't hurry up and grab her, she just might pass him by in favor of someone else.

Ha! That would be the day! It was Mark she wanted, and Mark she was going to have. She was just as positive about that as Martha had been about Luke, a story that Martha had told her times without number. It could be that Mark was so obtuse because girls grew up faster than boys, but he was still three years older than she was and it was time he got something besides politics into his head. Drat all this trouble, it kept him so occupied that girls and falling in love and getting married, had no room to crowd into a brain already overcrowded with tea parties and Liberty Boys and brave resolutions passed by the Congress!

Now that she was safely at home at last, she stood in the entrance hall and held her breath as she tried to identify the sounds she heard over the thudding of her heart that was beating fast because she had been startled already, half out of her wits, when she'd stumbled over a man and a woman coupling in one of the alleys, a redcoat and some street woman who had chosen the nearest dark place to complete their business together. The soldier had laughed at Tamara's startled cry and the woman had cursed, and Tamara had taken to her heels.

There it was again, that moaning, bubbling noise, directly in front of her and to the right. Her eyes were adjusting to the darker interior of the house now, and she made out a dark heap at the foot of the staircase.

She was so astonished that she forgot her fear. Her hands, searching to identify it, encountered something warm and wet and sticky, and in another instant she cried out, "Agnes! Dear Lord, what has happened to you?"

Even in the gloom she could see the whites of

Agnes's eyes as they opened and looked at her with mute appeal.

"Killed me," Agnes said. The words bubbled. "Killed me because I . . . knew. Ned's not the master's son. He's a . . . bastard. I knew, and they killed me. He did it. He . . ."

Her voice broke off in a deep gurgle that filled Tamara with horror. Then she was screaming for Mistress Gatesby, who took what seemed aeons to hear her before she lumbered down the stairs on her swollen legs, shielding a candle with her left hand. Tamara seemed to have been transported back to London, to a night when her father had lain at her feet in a pool of blood.

"Take care of her. I must fetch help, a doctor!"

Agnes was dead long before the doctor that the Armitages' nearest neighbor sent their son to fetch had arrived. And Tamara was left with Agnes's last words beating in her head, trying to send her mad.

Sixteen

She told no one. There was no one she could tell. The thought that her mother might have instigated Agnes's murder because of that dreadful knowledge was more than Tamara could bear.

She knew that she ought to tell, but how could she point the finger of suspicion at her own mother? She'd have to explain, and she could never do that. She'd rather die than have her father learn that Ned wasn't his son, that Millicent had betrayed him.

The physician had said that Agnes's death was an accident, that she had tripped and fallen down the stairs while carrying the sharp scissors. Only Tamara knew that it had been murder.

She could hardly force herself to look at her mother in the days that followed. Adulteress, murderess! Ned, her own Ned, a bastard! Every time she saw her brother her heart melted with love for him. If the knowledge would kill Charles, what would it do to Ned? Sometimes she thought she would go mad, but then she would tell herself sternly that she dared not lest she divulge what she knew.

Watching her, studying her white, expressionless face, seeing her almost imperceptible flinching away from him whenever he spoke to her, George's own suspicions were fomenting. He knew that Tamara had been the one to find Agnes's body. What he didn't know was whether Agnes had actually been dead when Tamara had found her. He hadn't had time to make sure, to be absolutely positive, because the snip of a girl had returned home earlier than she should have and interrupted him.

Look at her now! He'd barely arrived, along with Grace, to commiserate with Millicent over her shock at Agnes's death, and Tamara was already rising to her feet to leave the room. She'd only looked at him once when he had arrived and her eyes had slid off his face as though she couldn't bear the sight of him.

She knew, damn her! He'd have staked his life that she knew. Something was eating away at her and it couldn't be anything else.

She hadn't told anyone, he was sure of that. If she had there would have been repercussions before this. Charles Armitage's good name and popularity would not have saved Millicent from the closest of questioning. These provincials were stupid, the scum of the earth, but they knew the law and if it didn't happen to go against their own interests, such as defying Parliament and their rightful sovereign, they would have hastened to carry it out.

Millicent herself was a walking mass of nerve ends that quivered at the slightest sound. George had not told her, indeed he had not been alone with her for a single moment since it had happened, but she knew that he had killed Agnes.

The thought sickened her. She'd begged him to do something, anything, but she could swear to God Almighty that murder had never entered her mind.

But she was safe now. She reminded herself of that over and over. Agnes was dead and she was safe.

"You must take care of yourself, Millicent." Grace was filled with concern. "I know what a shock it must have been, the woman had been with you for years, but after all, she was only a servant. George, we must think of something to distract her, see how pale she is!" Grace patted at her friend and clucked like an agitated hen, denying even to herself that the death of Millicent's maid was serving to ease her own boredom now that her husband had drastically curtailed their social life, in spite of George's arrival, because of all the trouble with these provincials who didn't know where their loyalty should lie.

"I agree with Grace. We must plan a gala of some sort." George spoke gravely, but he watched Tamara out of the corner of his eyes as she left the room. She hadn't even excused herself, a breach of deportment that more than ever convinced him that Agnes had lived long enough to name him as her murderer.

The thought made the palms of his hands turn clammy and perspiration bead his forehead. Tamara wouldn't be as easy to deal with as Agnes had been. She wasn't a servant, she was Charles Armitage's daughter, and his favorite daughter from what Grace had told him, as well as Millicent's child. He was sure that Millicent suspected that he had done away with Agnes, but her own child was an entirely different matter even if there was little love lost between them.

He'd think of something. He would have to, because although Tamara had not as yet divulged her suspicions to anyone, there was no telling when she might have another of her frequent fallings-out with her mother and she would blurt it out to ears that would not only listen but also set retribution in motion. No doubt she was waiting for her father to return home, and she would tell him the instant he entered the house, and then everything would be too late, and all of his plans would be as nothing.

To be accused, arrested, imprisoned, tried, and hung! The thought filled him with desperation. He could almost feel the rope around his neck, feel it choke his life away, feel his lungs burst as he fought for the air that could not pass through his throat to them. His body twitched as he imagined how he would kick, struggling, until he finally hung limp and dead, his face blackened, his tongue protruding.

No! It mustn't happen, he couldn't stand it, he was young, he had everything to live for, if only he could carry out his original plans. Tamara must be taken care of. And perhaps in his grief at her loss, Charles Armitage would be more vulnerable, less alert to danger to his own life. He mustn't lose his nerve now. He could still win through, if only he hung onto his wits.

Henry Atkins had waited for four nights, as patiently as a cat at a mouse hole. Last night he'd thought he had her; he'd almost given himself away by leaping out of the shadows to seize her before he had seen that it was the wrong girl, the blond one called Annabelle.

There was no mistake this time. It was Tamara, a shawl thrown around her shoulders as she left the house by the back door to visit the necessary. The rest of the house slept and there was neither movement nor sound to bid him use extra caution.

Elation flooded through him as he thought of the reward that was waiting for him when his task was accomplished. This was a windfall the like of which had never come his way in all his unsuccessful life. Luck had been with him, long overdue, when the stranger, the man who was visiting those high-and-mighty Tories, the Gammages, had overheard him sounding off about Charles Armitage. He'd seen the stranger around once or twice before in the last few evenings. He'd noticed him because the man was so blatantly out of place in the sort of taverns that Atkins usually frequented, especially since he was no longer welcome at The Temptation. George Hartgrave had stuck out like a sore thumb, all the more because he took such an interest in eavesdropping on other men's conversations, as though he were looking for something in particular.

Still, Atkins had been surprised when Hartgrave had offered to buy him a drink, and then another, all the while sounding him out until Atkins had told him the whole story of how Charles Armitage and Luke Martin had done him dirt.

Hartgrave had been sympathetic. He'd been more than sympathetic. He'd wanted to know how badly Atkins wanted to get even with his enemies, and hinted that there'd be money in it if Atkins were interested.

He had the sack ready. It was coarse and harsh, and still retained traces of the rye meal that it had originally contained. He moved as silently as a shadow. A blow to the side of Tamara's head made her knees sag and then the sack was over her head and he hoisted her over his shoulder and set out.

He knew the alleys of Boston as well as any river rat who had grown up in them. The patrols were a problem but he had memorized their movements and was able to keep out of their way. When the girl stirred, he sat her on her feet and struck her again before he took the sack from her head and cast it aside. With his arm around her and under her armpits he was able to keep her moving. He used the bottle of rum he'd brought with him, and poured a liberal portion of it over her so that she reeked of it. It was a shame to waste good rum, but there'd be all the rum he could want for as long as he wanted it once this night's work was over. In the alleys, and with the shawl wrapped tightly around her nightdress, she could have been any streetwalker the worse for drink.

He had to be more cautious as he approached the docks. Someone might be around even though they were deserted these days, and there might be a British ship with a watch that was more alert than usual. But all went well.

He had made sure that the rowboat was ready and waiting. He'd checked to make sure it was still there before he'd taken up his post on the Armitage grounds. Its oars were muffled. He put the girl into the boat and shoved off.

He wished that he could do a few things to her before he dumped her in the harbor. He would have liked to strip her nightgown from her, take her, unconscious and helpless, in one of those alleys, pay back even more for the harm that Charles Armitage had done him all those years ago. He'd never had steady work since Mr. Armitage had convinced Peters that Luke Martin was a better workman than he. Lately he'd been doing odd jobs, some of them for the Gammages themselves, cleaning their yard, trimming shrubbery, work fit only for a servant or a boy.

Saliva gathered at the corners of his mouth when he thought about what he could have done to the lawyer's favorite daughter if only he'd dare to take the time and the chance of being stumbled over. He knew things to do that would have left her marked so that if the tide washed her up Charles Armitage would know what had happened to her.

There wasn't any use in thinking about that. He hadn't dared take the time and the chance. He'd have had to kill her first to make sure that she wouldn't wake up and scream and attract a patrol, and there wouldn't have been much satisfaction in doing those things to a corpse. The idea of it made even him feel queasy.

Just drowning her would be enough. He knew what store Charles Armitage set by her. And there was Luke, too. She walked out with Luke's son Mark, and the Martins regarded her as a daughter. It would hit them almost as hard as it would the lawyer. He'd always known that someday he'd find a way to get his revenge, but he had never dreamed that it would fall right into his lap and that he'd be paid for it as well.

He was out far enough now. He balanced the girl on the edge of the rowboat and shoved her over. She made a splash when she went in, and then she went under.

He heard a voice from the *Lively*. Sounds carried over the water, and he thought he had better get out of there. There was no chance that the girl would be spotted and rescued. It was a dark night and even if they'd heard her hit the water they'd never get to her in time.

He thought he saw her come up, once, as he pulled away, but he couldn't be sure. It didn't matter anyway. Even if she came up three times as some people claimed all drowning people did, she was still done for. His remaining, rotted teeth showed in a broad smile as he made for the wharf.

It was the coldness of the water that revived her. She was strangling, drowning, and she had no idea where she was or how she had come there. For a few seconds she thought that she was having a nightmare and that she would wake from it in a moment, but another mouthful of water, searing her lungs, set her arms and legs into motion.

Treading water, fighting off the shawl that entangled her arms, she saw the *Lively* and knew that she was in the harbor. She remembered then. Someone had struck her as she had walked the oyster-shell path from the house to the privy.

The ship was too far away. The wharf was nearer, directly in front of her instead of a distance off to the left. She took a deep breath and struck out, swimming strongly in spite of the throbbing of her head. It was a long way but she knew that she could make it. As her father had instructed him so long ago, Mark had taught her well.

The wharf loomed directly ahead of her now, within arm's reach. She reached out, her hands grasped the slippery, slimy pilings, and she hung on, gasping for breath, gathering her strength. The icy water was taking its toll of her now, numbing her. She was so exhausted that she had an almost overwhelming impulse just to let go and let the water close over her head.

If it had been Annabelle, or Lillian, or almost any other girl she knew, gently bred, who had lived her whole lifetime as a young lady of quality should, she never would have been able to pull herself up out of the water and climb the pilings until she gained the safety of the wharf. But Tamara had spent her life tagging after Mark, doing the same work Mark did, walking for miles, wielding hammer and saw. Her muscles were lithe and strong, her endurance was much greater than that of those other girls. Luke was fond of saying that she was as good as any boy, and on this night she proved it.

Shaking with cold, her teeth chattering, she lay sprawled on the wharf gasping for breath. But she couldn't stay there. Even in her state of shock, her mind kept working enough so that she realized that if she were found, questions would be asked. No young lady of her age could have any valid reason for having been swimming in the harbor, at this hour, in nothing but her nightgown.

And if questions were asked, what could she say? That her mother had betrayed her father, that her mother's sweetheart had killed her mother's maid to keep her from divulging the information, that now her own life had been attempted, by the same man and for the same reason? It would shake Boston to its core, and all of their lives, her father's, Ned's, Annabelle's, would be ruined.

Tamara had no doubt that George Hartgrave was her mother's lover, Agnes's murderer, and her own assailant. She had heard Grace Gammage talk about the time George had visited her for several weeks, here in Boston, before Ned had been born, to know that her mother and George had seen a great deal of each other then. Tamara's own memory of their stay in London was vivid in her mind. George had been around a great deal, although seemingly no one had suspected that they were having an affair. Now George was back in Boston, and Millicent saw him at the Gammage house, and George visited in theirs. It had to be George. There simply was no one else it could be.

If it hadn't been full summer, Tamara would have been a great deal worse off than she was. As it were, although her nightgown was still sodden and her hair dripping, she was cold but in no danger of freezing. She pushed herself to her hands and knees and then got to her feet. Now that she had regained her breath and her heart had stopped trying to pound its way out of her ribcage, her stamina came to the fore. She began to walk, keeping to the deepest shadows and the darkest alleys. With her father still away, for who knew how much longer, there was only one place she could go where she would be safe. It was a long walk, but she knew that she could make it.

So it was that later that night Luke stirred, wakened from his sleep by Tige's barking and whining at the door. "What, Tige, again?" he mumbled, still half asleep. "All right, stop your racket, I'm coming!"

He muttered to himself as he descended the steep staircase. The old dog needed to go out sometime during the middle of the night ever since he had become so decrepit, and Martha would no longer hear of him being left outside all night as a dog should be. What if it rained? What if it turned cold? Who ever heard of a dog being a house pet, except no-account scraps of fur that some ladies kept for lap dogs? Still, Martha wouldn't have been Martha if she hadn't been softhearted.

Tige had stopped his barking and was snuffling at the crack under the door when Luke reached him. Luke lifted the bar and swung the door open and his voice lifted in a startled shout as Tamara, wet as a drowned rat, fell into his arms.

"Martha! Come quick, strike a light! It's Tam, and something's happened to her!"

His shout roused the house. Footsteps pounded down the stairs as Mark and John and Tim came racing down, with Martha close on their heels.

The lighted candle showed a girl with her sodden hair clinging to her face and neck, her nightgown clinging to her body, her eyes almost black with shock and fright and fatigue, in a face so pale that Luke was afraid that she was about to die in his arms.

"John, fetch one of my clean nightgowns. Mark, bring a blanket. Tim, stir up the fire." Martha's voice shot out orders that were obeyed as if she were a sergeant and they her recruits. "Now you men clear out of here until I get her dry and decent. Luke, have we anything stronger than cider in the house? Did you and the boys leave any of that brandy Eli brought around for your birthday? Then fetch it!"

Wrapped in a warm patchwork quilt, one that she herself had helped Martha put together and that contained scraps from dresses she had worn as a child, Tamara sat in front of the fire that was now leaping up the chimney, her hands clasped around the pewter cup of brandy that Luke had brought her. He had warmed it with the tip of the glowing poker, brought to red heat in the flames. Slowly, as if in a daze, she told them everything.

Luke sat opposite her in the second ladder-back chair, while John and Tim squatted Indian fashion a short distance away, but Mark was pacing the floor, so angry that his face was white, and even whiter lines ran from his nostrils to the corners of his mouth.

Luke's big hands, hard and calloused, clenched and unclenched. Faced with the truth that Tamara had faced alone, he felt the same helplessness. For Charles Armitage to learn that Ned was not his son was unthinkable. As Luke's hands clenched, he could almost feel Millicent Armitage's slender white throat between them, choking out her deceitful life. As for George Hartgrave, he wished that he could tear him limb from limb with these same hands.

The servant woman Agnes murdered, and Tamara all but murdered, and would have been dead now if she and Mark hadn't defied Parson Eldridge and half of Boston for Mark to go on teaching her how to swim!

"George Hartgrave!" Luke said. "You must be

right, Tamara. Martha, when was it that we heard so much about that young man from England visiting Grace Gammage?"

Martha knew to the year and the day. Patience Bates, who was much more prone to gossip than Martha, had regaled her with tales of all the gala affairs that had been given in Mistress Gammage's cousin's honor. There was no doubt that the dates jibed. George Hartgrave could have been Ned's father as easily as Charles.

Having Martha confirm what she herself had not been able to remember clearly but what she had suspected made Tamara feel all the worse. She wouldn't have told anyone in the world what she suspected except the Martins, but under the circumstances, because she was in need of protection, she had had to tell someone, and she knew that the secret was as safe with the Martins as it was in her own heart.

"I'll twist Hartgrave's neck until it breaks, the minute I get my hands on him, the bastard!" Mark raged, so angry that his voice strangled in his throat.

"And what excuse would you give?" Luke's voice was as angry as his son's but his mind hadn't stopped working because of it. "Would you tell the truth, and have Charles Armitage shamed before the entire colony, as well as what knowing about Ned would do to him personally? And where's the proof? Tam never saw the man who kidnaped her and threw her in the harbor, and the servant Agnes is dead. Who is there to swear that George Hartgrave is the one?"

"Aye, there's that. And when Tam's body isn't found he'll know that she isn't dead. So what are we to do about it?" Mark resumed his pacing. "She won't be safe as long as he's at large, just waiting for another chance at her."

A smile spread across Luke's face. "Do you mind

last Christmas, when Tam said that she'd pass as a boy if she wanted to, and I said that she probably could the way she's grown up with hammer and nails? How would you like to be my 'prentice, Tam?"

"Luke, what do you have in mind?" Martha protested. "I never heard of such an outlandish scheme!"

"Can you come up with a better? He'll be looking for her, and she dassn't return home because that's the first place he'll look, and our house is the second. How do we even know that we can trust Mistress Armitage? A woman who'd betray her husband, and allow her lover to murder her maidservant, might not draw the line at having an accident befall her daughter. At least we can't take the chance."

Tamara's face went a shade whiter, but she made no sound. It was true. Her mother had done the other things, or at least condoned them. Millicent had never liked her, this third daughter of hers who wasn't beautiful as Lillian and Annabelle were beautiful and who refused to conform to the standards expected of a young gentlewoman. Lillian was the one she liked, and Ned was the one she loved. Annabelle with her porcelainlike beauty was an asset to her. But Tamara had never been anything except an annoyance.

"Tim's clothes will fit her. We'll have to cut her hair and that's a pity. But she's as good a hand at carpentering as any 'prentice I ever saw, and I'm still busy enough roofing a house that the lumber was paid for and delivered before all this embargo business. Who'll notice if I put on an extra boy? We'll keep Tim at home and say he's laid up, and I hired the boy to get the work done faster."

"She can't stay here," Mark said. "Even if George Hartgrave wouldn't know where to look for, and he probably does, her mother would."

"There'll be a hue and cry for her." Martha was matter-of-fact. "She can't just disappear without anyone asking questions. Even if her mother doesn't set up a search for her, 'Belle and Ned will demand to know where she's gone. What will we do about that?"

"We'll give them something to think about!" Luke said. "If Mistress Armitage knows nothing of the attempt on Tam's life, she'll accept it, knowing how headstrong Tam is when she takes a notion. As for Hartgrave, no doubt he'll be shaking in his boots, wondering how such a message got back to her mother."

"What will we give them to think about?" Martha glared at her husband. Men could exasperate a woman to death, with all their plotting and scheming and thinking they were smarter than anyone else.

"Why, we'll send John with a note from Tam, telling Mistress Armitage that she missed her father so much that she decided to go to New York to join him! We'll leave it to them to figure how Tam expected to get there, but you can lay odds that Tam's mother at least will believe that she's capable of it! We'll say a lad brought us the note, to be taken on to her, and that's all we know and we'll be as upset about it as she is."

"But she still can't stay here," Mark reminded his father impatiently. "If she stays here, that boy's disguise wouldn't fool anybody."

"There's Eli. She can bide nights at The Temptation. Charity will see that she comes to no harm. Outside of her and Eli, even Patience mustn't know. Not that Patience would let it slip on purpose, but you know how hard it is for her to keep her tongue from wagging, and she might trust some woman who'd trust her husband and before we knew it, we might as well have a broadside printed!"

Tamara sat as still and pale as a statue while

Martha's scissors snipped off her hair to queue length. As the locks fell to the floor, she felt that a part of her life was being cut off with them. Her hair would grow again, but after all that had happened, and knowing what she now knew, her life would never be the same.

From her perch on the roof, Tamara looked down and caught her breath as she saw George Hartgrave among the people passing on the street below her. His eyes flicked at the house as he went by, without actually noticing it.

George was in a black mood. The girl was gone, disappeared. Her body had not been washed in by the tide. Atkins had botched the job. Why hadn't the fool told him that story of Tamara's knowing how to swim? It didn't matter how Atkins protested that some parson had put a stop to it so she'd never actually learned; obviously she had, and just as obviously she had gotten ashore and was hiding somewhere, waiting for the right time to denounce him.

George himself had only heard the story after the note from Tamara had been delivered to Millicent. Distraught, Millicent had gone straight to Grace, and Grace had remembered how headstrong the girl was and brought up that old episode to prove her point.

Was there, as Atkins insisted, a chance that her body had been washed out to sea and would never be found? He stumbled, cursing. Of course there wasn't! His brain was becoming addled. A dead girl can't write a note. No, she was alive. But she couldn't connect him with the attempt on her life.

He had planned it so carefully that there had been virtually no chance of anything going wrong. Grace, that inveterate gossip, had told him of Atkins' enmity toward Charles Armitage and Luke Martin. It had been a simple matter to procure the man's services. He had promised liberal payment, a promise that he had had no intention of carrying out. Always belligerent and usually more than half drunk when he wasn't working, there would have been little interest in the finding of Atkins' dead body in some alley. The man could scarcely be in the company of any other man without picking a fight.

There had been no question of George's doing away with Tamara himself. In this case his alibi must be foolproof or Millicent would suspect that he had done it, and even Millicent would not have kept silent. No matter how self-centered and selfish a woman was, she could not be expected to turn a blind eye to the murder of her own child. And so as Millicent couldn't be trusted, George had made sure that his whereabouts were accounted for every minute of the time that Atkins had carried out his mission.

Three of the nights had been spent playing at whist with half a dozen young British officers, sessions that had not broken up until dawn. He had won a little but made sure to lose a little more so that they would want to go on playing, but he had never been out of their sight. Daytimes he had kept to Grace's house. On the fourth night, the night that Atkins had finally managed to waylay Tamara and carry her off, he'd feigned illness and kept his cousin popping in and out of his room with his complaints, an illness he had meant to continue until Atkins indicated that Tamara was dead. The man was to wear a red kerchief around his head while he worked around the Gammage yard, when his mission was completed.

Even Millicent would not have been able to suspect George. He would have put forth the theory that some drunken regular had waylaid her and then drowned her so that she could not accuse and identify him.

The scheme had been foolproof, absolutely foolproof! George gnashed his teeth in rage. That fool Atkins! He should have found someone else to do the job, but who could he have found who had such a hatred of Armitage that he would agree, and who would have been so easy to dispose of afterward? Atkins had been ready at hand as though Providence had sent him, and choosing him had been a calculated risk that any gambler would have taken.

George was so jumpy that he was instantly aware of it when three men fell in behind him. He quickened his pace but two of them drew abreast of him and the third put his hand on his shoulder, pushing him into an alley. He opened his mouth to shout and started to reach for the ornate but deadly dagger that he always carried on his person, times being what they were and the colonials' feelings against Tories making for danger even in broad daylight if a patrol didn't happen to be nearby.

"I wouldn't do that," a deep, strong voice advised him. "Just keep moving. We'll tell you when to stop."

"I have little money on me," George said. "Take it, and leave me be!"

"What you have, you'll be needing, Mr. Hartgrave." Luke now stood squarely in front of him, feet spread apart, balancing on the balls. A younger man who was obviously his son and just as big looked at him as if he'd as soon cut his throat as explain what this was all about.

"We know that you murdered the Armitages' woman Agnes. We know that you tried to murder Tamara Armitage. Boston isn't healthy for you anymore, Mr.

Hartgrave. We suggest that you set sail for England as soon as possible."

"You're mad! How dare you accuse me of such crimes? What proof have you?" George was sweating profusely but he was convinced that they could not back up their statements. If Tamara hadn't come forward she must have decided to hold her tongue in order to protect her father and her brother, and without Tamara's sworn testimony these men didn't have a leg to stand on.

A sudden thought made the sweat pour even more freely, beading his forehead and soaking his armpits. How could he have been so stupid as not to have thought of it before? Tamara's note to Millicent had said that she was going to New York to join her father. He didn't doubt that that was exactly what she had done. What if she'd gone for the purpose of telling Charles Armitage what she knew, and about the attempt on her own life? It was obvious, now, that she'd told these men. George was not acquainted with them, but he correctly surmised that they were the Martins, her best and dearest friends, almost a family to her. Even without proof, Armitage would make a dangerous enemy. He'd have ways of setting inquiries into motion, and if he were to lay his hands on Atkins and persuade the man to talk, things would go hard on George.

"We don't need proof. There are three of us here, and there's one more you haven't seen. Boston is full of alleys, Mr. Hartgrave. And bodies have been found in them before." Three pairs of blue eyes, staring into his, held a world of menace.

They turned and left him, leaving him standing there with nausea churning in his stomach. He was not a coward, but he knew that as long as he remained in Boston he wouldn't be able to step out of Grace's house without wondering when and where they were going to strike. As they had said, Boston was full of alleys.

And if Tamara had joined her father, and told him what she suspected, Charles Armitage would return at any moment, with fire in his eyes and a determination to lay the culprit by his heels. Everything was lost. His great gamble, his one final attempt to gain a fortune, was lost to him, and now his own freedom and possibly his life were in danger. More than possibly, because if Armitage was unable to come up with proof, there were still those three men, and another one they'd left unnamed, who had sworn to kill him if he didn't leave.

It took him two days to secure a loan from Grace's husband, who was reluctant to advance the money. With specie so scarce, Mr. Gammage was loathe to part with it. During those two days George did nothing but remain indoors except when he arranged for a pass to cross the Neck and make his way to Providence to arrange passage on the first available ship.

He told the Gammages, a lie born of necessity, that he'd heard of an opportunity in Virginia whereby a gentleman might find suitable employment, but that he would need a little cash to support himself and to invest before his profits would start coming in.

He told the story about Virginia in order to throw Armitage off the track if he came back from New York with blood in his eyes. Actually, he would be forced to return to England and sell up the last of his father's property to realize enough to buy himself a commission in the Army. There was no other door open to him now.

Seventeen

All of Boston waited for winter to come and for the Charles River to freeze over. The citizens of Boston waited with hopeful expectation, and General Gage waited with dread.

"Just wait till the river freezes, and then we'll see how much good Gage's fortifications do him!" Eli said. "Soon's that river freezes, men'll pour in here across it from all over New England and chase those redcoats out!"

Eli believed it, and General Gage believed it. The colonies were a hotbed of seething indignation at the depredations inflicted on Boston. Every day, resentments grew stronger. Supplies were at a premium. There was little wood to be had, and what little there was, was competed for by the redcoats themselves, as well as by the hordes of Tories who had come in to escape retaliation against them by the patriots.

"Gage is having his troubles, all right," Luke conceded. "He isn't telling how many desertions he has among his ranks, but it's a lot. Plenty of those lads from England are on our side, and they skedaddle the first chance they get."

"I hope they get across that river in a hurry when

it freezes," Eli fretted. "With firewood so scarce, we're goin' to get mighty cold till we drive the lobsterbacks out. I never saw so many down-and-out folks in Boston in my life as there are right now."

"I'm not doing so well myself. Nobody's building. Even if they had the money, which they don't, there's no way to get lumber in. You're better off than the most of us, Eli. Long's a man has a shilling in his pocket he'll spend it for drink, and the redcoats see that the taverns are fairly well supplied for their own use."

"Mebby, but who wants them in their place of business? And my supplies ain't all that good. We'll all be goin' dry if that river doesn't hurry up and freeze."

"I'm as anxious for it to freeze as you are, Eli. The way things are now, I'm having to send my boys outside of town to get what work they can. If the British weren't so lenient about issuing passes across the Neck things would be bad for us. As it is, they bring back part of their wages in supplies, or else there'd be nights we'd go hungry."

So they waited for the river to freeze. But there was just one trouble: The winter of '74 and '75 was the warmest that Eli or any other inhabitant of Boston could remember. Every night when they went to bed, even if they were shivering because of the lack of firewood, they prayed for a cold snap so that the river would freeze over and their rescuers could reach them.

And every morning, when they got up, the warm spell was still with them. Not warm enough to be comfortable, but too warm for the river to freeze. In his own snug quarters General Gage thought that Providence must at last be on the side of the British.

What King George and Parliament thought notwithstanding, the general had a healthy respect for the numbers and marksmanship of the provincials who would pour in on his troops when and if the river froze.

But the river didn't freeze that winter.

Tamara, at home again ever since George Hartgrave had left Boston, prayed for the river to freeze as hard as Eli did. It made her blood curdle to see redbacks wherever she looked, so that even Millicent's ranting and raging about her escapade, when she'd cut her hair and donned Tim Martin's clothes and worked as a 'prentice for Luke Martin out of sheer boredom and because she couldn't bear to hear her mother and her mother's friends talking against their own Bostonians, made little impression on her.

Millicent had been livid when Tamara came home, wearing one of Martha's taken-in dresses and with her hair cut like a boy's, but she'd accepted Tamara's story at face value. Tamara explained to Annabelle that she'd made her mother believe she'd gone to New York to join her father just to throw her off the track, so she wouldn't search for her in Boston.

"Tam, how did you dare!" Annabelle exclaimed. "But it must have been fun, for all it was so rattle-brained!"

"It was fun." Well, it had been, so that much at least wasn't a lie. With hammer and nails and saw so natural to her, Tamara had enjoyed the work, especially as it had kept her close to Mark daytimes as well as at night. But when George Hartgrave had left, Martha had told her that she had to go home before her luck ran out and her masquerade was uncovered, to the mortification of all of them.

Luckily, with George gone, without as much as an explanation, Millicent had other things to think about, and so she didn't tear Tamara apart as she would have done if her mind hadn't been seething with her lover's perfidity.

Mark hadn't particularly wanted to go over Concord way to reshingle Matthew Baldwin's roof, but times were hard, and when Eli had told him that his friend Matthew Baldwin had gotten word in by a man with a pass that he had the work and would Eli send one of those carpenters he set such store by to do it, Mark had felt compelled to go. It would bring in a little hard cash even if there wasn't much it could be spent on, and they had need of all the hard cash they could earn outside of Boston, not being able to earn any in the town itself.

It wasn't easy to get a pass to cross over the Neck. A man had to have a good and valid reason for wanting to get out of Boston. But passes were obtainable, and with a story of an elderly man who was suffering because of a leaking roof, and after a thorough search to make sure that he carried nothing that could be used as a weapon, Mark's pass was forthcoming, as it had been on other occasions. It was the searching that Mark hated, it made his gorge rise to have to submit to being searched by a lobsterback.

The British had a dilemma. A man outside of Boston was one less mouth for Boston to feed; on the other hand, he might come back with a gun in his hand along with hundreds or thousands of others. But taken by and large, General Gage was lenient, at least as lenient as he dared to be.

Luke said that General Gage was a good man, that Boston was lucky that some other man hadn't been sent in his place, and Mark supposed that his father was right. The general did his best to keep order among his troops as well as among the populace. Remembering the massacre all too well, Gage insisted that his men refuse to be drawn into a quarrel even if the other party was wrong. He clamped down on their shoving of the citizens around to show who was boss. But for all that, the troops were bound to get out of hand, and resentment ran higher with every day that passed.

It was a longish walk to Concord, and Mark's stomach was none too full. At least he had the hope of being well fed as long as the job lasted.

He didn't think much of Matthew Baldwin when he saw him. The man was older than Eli, and he lived a piece out of Concord on a parcel of land that he called a farm, and he turned out to be both parsimonious and cantankerous. His wife was some better; she insisted on giving Mark a meal as soon as he got there even if it was only bread and hard cheese and cider that wasn't near as good as Eli's. Matthew thought he should have put in a few hours of work before he was fed.

The roof was in bad shape and it was going to take longer than Mark had expected. Parts of it had rotted right through and he was afraid that his weight would send the rest of it crashing down through the ceiling and bring down Matthew's wrath on his head. The first day Mark worked lying on his stomach to distribute his weight and he sweated pretty freely, until he had enough of it fixed so that he had a solid place to work from.

"You're plumb slow. I can't see why Eli recommended you so high," Matthew Baldwin grumbled that first night, watchful that his wife didn't fill Mark's plate too full. But when Mark had gone to bed in the spare bedroom, Mistress Baldwin sneaked him in an extra piece of dried pumpkin pie. It helped to fill the empty corners.

The morning of Wednesday, April 19, 1775 found Mark working on Baldwin's roof, his stomach well filled with cornmeal mush, which Matthew had not begrudged him, and two eggs laid by the scrawny hens that scratched around the farmyard, which he had.

It looked to be a fair day, not too warm, and Mark hoped to get a considerable amount of the shingling done so that he could finish it up tomorrow and start on home. He had taken a liking to Mistress Baldwin but he didn't think much of Matthew's hospitality. Mark would have a word or two to say to Eli when he got back.

Mark was anxious to return because he was sure that something was in the wind. There had been rumors that Gage was going to attempt to take the military supplies that the patriots had stored in Worcester and Concord. Mr. Revere had been sure of it and there was some kind of scheme hatched to give warning if the troops sailed or marched out of Boston. Mark wanted to get back and find out what was going on.

If Revere wasn't careful he was going to end up kicking his heels in the air. All that express riding he'd been doing had just about run his luck out and he was bound to be caught sooner or later. Gage was becoming mighty upset about it, especially in view of all the directives he got from London ordering him to do something to put those rebellious colonists in their place and get the business over with.

What did Parliament expect him to do, repeat the Boston Massacre only this time kill every man in Boston? Mark was inclined to agree with his father that Gage was as good a man as they could have hoped to have put over them. He seemed to have no desire to go around murdering fellow Englishmen even if they were, according to his lights, in the wrong. He'd bent over backward to keep order in the town and keep his own troops in line. But King George was getting impatient and

Gage would have to do something pretty soon unless he wanted to see his career go down in ruins.

Mark, like all the rest of Boston, wondered uneasily when Gage was going to make his move. He was wondering about it, his mouth full of nails and his hammer raised to strike, when he heard the church bells. They were making an infernal racket, and they were coming from more than one direction, and they weren't tolling out the hour or marking the passing of some poor soul to his reward.

Nails spewed in all directions as Mark spat them out. His hammer dropped from a hand gone numb, and then he was scrambling down the ladder face forward and almost went a header before his feet touched the ground. He burst into the farmhouse kitchen where Matthew was scolding his wife for extravagance; one egg for Mark's breakfast would have been plenty.

"You got a gun?" Mark shouted. The man must be stone deaf not to pay any attention to those bells!

"Why aren't you on the roof? I'm paying you to work, not to come in here asking for guns!"

"Damn it, man, don't you hear those bells? The British are coming! If you aren't going to fight, give me your gun!"

"You aren't getting it. This ain't my fight. I don't care one way or another just so's things get back to normal as fast as they can. I'm too old to go off chasing redcoats over a few taxes that don't affect me much anyhow."

"Damn you to hell!"

Mark turned on his heel and ran from the room. He'd find a gun somewhere in this house, or get outside and find him a scythe, or a stave, anything he could use as a weapon.

Mistress Baldwin's voice stopped him as his feet pounded into the parlor. "Mr. Martin, here!"

Her face was flushed and her eyes were bright and she was panting. There was an ancient musket in her hands and she thrust it at him.

"Here! It doesn't look like much but it works. And God bless you!" Mark was glad that he wasn't in her shoes, having to face her husband's wrath for giving him the musket, but then he forgot it as he shoved past the old man who was trying to intercept him, and ran out of doors and pelted along the road to Concord. Other men were already hurrying in the same direction, some on horseback, and others, like himself, afoot. Before he got to the town he had fallen in with some of those who were trotting on shanks' mare, muskets in their hands and their faces set.

"You think they're coming?"

"Bound to be. Step it up, we'd better git there!"

There weren't any British in Concord yet when they got there so they went right on through and waited on the road that led to Lexington. They didn't have long to wait.

"It's Colonel Smith, bedamned!" the man Mark had spoken to earlier said. "And they're too many for us. Ain't a thing we can do."

They turned around and marched back into Concord, Colonel Smith and his columns on their heels. Mark thought he must be dreaming it. Some fifes and drums had joined up with them and they began to play a marching tune, and those British behind them began to play, too.

They marched right on into Concord and nobody lifted a hand or fired a shot to stop the British. The redcoats were hungry. They'd set out and marched for fifteen miles without any breakfast and they were ready to eat. They ordered food and drink and they were served and they paid for it.

Somebody set chairs out on the lawns and the officers took their ease under cherry trees that were already in blossom. Anybody'd think it was a damned picnic. Mark recognized Major Pitcarin, stirring a brandy and water with his finger and making some joke that made the other officers laugh.

"Aren't we going to do anything?" Mark demanded.

"Mebby, mebby not. Just heard some of our men's gathering at the far end of North Bridge. Could be there'll be a fight over there. Shall we meander on over there and see?"

"What's Smith going to do?"

For a time it seemed as if Smith weren't going to do anything. He finished his breakfast at leisure before he walked off at the head of his troops to go to the aid of Captain Laurie at the bridge. Mark and the others he'd come belting into Concord with were well ahead of him.

There was a fight at last. Mark aimed and fired. He couldn't be sure if he'd hit anybody but some at least of the provincials' balls hit their marks. He would see well enough through the smoke to see that it was mostly officers who were picked off. These minutemen knew their business.

He borrowed shot and powder from the man next to him. Mistress Baldwin either hadn't thought or hadn't had time to fetch him powder horn and a pouch of bullets when she'd given him the musket.

He loaded and fired again, and this time he had the satisfaction of seeing the man he'd aimed at go down. All that drilling with the militia, before the British had occupied Boston, had paid off.

The British, feeling their stings, fell back into Concord. "Aren't we going after them?" Mark wanted to know. If it were left to him he'd keep right at their heels like a swarm of wasps.

"Best not. I don't think there'll be any fightin' right in the town. Smith'ud burn it down around our ears if we attacked him there."

The man Mark had spoken to wiped a smoke-grimed hand across his eyes, leaving dark streaks behind. It put Mark in mind of the Liberty Boys and their sooted faces.

"Listen to them bells!"

Mark listened. They were everywhere, clanging wildly, sounding the alarm from village to village, from farm to outlying farm.

"That there's Bedford," Mark's new friend said. "And they'll be comin' from Westford and Acton and Watertown, from every damned place in New England!"

They came, in dozens and in scores and in hundreds, the ones fortunate enough to own or be able to borrow horses first, the men afoot after. All were armed, and every face was set in grim lines. Mark felt something akin to awe.

They'd been ready, every man jack of them. The whole of New England had been ready, and now they came and kept coming, not to join the men at the bridge but deploying through fields and behind trees and fences. Farmers, schoolmasters, storekeepers, artisans, each with one aim in mind, to drive the British back where they'd come from and teach them a lesson they'd not soon forget.

Smith had come to the same conclusion and he wasn't happy about it. He decided to get out of there, back to safety. They took the road that led through Lexington, where unknown to Mark and many of the others, men had been killed that morning before the British had marched on to Concord, preceded by those church bells, which must have been starting to get on the redcoats' nerves.

The provincials skirted them every step of the way. Not being fools, they didn't line themselves up and get themselves mowed down by British volleys. They kept to cover.

Every tree, every stone fence around a farmer's field, spat out death at the marching British columns. Redcoats went down, one after another, without finding a target to shoot back at. When a man fell the others closed ranks and they continued marching. But even these well-trained troops could not stand up under that gauntlet of blood indefinitely. They panicked and by the time they reached Lexington they were running. They ran past the square where they had exacted a toll only that morning, and on and out of town toward Charleston.

Half a mile out of Lexington they met Percy, who was bringing fresh troops and a couple of cannon. Smith's retreating men fell in their tracks, hysterical and panting, thanking God that Percy had come at last.

They reached Charleston at nightfall. All they'd accomplished along their flight was to burn a few farmhouses and shoot so few of the snipers that they needn't have bothered losing time by firing at them.

When they camped at last on Bunker Hill they thought they had been through hell. Twenty-four hours on the march and most of it had been under devastating fire. Who'd ever given them to understand that these provincials couldn't fight, that this expedition would be nothing more than a pleasant promenade?

Word spread through the camp that long before the rout had ended, Colonel Smith had been ready to surrender, except that he hadn't been able to locate an enemy of high enough rank so that he could hand over his sword.

"My mother never wanted me to be a soldier," an exhausted young subaltern said. "And I wish to God I'd listened to her!"

His companions were too spent to answer, but their silence was agreement enough. To a man, they never wanted to hear another church bell as long as they lived.

Eighteen

It was late when Ned woke with his mother's hand on his shoulder and her other hand pressed against his mouth to keep him from crying out. He didn't know what time it was but it had the feeling of being late, in the middle of the night.

"Shhh. Wake up, Ned! Get up and get dressed quickly, but don't make any noise."

He struggled against the sleep that still engulfed him. "But why?"

"Keep your voice down, and do as I told you! Hurry, now. Your father has sent for us."

That brought him fully awake. If his father wanted them, they must go.

He dressed as fast as he could, pulling on breeches, shirt, stockings, and shoes. His mother thrust a change of clothing in a small bundle at him. He was still fuddled from the dream he'd been having. It had been about his father, and the danger he might be in galloping here and there on errands for Sam Adams and the others who were struggling against British oppression.

There'd been fighting at Lexington and at Concord, and he'd dreamed that his father had been there and been wounded, although he knew that it wasn't true. The provincials had chased the British all the way back to Charleston and everyone was still talking about it, but his father was away somewhere and hadn't been in the battle.

They went down the front staircase, without a candle to light their way. A man was waiting just outside the door with a small traveling chest on his shoulder. Even in the darkness, Ned recognized him. It was Henry Atkins, who did odd jobs for the Gammages between what other work he could pick up, and that was almost nonexistent these days when work was so scarce that better men than Atkins were forced into idleness.

Ned didn't like Mr. Atkins. The Martins were sure that he'd been the one who'd burned down their work-shed years ago, to get even because Luke had licked him in a fight about a tax agent.

"But where are Annabelle and Tam?" Ned demanded, as his mother pushed him ahead of her down the drive. "And why aren't we taking the coach?" If they were going somewhere the coach should have been waiting for them at the door with Abel on the driver's seat.

"Hush. Your father doesn't want the girls to come. He thinks they'll be safer here. And no one must know that we're going. Your father will explain it all when we see him."

He walked along obediently, his mother holding fast to his hand, moving more quickly than he'd ever seen her move. She was dressed differently, too, and it took him a few seconds to realize that she was wearing one of Agnes's dresses and Agnes's old dark cloak.

"Are we in danger? Is that why you're dressed like that, so that no one will recognize us?"

"That's my intelligent boy! Of course it is, Ned. Now be still. We must hurry along."

"But where are we going?"

"To New York."

Ned was not only fully awake now, but also heady excitement was making his blood race. "Is Father there?"

"Yes, he's there. You'll like New York, but for now you must say your name is John Fletcher and I'm Mary Fletcher, your mother, who has lost her position as a maidservant. Can you remember that, if we're questioned?"

"Of course I can." Ned was disgusted. Did she think he was half-witted? He was almost grown, he'd been fifteen in February, and a great many lads, especially if they weren't from wealthy families like his own, were considered men at fifteen. But his mother seemed to think that he was still a little boy.

There was a wagon just ahead. It was a rough farm cart, but Mr. Atkins threw the chest into it and helped his mother up onto the high seat. Ned clambered up, still trembling with the excitement of this adventure. His father was in New York and they were going to him, and it was all very secret. His head buzzed with the amazement of it all.

His heart was in his throat when they were stopped by the British sentries at the Neck, but Mr. Atkins had passed back and forth many times, foraging for a day's work in the countryside as a farm laborer, even if he was only paid in food.

The woman and boy, he explained, were his niece and great-nephew, who were Tories and who wanted to stay with friends who'd give them shelter because she could find no employment in Boston since the people who had employed her could no longer afford to pay her or even to feed her and her son.

It was a good thing that his mother remembered to keep her hands hidden in the folds of the cloak, Ned thought. It was getting light now, and they were so soft and white that even a stupid Britisher would have known that she wasn't a maid.

The wagon was empty except for the small chest and his own change of clothing, and after the redcoat had examined the contents of the chest to make sure that no firearms were in it he waved them on. He'd seen Atkins before, and a woman and a child weren't apt to come back bringing a small army behind them. Ned guessed that after the battle at Concord he had other things to think about except an out-of-work serving woman and a lad.

They went all the way to Providence in the farm cart and there they boarded a coastal schooner for New York. They kept to themselves and no one questioned them. His mother kept the hood of the cloak pulled closely around her face, and her face itself was scrubbed clean of the cosmetics that she usually wore.

New York, with its bustle and strangeness, fascinated Ned, but his mother gave him no time to crane his neck or run around sightseeing. She hired a conveyance to take them directly to an inn. It was a poor sort of place and Ned couldn't understand why she had chosen it, except that it must be a part of keeping their identities a secret. A serving maid wouldn't be able to afford anything better.

"Stay right here," Millicent told Ned, when they had been shown to a small, mean room. "I don't know how long I'll be but you are to stay here and wait until I come back, do you understand? I'll bring you up some bread and cheese, in case I'm late, but you aren't to stir from this room."

Ned was hungry and he wolfed down the bread and cheese even if the bread was stale and the cheese tasted a bit moldy. After he'd eaten there was nothing to do but watch the street outside of the window and keep a sharp eye out for his mother and father, because of course his mother had gone to fetch his father, and then this masquerade would be over.

But it was dark before his mother returned, and Ned, exhausted by the journey, had fallen asleep on the most uncomfortable bed he had ever slept in. He came out of his sleep slowly when Millicent lighted a candle, and he felt alarm when he saw that she was not only alone but also that she was agitated, her face white and drawn with anxiety.

"Couldn't Father come with you, Mother? When will I get to see him?"

"We were too late. He has already left. But don't fret, love, everything will be all right. We're going to England! Yes, yes, that's the message he left for us, we are to go to England, and in the morning I will see about passage. Now go to sleep again."

"How could he sleep with his disappointment churning in his head like a sickness, like he had eaten too many green apples or was coming down with a fever? Going to England! That didn't make sense. His father despised England, and even if there was going to be a real war with the British before long, as so many of his friends had told him, Charles Armitage wasn't one to send his family away, much less plan to join them there. Charles thought that every patriot's duty was to stay right here in the colonies and fight to the last man.

And sleep was made further impossible by his mother's pacing up and down the room, ten steps this way, ten steps the other. But in answer to the questions he put to her she would only say, "We are going to England, and we will stay with Sir Basil, and we'll visit Lillian too, won't that be wonderful? That is what your father said."

Ned couldn't understand it at all. Why would Father

send them to England, and leave Tamara and Annabelle behind? He had the distinct impression that his mother wasn't telling him the truth. Ned grew more and more worried. Millicent had been acting strangely for weeks, it was as if her nerves had given way, sometimes she hadn't even noticed, or answered, when someone had spoken to her, and she had snapped at the servants and at Annabelle and Tam a good more than was usual.

"Mother, I don't . . ."

"Be still and let me think! Don't I have enough on my mind without you pestering me? This change in plans poses problems, but everything will be all right."

He fell asleep at last, counting his mother's pacing steps, and when he woke the sun had filled the room and his mother had gone.

By the time she returned, the sun had reached its zenith and his stomach was so empty that he felt ill, but he hadn't dared to leave the room to seek something to eat downstairs, and besides he had no money with him.

The sight of Millicent's face shocked him. If it had been white and strained last night, now it looked as if she were dying of some dreadful disease. But her temper was still there, and it manifested itself in raging.

"Thieves! Oh, Lord, the thieves! The money lender will not give me a tenth of what my jewels are worth, and I didn't bring enough cash with me for our passage!"

Actually, it would have been impossible for Millicent to bring enough money for any such enterprise. Cash was not only short in Boston, but also Charles was pouring all he could scrape up in the effort to help the colonists drive the British out of the country. The fool! Didn't he realize that there was no way that the colonists could win against the might of England? Couldn't he realize that when this madness was over with, Massachusetts would be crushed, its citizens impoverished, the ringleaders imprisoned or hanged and their families left to suffer the consequences with no means of support? There had been very little money in the house, and Millicent had had no way of raising more in Boston. Even if she had wanted to sell any of her jewels there, there were few who could any longer afford to buy them. And she hadn't expected to have to sell the jewels that she'd sewn into the hem of her skirt, she'd thought that they'd be taken care of as soon as they reached New York.

"But didn't Father leave us money for our passage?" Ned was completely bewildered.

"No, he did not. I expect that he didn't have enough with him but he assumed that I could sell my jewels and raise the passage money. Never mind, I'll find someone who will give me a better price! Some of the officers here will be wealthy, and they'll be glad to pick up such good pieces for their wives or sweethearts for a good deal less than they'd have to pay in a shop. If only I'd brought some of my own gowns instead of those rags that Agnes wore! But I was afraid to take the risk, the sentry might have been suspicious when he examined my chest."

At least they ate. The food wasn't what Ned was used to, but anything was palatable when your stomach was empty.

For the next week, day after day, night after night, Millicent went out and left him alone at the inn. It wasn't until they had been in New York for eight days that she returned early one evening with a flush on her face and excitement in her eyes.

"I have found a friend who knows someone who will probably give me the price I want for my jewels. We will be going to England very soon now."

She had spent some of the small sum she still had

left on ribbons and lace and she spent the rest of the evening refurbishing the best of Agnes's dresses that she had brought with her. She had also bought cosmetics, and she spent a long time making up her face to hide the lines of uncertainty and strain. Looking at her when she was ready to leave the next evening, Ned thought that she looked cheap and garish, but he kept his thoughts to himself. It wasn't safe to talk to his mother these days, she was too apt to turn on him and give him a tongue-lashing. He didn't mind that so much. It was the way she fawned over him and coddled and petted him afterward that bothered him, begging him to forgive her and promising him that she'd make everything up to him a hundred times over once they got to England. It seemed to Ned that she wasn't quite rational, that she was even worse than she'd been for the past few weeks back at home.

By now Ned was heartily tired of the room at the inn, its four walls hemming him in. He wished that he dared set out and explore the city on his own, but knowing his mother's temper he dared not after she had told him that he must not. Even though he had never felt the full brunt of it on himself until they had come to New York, she was so tired and worried now that if he disobeyed her she might easily fall into a rage that he wouldn't soon forget.

Even England would be better than this imprisonment, although personally he wished they could go back to Boston instead. At least he could ask Lillian if he could stay with her, and not have all those disgusting old men pawing at him and making remarks that would make him want to shove their filthy words back down their throats. He didn't care overly much for Lillian. She had never put herself out to be nice to him, as Annabelle and Tamara did, but staying with her would be better than staying with Great-uncle Basil.

Millicent didn't give Ned another thought once she had left the inn to keep her rendezvous. The man was waiting for her where he had said he would be. She had not wanted him to call for her at the inn, in case Ned might let something slip or he might later remember that she had a boy of his description with her. By now it was possible that Charles would have learned that she and Ned were missing and have set a search in motion. If she were discovered now, and forced ignominiously to go back to Boston, she wouldn't be able to bear it.

As a matter of fact, the gentleman she was meeting wasn't a friend of a friend. She had picked him out because he looked prosperous, making his acquaintance by the simple expedient of pretending to become faint outside of a much more respectable inn than the one at which she and Ned were staying. He had been solicitous, taking her into the ladies' parlor and buying her a glass of Madeira to restore her, and because of his kindness she had confided her problem to him, that of selling her jewels for a fair price.

Her strategy had paid off. The gentleman was indeed prosperous and he knew another man who might be interested if the pieces were as good as she said they were.

"Rich as Croesus, he is. If you'll bring the pieces tomorrow evening I can arrange a meeting."

At last! After all the frustrations of the journey and of finding that in spite of Grace's assurances George was not in New York, that he had been transferred somewhere else almost immediately after he had arrived with his regiment, things were beginning to straighten out. She had counted heavily on finding George. He would have helped her, seen to the sale of her jewels, put her and Ned aboard a ship for England. He'd have done it for the reimbursement she would promise him once Uncle Basil had died and Ned had come into his money, a reimbursement at an interest rate that would have tempted a much richer man, as well as the promise of her patronage once she was queening it in London and he returned there after this madness was over.

This dreadful rebellion! The rabble was actually frightening. They'd fought the troops at Lexington and at Concord, and Millicent was sure that soon the entire seaboard would be in open conflict. As long as she and Ned remained in Massachusetts they would be branded as traitors along with Charles. Charles would lose everything, very probably even his life, and they'd be left impoverished, and as long as they were branded as traitors there would be no chance of Ned's inheriting from Uncle Basil. Her only hope was to get to London as a refugee Tory, thereby safeguarding Ned's interests.

With Charles working openly for the rebels, there would be no stigma attached to her breaking off with him. She and Ned would be welcomed with open arms, made much of, and she would never have to return to America. Her only regret was that there had been no way that she could bring Annabelle, at least, with them. But she'd known that Annabelle would refuse to come, and both she and Tamara were old enough to ask questions that she couldn't answer if she'd told them the story that their father had sent for them. Knowing Tamara, she was convinced that Tam would refuse to board the ship, and if Tamara refused, Annabelle would refuse. Millicent hadn't dared to take the chance, but Ned, at least, would be safe, and so would she.

There was another man, a younger man, with the

one she had met yesterday afternoon, as honest-looking and prosperous-looking as the first.

"We're to meet my friend at an inn near here," Millicent's first friend explained to her. "We cannot take you to his home as we ordinarily would, as he wants the jewelry as a surprise for his wife for their anniversary."

The other gentleman was late in arriving but the time was passed pleasantly in a small private parlor. Before the prospective buyer appeared Millicent had drunk three glasses of Madeira and been amused by the younger man's open admiration of her.

The gentleman arrived at last, fortyish, balding, his ample figure attesting to richness of living, exactly the sort of prospect that Millicent had wanted. He examined the pieces over yet another glass of wine, and offered a price that Millicent accepted immediately. It was not what the pieces were worth but it was a good deal more than the money lenders had offered.

The exchange was made. The gentleman and the other older gentleman left her, while the younger insisted on escorting her back to her lodgings. "It's far from safe for a lady to be abroad alone after dark. I'm only glad to be of service."

Millicent's step was light as she walked beside her companion. How soon she would be in London, never again to set foot in these benighted colonies! She could hardly find words to express her gratitude.

The two men stepped out of an alley so suddenly that Millicent's companion was struck down before she realized what was happening. She screamed as one of them grasped her arms from behind, pinning them to her sides, while the other struck her on the side of her head with such force that she too plunged into instant unconsciousness.

She regained her senses with the knowledge that she was lying on the ground, in an alley so black that she could make out nothing around her. She held her breath, afraid that her assailants might still be there, waiting to do her even further harm, but she could hear nothing. Even her companion, the one who had been struck down before she had, was gone. Her head felt as if it were going to burst, and her body was so sore and bruised that she could hardly struggle to her feet.

Her dress was rumpled and muddied, her stockings torn, her knees were bruised, and her hands were scraped from her fall to the cobbles, but even so, her first thought was for the money she had carried in her purse.

It was gone, of course. She leaned against the grimy wall of the building behind her and wept. She'd been a fool, she'd been taken. The men had planned this from the start. She would hardly have handed over her jewels in some dark alley, she'd have been suspicious if she hadn't been taken to a respectable place, she might even have screamed for help, or managed to run away and elude them. They'd had to allay her suspicions, pay her over the money, and then strike while the youngest man had held her attention, feeling happy and secure because she had the money in hand.

Ned had been awake for some time before he heard the stumbling footsteps in the narrow corridor outside of their room at the inn. He'd slept fitfully after his mother had gone out to sell her jewels, starting up again every once in a while, worried because she hadn't returned.

The footsteps stopped outside their door, and he heard a soft thud. His alarm deepening, he hurried to throw the door open and he cried out as he saw Millicent lying in a heap on the floor, her shoulders shaking.

She was in a dreadful state. Her face was swollen and discolored from the blow she had taken and from her subsequent weeping, and the cosmetics she had applied before she had left had run and smeared from her tears. Her eyes were wild as she babbled "Thieves! They were thieves! Gone, all gone, my jewels, my money, oh God, oh God . . . ."

Staggering under her almost dead weight, Ned got her onto the bed. He started to run downstairs to fetch the landlord or his wife to help him but she called him back and clung to his hands.

"No, no! I'll be all right. We mustn't have inquiries set in motion! I'll find a way, I'll find some other way! I'll write to Grace, she'll send me money, she'll do it for our friendship's sake. Just let me rest, Ned. Everything will be all right."

Everything was not all right. When Millicent was able to rise from the bed the next morning, she wrote the letter to Grace and asked Ned to take it to the landlord to be posted. All the rest of that day and the next she paced the room like a madwoman, raging at herself for having been such a fool as to be taken in by scoundrels.

As her bruises worked out their color deepened, until Ned could hardly bear to look at her. Except for the time she spent eating, only nibbling at the food she had Ned bring to their room from the kitchen, telling the landlord that his mother was indisposed, she either paced and raged until she was exhausted, or slept restlessly, tossing and turning until he made his bed on the floor so that he could get some rest.

She'll soon be well, and when Mistress Gammage sends the money we'll go home to Boston, Ned told himself. He missed Tamara so much that it was an ache inside of him. He dreamed about his father, dreamed that Charles had come to take them home, and when he woke from the dreams he nearly wept because it wasn't true, and that shamed him because he hadn't cried for years.

In a few days' time, instead of getting better, Millicent fell ill—desperately ill, raging with fever, and a rash appeared on her face and body. She lay on the bed, tossing and moaning, and as her delirium deepened she raved, and Ned's life plunged into hell, shattered beyond any hope of repairing.

"His father, his father! Not Charles Armitage, but George Hartgrave. George, George," Millicent cried. "Why have you abandoned me? Come back, come back! I need you, your son needs you!"

In her delirium, Millicent told it all, relived her affair with George Hartgrave from its beginning until it had been taken up again when Mr. Hartgrave had returned to Boston. It had been weeks before Millicent had learned from Grace Gammage that he had returned to England and sold up the last of his property and bought a commission in the Army.

Ned listened, and tried to stop his ears to shut the words out. And he died inside.

Millicent's fever climbed, and she screamed and moaned, and Ned couldn't keep her quiet. The landlord came, and looked, and backed out of the room, cursing.

Other men came. His mother was picked up, and carried, raving, through the streets in a cart, with Ned sitting numbly beside her on filthy straw.

They called it a hospital. The inmates called it a pesthouse. Ned called it hell.

Smallpox, they told him, the disinterested doctor who saw Millicent but once, the slatternly women, dregs of humanity, who served as attendants.

There was straw on the floor to serve as beds. Slops, reeking and almost entirely lacking in nourishment, to eat. Odors that made Ned gag.

She's going to die, the slatterns told him. You'll get it too, you've been infected. They grinned their broken, gap-toothed grins, and shrugged, and kept their senses deadened with gin, creatures not quite human, surely not human, while the patients, the damned and condemned to hell, lay in their own filth and vomit and either died or got better through no fault of those who were supposed to care for them. Brackish water, wormy gruel, it was as much as paupers deserved, more than they were entitled to.

Ned waited for the disease to strike him, and while he waited he tended his mother as best he could. Then he too became ill, he saw the disembodied faces of the slatterns hanging over him, saw their witless grins, and he turned his face into the crawling, odorous straw and waited to die.

He was a bastard, Charles Armitage wasn't his father, he'd been cheated, cheated by this woman who was his mother, who had betrayed him.

Even death cheated him. He had only a light case, not severe enough to mark him. And somehow, they called it a miracle, Millicent also lived. A skeleton with clawlike hands, and the look of madness on her face, her face pocked, its beauty destroyed.

When they could both get on their feet and walk, they were turned out. Ned had never known before that a damned soul could be expelled from hell.

He took his mother, leading her by the hand, back to the inn because it was the only place he knew. He begged shelter for her, in return for whatever work he could do. The clothing they had left behind them had been sold to pay for the room rent that Millicent owed, and there was still some owing. They were human derelicts but Ned could still work.

There was no letter from Grace Gammage. With Boston occupied, cut off from the rest of the colonies, Millicent's letter had probably never reached her.

They were given a cubbyhole under the eaves. It was boiling hot, airless, another version of hell. When he could think, when he had time to think, Ned speculated on that. The preachers had never told him that hell was divided into compartments, each one different from the others, but equally bad. Maybe they didn't know it, never having been there themselves.

Ned was put to work in the stables. He was a strong boy, big for his age, and acquiring his services for only the unused cubbyhole and enough food to keep him and his mother alive was a bargain. Ned was also a handsome boy, his fair hair and blue eyes, along with the thinness and pallor from his illness, gave him the look of an angel. It took him only two days to learn that the brutal hostler liked boys. He had thought, in his innocence, that only the depraved old dandies of London had such strange appetites, like those friends of Sir Basil's.

He fought back, but he was smaller than the hostler for all his being big for his age, and he was still weakened from the sickness although his face had been left unmarked. He learned, that second night, about the third anteroom to hell.

He was given more explicit lessons on the following nights. If it hadn't been for his mother, he would have run away even if it had meant starving.

Instead, as his strength returned, he became adept at avoiding the hostler whenever it was possible. The innkeeper himself was a God-fearing man, dishonest only where it paid him to be, and unless the hostler had had too much to drink Ned could keep him off by threatening to tell. There was a great drawback to actually telling. The hostler's services were worth a great deal more to the innkeeper than Ned's. If he told, he would be the one to be sent away, and his mother with him.

If he had been alone, he could have managed to make his way back to Boston. But his mother was still his mother, even if she had betrayed him and even if she was a little mad.

He could find no pity for Millicent in his heart, but he could not desert her. As for himself, he would never return home. He'd rather die than foist himself off on the man who still thought that he was his son.

Nineteen

"We've made a mistake. Luke said it was a mistake and he was right." Mark wiped sweat from his forehead and squinted through the sunlight toward the British lines. "He said we should use Bunker's Hill, not Breed's. It's a deal higher, we'd have a better advantage."

His face was grimed and his shoulders felt as though they were being seared with red-hot irons. He'd done his share of digging, but so had they all.

The men around him were equally begrimed. They'd all worked all night, throwing up this redoubt and a hundred yards of breastworks to fill in a gap that had been left between the redoubt and a fence made of stone posts with wooden rails.

The British forces had left Boston about noon, with some fifteen hundred grenadiers, marines, light infantry, and artillery pieces transported by barge. They'd landed on the Charleston peninsula and now they were formed up on Moulton's Hill, except the ones who had moved up toward the bottom of Breed's Hill, and things were going to start popping, as Eli said, any minute now.

Eli had been as good as his word. Even Patience's broom had not been able to keep him from presenting himself geared for action and raring to fight. He was right there beside Tim, joining up with William Prescott's militiamen to fortify the hill and do his damnedest to defend it when the time came.

"The Committee of Safety told Prescott to fortify Bunker, not Breed's!" Mark went on. His throat was raspy from thirst and labor. "And it looks to me as if we've made a bad mistake."

Behind him a deriding laugh made all three friends turn. "That's Luke for you! Always sticking his nose in where it ain't wanted. I notice he ain't here, though. Skulkin' to home, lettin' the rest of us do his fightin' for him!"

"You keep that consarned trap of yours shut, Henry Atkins!" Eli bellowed. "Luke's over yonder on Bunker, helpin' fortify it, and you might turn out to be danged glad that he and old Putt's there. We're likely to need 'em before this is over, and Luke Martin'll do his share of fightin', don't you go worryin' none about that!"

"Yes," Tim put in. "What we want to see is for you to do the same!"

"You don't have to worry about me, you young whippersnapper. I'll pick off my share of them dirty redcoats. What I'd like to know is what you and Eli's doin' here. Eli's so old and blind he'll be shootin' our own men, and you're just a snot-nosed brat. I'm goin' to stay well behind you, you can lay your britches on that, so's there won't be any accident happenin' to me when you aim the wrong way!"

"Old man!" Eli started to leap forward to attack his tormentor. "Who're you callin' old? I'll show you who's old, you lazy, no-good lout!"

Mark grabbed one of Eli's arms and Tim the other to hold him back. "Easy, Eli. Don't let him get your goat. We've got other fish to fry."

"Just like his pa!" Henry sneered. "Always the

peacemaker! Comes from associatin' with Charles Armitage, I reckon. Your pa and Eli here was allers too good fer me once they started suckin' up to the lawyer. Used to be I was good enough to pay my money and drink my cider at The Temptation, but no more! Well, there's things I know about Lawyer Armitage, and his wife too, you'd like to know, only I ain't tellin'!"

Mark felt rage rise in his throat. Henry Atkins was a ne'er-do-well and a habitual braggart, but there had been a core of conviction in his voice that convinced him that the man knew something. Could it be possible that he had some idea where Millicent Armitage and Ned were? Charles had been frantic when he'd come home to find them missing, and so far there hadn't been a clue. Even Mistress Gammage had denied knowing anything about their disappearance, although Charles had told Luke and Eli that he thought that the woman was lying.

"What do you know about Mistress Armitage?" he demanded, loosing his hold on Eli and stepping threateningly close to Henry.

Henry's eyes shifted but he held his ground. "A lot you and Armitage'ud like to know, what's what I know! Don't you lay a hand on me, it's agin' the rules to fight amongst ourselves!"

"Damn the rules!" Mark reached out and grabbed Henry by his shirtfront, and the lanky man's feet left the ground.

"Hold it there! What do you think you're doing? Come to attention! Save your personal quarrels for later, you blasted idiots!" The barking voice was authoritative, and Mark had an idea that it was Prescott himself speaking, but the speaker had already turned his back and hurried off to bark orders at someone else.

"Here they come! It's General Pigot's men! And there's their right flank under Howe himself, circling around! Damn, they're going to use them cannon on us!"

Mark had no idea who had yelped out the words, and there was no time to speculate. The British, bayonets fixed, were advancing toward them. His throat felt like sandpaper, and once again, as he had for a moment or two when he'd helped chase the British all the way back to Charleston, he cursed himself for being a coward. His hands were so sweaty that he had to wipe them on his breeches before he could keep a good hold on his firearm. Not Matthew Baldwin's old musket, thankfully. Then, he had been afraid that the gun would explode in his face; now he was carrying a regulation militiaman's musket.

There was a volley of firing from behind the stone and rail fence where New Hampshire's John Stark had managed to get through British fire to reinforce Connecticut's Captain Knowlton. Through the smoke Mark saw the enemy go down in ones and twos and threes, but those coming up behind them charged right over their fallen comrades to get at the rebels before they had a chance to reload.

The rebels behind the fence went on firing in relays of three; fire, fall back, second man fire, fall back, third man fire. The British turned and fled and Mark rammed another ball down the barrel of his musket, wanting to cheer except that his throat was so dry that no sound would come out. They'd turned them, by God, they'd turned them back!

His elation was premature. Howe had his men charging the redoubt now. The British troops were crossing the field and jumping and clambering over walls and rail fences, the tall pasture grass coming up to their knees.

Mark fired again, wiped sweat and smoke from his

red-rimmed eyes, and saw the redcoats go down like wheat under a scythe. He wasn't afraid anymore. There was no time to be afraid or even to think about it. Fire, reload, fire again, hands steady because there was no time for them to shake, eyes clearing because there was no time to let them blink and fog over.

"They're falling back!" The cry went up all around him. "We did it again, they're falling back!"

"I've only got two rounds left. Anybody got any extra bullets?"

"Not me. How about you?"

The dryness had returned to Mark's throat. They were running short of powder and ball. Why hadn't the British fired those cannon? If they brought them into play it was going to be all up.

"Look! They're gettin' smarter!" That was Eli, at his shoulder. "They're comin' again and they've shed their packs! Their coats, too. They're comin' right this way and this time they ain't hindered by all that weight!"

He and Mark threw themselves flat as a cannonball landed nearby. The British had brought their big guns into play at last. Mark would not learn until much later that the first cannonballs the British had brought with them to the attack had been the wrong size, and they had had to send back to Boston for the right size.

"Fall back! Into the redoubt!"

Mark and Eli lost no time in obeying. Men ran and cursed and pushed against them on all sides as they dashed for the safety of the redoubt they had labored on all the night before. Wounded men, dead men lay under their feet, making them stumble. Groans and screams made the air thick with hideousness. Mark had the impression, fleeting because again there was no time, that he had been transported into Bedlam.

Inside the redoubt it was crowded, the air was thick, there were despairing curses as men's last balls were fired and there were no more to replace them. They tried to hold out but there was no stemming the tide of the oncoming British. They were on them, over the wall. Mark grasped his ammunitionless musket by the barrel and used it as a club, and others were doing the same. Rocks, fists, musket butts against bayonets. Was this how it was going to end, here on Breed's Hill? Wiped out, massacred, all their brave defiance coming to nothing?

Prescott was fighting like a madman, a demon, his sword against the bayonets that faced him. Mark found himself close behind him, trying, he didn't know why anymore, to protect their commander from attack from behind or the side. Eli and Tim were lost somewhere else in the melee.

They were driven out of the redoubt now, into the open, fighting step by step, retreating, from fence to tree to wall. They were making, desperately, for Bunker's Hill and the defenses there. How far now, how far? Mark swung his musket again, caught a man with a bayonet poised to jab into the man beside him, the stock catching the British marine on the side of his face, the bone crumbling, the flesh splitting. He felt vomit in his throat and ran on. They were going to make it, some of them were going to make it.

He stumbled over a fallen man and didn't know if it were friend or enemy, didn't have time to stop to look. Only a little farther now, a little distance that stretched endlessly in front of him. His breath was gone, there was a red haze in front of his eyes, his ears were roaring, and he had no sensation of running although he knew that his legs must still be moving because he was covering ground.

They'd been licked. They'd been licked all along the line. He fell to his knees as he reached the defenses on Bunker's Hill. Someone, he never knew who, grabbed him by the arm and dragged him forward into comparative safety. Still there was no time to rest, to catch his breath, to think. Another musket was thrust into his hands, and he had the irrevocable impression that this had been going on forever and would keep going on until the end of eternity.

"They got Joseph Warren," he heard someone say. "Deader'n a doornail. If I was a gen'ral I wouldn't of been fightin' in the damn ranks as a volunteer!"

Dimly, Mark's mind registered the name. Joseph Warren, the president of Massachusetts' Provincial Congress, fighting in the ranks? He shook his head to clear it. It didn't seem possible. Anyway, it didn't matter much. An enemy bullet or bayonet, or a cannonball, didn't give a hang whether a man was a plain militiaman or a general, just as long as he was vulnerable flesh and blood.

Somewhere off to the right he heard another voice, one he recognized in spite of the buzzing in his head. Tod! Oh, God Almighty, Tod Bates, Eli's Tod!

Fighting nausea-racked dizziness, Mark got to his feet and got over there. Tod was on the ground, his right leg gushing blood, the flesh mangled and mashed in with the cloth of his breeches. Eli was ripping his shirt into strips and trying to wrap the strips around the mangled flesh.

"That you, Mark? Give me a hand here before the lad bleeds to death. Patience's goin' to kill me for this. I never got a scratch, not one damned scratch, and here's Tod with his leg most shot off!" His voice was laced with anguish and rage. "Why couldn't it of been me, why'd it have to be Tod? I'm too old to matter much.

He ain't dyin', is he? He ain't goin' to die right here? Oh, Lord God . . . ."

"Get out of here," Dr. Peabody said. "All of you women get out of here."

Annabelle's breath caught in her throat, and she was so white that Tamara was afraid that she was going to fall over.

"You'll need help."

"Are you insane, young woman? I've got to take that leg off. I can't save it, no doctor in the world could save it after all this time. It's a miracle that he didn't die before Luke managed to get him back here, and it's a miracle that that rowboat wasn't caught with both of them in it, but if I don't get that leg off the miracles are going to run out. Now get out of here and send Luke in here to help me."

"You'll need more help than that." Listening, Tamara's heart felt as if it were going to break from sheer pity for her sister.

On the pillow, Tod's face was whiter than Annabelle's, whiter than Patience's, as though all the blood had been drained out of his body. Tamara thought, her throat constricting, that even if Dr. Peabody took off the mangled leg he would surely die, and then what would Annabelle do? Her own body felt taut as a tightly stretched bowstring. The strain she had gone through recently had been all but intolerable. Her mother and Ned gone, disappeared, no one knew where although like Mark, Tam suspected that her mother had made a last desperate bid to get back to England before hostilities came to full swing.

Mark and Luke and even Eli, and young John and Tim, were all off fighting. She and Annabelle had watched the battle from the roof of their house, had seen the smoke, had seen Charleston catch fire and burn from the incendiary fire from the British ships and the British artillery in Boston. It had been like the end of the world, made all the worse because they knew that their men were in the thick of it.

That had been two days ago. It had taken Luke all that time to get Tod back home, using a rowboat on the Charles River under cover of night after he had decided that he wasn't going to let the lad lie there and die without lifting a hand to try to save him.

Together, he and Eli had carried Tod to the river and along its banks, feeling their way in the dark, afraid with every step that they'd be surprised by the British. They'd been relieved when Tod had sunk into unconsciousness again, after brief periods of being aware of what had happened to him, because once he had fainted from the pain of being carried, there were no more stifled moans to betray their presence. And now, Tamara thought, Tod would either live or he wouldn't live, and if he lived it would be without his leg.

She looked at Annabelle again and saw that her sister had gone a shade paler, although she wouldn't have thought it was possible. Dr. Peabody saw it too.

"You wouldn't be able to stand it, child," Peabody said, his tone more gentle than it had been before. He himself was exhausted. He wasn't used to treating wounded men, not from bullets and bayonets. Gout and bound-up bowels and croup and once in a while a broken limb from a fall from a horse, indigestion, and scythe-slashed legs were what he knew, not attempting to patch together war-mangled bodies. He was too old for this sort of thing, but if the wounded men had had the courage to stand up and fight, then he had to find the courage to patch them together again.

Annabelle's face was still the color of paper but

she lifted her chin, and her eyes were steady. "If you can bear it, doctor, I can."

Peabody spread his hands in helpless surrender. "All right, then. Patience, fetch me the rum bottle. We have to get all he can drink down him."

An hour later, kneeling in front of the fire heating the poker that would cauterize the spurting flesh when the doctor's gruesome task was finished, Tamara swayed a little and gritted her teeth against fainting. How could Annabelle help Patience to hold Tod's leg in a firm grip, with the sound of the saw rasping in her ears as Peabody cut through the bone, while Luke held down Tod's shoulders with his great strength and Eli held his other leg, both their faces green?

In spite of all the rum they'd managed to get down him, another shriek tore from Tod's throat. It cut through Tamara like the knife Peabody had laid aside. Then there was silence, so deep and sudden that she felt as if she had been transported into a void. Only the continued rasp of the saw got through, and then the doctor's voice, gruff and filled with urgency.

"Bring that poker!"

She brought it, and gagged as the smell of searing flesh filled the room. Thank God, oh thank God that Tod was still unconscious, with only a protesting whimpering emerging from his throat.

Her hand reached out to take the poker back with no conscious directive from her mind, while the doctor eased the flap of skin he had left for the purpose over the stinking, charred flesh. She saw that his hands were shaking. He was an old man, and he was tired.

Patience had the needle and thread ready to sew down the flap. Peabody accepted it from her but when his hand continued to shake she took it back. By the door, Eli leaned over and retched. "Stand out of my light," Patience said.

Tamara closed her eyes. How can she? she thought. How can she hold her hands steady and sew on Tod's skin and flesh? But deep inside, she knew how she could. She could do it because it had to be done, just as Annabelle had been able to listen to Tod's agonized screams and go on holding his leg while the doctor had cut through flesh and bone.

"Good woman. Well, it's done. Whether he'll live is in God's hands now. As for me, I could use a drink. Some of that rum Tod left will be fine. I have to be on my way, there are other patients waiting for me."

Tam moved to put her arms around her sister but Annabelle gave no indication that she knew she was there. Annabelle was praying. Tam's lips moved as well, and her eyes scalded with the sudden tears that flooded them.

"It's going to be a long, hard pull. I wish I could stay around in case you need me." Luke's voice was ragged and he, too, took a pull from the bottle that Peabody handed him. "But I have to get along too. I have to get back to our lines before the British tighten things up until I can't."

Tamara nodded. She understood. It was up to them now, to the women. The men had to go and fight.

Mark was still out there, and John, and Tim. Once again she closed her eyes and prayed silently. Let Tod live, and protect Mark, and John and Tim, and please, God, wherever Ned is, let him be all right, and wherever Father is, let him be all right. God protect them all.

She remembered, later, that she had not included her mother in her prayer, but it didn't seem to matter. She might even be in England by now, living in the lap of luxury in Sir Basil's house, visiting Lillian and her husband, Freddie, triumphant that she had gotten away from Massachusetts at last. But poor Ned! He hated London, he hated his great-uncle's friends with their depraved, unnatural morals. If Father could never get him back, it would almost kill him.

"Go away," Tod said.

A choked-back sob caught in Annabelle's throat. He'd spoken, and his eyes held no trace of the delirium that had held him in its grip ever since his leg had been amputated just below the knee.

"Lie quietly, darling. You're home, everything is all right."

"Go away. I don't want you here."

Annabelle's color faded but she spoke firmly, her voice sure of itself even though it was soft.

"I'll never go away. You can't drive me away. I belong here, with you. Always with you, forever with you."

"A one-legged man!" Tod's voice was torn from the depth of his soul. "It was bad enough before. Me, a foster child, a bastard, father unknown, mother a tavern slut! And you Charles Armitage's daughter, sister to Lady Lillian, sister to the heir to Sir Basil's fortune! An heiress in your own right, blue-blooded, unattainable, and still driving me mad by hanging around me, by refusing to leave me alone even when you knew that being near you was killing me!"

"That was your fault. There was no reason for it to kill you. My father would have given his consent to our marriage any time you'd spoken up."

"I'll have my mother throw you out."

"Try it. She isn't about to throw me out. She knows I belong to you and you belong to me. Eli knows it.

Tamara knows it. My father knows it. You're the only one who doesn't seem to know it, but I'll get it through your head if it takes me the rest of my life."

"I'm a cripple!" Tod shouted. "A one-legged cripple!"

"Just because you lost your leg doesn't mean that our children will all be born with one leg."

Tod turned his face into the pillow and groaned, his shoulders shaking. Annabelle got up and went into the kitchen, where Patience was preparing the midday meal.

"He's all right, Patience. He's awake, but he isn't in his right mind, exactly. He told me to go away, that he won't marry me. How do you feel about a full-fledged scandal? Because I'm not going to leave him, not ever again, married or not."

"He'll have to marry you, then." Patience's face lighted up with joy that made tears come into Annabelle's eyes. "We can't have your name besmirched." Then, with a low cry, Patience broke. She groped toward Annabelle and the two women, one young and the other well past middle age, clung to each other, weeping.

They broke apart at last, laughing. It was wonderful to be able to laugh again. That Boston was under siege, that they were trapped inside with the British, meant less than nothing.

"And as for scandal, how about that sister of yours? Why, your compromising yourself by refusing to move out of my house isn't a patch on what she's doing! Your mother would have a seizure if she knew what Tamara was up to now."

Twenty

The Temptation was crowded, as it always was these days. Even if a man had no money to spend on spirits, he came to the tavern as a matter of course, to hear the latest news and to expound on the situation. The only difference was that Charity and Tamara often had to serve redcoats, a fact that made Tamara's gorge rise even as she thumped down the mugs of ale or hot, spiced wine or rum flips, things that only lobster-backs could afford, in front of them and accepted their money.

Patience and Martha had both protested volubly when Tam had stated her intention of helping Charity keep the tavern going. Charity couldn't do it single-handedly, and with Eli somewhere out there with the besieging Continental troops, someone had to step in.

"If Charity can do it, so can I!" Tamara had said when Martha had tried to dissuade her.

"Charity is a good deal older than you, a grown woman, and nowhere near as pretty. But you! Tamara, surely you know the danger you'll be in, exposing your-self to all those enemy soldiers! Charity won't be able to protect you. It's unthinkable! What would your father say if we were to allow you to run such risks?"

"There won't be any risks." Tamara had taken the pins from her hair, grown out again since Martha had cut it when she had been hiding from George Hart-grave, and shook it out over her shoulders. "Just get your scissors, Martha! Tim's clothes will still fit me. I'm going to be a boy again!"

"Tamara Armitage, you've taken leave of your senses!"

"Charity needs help, Eli needs to have his business intact when he comes back whenever this is over, and there's another very good reason why I'm going to do it. When men drink, they talk. And I have sharp ears. Anything I can pick up can be passed along. Our spies get in and out constantly. Maybe what I hear won't be much of anything, but anything at all might prove to be important. I won't learn anything that could help our troops by staying at home, or helping you. Not that I won't go on helping you whenever I can, of course."

"So you'll be a potboy half the afternoon and all of the evening and hoe in my garden in your spare time!"

"Certainly I will." Tamara had dimples when she smiled, Martha realized. They didn't show very often, only when she was full of mischief, as she was now. There was one right by the left corner of her mouth and another, less deep, in her right cheek.

Patience had been even more horrified but no more successful than Martha in dissuading her. "I can't just sit around and do nothing! Martha is perfectly capable of running their home place, and with both you and Annabelle here to look after Tod you don't need me. So I'm going where I can be useful."

She was glad, now, that she had never developed the lush curves that her mother had deemed so important. And she was glad that she had inherited nothing of her mother's and her sisters' ultraporcelain beauty. With her hair cut and in a queue, with Tim's breeches and shirt and stockings and shoes, with her nails cut short and square and her hands not overly clean, she could pass as a boy in any company and she doubted that anyone who knew her could detect her true identity.

Her mother's Tory friends did not frequent The Temptation, which was far too common an establishment for their tastes, and her father's friends would never betray her even if they should penetrate her disguise. Martha and Patience were worrying unduly. Tam felt that she had to do something useful, or she'd burst from the inside out. It drove her frantic that she couldn't take up a musket and go and fight, but even if she could get away with passing herself off as a boy and joining the Army, that was one thing her father would never forgive her for. She supposed that she could go as a camp follower, but she had no one to follow. Luke or Mark, or even Eli, would send her packing with a wallop across her nether regions if she showed up with the pretense that she was attached to them.

"You, boy! Another flip here and look lively!"

Tamara looked lively. Her face was grimed with chimney smoke, and her hair, where it had come loose from her queue, hung over her forehead and into her eyes and made her squint.

She walked with an awkward gait, practiced until she could do it automatically, just as an adolescent boy would walk when his feet had grown too fast for the rest of him. Tim's shoes helped, being too large for her so that she had to stuff wool into the toes to keep them on. All of her movements were awkward, angular, but she managed to be sufficiently awkward without spilling anything on a patron and drawing undue attention to herself. A clout on the ear just might catch her off guard enough so that her cry would sound more girlish than change-of-voice boyish.

She kept her ears open, as did Charity. The difference was that the redcoats were more likely to go on talking in front of her than in front of Charity, who was a woman and who looked bright, while Tamara, as a boy, looked stupid and completely disinterested in anything except working hard enough to earn her keep.

So far, in all these weeks, she and Charity had picked up only two or three bits of information that might be of some use to the besieging forces. The arrival of new officers, the arrival of extra supplies, a rumor that the British were going to attack the besiegers. There were plenty to carry the bits and pieces of information they picked up to the Continental lines outside of Boston. It drove the British crazy, knowing that spies were everywhere. They had to allow farmers and supplies to come in, and there was no way of telling who was loyal and who was not. But men in their cups still had a habit of letting their tongues loosen, especially when nobody was listening except a half-grown boy who appeared little more than half-witted.

Charity herself had little trouble in keeping the soldiers at arm's length. Never pretty in the accepted sense of the word, she had taken to pinning her hair up in a sort of rat's nest, to wearing shapeless, dirty dresses, and she had a trick of crossing her eyes that would repel all but the most desperate and he'd have to be so high-flown that it would be easy to fend him off. She never appeared in the common room without her disguise, soot marks on her face, her expression sullen and surly, sighing and overworked. There were enough other women, better endowed and much more willing, in the city to keep her as safe in her disguise as Tamara was in hers.

Tod was horrified. "How could you have let her?" he demanded of Annabelle. "Your father will be furious when he finds out! This is the worst thing she's ever done, and she's done more than most girls of her age manage to do in a lifetime!"

"How could I have stopped her? I'm only her sister, not her mother or father."

"Her older sister! In the absence of both your parents, you stand as the head of your household and you have full authority over her. You Armitage women are the most stubborn, recalcitrant creatures in the world! I'll be glad when your father returns and takes both of you under his control again."

"He'll have no control over me." Annabelle's voice was sweet and soft. "I'll be Mistress Bates by then."

"You will not!" Tod could hobble around the room by now, leaning on a crutch that Tamara had fashioned for him with her own hands. "Your father will find you a suitable husband, and you'll obey him, and be glad that you did."

"You'll be well enough in another month or two," Annabelle said dreamily. "Your mother is upset because we can't be married in Old South. She's so indignant about the British ripping out the pews and using it for an indoor riding academy that I'm afraid that she'll take her broom one of these days and try to sweep them out single-handed! I'll wager she'd lay open a few heads before they subdued her, too. I was afraid she was going to burst, the first day she walked past the church and saw what they'd done. She was so angry she was shaking and I had to practically force some rum down her throat when we got home, to calm her enough so she wouldn't actually take her broom and go back there after them."

"Stop changing the subject."

Annabelle looked at him with wide-eyed innocence.

"I'm not changing the subject. We were talking about our wedding and that your mother wishes that we could be married at Old South. But I have more news, Tod. Tam picked it up at The Temptation."

"Go away. I don't care about your news. I only want you to go home where you belong."

Annabelle stayed where she was, in the chair beside Tod's bed. She picked up her knitting and the needles clicked and flashed.

The silence lengthened out until Tod, with something like desperation in his voice, said, "Well, what did Tam hear?"

"It was about the battle. The British lost over a thousand men, nearer eleven hundred, killed and wounded. They'd been reinforced, too. Tam has it that another thousand were sent in. Against odds like that you did very well. Sir William Howe was certainly impressed. They say he hasn't got over it yet."

"We lost men, too," Tod said, staring straight ahead of him with his face gone grim. A muscle at the corner of his mouth twitched.

Annabelle bent her head to count stitches. "Yes, we did, but not nearly as many. About four hundred. Or a few more, but not many. And many of them were only wounded, like you. With the British overrunning the town we won't be able to have a very fancy wedding, but I don't mind. I always thought it was silly to get all dressed up and be stared at and have to go through a party afterward when all you want to do is get away from everyone and be alone. I'll wear my blue shot-silk, I think. And there'll still be flowers. Shall I wear flowers in my headdress or do you think it would be frivolous? Mother had a lovely piece of gauze that Father bought her before all this started and she didn't take it with her. Your mother and I are working on it, it'll make a beautiful head, but you can't see it until the wedding because it would be bad luck."

She broke off because she'd glanced up and seen that Tod's eyes were filled with tears. She was beside him instantly, the knitting dropped forgotten to the floor, her arms around him as she pressed him back down onto the bed.

"You're tired and you hurt! You shouldn't practice walking so hard!" Off-balance, because Tod was trying to sit up while she was trying to force him down, they both fell over and the crutch that was leaning against the side of the bed crashed to the floor. Annabelle ended up still on top of him, her arms around him.

"Get up! What do you think you're doing? What if someone came in?"

"It wouldn't matter. We'll be married soon anyway, and people make allowances for lovers. Besides, your mother has gone shopping and there's no one else in the house."

Her mouth was warm and sweet on his, filled with a leashed-in passion that shook him. Her arms tightened and she kissed him harder, all of her love for him that she had had to suppress for so long breaking its bonds and flaming up with a fire that shook both of them to the core. Her body was trembling, crying out against the restrictions she'd had to put on it, demanding the freedom to express her love for him at last.

"Annabelle, for the love of God!"

"You love me. Say it, say you love me! Say you want me as much as I want you!"

Annabelle's eyes were shining behind her tears and her face was flushed and her breath came quickly. She found one of his hands and pressed it against her breast. She laughed, a triumphant, delighted gurgle, as she felt his manhood swell into life against her thigh. She pressed home her advantage, kissing him again, turning both of their bodies into pillars of flame. "Say it! Say I'm your woman!"

All of his own years of frustration exploded in Tod, and Annabelle cried out again as his hands explored her body, as they fumbled with her clothing. There was no turning back now. Flesh and blood can bear just so much and both of them had had to bear far more than their share.

There was pain in her cry as he found what he was looking for and entered her, but the pain was overlaid with triumph and a rapture that was almost beyond bearing. She arched against him, her body throbbing, seeking, tears of joy streaming down her face. Their climax was like an earthquake, leaving them spent and shaken and completely fulfilled, while Tod stared at her with his face white and stricken.

"Oh, my God, what have we done?" he moaned.

"What God intended us to do from the moments of our conceptions," Annabelle told him. Her face was radiant. "Only he intended us to do it a whole lot sooner."

Half an hour later she was downstairs, sweeping the kitchen floor, which didn't need sweeping, when Patience arrived home.

"My goodness, but you look happy!" Patience said as she set her carefully bought purchases down on the deal table. "Has anything happened?"

"You can bet your Sunday mittens something's happened. I've just seduced your son."

The goose that would have cost Patience tenpence a year ago and that she had paid twice that amount for slipped from her hands and fell to the floor. "May God have mercy on us!"

"Yes," Annabelle said, her eyes shining. "He finally has!"

Twenty-one

Eleven months, Luke thought, as he geed and hawed his oxcart up the steep grade of Dorchester Heights. Eleven long, dreary, hungry, thirsty, lonesome, and endless months, but now at last they were doing something. Pray God that after tonight this siege would be over, and they'd blow the British clean out of Boston and he could go home and see Martha again.

He knew that Martha was all right. Tam had gotten word through to him as often as she could. Imagine the lass getting herself into Tim's breeches again and working as a potboy at Eli's tavern, just to help Eli and Patience out and to keep her ears open. Only a few days ago she'd sent a message that it was a certainty that Howe was expecting reinforcements that would enable the British to strike in force, and they'd probably be scattered from here to beyond and thoroughly licked if that happened. Her message had stirred the officers to action, and Luke thought that it was a good thing that Washington had finally decided to make a move before it was too late.

This was one tarnation of a big job they were about. Luke hoped that the artillery fire would keep up. It had been going on for two days and they'd better not quit now or the British would hear what they were up to and then it would be all up with them.

The slope literally crawled with men and heavy carts. Two thousand men, Luke reckoned, and he knew for a fact that his cart was only one of three hundred and fifty hauling up those cannon that Harry Knox had dragged all the way from Fort Ticonderoga last winter. Knox's Novel Train of Artillery, the men had come to call it, and that had been a job to make this one look like splitting out shingles under roof on a rainy day, more pleasure than task.

Luke ought to know. He'd been there. Good drivers were at a premium and he was one of the best in Massachusetts, besides having the heft to stand up under the heaviest work. He and Mark had both been there, and Eli'd raised cain because he'd been left behind. Not that Eli would have been much help, old as he was and as skinny as a rail, unless his monumental fund of cussing could have helped egg the men along. Anyway, he hadn't got to go.

But that was behind them now, and the task at hand loomed ahead and it was going to be touch and go. They had to get these prefabricated redoubts up, both of them. At the beginning of March the ground was still frozen and the breastworks had to be put together before they were hauled up the hill. Luke and Mark had had a hand in that, too. Carpenters and haulers, by God, when they'd turned out to fight, to drive the British clean out of these colonies, and they'd ended up being carpenters and haulers again.

Charles Armitage didn't look at it that way, though. He was in and out, staying and helping when he was needed but mostly galloping off again on whatever errand the bigwigs had dreamed up for him. Luke hadn't been so sure about this man Washington, up until he'd finally decided to do something. In the first place, the man was a Virginian, and in the second place, he hadn't done much proving that he knew how to win battles.

Luke knew that he wasn't the only militiaman who held that opinion, either. There'd been more than one fight between Massachusetts men and those buckskin-jacketed, Indian-legginged troops from Virginia, with those coonskin caps and those long rifles that had an accuracy and range that made the Massachusetts muskets seem like children's toys.

General Washington, now, liked those sharpshooters from down his way. Luke had heard how the general had said that just the sight of them was enough to scare the lobsterbacks into turning tail and running, because any man who looked like that and who carried that kind of a rifle and knew how to use those tomahawks they toted was bound to be able to shoot the eye out of a squirrel at a hundred yards. No just aiming someplace in front of you, like the British had been trained, and trust to luck that because there were so many firing somebody was bound to be hit.

Those Virginians, and Patrick Henry's boys in particular, were going to aim right between a man's eyes or his breastbone and they were going to hit what they aimed at. Washington liked their style of dressing so much he'd ordered Indian-style leggings for all the Continental troops. Maybe one of these days they'd get them, too, but Luke wasn't holding his breath waiting. That Congress down in Philadelphia wasn't any great shakes at raising money or supplies.

That was one of the things that Charles Armitage did, get himself around and try to drum up what was needed. Mr. Armitage didn't like not fighting any more than Luke did, but he'd told Luke that if they were going to win this war every man had to do what he was best at, and every woman too. He knew about Tamara, and he hadn't turned a hair. "Good girl," he'd said. "I might have known that she'd find a way to be useful."

Tamara wasn't the only female making herself useful these days. Luke knew that the wives and daughters of the men out here had taken over their husband's farms and businesses and were keeping them going. Mistress Arthur, for instance, was running Arthur's upholstery shop, and merchants' wives were right there behind the counters making change and keeping the books, and on the small farms the women were doing the plowing and planting and tending the livestock and fighting through sickness and accidents alone.

Luke shook his head as he shouted at his off ox to keep it in line. He'd never thought to see the day when women would take on men's work. He wouldn't have thought that they could do it. But they were, in their hundreds. A wry grin twisted his tired face and any observer able to see him that well in the dark would have seen that there was a twinkle in his eyes. He'd lay any odds asked that the British hadn't counted on those womenfolk, either. Who'd have thought they'd be a deciding factor in whether the Continentals lost or won? But for himself, he was ready by now to concede that without the women behind them, keeping things together, there'd be a mighty slim chance of winning through.

The world was turned upside down, all right. He'd come over to Massachusetts all those years ago as a young man with hardly more than the shirt on his back and a few tools, to find a better life than he'd known back in England. And he'd found it. He'd found Charles Armitage, who was the best friend any man could hope to have, and he'd found Martha, and they had three fine, strapping sons, and he'd found Eli, and his business had prospered.

Now here he was, manhandling an oxcart up a hill to try to hang onto all he'd found. A carpenter he was and that's all he'd ever wanted to be, a builder, with his sons following in his footsteps and adding to the family prosperity, and all because some fools over in Parliament had decided to lay taxes on the colonies he was out here on this hill and he'd almost forgotten what Martha or his house looked like.

He hadn't had a word to say in the matter but he had to fight, all the same. The same as Charles Armitage, an aristocrat, a man of substance, a man who'd never done any manual labor in his life, had to fight. Yes, and put his shoulder to a bogged-down oxcart when it was needful, or wield a shovel or tote supplies on his back.

Charles could have gone on back to England and lived high on the hog all the rest of his life, what with his own fortune and that that young Ned would get from Sir Basil, and been well out of this, but here he was, standing with the common men and trying harder to win this war than most of them put together even though he had a whale of a lot more to lose.

Charles carried more than the burden of the war on his shoulders, too. He'd never been able to find a hint as to what had happened to Mistress Millicent or Ned. He hadn't had much time to go searching himself but he'd had inquiries made every place he could think of. The only thing he'd come up with was that as far as he could find out the woman had never boarded a ship for England. It weighed heavily on him but you'd never know it from the way he had a smile and an encouraging word for every man he came into contact with, from the common militiamen to the officers.

How's it all going to end? Luke wondered as he helped to wrestle the heavy timbers from the cart when he reached the top of the hill. Mark's right here, and

John, and even young Tim, although Tim was mightily put out because he'd been pegged as an orderly for one of the minor officers. He shouldn't complain; at least it gave him something to do while the rest of them had sat around chewing on their knuckles and going crazy from inactivity.

Was there any chance that all of them would come out of this alive? How'd he be able to face Martha if he had to go back home and tell her that one of her boys was dead? Only Martha'd be the one to try to comfort him, he realized, shaking his head again. She'd cover up her own agony to help him over his. She hadn't said a word even when Tim had taken off to join up, not one word except that they mustn't worry about her, that she could keep the home place going and she'd be just fine.

Women! The men were going to have to go some to measure up to them.

He wished he could lay his hands on Henry Atkins. Ever since Breed's Hill, Luke had been convinced that the man knew something about Millicent Armitage's disappearance. But Henry had dropped out of sight, he hadn't laid eyes on him since then, and neither had Charles, although he'd looked for him after Luke had finally had a chance to tell him what the man had said. If he could just get his hands on him, he'd choke it out of him even if he had to make it Henry's last breath that spilled it out.

Luke put his shoulder to the timber and heaved, throwing his vast strength into the task, and he grunted with surprise as he saw Charles Armitage himself take his place beside him.

"Kinda demoting yourself, aren't you?"

Charles smiled through the strain on his face as he exerted all his strength to help heave the timbered section into place. "It has to be done, and time is short." Damn, what a man! If there was any way in the world Luke could take some of the burden off his shoulders, he'd do it no matter what it cost him. Only there wasn't. A man's burdens, some of them anyhow, were his own.

Luke had been a hard worker all his life, but he worked all that night of March 4, 1776, as he had never dreamed of working. All around him, other men were also driving themselves to their limits. A few of them dropped from exhaustion and had to be carried or dragged out of the way so that the others could take their places.

Hurry, hurry! Thank God for that artillery bombardment the Continentals were keeping up, to cover the noise of their work. There were hundreds of men, slaving like worker ants, swarming all over the hill, all under cover of that blessed bombardment. If they couldn't drive the British out of Boston before their reinforcements arrived there'd be the devil to pay.

It was done. When the sun came up the redoubts were finished, the cannon in place. They waited. The British down there in Boston had seen the batteries pointed right down their throats by now. What were they going to do about it? That was the question. If Howe had any sense, he'd attack.

The work had been hard, but the waiting was harder. Men's nerves were stretched to the breaking point from tension as the hours passed and nothing happened.

"He'll attack. You wait and see, they'll be swarming up here against us any minute now," was the word that went around. But when night fell, the British were still sitting on their haunches in Boston.

Clouds gathered, and thunder and lightning rent the air. Rain came down in torrents, lasting until well after daybreak. And when the storm finally abated and cleared away, there was still no attack. As stolid as he was, even Luke felt the strain.

"If I was in command of those British ships in the harbor, I'd move on out of there to a place of safety unless Howe takes this position. We could blast them right out of the water," Charles said.

"Then why don't we? What're we waiting for?"

"I don't make the decisions." Charles ran his hand over his face, leaving streaks across the grime that was already there, but he managed to smile in spite of his grinding fatigue. "We'll just have to wait some more."

"As far as I can see, that's what this war is all about—waiting," Luke said sourly, squinting down at the harbor again. "How're we going to win a war by waiting? I always figured it'd take some fighting, too."

But Charles had already gone before Luke had finished his sentence. Luke shrugged. So they'd wait. But if it were up to him, he'd give the order to fire right now. What the hell, that was what they were here for, wasn't it?

They'd pulled out, lock, stock, and barrel, every man jack of them, sneaked aboard their ships and skedaddled for safety. Stunned disbelief struggled with elation on that day of March 17 as men slapped each other on the back, their voices raised in near hysteria.

"What do you think of the gen'ral now? He can win a battle without even fightin'!"

"Damn, man, we can go home! You realize that! I'm goin' to git to see my old woman again!"

"Me for the first tavern. Gonna wet my whistle first thing I do, in a town that belongs to us agin! You thought of that, man? Boston's ours agin, we done driv 'em out!"

Tamara's face was shining like an Easter sunrise

as she threw herself into Mark's arms. "You're here, and all in one piece, too! Is Luke all right, and John and Tim and Eli?"

"Eli's right here." And so he was, Tam realized, standing on her tiptoes to look over Mark's shoulder. Mark was so broad that she hadn't even seen the older man behind him, grinning from ear to ear at the sight of what appeared to be a half-grown boy hugging and kissing a man. If any of those lobsterbacks had still been in Boston and in The Temptation, their eyes would be buggin' right out of their heads. Right comical-lookin', it was, and the colonials who were in there were just now beginnin' to realize that Tamara wasn't a boy after all, but very much a girl. She was a caution, Tamara Armitage was, but it was the likes of her who would help win this war, if it wasn't all over with but the shoutin' right now.

"Mark, I can hardly take it in! When the ships left we almost went crazy. I could have drunk up Eli's entire stock of brandy myself, just to celebrate."

"Looks to me like you went crazy a long time ago!" Mark's fingers dug into her shoulders and incredibly he began to shake her, so hard that her head bobbled. "Dressing up in Tim's britches, working in the tavern where you'd have been hung for a spy if you'd been caught! I ought to wring your stupid neck, that's what I ought to do!"

"Wouldn't that have the same effect as hanging?" Tamara wrenched herself free and stood glaring at him, her mouth and chin stubborn, her eyes defiant. "I had to do something, you great moron of a male! And I wasn't caught, and I did send in a little information, even if it wasn't much!"

"Wasn't much!" The voice Tamara heard now was laughing, and she gasped as her father walked into the tavern. "I must agree with you, Tamara. It wasn't much. But every bit of nothing much that we learned was important. You helped to confirm that the British expected reinforcements, and that helped to get our commanders moving, and that was why we were in a position to fire on the ships in the harbor, and that's why the British pulled out. I'm proud of you, lass."

She threw herself into his arms and womanlike, she had to blink to keep from crying and spoiling all this praise about doing her duty and helping with the war effort. Think what a sight she'd be, still dressed like a boy and with her face all grubby, bawling like a female idiot, right here in public! She wouldn't be proud of herself then, even if these men who meant more to her than anyone else in the world still would be.

"I've got to get busy. People are waiting to be served," she said. "Charity can't do it all, with the place bursting at the seams. Isn't there any place else in Boston for people to celebrate?"

"Whoa up, there!" Eli exclaimed. "What you're goin' to do is git yourself to home and git outa them boy's britches, and git yourself all prettied up so's we kin all celebrate together, and to the devil with the tavern! Patience'll have a conniption if we don't all git over there pretty quick. And our celebration's got to be there, because of Tod. Now git, an' don't let me see you agin till you look like Tamara Armitage, not like a gol-durned smutty-faced pot boy!"

Tamara had never been happier in her life than she was when she walked arm in arm with her father through streets that were no longer filled with redcoats, to go home for the first time in she couldn't think how long. British officers had taken over their house on Beacon Hill. Poor Mistress Gatesby! It must have driven her into near madness to have to cook and clean for them. Louise had got away before they'd moved in, and not come back, but Mistress Gatesby had been determined to remain and take care of her master's property as best she could until his return.

Jonas was already there when they arrived, trying to comfort Mistress Gatesby, who was in a state of hysterics at the thought of Mr. Armitage and Tamara being able to come home. And Abel was there, cleaning up the lawn, a broad grin splitting his face in two as he explained that he'd been pressed into service by the British officers and that they'd tried to make him go with them to the ships, but he'd managed to get away from them in all the confusion and hide until they'd sailed.

The house wasn't badly damaged, as some other gentlepeople's houses were, from abuse by their red-coated occupants. Apparently the soldiers who had taken over this house were really gentlemen. There were no holes burned in the woodwork or spur marks on the tables. Everything needed a good dusting and cleaning, because Mistress Gatesby hadn't been able to keep up with all the work with no one to help her, but that was of so little importance on such a day as this as not to deserve a second thought.

Two hours later, wearing her pink dress with a lace fichu, Tamara was in Martha's parlor. Lordy, but it felt good to look like a girl again. Slopping around looking like a half-witted boy hadn't been as much fun as she'd let on it was. There was no way she could make her hair grow back instantly, but she'd caught it back with a pink velvet ribbon, and her face was scrubbed and she'd even found some of her mother's choicest scent and dabbed drops of it behind her ears and in the cleft between her breasts. Just let Mark dare to treat her with a lack of respect now! You don't go around shaking ladies, and she was a lady again, and if he didn't notice it she'd . . . she'd spit in his eye!

In spite of his urging them all to hurry, Eli was the last one to arrive. Patience, her broom in hand and her dustcap still on her head instead of a headdress proper for such a celebration as this, quivered with joy laced with indignation as she clasped her husband to her bosom, without relinquishing the broom, so that he yelped as its handle dug into his chest.

"Leave off, woman! I come through the siege and the Heights without a scratch, and now you're tryin' to do me in the minute I git home!"

"And you're staying home from now on, you old fool!" Patience said, the shrillness of her voice undermined by its tremor. "You're too old for such goings-on, and I know it if you don't! Home you are and home you're going to stay, if I have to tie you up to see to it!"

"You'll play hell. I'm goin' when the rest go, where they go. I ain't got me a redcoat yet, that I know of for sure, and I aim to get me half a dozen to make up for what they did to Tod. How is Tod? Where is he? He ain't, he didn't. . . ."

"You know he's all right, you addlebrain! And don't you go using language like that in my house, much less in front of Tamara and Charity! Being in the Army's coddled your senses, I can see that, and you never had any great overdose of them in the first place!"

"Where is he, then? Up in his room?" Eli made to hurry upstairs, but Patience held him back, the force of her grasp almost unbalancing him.

"He and Annabelle have gone out to look around town. He can walk so well with the crutch that Tam made him, you wouldn't believe it. And Tam says that she can make him a peg, as soon as he thinks he's ready for it. Is that so, Mark?"

"If she says she can, she probably can." Mark's voice was sour. "Only she won't have to, now the real carpenters are home for a spell. Father and I will do it and then it'll be done right. Whatever possessed you to let her work at the tavern, and in britches, Patience?"

"It isn't your place to say what Tamara can do and what she can't do. That's up to her father, and to Tam herself. Besides, do you think I could have stopped her? If Mr. Armitage doesn't mind I can't see that you have any call to go running off at the mouth about it."

Mark's face turned black. That was women for you, they'd side with each other no matter how wrong they were. Besides, he had to be getting on home. Luke had already gone on ahead, to pick up Martha, but he wanted to see the place for himself and see how it had gone down since he and the other men had been away.

"That's right. You aren't my lord and master. Not yet you aren't, anyway. If I remember rightly, we aren't married."

"You're right we aren't married, and we never will be unless you stop acting like you've acted all your life!"

"Oh, then you have given some thought to marrying me! I thought it had never as much as entered your dense mind!"

"There's a war on, you little idiot! You think I want to leave a widow with a young'un or two to raise all by herself?"

"Do you think I wouldn't be capable of raising them by myself?"

"Not in britches you wouldn't! It, or they, wouldn't know whether you were the father or the mother!"

"*She* wouldn't be that stupid! Only a boy would be stupid enough not to know the difference!"

Mark raised his hand. Tamara's eyes flashed fire.

"Don't you dare! You do, and I'll take Patience's

broom and you'll be laughed out of the militia for being chased all the way to the common with a woman beating you over the head with it!"

"Just you try it! I'll tan those britches!"

"What britches? I'm not wearing britches, or hadn't you noticed?" Tamara's cheeks flew warning flags of color, and Mark's flamed with an anger to match hers. Charles was debating whether or not he ought to intervene before these two hotheaded youngsters came to actual blows when he heard the sound of footsteps and a stick mount Patience's well-scrubbed steps outside the house, and a moment later Annabelle and Tod entered the room.

A great lump rose in Charles' throat. Even under her voluminous skirts it was obvious that Annabelle was pregnant. Tamara had gotten word out to Luke that Tod and Annabelle were married but she hadn't mentioned that he was about to become a grandfather. She probably hadn't wanted to worry him. Worry him! The sight made him happier than he'd been in months. Annabelle was positively glowing, and Tod looked fit and well. Wordlessly, he gathered his middle daughter into his arms and reached out to shake Tod's hand.

"The fight's over, Mark. For the moment." Tamara's eyes still flashed, but she couldn't spoil her father's homecoming. "How do you like our surprise, Papa?"

Charles shook his head, but it was only because in spite of being a lawyer, he couldn't find a word to say.

Twenty-two

"You've had no word from the young master?"

Mistress Gatesby, her mopcap askew on her white hair, stopped in her task of rubbing one of the walnut tables in the library to a high gloss, something that hadn't been done since the British officers had taken over the house. Her faded eyes were filled with concern and surrounded with lines of fatigue.

"I'm afraid I haven't." Charles did not fail to note that the servant hadn't included his wife in her question, but he didn't blame her for that. Millicent had been a difficult mistress to work for, and he was well aware that none of his household staff had been fond of her. Their loyalty was to him, and to Annabelle and Tamara and Ned. They had never, he thought ruefully, cared for Lillian either.

"You must find someone to come in and help you with the work," he went on kindly. "It's too much for you, you're overtiring yourself. I'll ask Tam to see who she can find."

"Louise is coming back, sir. She let me know only this morning. Only today she's biding at home because her brother's back, you see, and no telling how long he'll get to stay. She says he's determined to get into some real fighting and drive those redcoats right into the ocean where they came from!"

"And that's the kind of man we need. Louise's brother, and thousands more just like him. Only I'm afraid that few share his enthusiasm, and fewer yet will share it before this is over."

"Then maybe we womenfolk will have to fight!" Mistress Gatesby's eyes flashed, and her chin came up firmly. Charles struggled against his smile of amusement at the mental picture of the elderly woman carrying a musket and marching off to war.

Come to think of it, they were fighting already, Charles murmured to himself as he left the house. Even Mistress Gatesby, already entered into her seventies, suffering from partial deafness and swelling of the limbs, had done her share of fighting simply by remaining at home and protecting his property as best she could. He had a very good idea that her looks of disapproval and her sharp tongue had saved his house from the damage that had been inflicted on so many others. He'd inspected half a dozen of them already, and what he had seen had sickened him. It was almost inconceivable to him that Englishmen, even though they were on opposite sides of an armed conflict, could hold other Englishmen in such contempt that they'd deliberately destroy priceless cabinetry and furnishings.

It was drawing toward evening, but Charles walked through the town, estimating the damage that the British had left behind them. Bile rose in his throat as he glanced into Old South Meeting House and saw that the pews had been completely stripped away and that no trace of them was left. A group of determined citizens were already cleaning out manure left by the horses that had been there. Did the British think that their God was different from the colonists' God, that such contempt for a house of worship was not blasphemy because it belonged to the provincials?

"What did they do with the pews?" he asked.

"Chopped 'em up and used 'em for firewood" was the answer, the voice grim with anger. "Just like they chopped down the Liberty tree and used it for firewood. Fourteen cords they got from it, and I wish it'd burned them up with it!"

Charles' throat was tight as he turned his steps toward The Temptation. How many meetings had been held under that tree, the giant elm that had been planted in 1646? He himself had been there on the fourteenth of August 1769, when the Sons of Liberty had celebrated the withdrawal of the Townshend Acts.

Three hundred people had moved from under its shelter to feast at the Liberty Tree Tavern. Eli and Luke had been there too, he remembered, and Eli had almost made himself ill on barbecued pig. John Hancock had come in his famous chariot, known by sight all over Boston. He remembered the last toast of that day, "Strong halters, firm blocks, and sharp axes to all such as deserve them!"

It had been a proud day for Sam Adams and his Sons of Liberty. Now the tree was gone, and unlike the Old South Meeting House and the private homes that had been left in a shambles, the damage could never be repaired.

At Eli's house, Eli and Patience would be making the most of the time they would have together. Mark was there as well, continuing his dispute with Tamara, who was perfectly capable of holding her own. Luke and the other boys, John and Tim, were at the Martins', having their own reunion. But for Charles, there was no place to go but to his own house that taunted him with its empty rooms, with its lack of a boy's running footsteps, a boy's laughter. He could have gone either to Eli's or to Luke's, but he had no wish to inflict his present morose mood on them while they had this chance, at least for the moment, to be happy, no matter how welcome he would have been.

The tavern was well filled, and Charles was greeted by name and with enthusiastic handshakes when he entered. The patrons vied for the privilege of sitting beside him and learning firsthand his views on what had just transpired and what he thought General Washington would do next.

"I'm afraid that I'm not in the general's confidence to that extent. He keeps his plans pretty much to himself."

"I seen you up on the Heights, puttin' your shoulder to them timbers just like the rest of us." The respect in the speaker's voice was obvious. "Hear tell your middle girl got married whilst we was makin' siege. Fine lad, Tod Bates. Boys, how about a toast to the bride and groom!"

Mugs were raised as all the men in the tavern rose to their feet. Now Charles' throat was tight for a different reason. When they had drunk, he himself rose to his feet and lifted his glass.

"To General Washington, and may he confound the enemy!"

They drank again, and a cheer went up. Since that morning when they'd looked down from the Heights and seen the British had sneaked away, Washington's popularity had increased a hundredfold. It didn't matter now if he held himself aloof from the common men, as though he was well aware of his own aristocracy, and that he expected explicit obedience without explaining his purpose. As long as he could make the lobsterbacks turn tail, he was their man.

Charles stayed late at the tavern, reluctant to return to his empty house. Two or three times he rose to give Charity a hand. She was rushed off her feet by this continuing celebration of the retaking of Boston, but she had refused to let Tamara or Eli come in to help her. Men nudged each other to see Charles carrying mugs and drawing cider.

"Will you look at that! Just like he's no better'n the rest of us! Who says that the rich men ain't on our side?"

"The gen'ral's rich, and he's on our side, I reckon. And Hancock's rich and he's on our side."

"Yes, but you don't see them in here drawin' cider!"

"Shut up, you," a more serious voice warned. "Likely he ain't hankerin' to go home, with his wife and his boy missin'."

Eyes were lowered, and voices along with them. There wasn't a thing they could do for the lawyer, but they all wished that there were something.

It was late now, but Charles sat on alone, staring moodily into the dregs of his flip. He should leave so that Charity could throw the bolt and go to bed. The girl must be exhausted after tonight's rush of business, but still he couldn't steel himself to face his empty house.

Charity had been in the kitchen for the past few minutes. Poor girl, maybe she'd already fallen asleep and he'd have to wake her so she could lock up behind him. Conscience-stricken, Charles started to get to his feet, but at that moment Charity re-entered the taproom.

She had changed her dress and brushed her hair. Her dress was of a soft rose color that brightened her skin and made her look younger. She'd left her hair loose and caught it back with a ribbon, and she looked clean and fresh and wholesome.

"I was just about to leave," Charles apologized. "I take it that you have an engagement. You should have asked me to go half an hour ago. Do I happen to know the lucky man?"

Charity flushed, but she met his eyes directly, with no hint of coquettishness. "I have no engagement. I don't have a man, young or old or otherwise. I just like to get cleaned up and look like a human being for a little while before I go to bed. And I wanted to tell you how sorry I am that your wife and son haven't been located yet."

Charles sat down again and indicated the bench. "Have a glass of wine with me, and then I'll go. I confess that the prospect of going home doesn't appeal to me. Tamara may be there, it'll be pretty crowded for her to stay with Martha tonight with all the men home, but I mislike inflicting my rather dark mood on her when she's so happy about having Mark back. There'll be plenty of time to see her later."

"I thought as much. That's why I didn't tell you that it was time to close the tavern." Charity moved across the room to throw the bolt and blow out all the candles except the one on the table in front of Charles. She brought wine, the best the tavern still had to offer, although it wasn't up to Eli's prerebellion standards. The redcoats had drunk them out of their better stock long since.

"I have a couple of nutmegs I hid away," Charity said. "I'll get them. It'll help make the wine more palatable."

Charles watched while she grated a nutmeg into the glasses. He wondered how long it would be before supplies began to pour into Boston again. Not long, he hoped. A good many cupboards must be all but bare.

Charity sat down again with a little sigh. "It's been a long day. It's been a long eleven months. It's been a long war."

"And it will be longer." Charles spoke with conviction. "But hopefully, the worst is over for Boston."

They raised their glasses and drank.

Charity was as tired as Charles had thought she would be, but she sensed that it would ease him to talk about Ned. Her heart ached for Charles so that she could hardly bear it. He had friends, true, good friends, but they were men. It takes a woman to listen with the kind of sympathy that helps to heal—even a tavern girl, as long as she wasn't a whore, and she wasn't and never had been in spite of what had happened to her before Tamara had discovered her hiding from the man who'd bought her and prevailed upon her father to rescue her. Mr. Armitage knew that she'd never sold herself to men, that her life had been spotless ever since she had come to work in Eli's tavern. Even if she hadn't wanted it that way herself, Eli would have sent her packing if it had been otherwise.

"Ned is a fine boy. Handsome, and intelligent." She was careful not to use the past tense. "He'll be found, Mr. Armitage, I'm sure of it. I pray for him every night, before I go to sleep." She said it simply, because it was the simple truth. She didn't add that she also prayed for Charles.

"So do I." Charles felt no embarrassment in the admission.

Her hand, when she reached to lay it over his to give him comfort, was strong and warm in spite of its roughness. A human hand, reached out in human compassion.

"I wish I could help you. I wish there were something

I could do. But even here, although I've listened and so has Tam, we've not heard a word. But they'll come back, I know it."

"Thank you, Charity. It's helped me just to hear you say it." Charles rubbed his hands across his forehead, a habit he used frequently these days. The work he did for the Congress was exacting, filled with danger, and always held the possibility of capture. He spent grueling hours in the saddle, often riding until his horse faltered under him before he could find another to take its place. Much of his riding was done at night. Sometimes it was twenty-four hours between anything that could be called a decent meal. He was tired, that was the trouble. He was so tired that he could die of it.

It almost seemed as if Charity could read his mind. "Let me get you something to eat. It won't be much, but there's some cheese and a piece of goose." Once again she held back telling the truth in its entirety. Patience had sent her the goose, a drumstick and thigh; she simply hadn't had time to eat it and now Charles needed it more than she did. "The bread isn't too fresh but I can toast it over the coals, that always helps."

He was imposing on her, but he was hungry. He should have accepted either Patience's or Martha's invitation to have supper with them instead of letting himself feel that he'd be a fifth wheel at these reunions, where everyone but he would have someone special. Even stale bread, toasted over the fire that had burned down to its last coals, sounded attractive to him. Perhaps men didn't realize how much the company of a woman, no matter how casually known, meant to them at mealtimes.

He watched Charity as she kneeled to toast the bread on a long fork. When it had browned, she put the cheese on the tines and softened it as well before she placed it on the bread. The flickering embers cast a soft glow over her face and he noticed, for the first time, that her body was slender and well made. The thin sharpness that had characterized her features when he had first met her had softened as she had matured. With something like surprise, he saw that she had turned into a very attractive woman.

He brought himself up short. Woman, indeed! She was years young than he was, almost young enough to be his daughter. Suddenly he felt old and bereft.

Charity placed the food in front of him and sat down again. "Eat," she said. "You'll feel better for it."

Surprisingly, it was true. He felt a great deal better after he had finished.

"I've kept you up much too long." He stood up, and she stood with him. They walked to the door together, and stood for a moment to say good night. The desolation that swept over him stunned him. He didn't want to leave this warm, dimly lighted room, he didn't want to leave this woman who had eased his heartache merely by her presence.

She stood very close to him, her face upturned, her eyes soft, filled with tenderness, a tenderness that he had never had from Millicent in all the years they had been married. For a little while, before Ned had been born, she had seemed to change, to return his love, but that had disappeared soon after Ned's birth. He was starved, starved down to the core of his soul, and empty, and needing. Millicent was gone, Ned was gone, and this war would be a long war and no telling how it would end.

He hadn't intended to kiss her. Or if he had, he'd intended it to be in friendship, in gratitude only for the kindness she'd shown him tonight. But her mouth was warm and parted and giving, giving of herself, loving him, suffering for him, wanting to ease his hurt.

He wouldn't have been human if he hadn't responded. He needed someone, God, how he needed someone! He'd been all his life alone, except for his children. Lillian, lost to him through her mother's machinations, Annabelle married and soon to become a mother, Tamara who would leave him for Mark if she had her way, and he didn't doubt for a moment that she would. Tamara had always been one to get what she wanted, through single-minded strength of purpose. And Ned, who was either alive or dead, and the inability to find out which driving him mad.

The shutters had already been drawn across the windows. On the table, the single candle had burned down to where it had begun to flicker. Charity's arms held him close, held him safe, sheltered from a world that was harsh and uncaring.

She took his hand and drew him back to the fire. "Wait," she said. She disappeared into the kitchen where she still slept on a pallet. When she came back she was carrying a blanket. She spread it in front of the fire and slipped a pillow under his head when she had urged him to lie down on it.

She undressed quickly but without hurry. There was no shame in her movements as she revealed herself to him. Her breasts were firm and high, her waist small, her hips flowed into long, well-shaped legs that tapered into slender ankles and delicately arched feet. She was neither ashamed of her body nor proud of it. Right at the moment, it was what she had to offer him to bring him comfort, and so she offered it as simply as she offered him her love.

The fire was almost entirely out now but the floor in front of it still retained heat that warmed the blanket. Her hands were capable and gentle as she helped him divest himself of his own clothing.

She gave herself freely, gladly, reveling in the giving,

asking nothing for herself except the pleasure of giving him pleasure. She had loved this man for so long that it seemed that she had loved him always, even before she had been born. If this was a sin, then she must go to hell, but she would still give him everything she had, every hope of salvation, and rejoice in it to know that she had brought him a moment's comfort.

Charles lost himself completely in her. She was not a virgin. The brutal landlord of The Jolly Tar had seen to that, before she had run away from him, choosing even to starve rather than go on submitting to him and the men who had wanted to buy her for their pleasure.

But Charles knew that this woman had never given herself to any man before of her own free will, and his burgeoning passion, that exploded at last into a completion that he had never experienced in all his years of marriage, was laced with humbleness and gratitude.

Twenty-three

Tamara approached the shipyard with rapid strides, her chin in the air and the light of determination in her eyes.

Annabelle was a married woman now, so happy in her coming motherhood that it hurt to look at her. And Tod was happy. There was a stunned look about him as if he couldn't actually believe that Annabelle was his.

And Mark was gone. Drat him, he'd gone, along with Luke and Eli and John and Tim, to help General Washington man the defenses around New York City, and he hadn't backed down an inch about marrying her before the war was over, if then.

He'd even made it plain with that "if then" that he'd have to do a lot of thinking about it before he'd saddle himself with a girl who'd been nothing but a pest to him all his life and now had the temerity to run around in breeches and still expect a man to marry her as if she were a real female who knew her place and was content to stay in it.

Her place! Raging, Tamara's chin thrust itself still farther forward as she stepped up onto the wharf.

The ship that was under construction was not going to be a thing of beauty. It was to be a practical, no-

nonsense ship that would help chase the British off the seas. Boston was a beehive of activity now that the red-coats were gone, and not the least of it was the building of ships where men labored from first to last light to get the job done, to get the vessels into action. And they needed people to help build them, didn't they? People who knew one end of a hammer and a saw from the other.

She wasn't needed at The Temptation anymore. Patience herself had won the battle with her principles and undertaken to help Charity operate the tavern. Annabelle was perfectly capable of running the house and looking after Tod, and Patience wanted to be out from under their feet and let them have the house to themselves as a young couple should.

Besides wanting to leave Tod and Annabelle in reasonable privacy, there was the practical side of the matter to be considered. Now that nearly every young man in Boston was away with the Army, Patience no longer had boarders, and the loss of income made it imperative that The Temptation keep in operation and turning a profit. Tod was taking care of Charles' affairs, he already knew enough law so that he was able to handle nearly everything that came into Charles' office in his absence, but Patience wanted him to be able to keep the salary Charles paid him to lay away for himself and Annabelle and the little one when it was born.

So it was up to her, as it was up to so many women these days, to take over and keep things going against the time when their husbands would return. She wasn't about to sit at home and busy herself cooking and dusting when her talents were needed elsewhere. And the way she could cook, turning even the commonest and most coarse of materials into delicious meals, her particular talents should draw more patrons to The Temptation and turn a profit that would make Eli's eyes bulge out when he came back.

Tamara was not about to sit on her own nether parts and do nothing to further the war efforts, either. Before he had left, Luke had found a twelve-year-old boy to stay with Martha and help her with the garden and the livestock, so she wasn't needed there. But there was one place where she was needed; all she had to do was convince Mr. Potts that she could do the work and that it wouldn't mean that the gates of hell would yawn open for him if he put a woman on his crew.

Mr. Potts looked at her with his mouth hanging open and his face red with indignation such as Tamara had never seen when she accosted him with her request to be put to work.

"You? A female? You're daft!"

"Why am I daft? I can do the work and you need every hand you can get."

"What would people say?"

"What will they say if you don't get this ship built as fast as you can? Other women are working. What's so different about building a ship and doing the heaviest kind of farm work? If women can plow and plant they can saw and hammer."

"Not in my shipyard they can't! How can a creature in skirts climb around the way a man does, I ask you?"

"I'm fully acquainted with breeches, Mr. Potts. And you know that if Luke Martin and Mark Martin taught me, I know what I'm doing. I'm young and I'm healthy and I'm strong and I'm an extra pair of hands."

"Lawyer Armitage's girl! I know about you. Been down to The Temptation, in breeches, passing as a boy whilst you spied for our Army!"

"That's right." Tamara's eyes refused to waver. "It was a necessary job, wasn't it?"

"I'll be dad-blasted." Normally the most temperate-speeched of men, the epithet was forced from the flabbergasted shipbuilder. "It'ud throw the rest of my workers into a dither, don't you know that, having a pretty young woman working alongside of them?"

"If you're afraid of what people would say and that I'd be a distraction I could pass as a boy again. It would be more practical anyway. Skirts are a nuisance, as you'd know if you'd ever had to wear them."

"Oh, no you won't! Not on my ship you won't! It would be bad enough to have a female working in the shipyard, but a female pretending she's a boy? I'd be read out of my Church, maybe run out of Boston altogether! I could be tarred and feathered. It's happened here, you know. The whole thing is out of the question. My men would never stand for it even if I was fool enough to put you on."

"Who's the master here, you or your men? I had the idea that if you told them something, they'd have to abide by it."

That stung, as it had been meant to do. And Mr. Potts was shorthanded. Most of the able-bodied men, those who weren't farmers or haulers or at some other essential job were off with the Army someplace, and even some of those he had managed to hire were hardly worth their salt.

Henry Atkins, for instance. Mr. Potts had hired him out of desperation but he'd had to let him go last week because he was too fond of rum and cider and he couldn't get along with the other men. If Luke Martin had taught her, this girl ought to be at least as capable a carpenter as Henry Atkins was, and she wouldn't show up drunk. Luke was good at his trade, none better.

He wavered, and Tamara pressed her advantage. "I'll make a bargain with you. I'll go to work right now and if by the end of the day you think I won't do, I won't come back tomorrow. Agreed?"

She held out her hand, and being a gentleman, Mr. Potts had to take it. And then it was too late; they'd shaken hands on the bargain, which was exactly what Tamara had had in mind.

It wasn't easy, but then she had not thought that it would be easy. Her fellow workers went from indignant outrage to treating the whole thing as a joke. They treated her with excessive politeness, waiting on her, handing her her tools, showing her how to pound a nail, cautioning her against smashing her thumb.

They jumped to assist her over piles of seasoned lumber. They bowed to her with exaggerated formality every time they had occasion to pass her. All the while they grinned those fatuous men's grins that set Tamara's blood to boiling, and winked at each other, until she'd as gladly have brought her hammer down on one of their heads as on the head of a nail, and with a great deal more satisfaction.

But by the end of the day, Mr. Potts scratched his head and hemmed and hawed. She could do the work, all right. Luke Martin had taught her well. She needed a lot of pointers, because building a ship wasn't like throwing up a house or putting a pretty cabinet together, but she knew which end of a nail to pound and she didn't toe them, and she could handle a saw and an adze as well as any 'prentice he'd ever had and better than most.

Smarter than most, too; she'd learn fast. The Lord knew what people would say. Parson Eldridge would probably flay him, come Sunday. All the same he was going to try her for a full week. Even his men had settled down, once they'd seen they couldn't get a rise out of her and she meant business.

"Only what I'm going to tell Mr. Armitage, I don't know," Mr. Potts muttered to himself when he reluctantly told Tamara that she could come back in the morning.

"He won't mind. He didn't mind my working at The Temptation dressed as a boy, and he won't mind me helping to build this ship. He'll be proud of me."

It wasn't her father she had to worry about. Mark would be fit to be tied. But when he came back, if they still needed ships, she'd still be helping to build them and he could like it or not, she was still going to marry him even if she had to use Patience's broom to chase him to the church.

Thinking of churches made her think of Old South. The parishioners had already gotten it cleaned up but when she'd visited it she had imagined that she could still smell horse manure. If she hadn't gotten this job she would have volunteered to help build new pews. Maybe Mark wouldn't have complained so much about that. Even a woman was sometimes allowed to help with the Lord's work.

She was tired, it had been a long and exhausting day, especially with all she'd had to contend with from the men, but she still turned her steps toward the Martins' house before she went home. Martha would be tired too, and Martha was all alone except for the boy Luke had installed to help her. She'd stop in there for an hour and tell Martha about how she'd beat Mr. Potts down until he'd hired her. Martha would be pleased about that, and it would help to take her mind off worrying about her menfolk.

She wasn't too tired to spin for an hour, or to sew. General Washington had asked all the women to make coats for the soldiers, because Congress hadn't gotten around to supplying enough and winter was coming on. There was a lively trade in possible romance connected with the making of the coats. Young single women had taken to writing their names and addresses and putting the slip of paper in the pocket, and Tamara already knew of two girls who had had hastily scrawled and misspelled letters to the effect that the recipient meant to look her up once the war was over. It would be funny if Tamara were to put her name in the pocket of one of the coats and Mark should be the one to end up with it.

There was so much work to be done, every hour of the day and often far into the night, work that the women had to do with their men away. Tired or not, Tamara would either sew or spin before she sought her bed that night. Come hell or high water, the work would be done, because the women were determined to do it.

I'm blaspheming, she chided herself, but then she smiled. She wasn't really, she'd just used the words that came naturally, and God would understand. Mark was the one who wouldn't understand, but as much as Tam loved him, she had never made the mistake of confusing him with God. Mark was human right to the core and she was glad of it, because so was she.

She quickened her steps. Martha would be glad to see her, and they could talk as they worked. The thought that it was funny that the tongue never got tired even when all the rest of the body was exhausted brought another smile to her lips. Or was it only women whose tongues never got tired?

Twenty-four

Nineteen thousand men, Luke thought, and still all they'd done for months was wait. Nineteen thousand, but by the best reckoning, at least five thousand of them were sick, too sick to fight if a battle got underway.

And they were split up. Five thousand were here, under Putnam in the city, and nine thousand under General Heath to defend the northern part of the island from Harlem to Kingsbridge, and the rest were deployed along the East River to stave off attack from Long Island.

Damn Congress anyway! As far as Luke could see, they were a bunch of vacillating incompetents who wanted to give the orders but didn't want to take any responsibility for them. Washington had wanted to burn the city and pull out, but Congress had disagreed with that, wanting to hold it against future need, only they'd stipulated that Washington had to be responsible, in the end, for anything that was done.

Well, they were going to move now, and any kind of movement was better than just waiting, no matter how much it galled him to have to turn tail and run again. Two days ago, on September 10, the British had occupied Monstresor's Island, right there at the mouth of Harlem River, and that meant that they could land either at Harlem or farther north and march on King's Bridge and that would cut off the entire American force on Manhattan Island.

And on the thirteenth, some men-of-war and transports had come sailing up the East River and taken positions there right opposite Kips Bay, and a smaller force of ships had sailed up the Hudson itself and dropped anchor above Fort Washington, so their own force now could not make a move between Manhattan and New Jersey.

There'd been fighting at Kips Bay. It had happened on Sunday, September 15, with five British ships giving shelter to about eighty flatboats that swarmed with four thousand redcoats and those devil-cursed Hessians, with Harry Clinton himself in command. All the Continental Army had to defend the bay were a few Connecticut militiamen in a ditch up beyond the rock-strewn beach.

Eighty-six ships' guns, loaded and aimed right at them, and they'd opened fire with a two-hour bombardment before they'd come ashore. Of course the militia had skedaddled. How in tunket could they have done anything else? What in blue blazes did Congress expect, miracles? Putnam and Washington himself had tried to rally the running men, but there was no way on earth they could set up a defense line. Luke'ud have run too if he'd been there, and nobody had ever yet called him a coward.

Now the redcoats were at Murray Hill, and nine thousand more of the devils had come ashore. Some Hessians had captured three hundred militiamen, and the rest of Putnam's men making tracks along Post Road would have been taken too, or at least there'd have been one tarnation of a massacre, if Aaron Burr, Putnam's aide-de-camp, hadn't gotten there in time to warn him and lead them on west to Bloomington Road and on north.

So they were running again, and it galled. Get out of the city, the orders were, as fast as you can, before you're cut off and can't get out at all. Only how they were to get the supplies out in time was something else again, there weren't enough wagons and that was the truth of it, there simply weren't enough.

It was going to be slow and if they made it at all it'ud be one of those miracles Congress seemed to expect, and Congress'ud probably say they should have stood and fought when there was no way they could win. Those Congressmen ought to spend a few months with the Army, and then they'd see how fast they'd be to criticize.

The heavy team strained, sweating freely, as Luke maneuvered the supply wagon along Wall Street to Broadway. There was Trinity Church just ahead. Luke had taken particular care to take in all the details of Trinity because Martha and Patience would be interested, once he got back home when this was over, if he got back and if it was ever going to get over, and right now he had his doubts.

What the . . .! Luke hauled back on the reins and sat staring, not believing his eyes. That boy there, that near-grown lad, ragged as any street urchin, and as dirty, if that wasn't Ned Armitage he'd pick this wagon up and haul it the rest of the way on his back. What would Ned be now, fourteen, fifteen? Fifteen, he reckoned, although where in the world all the years had gone in between Ned's birthing and today he couldn't fathom.

The street was jammed, the scene was pandemonium as the Continentals struggled to pull out. But Luke could swear that that was Ned, and he jumped off the wagon seat and began to run toward the boy, shouting his name as he went.

The boy jerked his head up and looked at him, startled, his mouth half open. There wasn't any doubt now, it was Ned. And the next second the lad had plunged into the crowd and turned the corner. Luke gave chase but by the time he reached the corner Ned was nowhere to be seen.

Luke wasn't naturally a cursing man. He hadn't tended to be a cursing man even back in London, when he'd been young and bent on raising all the hell he could get away with and still do a day's work every day and keep his father's wrath from skinning him alive. But he cursed now, turning the air blue.

Damn the boy! Why had he run like that? And the expression on his face, he'd recognized Luke, all right, and he'd turned tail and run, and now there'd be the devil's own time finding him again.

Was that woman, his mother, here too? Luke cursed again. He didn't care if Millicent Armitage were dead or alive and if he was going to be truthful about it he'd as soon she was dead, but the boy was another story. Millicent had given Charles nothing but trouble and heartache from the day he'd married her, but Charles would give half his life to get that boy back; losing him the way he had had nearly killed him.

"You, there! What the devil do you think you're doing?" an officer on horseback shouted at him. "Get back to your wagon! Get it moving! I'll have your hide nailed to a barn door if you don't get back where you belong, damn it. You think this is a picnic?" The officer's face was purple with rage, and for a moment Luke thought he was going to ride him down.

"I saw a boy. . . ."

"I don't give a damn what you saw! Get back to your wagon, you're blocking traffic!"

It was too late anyway. He'd never find Ned now. Still cursing, cursing the Army, cursing the British, but cursing Millicent Armitage the most of all, Luke obeyed orders. They had to get those supplies out and one lost boy wasn't as important to the scheme of this madness as a spit in the ocean.

Two more corners now away from Luke, Ned stopped running, doubled over from the stitch in his side. He was panting, breathless, and his heart pounded against his ribcage until he thought it was going to puncture itself against the bones.

It had been Luke Martin back there. He'd have known him anywhere, he'd almost been caught.

He swallowed, and his mouth and his throat tasted sour. Luke would have made him go along with him, made him go home, and he couldn't do that, not ever. He swallowed again, and fought against the tears that stung his eyes, and for a moment he leaned against the side of a building and his shoulders shook with unbearable grief.

He couldn't stay here. He had to keep moving, get out of sight, back to the inn and the stable where he still worked as a stable boy, where Luke would never find him. It had been a close call and one he had dreaded ever since the Continentals had moved into the area. He'd lived with the dread of being discovered by someone he knew from back home for so long that keeping his eyes peeled, being cautious, had become second nature to him.

His shoulders sagging, his breath still coming fast, he moved on, his mind filled with thoughts that beat and pounded inside his head, that hurt, that threatened to engulf him and drag him down into nothingness with their blackness.

"You there! Where've you been, you worthless little guttersnipe?" A blow to the side of his head made him reel as the hostler let go at him as he entered the stable yard. "Get a shovel in those useless hands of yours and get them stalls cleaned out!"

Ned wanted to kill him, but it wasn't the first time and he didn't try to retaliate. He'd learned a lot about survival in these past months, and the hostler would make two of him, and even if his inborn instinct for survival hadn't kept him from getting himself beat to death or so battered that he wouldn't be able to work, there was still his mother.

His mother. He picked up a shovel and started working. She was still that, there was no way to cut free from her, to say no, it isn't true, I deny her. She was his mother and he had to take care of her no matter what she had done to him and to his father.

No, not his father! Charles Armitage wasn't his father. His mouth clamped hard, his jaw rigid, his eyes were like stone. Not his father. Say it, say it over and over until it didn't hurt anymore. He'd get used to it sometime. Only it still hurt, even though he'd known it for a long time now. It hurt so bad he wanted to die. It was worse than the things the hostler did to him, or tried to do to him, when he'd been drinking and managed to catch him if he wasn't quick enough to get out of his way and hide until the man had sobered up again.

It didn't hurt anymore to look at his mother. When Ned looked at Millicent now all he felt was a kind of numbness.

Millicent's recovery had been slow. When she had regained sufficient strength she had been put to work as a scullery maid to help earn her keep, and to act as a sort of chambermaid when they were exceptionally busy. But even in her weakened state, Millicent had not forgotten who she was. Drawn up to her full height, her voice dripping scorn, she would say, "My good man, to whom do you think you are speaking? I am a lady, and I'll thank you to remember it!"

They didn't even bother to curse her for her clumsiness anymore. She received only a pittance for her labor and the landlord knew a bargain when he had one. The other chambermaid and the cook sometimes taunted her but Millicent ignored the taunts as if they were beneath her notice.

But that was when she was sober, and she was seldom sober anymore. Ned knew, without even the feeling of shame he would have had before he had learned the truth, what she did to get the wine that sustained her against complete madness every time she looked into the mirror and saw the ruin of her former exquisite beauty.

The inn being far from genteel, it was largely frequented by gentlemen without the company of their ladies, gentlemen who considered the price of a bottle of wine fair enough for the services she rendered them. It was true that she was no longer in the first bloom of youth and that her face was pocked, but her hair was still lovely when she remembered to wash it, and she was undoubtedly a lady, and the novelty appealed to them.

"Mother, you could still go home. You could write to Tamara and Annabelle, they'd find the money for your fare. Tamara would take care of you even if Father isn't home."

"I'll hear no more about it. We are going to England,

Ned. This is only a delay, a minor inconvenience. Mr. Hartgrave might return to New York at any time and he will see to our passage."

"He isn't coming back." Ned's face was stony as he said the words. "Let me write to Tam." He'd put his mother aboard the coaster, but he would not accompany her. Without her weighing him down he'd be able to make out on his own. He'd make his way to wherever the Continental Army was and join up. He was big for his age and boys as young as he was had already joined. He'd hold a musket in his hands and he'd kill redcoats, he'd kill more of them than anyone else because he had more reasons. George Hartgrave was British, a redcoat. But he had to get his mother off his hands before he could go.

But Millicent was adamant. If Mr. Hartgrave did not return, she would find other means. There were wealthier gentlemen in New York than the ones who stayed at Brown's Inn. She would save whatever she could from the few pence the landlord gave her for her work, and she would ask for hard cash instead of accepting wine for her extraordinary services to the gentlemen patrons.

What did it matter where she got the money, or how? Only her ultimate goal mattered, England and Sir Basil's town house, and Lillian, and Ned the petted heir apparent and herself made much of, once again a reigning queen of society, come once more into the life that Charles had cheated her of. The pockmarks on her face wouldn't matter then. As long as there was money and position, people tended not to notice such minor flaws, and in London there were cosmetics and skilled people to apply them that would all but hide them in any case. Millicent thought of London as other people dream of heaven, the place where all her troubles would be over and she'd live happily ever after.

All she needed was decent clothing again, fine cosmetics, the services of a hairdresser. All she needed was passage money, and then she and Ned would be in London and all this dreadful time would be forgotten as if it had never happened.

The trouble was, she'd look in the mirror again and see herself for what she was, and then she'd need the solace of the alcohol that dulled her anguish. And one drink led to another, and another. Millicent was now an alcoholic, unable to do without it. Only her dreams, and the alcohol, kept her alive, and the alcohol made the dreams so much more believable.

Ned had begun to get away, whenever he could, for an hour or two to find other jobs to do, to beg errands to run, to carry parcels or luggage, anything to pick up a few extra pennies. He hoarded the coins, a hoard that grew with agonizing slowness, against buying decent clothing to replace his threadbare things. The clothes he had were not presentable enough for him to seek better employment. He could read and write and figure, he could read and write and speak Latin and a little Greek, his mind was quick, somewhere there would be decent work that would enable him to take his mother from this place and find her a clean room, to try to keep men and alcohol away from her until her mind cleared enough so that she would agree to being sent home.

Ned's face was set and grim as he continued to shovel manure. Don't think, he told himself. It's all right. Luke won't be able to find you, he'll be out of town soon with his cart, they're evacuating New York, we're losing again.

He was well acquainted with losing. Ever since the

night his mother had waked him to go with her to join his father, his life had been nothing but defeat.

But like the rebels, the flame of hatred was still there, giving him the will to go on fighting.

Twenty-five

Luke had given his wagon over to John. There weren't enough wagons anyway and John was as good a driver as he was, or so near that it made no difference.

He hadn't asked for permission to come back to the city. It wouldn't have been given. But in this chaos likely nobody would miss him, and if he found the boy and got back to his outfit he'd face what came when it happened. If he didn't find Ned, and got back, he'd just melt in and nobody who saw him coming would report him. If he didn't get back at all they couldn't court-martial him, and stand him up against a wall and shoot him. It'ud be the British who'd do that if they caught him.

It was a fool's errand, and he knew it. He hadn't had what amounted to a uniform yet, he was kept busy driving wagons and all he had was a cockade for his hat, so if the British laid hands on him and learned that he was a rebel he'd be shot as a spy because he wasn't in uniform.

But they weren't going to catch him, he'd see to that. He'd left the cockade back at the wagon, and he was already wearing a farmer's clodhopper shoes and threadbare homespun breeches and a coarse jacket over his shirt. He'd be taken for a manual laborer of some sort, and he had a story ready for his tongue of looking for a runaway nephew to return him to his parents' farm.

He didn't have any idea of where to start looking, so he started from Trinity Church and went on from there. He'd called himself all kinds of a fool for coming back in the first place, but he knew it had been Ned he'd seen and he was going to find him for Charles if it took him a week.

That thought wasn't funny anymore. He'd already been back for four days and he hadn't seen a trace of the boy, or been able to learn a thing, and if he didn't get out of here while the getting was good and catch up with his part of the Army, there'd be hell to pay. But Ned was Charles Armitage's boy (and here his mouth went grim as he thought that even if he wasn't, Charles didn't know that), and he was going to find Ned for him if it was humanly possible. As for Millicent, he hoped that she'd gone somewhere else, to London maybe, or to hell.

It was the night of the twentieth now. Luke's stomach was empty enough to hurt. He hadn't been able to stash many provisions in his pockets when he'd set off on this wild-goose chase, and he'd only picked up a few hours of work from a suspicious local hauler helping to load and unload kegs of spirits. With the redcoats crawling all over the place it wasn't going to be easy to pick up any more.

He might as well give up for the night. He wouldn't be able to spot the lad even if he passed across the street from him and it wasn't likely that the boy would be out roaming around in the dark anyway.

It wasn't only the emptiness of his stomach that made him feel nauseous. New York was nothing more, these days with the world gone mad, than an oversized brothel. Women everywhere, soliciting, and you couldn't even walk across a park after dark without stumbling over couples locked together right there on the ground, and get yourself cursed for your clumsiness. He'd never seen anything like it even in London. It was beyond all belief.

He'd give his soul, or as near it as he dared, for one breath of clean Boston air, without all this hellish evil that seemed to emanate from the very walls and cobbles. If he didn't find Ned tomorrow, he'd have to give up and try to get back, and that wasn't going to be easy, either. Likely he'd end up getting shot by one side or the other; there wasn't much to choose between.

Sleeping on the ground in the open was no novelty to Luke by now, after all this time with the Army, but sleeping in an alley in the middle of enemy territory was definitely not to his liking. He hid himself as well as he could behind some barrels, hoping that no patrol would come along and discover him. As tired as he was, he'd likely be groggy enough not to say the right thing if he was jerked to his feet in the middle of the night with a bayonet pricking his belly. But he had to sleep, he was staggering with need of it now, and he had to get off the street because his size and his lack of feminine companionship made him conspicuous.

He had no idea of what time it was when the clamor woke him. Full wakefulness came slowly, in spite of the training of all those months when his senses always had to be on the alert.

It was the smell of smoke, a great deal more smoke than there should have been even in this town, more than the noise itself, that brought him to his feet. He cursed as he lurched against one of the barrels and it clattered over, but the noise of its falling was scarcely discernible in the general shouting and screaming that grew in volume with every passing moment.

Fully awake now, his senses prickling with alarm, he walked to the end of the alley and stopped, frozen in his tracks.

It looked as if half the city were burning. Had Washington decided to fire it after all? Luke wasn't sure that that wasn't what he would have done, in the general's place. It was a damned-fool mistake to leave New York intact for the British to snug down in for the winter.

It was a scene of utter pandemonium. Everywhere people were trying to fight the fires that spread from one building to another. Redcoats, Hessians, and common citizens alike were battling the flames, trying with hopeless desperation to check them, to save something from the inferno before homes and businesses and livelihoods were reduced to smoldering ashes.

Smoke stung his eyes and nostrils and choked and blinded him as he plunged into the crowd to lend a hand. Even if his own Army had set fire to the city deliberately with the intention of destroying it, it went against human nature to stand aside and let it burn. Every generation of man since time began had battled the common enemy, fire. He could no more have stood idle than he could have stopped breathing; pitching in to do what he could was a reflex action.

Not that there was much that could be done. The fire had too great a start, there wasn't enough water, there weren't enough buckets.

"There's one of the bastards! He helped set it!" he heard a redcoat shout. Luke's eyes glazed with disbelief, his mind boggled with horror as he saw half a dozen British soldiers give chase to a civilian and catch him and drag him back toward the flames.

With utter disbelief, he saw the soldiers throw the struggling man, screaming his innocence, into the inferno. The man ran out again, his clothing and hair engulfed in flames, and the screams that issued from his throat froze the marrow of Luke's bones.

Sickened, he tried to fight his way through the mob to help the man, but other civilians had him down on the ground now and were rolling him over and over to smother the flames. Someone ran with a bucket of water to pour over him and was flattened by the butt of a redcoat's musket for his pains.

Even as citizens and redcoats swarmed into a small-scale battle with each other on the spot, an ax was thrust into Luke's hands and a British corporal shouted at him to help hack down a house that was still untouched. A futile effort, Luke thought. The fire had spread too far, it was completely out of control, it looked as if the whole city were going to go.

The heat blistered his hands, his face. A flying brand landed on his sleeve and he burned his hand beating it out, but not before it had burned through his sleeve and seared the flesh underneath. He picked up the ax again and then, more than half blind from the smoke, he saw Ned.

He threw down the ax and plunged into the crowd, fighting his way through it, pushing, shouting, his face as black with fury at the impediment to his progress as it was with smoke and soot. There he was, just ahead, and running. Strength to make Luke's own legs churn in pursuit came from somewhere. He gained on the shorter boy, whose strides couldn't cover the ground as fast, and then he was close enough so that he could reach out and grasp his shoulder. "Ned, wait up!"

"Let me go!" Ned struggled like an imp from Hades. "I've got to get to my mother, the inn may be afire by now, let me go!"

"All right, we'll get her." They ran together, but Luke kept a firm grip on Ned's arm in spite of the pain that tore through his burned hand.

Ned had been right. The inn was already engulfed in flames when they got there. A few people, some of them patrons of the place, were attempting to fight the holocaust, but it was a lost cause. The timbers were old and burned like so much tinder. It would be leveled to the ground without adequate means to bring it under control, and the means were lacking here as they were wherever fires were raging.

Already, daylight was struggling to make itself seen through the pall of smoke that hung over New York, but the light from the fires cast more illumination than the first sickly rays of the sun. Luke thought that the great fires of London, in ancient times, must have been like this, and for the first time in his life he could imagine the horror and despair of the people who had seen everything they knew and owned swept away by forces that were beyond their powers to cope with.

"There she is!" Ned yanked his arm loose from Luke's grip and darted forward to pull a woman from a huddled group that was watching the destruction, numbed by the disaster into mindlessness. Luke was at his heels, fearful of losing him again now that he'd found him.

Luke's smarting eyes blinked through the half light that was thickened by choking, blinding smoke. Lord in heaven, was that Millicent Armitage, that pocked, haggard bag, dressed in the remnants of a dress that one of her lowliest servants would not have worn at home? Dirty, bedraggled, her hair hanging lank around her shoulders, her face and hands grimed with soot and smoke so that her eyes stared from her face like those of a specter from the grave?

"Come along! We must get out of the city while everything is disorganized. It's the best chance we'll ever have!"

"No!" The scream was torn from Millicent's throat. "I can't go, he'll come back, I must wait for him!"

"Mother, you must go with Luke." Ned's voice was desperate. "He'll get you to safety and see that you get home."

"I won't go." Millicent stood there, her old arrogant stubbornness evident even on her ravaged face.

She wouldn't come along of her own accord, whatever her reasons, Luke could see that. There wasn't time to argue so he struck her, his fist landing on the point of her chin just hard enough to stun her, sending a flash of agonizing pain up his own burned arm to his elbow. As her knees sagged he lifted her, motioning to Ned to follow him.

There was no response. Luke looked back over his shoulder and saw Ned melting away through the crowd. He dropped Millicent where he stood and bolted after the boy. It wasn't too hard to catch him but it was hard to hold him once he'd laid his hands on him. Ned struggled even harder than he had before; it was like trying to hold onto an eel.

"Take my mother! I'm not going, you can't make me go!"

For the second time within the past sixty seconds Luke's fist struck, harder this time. As he had with Millicent, he lifted the unconscious boy in his arms.

Millicent was stirring, soft moans emanating from her throat, when he reached her again. No one interfered as he prodded her to her feet. Her eyes were glazed, she didn't seem to realize what was happening. Still Luke dared not take a chance. By choice, he'd have left her there, to survive any way she could, but she was Ned's mother, Charles Armitage's wife, and Charles still loved her. During the few times Luke had seen the lawyer since this conflict had started, his love had been evident in his somber eyes, filled with an unspoken sadness that had twisted at Luke's heart.

He flung Ned over his shoulder and anchored him there with his hand. With his other, he grasped Millicent's wrist and dragged her along beside him. Plodding, his face as grim as death, he put one foot in front of the other.

Trinity Church was afire when he passed it, completely engulfed, there'd be no timber left of it standing by full daylight, Luke judged, but he gave it only a fleeting thought.

Few of the people he passed on the streets gave the strange cavalcade more than a fleeting glance. Refugees were everywhere, homeless, swarming together, stunned, some milling around aimlessly, others, like Luke, making for the countryside and safety. A squad of redcoats approached and Luke stiffened, but they only glanced at the big, smoke-filthy man, with part of his coat burned away, carrying a scrawny, unconscious boy and dragging a pockmarked hag along with his other hand. They had other things to do than question every civilian who had been made homeless in this night's atrocity.

Right foot, left foot. Ned was heavier than he would have thought, considering how thin he was, and Luke had already been exhausted when he'd found him. Millicent dragged back, whimpering, once or twice demanding, imperiously, to be set free to return to the scene of the holocaust. Luke didn't bother to answer her. Right foot, left foot, right foot, left foot, one, two, three, four, five, six, seven, eight, nine, ten, start over again, right foot, left foot.

Landmarks were gone. Luke had the lightheaded impression that he was walking through the center of hell. Everywhere there were blackened ruins, still belching smoke as pockets of flame flared up again. The smoke made twilight out of the daylight. All around him people were crying, sobbing, cursing, faces were either stunned or filled with despair. He had to keep going, he had to make his way out of it, to regain the Army. No matter what he'd have to face for this desertion, Ned and Millicent must be cared for, and returned home whenever it became possible.

As he went on, he knew he must look as mindless as some of the others he saw. Right foot, left foot. He had a long way to go.

It was no wonder that the Weckquaeskecks had named this place Quaroppas, their word for White Plains, Luke thought. The Weckquaeskecks were Mohicans, subject to tribute from the more powerful Mohawks, he had learned that much since coming here. The marshes and swamps that covered the flatlands emanated a white mist that hung perpetually in the air, like a scene from another world. It was eerie and it made some of the men uneasy, as though this were a place of ill omen, another anteroom to hell.

Luke's hand was healing now, the bandages he'd had to wear on both hand and arm for so many weeks had been removed, and although the scars were stiff he was gradually recovering their full use. It was a miracle that the surgeons with the Army hadn't taken the arm off.

Luke thought wryly that the doctor who'd tended him was glad that he'd roared that he'd tear him apart if he attempted to take his arm away, because the man simply hadn't had the time, let alone the supplies he needed. With over twenty-five thousand men here under General Washington, more than half of them were sick, or wounded, or otherwise unfit for combat. The doctors, the few of them who there were, had enough to do without hacking off another limb, especially if the powerful man it belonged to was going to resist their efforts.

Maybe he was lucky at that, maybe if they hadn't been so busy and so harassed they'd have taken it off as a matter of precaution. The thought was enough to chill him to the bone, a chill far worse than that engendered by the crisp late-October mist that came off the marshes.

He hadn't been as lucky as he'd hoped, when he'd set off on his insane search for Ned in New York City, about easing himself back into his place once he'd found the boy. Easing a boy in wouldn't have been all that difficult, Ned could have come from anywhere, he wouldn't have been the first to wander in and attach himself to the Army, convinced that he was old enough to be a soldier.

But a woman was a different matter, especially a woman who looked like a gutter hag and acted like a queen. There had been no way to make Millicent Armitage inconspicuous. Even if he'd been able to place her among the wives who were camp followers, they would have raised such a gaggle of questions that it would have been bound to come to the attention of the officers.

These women who tagged along with the Army were not camp followers in the accepted sense of the word. They were wives of soldiers who were so poor that they had no other place to go. They washed and mended and cooked, when there was anything to cook, and they were issued half rations. They lent a hand at any work that a woman could do.

So he had had to walk in cold, and put a bold

face on the matter because it had been the only thing he could do. He was having trouble enough with Ned and Millicent as it was, both of them doing their damndest to get away from him.

Not that he blamed Ned. In his place, maybe he'd want to disappear too. Because Ned knew. His mother, that aristocratic slut, had let it all out when she'd been raving with the smallpox that had ravaged her face. He knew that he was a bastard, and he was determined never to return home and face the man he'd grown up believing was his father. Better that Charles Armitage should think that he was dead. Ned had figured that out for himself a long time ago. A boy as quick and as smart as Ned could have managed to make his way home if he'd been of a mind to, and if he'd been capable of deserting the mother who should have been smothered in her cradle when she was born.

It was Charles Armitage's name that had saved him. "Armitage's lad, you say? You brought him out of New York? And his wife as well?"

The officers chose to assume that Luke had been caught in New York during the general exodus, and only managed to get himself and the boy and the lady out when the city had burned. Luke, as spent as he had been, had realized that he was not supposed to correct their misconception. Charles Armitage was highly thought of, and Luke himself was the best wagonmaster they had, and would be again if he didn't lose that arm. In the madness that had accompanied the evacuation, who'd had time to call the roll?

The women had accepted Millicent into their encampment, filled with sympathy for her ordeal. Luke had spread the word that she and Ned had been visiting there at the outbreak of hostilities, and that when Millicent had become ill they hadn't been able to leave.

The story of her money being stolen was true enough, and her battle with death, and their hearts went out to the boy who had cared for his mother, and him only a lad with too much lain on his shoulders. A young aristocrat at that, working in a stable to keep bread in his mother's mouth! It went to prove that blood would tell. His father was a fine man and Ned was only following in his footsteps.

But that had changed now. Although she was cleaner than she'd been and slightly better clothed, because the women had been generous with the little they had at first, she still assumed a haughty manner and took it as a matter of course that she could not be expected to help with the menial work of washing and mending and cooking. And there was the matter of her screaming deliriums when she couldn't manage to get her hands on any rum. So now she was shunned, left alone, and the women talked about her behind their hands and cast looks of dislike at her, closing their ranks against her. There was only one blessing: She still had the sense not to drop a hint of her real reason for having been in New York.

Ned was the more immediate problem. He was as determined as ever to drop out of sight, and it took Luke and Mark and John and Tim, all four of them as well as Eli, who was still stubbornly hanging in there, to keep an eye on him twenty-four hours a day. They never let him out of the sight of at least one of them. They didn't doubt that given the slightest opportunity he'd be gone, and as much as they sympathized with his problem they couldn't let that happen.

If Millicent Armitage had one grain of sense left in her head Charles Armitage would never learn the truth about Ned's parentage. Let him know that she'd run off to join her lover, that couldn't be helped; but not that Ned wasn't his own son.

Ned himself had to be convinced of that before they contrived to send him home. If he loved the man he'd believed to be his father, then he'd want to keep him from being hurt as Ned had been hurt. They told him that, over and over, until they were almost sure that they had him convinced, but they still didn't dare to take a chance. Sometimes the bleakness in the boy's eyes sent chills through them.

The general had taken lodgings in the town of White Plains itself when they had first arrived in this place, determined to make a stand. He'd quartered at John Purdy's house, but that was in the path of the British advance and so he had removed to a farmhouse belonging to the Widow Miller, a pleasant slope of farmland ending at the Bronx River close by the foot of Chatterton Hill. It was a well-built, pleasant farmhouse, two stories with a root cellar off a ways to the right and a huge old sycamore tree to the left. The general had two rooms there, and Charles Lee, his second in command, was quartered there as well.

"Sunday again," Eli said. "Doesn't seem like Sunday without Patience nagging at me not to make us late for meeting."

"You think the British are going to attack?" Tim asked. The slightest-built of Luke's boys, Tim was wiry and agile, quick on his feet, the sunniest-dispositioned of them, too, the easiest to get along with. John, now, was a serious young man and always had been, his mind filled with plans for the future. It wasn't likely that John would stick to building houses and pretty cabinets once this was over with; he was interested in ships, both the building and the sailing of them. Mark was Luke's mainstay, the one who was the most like him, solid, steady, content to master his trade and prosper at it.

"They're bound to." It was John who answered Tim's question. "The general's made a bad mistake, not fortifying Chatterton Hill."

"We outnumber them, though. Most two to one. Don't we have upward of twenty-five thousand? And Howe's only got around thirteen thousand with him, leastwise that's what the scouts say."

"But half of our men are sick, and most of them as green as a man can be and manage to stay alive. Howe's troops are veterans, and he has a force of mounted dragoons. They aren't going to be easy to lick."

"What's the date, anyway?" Eli wanted to know. He grinned sheepishly and settled his knitted cap more securely on his bald, half-scalped head. "Just in case I meet a ball with my name on it, it'ud be nice to know what day I died."

"It's the twenty-seventh," John told him. "And it's your own tom-fool fault you're here, Eli. Nobody would have expected you to join up in the first place, much less not go on home when your enlistment ran out."

"You young'uns think you're somethin', don't you?" Eli snorted. "Let me tell you, whippersnapper, when it comes to a fight, I'm as good as any man half my age! You sound like Patience, and that's no lie. A man oughta be able to git away from naggin', in the Army. 'Cept by officers, of course."

John had been right. Howe had advanced, and they had to fall back, and now, at this late date, Washington had seen his mistake in not fortifying Chatterton Hill. The hill overlooked his own right flank and it was too vital to be left vacant. Captain Alexander Hamilton was sent with sixteen hundred men and two cannon to man it, that was all the general could spare. It would have to be enough.

The top of the hill was open farmland, interlaced with stone walls that divided it into planting plots. The sides were wooded and steep. Some of the hated Hessians were moving around now to cross the Bronx River, down at the foot, and redcoats moved around the hill itself to enfilade the defending Continentals. That left the men on Chatterton under fire from both directions, and it was not a comfortable place to be.

"Here they come!" Mark yelled, and then all hell broke loose.

To Luke, it didn't seem possible that they had driven the first assault back, forced the British to retreat. But the Continental Army's elation was short-lived. They'd re-formed and they were coming again, they were gluttons for punishment, they didn't know when to quit. Or maybe they didn't know how to quit, trained as they were, knowing that any man who turned tail and ran in the face of the enemy would have to face court-martial and likely the firing squad for desertion under fire.

The Germans probably didn't know the difference. To the colonials, the Hessians were stolid, impassive, trained subhumans who obeyed orders with no thought for their own risk. It was one of the things that rankled the most, Englishmen sending mercenaries against Englishmen. If nothing else could keep them fighting, the memory of that last, intolerable outrage would.

Luke took aim and fired, reloaded, and fired again.

"A ball. Give me a ball!" a voice beside him demanded. Luke's finger tightened on the trigger and he thought, he was almost sure, that he saw a redcoat go down.

"Ned! What in blazes are you doing here?"

"I'm fighting. I have the right. I'm going to kill some of them. I'm going to kill all of them I can." The meaning of the boy's words was clear. George Hartgrave was a redcoat. Every time Ned took aim and fired, he was killing the man who had fathered him.

There was no way to send the boy out of it. Muttering under his breath, Luke shared his shot with him. Sometime later he saw that Ned had helped himself to the shotbag and powder horn of a man who had fallen, and he was still holding firm, his slitted eyes pools of hatred. The lad crouched behind a stone wall with Luke and fought like a grown man. Fifteen, Luke thought, and he had to swallow against the lump in his throat.

Aim, fire, reload, fall back, they were retreating, they'd been caught between Howe's pincers, the damned Britisher was famous for that, and they were being licked again. Licked again, was there nothing in this Army but defeat, nothing but retreat? Wait, fight, retreat, licked again, the words pounded in his head until he couldn't think for them.

God, oh God, Ned was down, and they were in full retreat now, forced to withdraw from their position. There was no time to try to see how badly the boy was hurt. Luke scooped him up and ran with the others, to lay him down and fire, reload, and pick him up again and keep going. This wasn't an anteroom to hell, it was one of the inner chambers.

What am I going to tell Charles? Luke thought. I took your boy out of New York, only to have him killed.

Twenty-six

Charity took off her apron and hung it behind the kitchen door of The Temptation and left the tavern, locking the door behind her. She'd cleared out the last of the patrons five minutes ago, and now she carried a small bundle, wrapped in a piece of calico, that contained all of her worldly possessions.

They were not many in spite of the fact that Eli had always paid her a fair wage. She had little need of material things. One extra workday dress, a better dress for meeting on Sunday, a comb, a small mirror, a few items of underclothing, and an extra pair of shoes and stockings. She wore her cloak around her shoulders, its hood pulled close around her face, because it was a crisp day and she had a long walk ahead of her.

Millicent Armitage was home, and Ned, Millicent ill and Ned virtually helpless from the wounds he had received at White Plains. Eli was home, his arm shattered at the elbow; how he had ever kept the Army doctors from amputating it Dr. Peabody would never know.

But he had kept them from amputating it, probably with his scathing tongue, and although his arm was always going to be stiff it was certain now that he would keep it. Patience said that it was a pity that it hadn't been his right arm, the one that's elbow was forever bending to carry either cider or rum to his mouth.

Mark was home. It was Mark who had gotten the rest of them home, wounded himself and so weak he couldn't even stand, so thin he was little more than a skeleton, with months of recuperation in front of him unless the winter killed him off, as weak as he was.

They'd come in a rickety farm cart, pulled by a horse that was more dead than alive. Mark had pulled the cart to a stop in his mother's yard and tried to shout to attract attention from the house, and keeled over and fallen off the seat. Martha herself had picked him up, with only the help of the young lad who stayed with her, and carried him inside before they'd gone back for the others.

Martha was a capable woman, but flesh and blood can accomplish only so much. She had her house to run, and Mark to nurse back from the death that lurked just behind his shoulder waiting to pounce. And Mistress Gatesby, although completely loyal to Charles Armitage, could scarcely move around anymore because of the swelling that affected her legs. She could no longer climb the stairs, let alone take care of a sick woman and a badly wounded boy. She had a pallet in the pantry off the kitchen, and did what she could to keep the lower part of the house in order, but that was all she could manage.

Charity walked fast. She wanted to get Millicent and Ned to their own home and settled before dark came on. She would have to care for them herself because there was no one else. Tamara had come to The Temptation that morning and said that this would be her last day at the shipyard because Martha could not care for them all. Patience had come on Tamara's heels and said that Charity was to take over Millicent's and Ned's care at the Armitage house, just Millicent and the boy. She and Annabelle between them, working in shifts, would manage to keep the tavern open, and Tamara would help Martha with the constant attention that Mark needed.

Charity didn't resent being ordered to care for Mistress Armitage and Ned. She was the logical choice. She was far stronger than Annabelle or Patience, strong enough to lift the boy when he needed lifting, to do all the heavier work, to hold up under the strain.

There was another reason she was glad to go. Annabelle didn't know about Ned's parentage, and Millicent, or the boy himself, in some delirium, might let it slip. Until both Millicent and Ned were well enough to negate that possibility, no one but Charity must care for them. If Mistress Gatesby learned the truth through any babbling on their part her lips would be sealed as closely as Charity's. It wasn't that Annabelle couldn't be trusted, it was because her tender nature would make it hard for her to dissemble in front of her father when he came home.

Charity's mouth tightened. For the love of Charles Armitage, she would care for his wife, and do her best for the woman who had betrayed him.

Mark lay on the bed that Martha had set up for him in the parlor, his face unnaturally red from the fever that racked him. Tamara was there, her face as pale as Mark's was flushed, and her eyes were deep pools of fear for Mark's life.

Still, it was Tamara who helped carry Ned to the farm cart and tuck a patchwork quilt around him, and Tamara who supported her mother, who could walk but who lapsed into incoherent mumblings every once in a while, to a place beside Ned in the wagon. "Thank you, Charity. I can't imagine how we'd manage without you."

Charity put her hand on the younger girl's. "We all do what we can." Then she climbed to the driver's seat and gathered up the lines and clucked to the ox that Tam and Jimmy, the hired lad, had hitched to the cart. The decrepit old horse was in the shed, only beginning to recover a little from its grueling odyssey. Tamara had to hit the ox on its shoulder with a stick before he would move out, but then they were on their way. Jimmy, supporting Ned in the back of the cart, would fetch the cart and ox back later, after he'd helped to get Ned and Millicent settled.

The only thing that Mark was really aware of in the days and weeks that followed was the hands, brutalized by hard labor but as tender as an angel's as they attended to his needs. Square hands, rough and calloused from hoeing in the garden, from splitting wood, from doing laundry with strong lye soap. Small, slender hands, as hard and as calloused as the square ones, the nails cut short, small scars from cuts and scrapes on their skin. Two pairs of hands, the larger and the smaller, but one pair or the other was always there, fluffing his pillow, smoothing his quilts, lifting him, sponging his burning forehead, putting a pan under him when he needed it, feeding him. Patient, loving, caring hands.

Gradually, as his fever from the infected wound in his shoulder abated, he coupled hands with faces. His mother's face, older, her hair showing more gray now, lines where there had been healthy plump smoothness when he had left the last time. Tamara's face, older too, thinner, but having a beauty he had never realized before that she possessed, a face filled with determination and steadfastness, her beautifully sculptured mouth seldom smiling but a smile appearing, when he indicated at last that he knew her, that spread to her eyes. Charles Armitage's eyes, her best feature, everyone had said, when she had been a pesky child who had tagged his footsteps and driven him to distraction.

"I'm better."

"Yes, you are. And about time, too! All we have to do now is strengthen you up and get some meat on your bones and you'll be as good as new, or almost."

"It's winter."

"Full winter. There's snow on the ground. Open your mouth."

The stew was good. It had been broth at first, Mark remembered hazily. Day after day, one spoonful of broth after another, insistent, forcing his mouth to open. But now there were chunks of meat in it, and turnips, and carrots and onions. Mutton?

Tamara read his thoughts. "It was an old ewe. We had to stew it for two days to make it fit to eat. You're lucky to have it, all the same. Prices are outrageous. Everything's scarce, and some people are going hungry. With so many farmers away with the Army the crops weren't what they should have been, and the Army has to be fed out of what little there is."

She was talking to keep his mind off other things, but it didn't work. "Have you heard anything of my father, of John and Tim?"

Tamara shook her head. "I don't know where they are now. Tod told us that General Washington sent guns up to some place called Miller Hill after he had to withdraw his right flank, and the British manned Travis Hill. Tod said that Travis isn't as high as Miller. He said that Colonel Glover held back his fire until the British had dragged cannon up Travis, and then he let them have it and the British only got four shots off because they pulled out because their position was too exposed to be tenable."

At least that news was good, that the British had had to do the running for once. It must have tickled Luke and John and Tim, they were sick and tired of retreating, always retreating.

"That isn't all." Tamara's eyes were shining now as she went on. "It seems that Howe wasn't too sure of himself and he delayed attacking again. Tod says he was waiting for reinforcements."

"Howe's good at that." Mark nodded. "He never was one to want to fight unless he had us outnumbered."

"And then it stormed. Tod says it rained like anything, it was a deluge that went on for hours, they thought it would never stop. And General Washington used the rain as cover to get to a stronger point at North Castle. I think I have all the places right, but Tod will tell you himself, anyway. For some reason, Howe didn't go after them there."

"How many did we lose?"

Tamara had to shake her head at that, because she didn't know. It wasn't until Tod came three days later that Mark learned that Washington had lost somewhere near a hundred and fifty men, fifty of them killed. From the best reports Tod had heard, Howe had lost a little more than three hundred.

Mark was impressed by the ease with which Tod got around on the peg that Luke had made for him right after the siege had ended and they'd been able to get back into Boston. His friend looked fit again, except for the loss of his leg, and he put in his time between keeping things together at Charles Armitage's office and helping out at the tavern.

"And they never came after us? There wasn't another fight?"

Tod's face held a grim satisfaction. "Howe made another of his mistakes. His reinforcements got to him, all right, he had twenty thousand men by all reports, and if he'd pressed his advantage he'd have had us. But he turned south instead, to Fort Washington. He'd have won the war, Mark, as sure as I'm sitting here talking to you, if he'd attacked instead. There's no doubt about it, it would have been all over. Most think he went to Fort Washington because it kept supplies from getting to him overland, and he had to depend on ships on Long Island and the Harlem River."

Tod shook his head, wonderment still on his face. "Sometimes I wonder which side Howe is on, ours or the British. Seems to me that if any one man wins this war for us, it'll be Howe, by always doing the wrong thing!"

"I'll be damned," Mark said. "You know, I think I agree with you. We'd have been finished for sure if he'd gone after the general instead of the fort."

"He's too cautious. We showed him a thing or two at Breed's Hill and he's been like an old woman ever since, afraid to go in if the odds aren't perfect. If I were a member of Congress, after this war, if we win, I'd vote him a pension!"

Three days after Tod's visit Tamara came downstairs dressed to go out in a serviceable woolen dress and an old sheepskin jerkin that he recognized as having once belonged to Eli.

"Where do you think you're going?" he demanded, pulling himself up to lean against the pillows against the headboard of his bed. "It's pretty cold out to go strolling around town, isn't it?"

"I'm going to work. Martha doesn't need me to help her take care of you anymore, and the weather's cleared enough so the work can go ahead. I told Mr.

Potts that I'd be back as soon as you were well enough so that Martha and I didn't have to stand shifts watching you."

"Work?" Mark's eyebrows shot up, and Tamara braced herself. So far, they'd managed to keep Mark from finding out what she had been doing while he'd been gone. No one who had come to see him, and nearly everyone they knew in Boston had come as soon as he'd been strong enough to receive visitors, had dropped even a hint.

"Work." Tamara edged closer to the door.

"What work?" Mark stared at her, and then his face relaxed. "Oh, of course. Potts is the shipbuilder. You must be keeping his accounts for him. Well, at least you can do that dressed as a woman, not like a boy. It's a nice, ladylike position, if you're determined to do something to help the war effort."

"Not the accounts."

Mark pulled himself up higher on the pillows, and then swung his legs over the edge of the bed and stood up and went to put another log on the fire. Tamara steeled herself against protesting that she'd do it, or that he should call Jimmy or his mother. Being able to do so little for himself or to help keep things going was beginning to make him pretty testy.

The applewood gave off a delicious aroma as it crackled and caught. Tamara thought that applewood made the best firewood of any, and her father agreed with her. He'd always specified it when he had put in his order for a winter's supply.

Mark straightened from his task and instead of going back to bed, sat down in the ladder-back chair beside the hearth. Dark suspicion flooded his face.

"If you aren't keeping the books, then what are you doing?"

Tamara's chin went up. "I'm helping him build a ship."

Mark's hands gripped the sides of the chair until the knuckles showed white, and his face turned an alarming red. Tamara raised her voice. "Martha! Martha! You'd better come and sit on Mark, he's about to fall in a fit, and I have to leave."

Martha came hurrying down the stairs, the sheets she had stripped from the beds still in her arms. Mark was struggling to get to his feet, his eyes flashing fire.

"Mark, you sit down again this minute! Are you trying to undo all the progress you've made? Tamara is going to work. All of Boston knows where she works and so far there have been very few objections. She's a good carpenter and we need ships. Even Parson Eldridge had to back down when some of the men talked to him and pointed out that there's mighty little difference to a ship whether a man or a woman pounds the nails!"

Mark might not have heard her. "The shipyard!" he bellowed. "I won't have it!"

"I believe that I pointed out to you once before that you aren't my lord and master . . . yet. It's a very strange thing that both my sister and I have to have our men wounded and helpless before we can get them to marry us. And we are going to be married, Mark, as soon as you can stand on your feet long enough to get through the ceremony. In the meantime, I'm going to work." Without another word Tamara pulled the door open and stepped outside and pulled it closed after her.

Well, now he knew. She didn't envy Martha, being left alone with him. It would be cold at the shipyard, her hands would be chilblained before nightfall, her feet half frozen, but all the same she'd rather be there than at home.

Her mouth curved into a smile as she realized what

she had just thought. Home. She had been born, and lived all but a few months of her life, in her father's house, a house that was considered a mansion by most of the residents of Boston, but now when she thought of home she thought of the Martins' house, a simple, unpretentious workingman's house, its main source of pride the new parlor floor that she herself had helped to lay when she was fourteen. That big house where she'd grown up, with all its luxuries, could never seem as much like home to her as Martha's kitchen; furthermore, it never had. Except for the times when her father had been at home, the mansion had never held attraction for her.

Her smile turned to a sigh as she reflected that her mother was once again in residence. As much as Tamara loved Ned, and she loved him wholeheartedly, it grew more difficult daily for her to visit there. Whenever she approached that house out of duty, her footsteps slowed of their own accord, and she had to steel herself to pass through the doorway.

Did her mother know that her lover, George Hartgrave, had murdered Agnes? Did she know that he had also attempted to murder Tamara as well? The thought was unbearable. It sickened her to have to look at her mother, to talk to her, to humor her as she had to be humored these days. The older woman's raddled face still retained its former haughtiness, her once perfect body, slat-thin now, still wore the lovely gowns that had either been sent from London to her own measurements or fashioned by the best Irish mauntamakers in Boston. But the face was a face that Tamara could not penetrate, the body a shell that had once housed a woman and now housed a stranger.

Murder! Tamara thought, as she plodded the frozen ruts. To kill your father was fratricide, to kill your mother was matricide, but she could not locate the word for killing your own child. Infanticide? Tod would know, but she couldn't ask him. It wasn't a word that came up in ordinary conversation.

Tightening her lips, Tamara wondered where George Hartgrave was now. It was a sin, almost certainly it was a sin and one of the most deadly, but she hoped that he was either dead or suffering as he had made Ned suffer, as he was making Tamara suffer every time she thought of him.

Tired and chilled to the bone, her hands smarting from chilblains, Tamara stopped in at her own home after work that evening. She wanted to see Ned, even if she would have to see her mother in payment for the privilege, and to be truthful she was in no hurry to face Mark again now that he knew what she was doing. Martha must have had a time getting him settled down again after she had left this morning, and now he had had all day to seethe and fester and work up his bile.

Because of her dirty shoes she entered through the kitchen. Charity had enough to do without having to clean floors and rugs, and Mistress Gatesby was no longer able to get down on her hands and knees to do such tasks. The poor woman's edema had worsened until Charity had had to take over the entire burden of caring for the house while Mistress Gatesby sat with Millicent and listened to her mistress's accounts of her former glory when she'd been a young lady in London with all of society at her feet. Listened to her complaints, too, bearing the brunt of them as Millicent raged because her former friends had deserted her after calling once or twice since she had come home after her horrible ordeal in New York and then having to travel with the Army.

"You didn't send the invitations! You neglected to

see to it, you worthless woman! Not one answer of acceptance, of course you didn't send them, I'll see that you're discharged directly Mr. Armitage returns!"

"Yes, Mistress Armitage." Mistress Gatesby went on knitting stockings and scarves for the soldiers, her racing needles turning them out as fast as her fingers could move. Pausing in the doorway to the drawing room, Tamara heard the exchange and drew a deep breath, willing herself to go in and get this brief duty-visit over with before she went upstairs to see Ned.

Her mother looked up and saw her standing there and an expression of distaste further marred her pock-marked face. "Tamara! What on earth are you wearing? Are you masquerading as a street slut these days? It's no wonder that my friends neglect me. Not one invitation this past fortnight, not one! Even Grace has abandoned me!"

"Mistress Gammage came to visit you only yesterday afternoon, Mistress Armitage," the long-suffering cook said, without looking up from the heel she was turning.

Millicent's forehead creased in a frown. "Did she? Well, yes, I do believe that I recollect it now. But Grace is the only one who comes, and she not often. And she doesn't invite me to her home anymore, to any of her gatherings."

"Mama, there is a war. There are very few galas this winter. Most of the men are away, and in any case no one can afford it."

Millicent's eyes focused on Tamara again. "Look at your hands! A scrubwoman's hands! You've been helping that servant of mine again, I suppose. Why your father allows it I cannot understand. I must certainly speak to him the moment he returns. This creature fails to send out my invitations, and you disgrace yourself by consorting with former bondspeople! We'll be in England next season, I vow. Things like this do not happen there. Yes, yes, we will return home to England; Mistress Gatesby, please do stop that eternal knitting and help me check over my wardrobe to see what I will have to order made up for the journey. Everything I have is in rags, utter rags, nearly the whole of it will have to be replaced."

"We checked your wardrobe the day before yesterday, Mistress Armitage. You decided that it is quite adequate until you arrive in London and can have more fashionable things made than you could get here in Boston." The needles went on clicking.

"Did we? Yes, I think we did. . . ."

Tamara slipped away. As unlikable as her mother was she couldn't help the pity that welled up in her heart. There was no longer any doubt: There were days when Millicent was addled in her mind. It was an aftermath of her dreadful illness, Tamara supposed, and all the drinking she did. She wondered if her mother would ever get better, or if she would get worse and worse until she became a mindless creature who had to be hidden from the world.

Charity was in Ned's bedchamber, having brought him his supper on a tray and prepared him for the night.

"This is one of my mother's bad days, I see," Tamara said. "Is she like this more often now, Charity?"

"It's hard to tell. Some days she seems perfectly lucid, and some days she slips into fantasy for only an hour or two, but today she had been restless since breakfast. I'm sorry for Mistress Gatesby, she's the one who's had to bear the brunt of it."

"There has been no word from my father?"

Charity went on plumping up Ned's pillows, not

looking up from her task. "No word. But otherwise things are going well enough. Ned is stronger, aren't you, Ned?" She gained control of her emotions and smiled, her face filled with pride. "He walked a little this afternoon, Tamara! Come now, Ned, tell your sister yourself, it's your triumph, she doesn't have to hear it secondhand! I'll just clear this tray away and leave you alone unless you need me."

"Ned, did you really?" Tamara's face flushed with excitement.

Ned shrugged. His face against the linen of the pillowcase was still white and thin, his eyes dark and haunted in contrast. He knew about his parentage, and the knowledge tore at Tamara's heart. How many hours had she spent telling him that it didn't matter, that it was no fault of his, that he was still her brother and she loved him and that nothing could ever come between them?

"Only as far as the chest and back, and I had to lean on Charity."

"But that's still wonderful! You're growing stronger every day. Do you know that you're a hero here in Boston? Everyone knows how you fought right beside the militiamen at White Plains. Mark says that you killed at least two redcoats, he had it from Luke."

"And there were hundreds I didn't kill." Ned's face was stony.

Tamara crawled up beside him on the bed and took him in her arms. "Stop it! You must stop it, Ned! You can't kill the whole British army single-handed! You did more than your share, you're still a boy, and Father will be proud."

But I won't be here when Father comes, Ned thought. That was the reason he tried so hard to regain his strength, to walk again. They'd brought him home, and he had been too weak to protest and too weak ever since to leave, his wounds had healed slowly, but he had to be strong again soon. He had to leave before Charles Armitage came home.

There would be no disgrace reflected on his father's name by his running off again to rejoin the Army. Maybe he'd be killed this time. If he wasn't, after the war was over he simply wouldn't come back. Let Charles Armitage think that he had been killed in battle and not accounted for, or had met with some fatal accident on his way home. It would be better that way, better for both of them, he'd head on West, or maybe South to New Orleans, and no one would ever hear of him again.

Tamara kissed his cheek even if he was almost a grown man and a hero. Her heart broke into splinters because she couldn't find a way to help him over this torment that ate away at him like some dread disease.

"I have to get back to Martha's. But I'll come again tomorrow, Ned. Go to sleep now, and wake up stronger."

Wake up stronger. He had to wake up stronger, strong enough to leave. He turned his face into his pillow, and his shoulders shook as the familiar desolation settled over him like a black and crushing cloud.

Twenty-seven

It was a long, hard ride from Philadelphia to Boston, and Charles was bone-weary as he slumped in his saddle. He wasn't a young man anymore, he was forty-seven years old, crowding the half-century mark, no longer a young man in anyone's language.

How fast the years had gone since he had been a young man first setting foot in Boston with his beautiful and reluctant bride! How filled with hope for the future he had been, certain in his youthful arrogance that Millicent would come to love him as her memories of London and the dissolute life that she loved there faded from her mind.

All those years, and sometimes it seemed no more than ten. And his hopes blasted as the years had passed and Millicent had hated him more with every one of them, hated him for marrying her, hated him for taking her away from England, hated him because their children had been daughters when all her hopes had been based on bearing a son to inherit from her uncle. For less than one year out of all the others, Millicent had seemed to change, kindling bright, false hopes that had burned all the deeper because they had proved to be false, and that had been when Ned's birth had been expected.

There had been compensations. He had loved his children, just as he loved them still, and he had made good friends, among common men as well as the more exalted.

His affairs had prospered, and as long as he had left Millicent alone she had tolerated him, except when she nagged him about returning to England to live. In that at least he had had his way. There would be no England for him or for his three remaining children. Lillian was lost to him, but then Lillian, of all of the children, had always been her mother's daughter. To Lillian, he reflected grimly as he hunched his shoulders against his fatigue, he was now an enemy.

This war had taken its toll of him more than physically. Where was Millicent, where was Ned? Would he ever find them again, ever see his son again? Or had Millicent managed after all to get Ned to England, had she by now turned him into a young fop intent on his own pleasures, holding Boston and all of the colonies in contempt?

No! Ned wasn't like that and he never would be. His son had hated England when they'd been there, and made it plain that he never wanted to return there. If he lived through this war Charles would find him and bring him home. Even if the British won, and it had begun to look as if that were more than a possibility, he'd find him and bring him home.

As for Millicent, Charles had at last conceded defeat. If her heart was still set on England then he would raise no hand to make her return to Boston. She could make her home with Sir Basil or Lillian in London. It had taken him all these years to admit unqualified defeat.

He was halfway through his journey now, traveling through sparsely settled countryside, woods interspacing stone-fenced fields and an occasional lonely farmhouse. A few miles ahead there was an inn that he knew where the proprietor was an avowed patriot. Charles would have to put up there for the night. It was already growing dark and even if he himself hadn't been ready to drop, a horse could only stand so much.

He missed having Jonas for company, but the nature of Charles' work made it imperative that he travel unrecognized, and that could not be accomplished if he had his black servant at his side. Jonas was in Washington's troops, serving as a private. Having once been a slave himself, the black man was ready to lay down his life to insure freedom for all men.

Still, Charles missed him sorely. Although Jonas was only two years younger than himself, the servant's energy never seemed to flag. It would be a comfort to have him with him now, to carry hot water up for a bath, and to take care of the travel stains on his clothing, but much more than that, because those were things that Jonas did of his own insistence, to have someone to talk to.

Except for men he had known for years, men he knew to be undeviating patriots, Charles dared talk to no one during these flying journeys as what he wryly called errand boy, running messages from Congress to Boston to General Washington wherever he happened to be. Nobody knew for sure how many patriot faces hid Tory hearts, and it made Charles' tasks the more difficult because of his essential solitariness.

Deep in his far-from-pleasant thoughts, brought on by fatigue and mental stress over Millicent's and Ned's disappearance, it was only his instinctive reaction to danger, cultivated to a sharp pitch from all these months of evading British patrols, that saved him.

He was riding past a copse of trees, his mount's pace slow because the horse was as tired as he was, when the faint sound of a pistol being cocked made him jab his heels into his horse's flanks and rein aside so fast that the beast stumbled and almost went on its knees. He hauled up on the reins automatically to keep the beast on its feet, but it was that stumble that saved his life as a bullet whistled past his ear.

Without pause, without thinking, acting again by instinct, Charles dug his heels in again and sent the horse headlong into the trees, charging the unseen marksman. If there were only one, then he would be on him before the man had time to reload. If there were more than one then it would be all up with him anyway because his exhausted mount could not possibly outrun fresher horses, and the other man or men would also be armed and this time he'd present a much more strikable target.

His horse crashed into the man as he was still trying, frantically, to reload, and knocked him sprawling. A scream escaped his would-be assailant as the horse's hoofs trampled over him before it could be checked.

Charles had reined up and was off in less than an instant, to kneel beside the writhing man and twist his arms behind his back. The man's eyes were open, looking at him with fury and loathing even through the pain that twisted his features into near unrecognizability. In the swiftly gathering twilight, it was a moment before Charles realized that he knew the man who had tried to ambush him.

George Hartgrave! He was in civilian clothes, but Charles had no doubt that he was attached to the British Army. No doubt Hartgrave had been sent on this particular errand to track him down and waylay him, because he knew him by sight.

"Damn you! Damn you to hell. . . ." Hartgrave's

voice broke off as his head fell back and his eyes closed. He was badly hurt. It looked as if one or more of his ribs had been broken, as well as his arm, when Charles' horse had overrun him.

By rights, Charles knew that he ought to finish him off where he lay. Hartgrave was an enemy, and this was war. Instead, he loosened his hold on the broken arm, feeling compunction because he had twisted it before he had realized that it was broken. The idea of killing an unconscious man filled him with revulsion. He couldn't do it, it was against everything in his nature, although he knew that if their positions had been reversed Hartgrave would have lost no time in dispatching him.

He worked swiftly, stripping off Hartgrave's coat, divesting him of his linen shirt, which he tore into strips and wrapped around the man's chest. He used a third to bind the broken arm close against Hartgrave's side, to save it from swinging and jolting. It was the best he could do.

Hartgrave's horse, tethered to a tree, was plunging and whickering, so close that Charles had to drag Hartgrave out of the danger of being trampled before he could finish his crude first aid. No doubt Hartgrave had had his hand over the beast's muzzle to keep it from whinnying as he had approached.

The crude bandaging done, Charles quieted the plunging animal but in the end he had to sling Hartgrave's limp body over his own mount to transport him because the fresher, more spirited animal refused to stand for it. His own was too tired to care, and plodded along docilely as Charles mounted the other and led it along to the shelter of the inn.

The landlord was agitated when he saw the burden that Charles had brought with him. "What happened, Mr. Armitage?"

"He took a potshot at me. For public consumption, though, he met with an accident when he was thrown from his horse and trampled."

"You should have finished him off!" The landlord's face was indignant.

"I know. I didn't, though, so I hope you will find a bed for him and get him some kind of medical attention once I'm on my way again. In a way, he did me a favor. His horse is fresh, and I'll be able to press on again after I've had something to eat and an hour or two of rest. So now I'm a horse thief, Caleb, among other things."

"I hardly think he'll press charges." The landlord was still glum, little liking having to give aid and shelter to an enemy. Still, Mr. Armitage was right. You couldn't kill a man who was helpless, not and live with your conscience all the rest of your life. "It's only mutton again, I'm afraid, and lucky to have that. I hope the damned British find it as hard to come by decent rations as we do!"

"I doubt that, Caleb. Some of our own farmers are selling their crops to the redcoats, for hard cash, because they can offer more than we can and they don't have to wait for their money." Charles' face was white at the enormity of it, and two deep lines etched his face from his nostrils to his mouth. "They call themselves Americans, but when it comes to their pockets, they rationalize that they have to live even if there's a war going on. I admit it's hard not to judge them."

"Judge 'em! I wouldn't wait to judge 'em, I'd shoot first and judge 'em afterward!"

"And leave their wives and children in want," Charles said tiredly. "Well, we can't do anything about it now, Caleb. Bring me the mutton. It'll taste good to me no matter how you've managed to ruin it."

"Ruin it! Why, you . . ."

Caleb broke off. It wouldn't do to say what he'd been going to say to a gentleman like Charles Armitage, who was close to killing himself in the service of his country even without enemy bullets to help him along. Besides, Mr. Armitage had only said that to take his mind off his anger about those dad-blasted farmers who'd feed the enemy and let the American troops go hungry.

Still groggy with weariness, Charles was back in the saddle, on the fresh horse, two hours later, after having slept like a log for an hour and a half. He'd looked in at Hartgrave before he'd left, but the man had still been unconscious. He'd probably live to try again. Charles' mouth was grim as he turned Hartgrave's horse's head toward Boston.

Upstairs in the inn, George had regained consciousness only enough to realize that Charles Armitage was gone. He lay there, despair numbing his body even more than the pain of his injuries.

Thinking about his failure served to bring him fully awake. He gritted his teeth so hard that his jaw ached. He'd asked for this assignment, he'd pushed himself forward to volunteer for it. Fighting the colonials was pleasurable enough, he was no coward, and it gave him satisfaction to help put down the rebellion of such scum, but the chance to do away with Charles Armitage himself, when the opportunity had offered, had been something that he had to have.

To put an end to the man, to have him, irrevocably, out of his way, was a thing he'd dreamed of ever since he'd had to flee Boston after his abortive attempt to have Tamara Armitage murdered. To do it in a way that no blame could attach to him was opportunity tendered by the fates. With Armitage dead, there'd be nothing to keep him from claiming Millicent when this war was over. Even if Armitage's fortune was dissipated by that time, through wasting it on a lost cause, there was still Sir Basil's fortune, and the life he'd always wanted in London.

He'd had his chance. His superior officers had been pleased to learn that he knew the man by sight, and had assigned him to the task of removing that particular thorn from their sides. But then the devil's own luck had saved Armitage after he'd picked up his trail and placed himself to waylay him where there could be no chance of missing.

George closed his eyes but he couldn't shut out his fury and his overwhelming disappointment. He wasn't going to die, and he should be grateful for that, but he doubted that he'd ever have another opportunity to remove Charles Armitage from blocking his path to everything he had always wanted.

"But you can do something, surely there's some treatment!" The despair that had engulfed Charles since his arrival at home deepened. Finding Ned and Millicent here had been almost an anticlimax to his brush with death, but his joy at their safe return had plunged into consternation at Ned's debilitated state from the wounds he had received at White Plains and at Millicent's condition.

Ned, thank God, was going to be all right. The lad had given good account of himself, killing two redcoats before he himself had been felled by two different balls fired at the same time. He was still weak, recuperation would be slow, but Dr. Peabody had assured Charles that recovery was a certainty. But Millicent! The horror of her condition had stunned him, and he still felt its effects.

"If she had had proper medical attention from the

first, her condition might have been alleviated to some extent, but I can't be sure even of that. I'm afraid that outside of the effects of the smallpox, her trouble is mental, and I have to confess that we doctors know almost nothing about its treatment."

"Her mind . . ."

"Alcohol eats at the mind, Charles. You yourself know that, you've seen its effects on too many men not to know it. Why some people can drink moderately with no ill effects, and why others can't leave it alone, and drink until their health and their sanity suffer, is something we have yet to discover."

"Charity tells me that she has days when she seems completely rational." Charles was pleading for hope, any hope.

Peabody spread his hands. "If you could prevent her from drinking, her condition might improve. But don't pin your hopes on it." This war had destroyed anything that was left of the doctor's bedside manner. Better to force people to face the truth, then it wouldn't hurt so much in the end. A doctor was only a man, not God.

The wine Charles had been drinking tasted sour, and he set his glass aside although Dr. Peabody finished his own with appreciation. Good wine wasn't easy to come by these days, and the British had all but drunk Boston dry during their occupation, and supplies were hard to get, and Charles' own cellars had been virtually exhausted by the officers who had taken over his house during that period. He supposed he should consider it lucky that they had not had the time or the opportunity to take the last of it with them when they had evacuated the town.

"About Ned. I sense a difference in him, a reticence he never had before."

Again Peabody spread his hands. "His experiences,

at too young an age, account for that. But his very youth is in his favor, Charles. The young are resilient, they can absorb things that would kill an older man, with no damage to their minds or personalities."

All the same, Charles was troubled. It seemed to him that it went deeper than that. He could swear that Ned had not looked directly at him since he'd returned home two days ago.

Thank God for Charity Babcock! What would have happened to Ned and Millicent without her? The young woman gave of herself unstintingly, just as she had given herself to him on that night so long ago after the siege, when Charles had returned to find Ned and Millicent gone. He had been near the madness of despair that night, and Charity had been there, with her warm arms and her warm heart, to draw him back from the brink.

He hadn't made the mistake of offering her money. There had been no way then for him to repay her for what she had done for him, any more than there was any way now. Privately, Charles determined that she would never want for anything for as long as he lived, and that if he had anything left after this war was over, he would insure that she lacked nothing after his death. At the moment, even trying to express his gratitude in words seemed like an insult.

Nor was there any repetition of that night at The Temptation, or even a hint of such a thing. With Millicent back under his roof it was impossible, no matter that she had tried to leave him and return to England against his wishes, no matter that she was destroyed, both mentally and physically. She was still his wife, and so she would remain for as long as her tormented soul and body remained together.

Millicent joined him at the supper table that night. She was dressed in one of her favorite gowns, a pale green brocade that had been immensely becoming to her while she had retained her beauty. Now it hung on her, its color emphasizing the pockmarks on her face that the cosmetics she still had left failed to cover, and her straw-like hair, combed into a travesty of her former elaborate coiffures. She would not let Charity dress her hair, she considered the girl too base to be allowed such an intimate service, and Mistress Gatesby was incapable of fashioning the puffs and curls and swirls that Millicent demanded.

"I think we must begin packing, Charles. We must take the first passage available, or the season will already be over before we arrive at my uncle's. We should have gone months ago. I don't know what you were thinking of to delay it for so long."

She sounded perfectly rational, hardly more unreasonable or stubborn than she had been for years.

"I'm afraid we'll have to delay yet a little while longer. You seem to forget that we are at war."

"At war!" Twin spots of color flamed on Millicent's face. "An insignificant rebellion of the lowest rabble! A thing to be ignored. Surely we cannot let such a farce interfere with our plans. You have influence, you can arrange it."

"It is hardly a farce, Millicent. I'm sorry, but you will have to postpone your plans."

Millicent stood up, her wine glass crashing against the scenic wallpaper at the far side of the room as she flung it. It shattered into a hundred pieces, its contents staining the carpet.

"I will not wait! I will not delay! I have waited and delayed too long, I have waited all these years and I am done with waiting!"

"Millicent, control yourself!" Charles spoke sharply, using a superhuman effort to control his own temper. He saw no point in treating her as if she were a complete moron, that would certainly only hasten the disintegration of her mind. "What you are asking is impossible at the present time."

"It is not impossible!" With a scream of rage, Millicent virtually threw herself across the table at him, her fingers extended like claws, her face contorted. Before he could secure her hands she had raked long furrows across his face with her nails.

Charity came rushing in from the kitchen, and it took both of them to subdue her and get her upstairs to bed.

"Is she like this often?" Charles asked, when Millicent's struggling and her wild screaming finally subsided.

Charity met his eyes with perfect candor. "Never as bad as this, but two or three times I've had to use force to restrain her. It happens when she's crossed, when something upsets her."

"I'll stay with her until she falls asleep. You'd best see if her outburst upset Ned."

He sat beside her bed, this woman who was still his wife, this woman he had loved for so many years that it tired him to count them. Her sobbing eased and he thought that she was falling asleep when she began to mumble and mutter incoherently.

At first he paid little attention, only watching to see that she did not grow violent again and try to leave her bed. God in heaven, was this to be his life from now on, keeping watch over a woman who was more than a little mad?

Then words and phrases began to string themselves together in his mind, intruding on his thoughts. "George," she said, over and over. "George, George."

They knew only one George, and his last name was Hartgrave.

Two hours later, when Charles left the room after Millicent had fallen into a deep sleep, his face was gray.

His father knew. His mother had been raving, as she had raved when she was burning with fever when she had had smallpox. She had let it all out and now he knew the truth, that he wasn't his son, that he had never been his son, that it was all a lie and that he was George Hartgrave's bastard.

He hadn't told him. He hadn't come into this room to say good night the way he had the last two nights since he had come home. But Ned had stood in his own bedroom doorway, the door barely ajar, and he had seen Charles come out of his mother's room, he'd seen the grayness, the utter despair, on Charles' face, he'd heard enough to know that Millicent had held nothing back.

He couldn't even look at me, Ned thought. He didn't as much as look toward my room, he will never be able to look at me again.

He was still weak, although he had practiced moving about, practiced walking, a great deal more than Charity suspected. Charity had her hands full taking care of this big house and doing all the cooking and laundry, so Ned had had plenty of time for his secret practicing.

He moved slowly, only his hands hurried as he threw one change of clothing into a square of cloth he'd fashioned from an old nightshirt by ripping out the arms. His father had gone to his own room, and his mother hadn't shared a chamber with him since Ned could remember. There was no sound from either room now, but Charity still moved about downstairs, cleaning up the supper dishes and tidying up the mess that his mother had made when she'd thrown her wine glass against the wall and sent dishes flying from the table. He'd have to wait.

He heard Charity come up the stairs half an hour later, and he got into his bed, the bundle he had packed tucked safely under the covers, and blew out his candle. When she opened the door of his room he pretended that he was asleep.

She came inside, walking softly so as not to disturb him, and he felt a feather-soft touch as her fingers brushed against his cheek. It took all his effort not to swallow. He'd miss Charity. Outside of Tam and his father . . . when would he learn not to think of Charles Armitage as his father? . . . and Annabelle, Charity was the person he loved the most. She'd been good to him ever since she had come to take care of him and his mother, and her patience and tenderness and the warmth of her affection for him had bolstered him when he had been at his lowest ebb. She'd nursed him and encouraged him and helped him to sit in a chair, to stand for the first time, to take his first faltering steps, bearing all of his weight on her shoulder.

To walk. He must walk now, as soon as he was sure that the house was quiet for the night, as soon as he was sure that no one would hear him leave.

He waited for a long time, it seemed like hours, before he rose again from his bed and took his coat and hat from the wardrobe, and made his way down the stairs with his bundle clutched in his arms.

He unbolted the front door, slowly so as to make no noise, and opened the door as slowly to prevent any creak that might have alerted Charity, who had learned to sleep with her ears still awake in case he needed her in the night. He pulled the door as slowly shut behind him.

It was very cold, and the sky was black with clouds that were burdened with snow. Even as he moved down the drive, the first flakes began to fall. The wind came up, sharp and bitter, and he hunched his shoulders under his coat and plodded on, trying to ignore the pain in his side where the worst of his wounds still bothered him.

He didn't know exactly where General Washington and his Army were at the moment, but he'd find them. He was going to fight again, to hold a musket in his hands, to kill as many British soldiers as he could. And every time he fired, he'd pray that it was George Hartgrave his ball would reach. His father, his biological father, the man who had betrayed the man he had idolized with what amounted to worship since the day he could walk.

The pain in his side grew worse, but he kept on going. He had been walking for a long time now, and the snow was thickening. Every step was an agony. One thing was good, though: He didn't feel so cold anymore. The exercise, and the pain of walking, had almost made him forget it. Or was it that he was becoming too numb to feel it?

It didn't matter. Somewhere at the end of his journey he would come up with Washington's Army.

Twenty-eight

Charles had no idea what time it was that Charity came into his room where he sat by the last dying embers of the fire, staring into the coals with unseeing eyes.

"Mr. Armitage, I'm sorry to disturb you, but Ned isn't in his room and I can't find him anywhere in the house."

Charity's face looked calm, but her hands were clasped tightly in front of her breast. "I can't understand it! When I couldn't find him I hoped he'd be in here with you. The lad can hardly put one foot in front of the other yet, so where could he be?"

"He wouldn't have gone outside to the necessary, in this weather?" It was the first logical explanation Charles could think of, but even as he spoke he knew that it was a futile one. His surmise was confirmed as he noticed that Charity's slippers were wet, and also the hem of her gown.

"No, I looked there. He's gone, Mr. Armitage."

Charles rubbed his hand over his throbbing forehead. "But where could he have gone? And why? What possible reason could he have for leaving the house in the middle of the night, as weak as he is?"

For the first time he became aware of the wind that

had blown up, of the snow that was hissing against the windowpanes, the very sound of it so cold that it made a shiver pass through his body even in the warm circle that still remained in front of the dying fire.

Charity met his eyes frankly, without dissembling. "He knows about George Hartgrave and his mother, that you aren't his father." From her own room, waiting there within easy earshot in case Charles should need her again to help control Millicent, Charity had heard Millicent's ravings, and she knew that he had also learned the truth. Her heart ached for him, so hard that it was an actual pain in her breast. She would have given all the rest of her life, gladly, if there had been anything she could do to spare him this.

"Oh, my God!" Charles' face blanched. He leaped to his feet and lurched, his legs stiff from having sat unmoving for so many hours. "I must find him!"

A picture of Ned's face, the last time he had seen it, rose in front of him. White, and the eyes clouded with pain, but now that he knew that Ned knew, he realized that there had been more behind that look of pain than the physical discomfort of his wounds. The boy had been in agony because of the knowledge, because of his shame at facing the man who thought that he was his son.

It took Charles only moments to get into his heaviest riding clothes, minutes more to go to the stable through the blowing wind and snow and saddle Jupiter, the Narragansett that had replaced Sheba several years ago. His hands turned numb as he worked with girth and buckles, and before he had finished, Charity was beside him thrusting a napkin-wrapped package at him.

"It's cold fowl and a flask of brandy, you might need it," she said. Bless her, he hadn't even thought to bring a stimulant, much less food. He would have no need of it himself, of course, but if he didn't find Ned at one of the only two places he could be, either at Luke's or at Eli's, the boy might be the better for it when he did find him, he'd be chilled to the marrow.

It was Eli himself who opened to his knock. Eli no longer slept well, and he wakened at the slightest noise. He had a shawl wrapped around his shoulders over his nightshirt, and a knitted nightcap on his bald head.

"Lord Almighty, Mr. Armitage, what are you doing here this time of night? It's gone one in the mornin'! I heard the watch call it out just a piece ago."

Alarm replaced the look of astonishment on his face. "Don't tell me the British are comin' agin! By thunder, stiff-armed or not I can still fire a gun! Why aren't the church bells sounding the alarm?"

"The British aren't coming, Eli. I'm looking for Ned." Charles' heart had sunk, because it was obvious that the boy wasn't here.

"Ned? What in tunket would he be doin' out on a night like this? It's blowin' up a blizzard, and he can't hardly walk!"

"I'll explain later. He's probably with Martha and Tam."

Tamara answered to his knock at Luke's, enveloped n a heavy flannel nightgown, her bare toes curling away rom the cold floor under them, her hair in a long hick braid down her back, her eyes wide with alarm. "Father! What is it? Has Mother taken ill? I'll come at nce. . . ."

The boy wasn't there, either, and when Charles xplained in a few terse words before he turned Jupiter's ead toward the Neck, Tamara's eyes darkened with ain and understanding. Oh, God, where could Ned be, nd on a night like this? If she'd had anything to ride except an ox or the poor, decrepit horse that Mark had driven Millicent and Ned and Eli home with, she'd have dressed and gone to help search for him. As it were, she'd only be a hindrance to her father, who would make better time without her.

Charles' heart was bitter as he pushed through the silent streets, past the oil-burning street lamps that Mr. Revere had designed years ago and that were never lighted during the summer months or on moonlit nights. The town was sleeping, there was only the sound of Jupiter's hoofs on cobbles that were rapidly becoming so covered with snow that even they were muffled.

How many others knew? It seemed to him, at that moment, that he himself was the only person in Boston who hadn't known.

But that made no difference now. Ned must be found. Who knew what thoughts were running through the boy's head? It was no fault of his that his mother had made him a bastard. If he died for it in this cold and storm, it would be a blacker mark against Millicent's soul than the betrayal itself.

He pulled his cloak collar up around the lower part of his face and bent his head into the teeth of the wind-driven snow. How long could Ned last, as weak as he was, scarcely able to stand on his feet, in conditions like these? The snow would cover any tracks he made almost as soon as he made them, and once open country was reached he could turn in any direction and Charles would have no idea which way he had gone.

If Jupiter hadn't snorted and tossed his head, half shying, Charles would have passed him by without knowing. Ned lay just off the road where he had fallen and he was so covered with snow that it was almost impossible to see that the hump his body made was that of a human being.

Charles had to shake him before Ned opened his eyes. "Fell," he muttered. "I can get up now. I'm all right."

Charles' fingers were without feeling, numbed by the cold, as he removed his gloves and held the brandy to Ned's lips. "Swallow," he commanded. "There, that's right. Now again."

Ned coughed and spluttered, choking. His eyes were filled with a despair that made Charles' heart twist. "You shouldn't have come after me, sir. I would have been all right. I was just resting a little."

"I'll help you to get on Jupiter. You'll have to hang on and try not to lose consciousness. It's going to be a long trek home through this snow. Do you think you can do it?"

"I'm not going back, sir. I'm going to find the Army. You needn't worry about me."

There was a strangling sound in Charles' throat. "You're coming home, where you belong."

"I don't belong there, sir."

Charles' arms went around him, held him close against his chest. "You're my son," he said. "You always were and you always will be. We'll talk about it later, after I get you back to safety, if you want to talk about it. But remember this, Ned: You're mine. I won't relinquish you, now or ever."

The tears on Ned's face froze as they fell, as Charles lifted him onto Jupiter's back.

A fine mist was falling. If it turned into a driving rain, as a look at the sky promised it would, work would have to be suspended until it cleared.

Tamara glanced up from where she was fitting the last section of a rail, to see if she would have time to finish before the deluge began in earnest, and she frowned as she saw Jake Clement on one of the yardarms. His stance was unsteady and she suspected that he had brought a bottle of rum with him in spite of the strict rule against drinking on the job.

The man Clement was an off-and-on drunkard, a fine craftsman when he was sober, but erratic and unsteady on his feet when he'd been drinking. He wasn't supposed to be up there anyway. Mr. Potts had told him to leave that questionable brace until he had time to check it himself.

There! She'd known it, the man was drunk and he wasn't taking proper care, he'd just slipped and if he didn't watch out he'd fall and then they'd be short a workman when they hardly had enough as it was. How he'd managed to get that bottle past Mr. Potts was a mystery.

"Mr. Clement, come down!" Tamara shouted.

Clement paid no heed to her call, but went on with what he was doing, his hands unsteady. Scowling now, rage filling her breast, Tamara laid aside her own tools and began to climb. The dratted fool hadn't even heard her, she'd have to get closer to him, and while she was up there she'd check to make sure he hadn't done something that would cause even more trouble later. Mr. Potts was at the other end of the ship and none of the other workers were in sight at the moment, so it was up to her to get Clement down.

Her skirts were damp from the misty rain and they clung to her legs as she climbed, hampering her. She raised her face and called again. "Mr. Clement! Wait! You aren't getting that right!"

Clement heard her that time and he looked down. He leaned over a little to get a better look and then he shouted, "Get down from here, you fool girl! You got no business comin' up here in them skirts! Potts was crazy ever to hire you in the first place!" Of all the men she had worked with since Mr. Potts had put her on, Clement was the only one who still resented the fact that she was a female holding down a man's job and doing it as well as a man could do it.

He started down to intercept her and make her return to the deck, filled with the superiority of his manhood. But he'd drunk more than he'd realized, and he slipped, and banged into Tamara, and recovered himself with that sixth sense that protects drunken men. His mouth dropped open as he saw Tamara jarred loose from her hold and plummet to the deck below.

His shout brought Mr. Potts and the other men running. Tamara lay where she had fallen, her leg twisted at an odd angle under her. Her face was so white that Mr. Potts said "Godalmighty" before she opened her eyes and he saw that she wasn't dead.

They carried her home on a shutter hastily requisitioned from a countinghouse. Because the Martin house was the nearer, that was where they took her. Ordinarily they would have taken her to her father's house but they all knew that she had been making her home with Martha Martin ever since this cursed war had started.

Mark was on his feet now, in this early spring of 1777. He was so well recovered that although Dr. Peabody had told him that it would be the height of foolishness to try to rejoin the Army just yet, he was able to potter in the garden and do odd jobs of carpentry, repair work for the most part because nobody had money to pay for building, and mostly having to accept promise of future payment for the same reason.

"Tam!" Mark's face blanched as he opened the door and saw the burden that the men were carrying. Tamara's face was dead white, her eyes filled with pain.

Her face was wet from the rain that had started to come down in earnest, and her upper teeth were sunk into her lower lip until a drop of blood appeared and ran down her chin, its color diluted by the rain.

"That damned drunken fool Clement knocked her off the yards." Mr. Potts had been upset enough to leave his work and be one of the stretcher bearers himself. "Near as I can figure it, she saw he was drunk and making a mess of things, and he didn't hear her when she yelled for him to come down so she started up there, in those skirts of hers, to stop him. It's partly my fault, I should've let her wear breeches the way she wanted. She wasn't supposed to do any high work anyway but she did aplenty of it just the same. You know Tam. When she sees something that needs doing, she does it. If we had a few thousand more like her, we'd have this war won by now. She's as much a patriot as those men fighting battles, makes me wish she were my daughter. It's no wonder that Charles Armitage is so proud of her!"

Tamara took her teeth out of her lip for long enough to speak. "Patriot! Better call me the fool I am! Breaking my leg when there's so much to be done! General Washington ought to shoot me as a traitor!" she said with a sense of humor that she did not feel.

"Are you sure it's broken?" Mark asked and gave a shout for his mother.

Martha came hurrying in from the back yard where she had been laying out the garden as part of the spring planting.

"No, don't go lifting her, put the shutter and all on the bed," Martha directed, throwing back the blankets. "Has anyone sent for Dr. Peabody?"

"I sent a man to tell him before we started. Likely he'll be along directly. Tamara, I'm sorry about this.

I'm going to fire Clement as soon as I get back to the yard."

"I'm sorry too. But it was my own fault, I should have gone to find you instead of trying to get him down myself when I could see he was drunk."

"You still wouldn't have fallen if he hadn't been drunk and bumped into you!" Mr. Potts' face was red with anger. "The tarnation so-and-so tried to tell me he hadn't been drinking, when he reeked of it! But the Lord knows what I'm going to do now, with you laid up and Clement sacked, as shorthanded as I am."

"I can take over Tam's work." Mark's face was set and there was a white line around his mouth. "I intended going around to your yards the first of the week anyway, to see if you could use me. Barring that, I'd have seen if I could at least drive a wagon to do some of the hauling the Army needs even if Peabody said I'm not fit for it yet. I could still handle a team even if I couldn't do much lifting."

It had driven Mark almost out of his mind these last weeks, to be so helpless while his womenfolk did all the work, men's work at that, the way Tam had been doing. A girl in a shipyard, while he'd had to stay at home, utterly useless! Now his mind was made up. Fit or not, he was going to be at the yards in the morning, just as soon as he was sure that Tam was going to be all right.

It was over an hour before Peabody arrived, and he was in an ugly temper when he walked in.

"Broke her leg, did she? Well, we'll see about that! Likely it's no worse than a bad sprain. Everybody thinks he's a doctor these days."

"It's broken, Doctor," Martha said, her tone final. The doctor glared at her and then he relaxed and had the grace to smile.

"If you say so, I'll take your word for it and set it even if it isn't. Spent all day tending a man who was hemorrhaging. Caught the lung disease last winter, with Washington's Army, and I couldn't do a blessed thing for him but sit there and watch him die. So many of the boys who had to winter out, without adequate warmth or shelter, wet and cold most of the time, have come down with lung fever. I'm almost glad you broke your leg, Tam. It makes me feel useful again."

Tamara had never been drunk before, but she was thoroughly, deliciously drunk before Peabody, with Mark's strong hands to assist him, went about setting the simple fracture. They'd poured enough rum into her to make sure that the pain would be dulled.

"You see that you set it straight, Doctor!" Tam hiccuped. "Set it good and straight, mind you, because Mark might not want to marry me if I had a gimpy leg. Oh, yes, he's going to marry me, he just thinks he isn't, who ever heard of an Armitage girl who didn't get the man she wanted? Annabelle had to wait till Tod lost a leg and couldn't run away from her anymore before she got him, and I'm going to get Mark, so you mind you set it straight or I'll make you sorry!"

"Tam, for the love of Goshen, stop it!" Mark's face was hot with embarrassment. "You're drunk."

"I'm drunk. I never was drunk before. It's lovely being drunk. Nobody ever told me how much fun it is or I'd have done it long before this. That's just like men, having all the fun and not letting us women in on it! Well, if I can build ships, I can get drunk. Do a man's work, you can get drunk like a man!" She hiccuped again. "And do the proposing like a man. Mark, will you marry me?"

"Yes, damn it!" Mark shouted.

Tamara giggled, a fatuous look of satisfaction on

her face. "You're a witness, Dr. Peabody. Do you think I ought to make him put it in writing? Martha, you're a witness too. How soon will I be able to walk, Doctor? It doesn't matter. I'll just use a crutch. Then if he tries to back out I'll have something to hit him with."

"Tamara, shut your mouth," Peabody said. "Ready, Mark? Get a good hold on her shoulders, now. And Martha, be ready with those splints and bandages. We might as well get this over with, the state she's in she'll never know the difference."

That wasn't quite true. Tamara gave one shriek before she fainted, and Mark, sweating blood, cursed himself for a hundred kinds of a fool for not having asked her to marry him before she'd had to do the proposing in circumstances like this. Tam had gone on about their getting married, for years now, ever since she'd been fifteen or so, but he'd never been absolutely sure that she'd meant it. Besides, he hadn't felt like getting trapped for all the rest of his life, especially by such a hardheaded female as Tamara.

He didn't feel trapped now, he just felt mortified out of ten years' growth because of the way it had come about. Likely Tam would feel queer about it all the rest of her life, if she wasn't too drunk to remember. Maybe she wouldn't remember, and she'd back out when he told her.

Back out, hell! He wasn't going to let her get away from him now. Look at her hands, rough and chapped and calloused like a man's, only small and beautifully shaped. She'd worked like a man, she'd driven herself to the limits of her endurance, and there'd never been a word of complaint out of her. She'd put up with his surliness and his ignoring of her, with his bad temper and putting her down, all of her life, and she still loved him and wanted him although only the Lord knew why.

His mother should have belabored him with her cast-iron skillet until she'd pounded some sense into his head.

Tamara's faint didn't last long. Her eyes opened as Peabody was finishing winding the bandages around the splints.

"Mark, what are you doing just standing there? Get busy making me a pair of crutches. I'm not going to be carried down the aisle, I'm going on my own two feet!"

"One foot and two crutches," Peabody grunted, suppressing a rare smile. "There, that ought to do it. Mark, I'm going to be one of your witnesses at the ceremony. I'll accept that privilege as my fee for setting the leg."

Twenty-nine

It was planned as a small wedding, with only Eli and Patience, Annabelle and Tod, Martha and Ned and Charity and the doctor. Her father couldn't be there, at the moment no one knew where he was. He'd been gone for weeks again, express riding for the Congress, relaying messages from Philadelphia to wherever he was sent. It hurt Tamara to know that her father couldn't be present to witness the happiest day of her life, but this was wartime and she knew that he would not want her to put off her marriage until he had been located and could manage to be at home. In times like these, you grasped your happiness when you could, and were grateful for it.

She did not, after all, walk down the aisle on crutches. Ned, his face almost stupefied by the importance of the occasion, gave her enough support as he walked beside her. In the absence of Charles Armitage, Ned, bursting with pride, was the one to give her away.

They were married at Old North because Tamara insisted that they be married in the church where Robert Newman had flashed his two lanterns in the steeple, for the briefest of seconds, to give warning that the British were going by sea, a warning that Mr. Revere had asked him to give so that friends on the other side of the river would have a horse ready and waiting for him when he had rowed across because he could no longer leave Boston by the heavily fortified Neck. But although outside of the family only Charity and the doctor had been invited, word had gotten around and the church was filled to its doors.

They shouldn't have been as surprised as they were. The lawyer was both well known and well respected, and everyone who knew him liked Luke and Mark equally well. Tamara herself was something of a celebrity for her work at the shipyard, as well as her potboy performance at The Temptation, and those who were not too set in the old ways held that the breaking of her leg had been the same thing as being wounded in the line of duty.

If Tam suspected that some of the people had come out of curiosity, she didn't mind. Let them gape all they wanted. Her head was high and her chin was firm, and happiness radiated from her like an aura of pure beauty. Mistress Mark Martin! As she spoke the words that united her with Mark for all the rest of their lives, she was crying inside with that happiness.

Once again Eli threw the doors of The Temptation open to females as well as for men. Charles Armitage's girl and Luke Martin's boy, that was an occasion, and one that he couldn't pass by without throwing the gol-durndest shindig it was in his power to give in honor of it. The long tables were laden with all the fare that Patience and Martha and Charity had been able to scrape up, and Mr. Potts' wife, Mistress Emily Potts, sent home to clean out her own larder to add to it, and the drinks flowed freely without a ha'penny changing hands. Even Ned got a little tipsy, he'd given his sister away, he was an Armitage, it was his right. Hadn't his father, Charles Armitage, said that he was an Armitage, that he was his son? Hadn't he fought at White Plains? Who was to say that he wasn't a man, with all of the rights and privileges that went with that estate?

If the guests at the impromptu celebration noted that Millicent Armitage had not been present at her daughter's wedding, they were all too polite to remark on it. They understood that Mistress Armitage, poor lady, was too ill to attend.

At the Armitage house, Millicent spoke sharply to Mistress Gatesby. "You will be kind enough to stop that doleful sighing! I couldn't prevent that common tavern-wench from going, she is in my husband's employ, but you are in my employ! My daughter, married to a common workman! My other daughter, married to a nameless bastard!"

Millicent rose from her chair and began to pace. She, too, had had more than a little to drink. Two daughters lost, and all because of her husband, who had refused, criminally refused, to allow them to live in London, where such things could never have happened!

She lifted her glass and drained it, and she held it so tightly that it broke in her fingers and blood fell, unheeded, to the carpet.

"I have only one daughter," she said. "You will please to remember that. Lady Lillian is my only daughter."

Mistress Gatesby sat stolidly in her chair, her fingers busy with their knitting. She made no move to fetch water and bandages to look after her mistress's cut hand. "Yes, Mistress Armitage, I'll remember."

One daughter indeed! And well she and Mistress Armitage deserved each other! If it hadn't been for young Ned, Mistress Gatesby would have wished that Millicent had been able to carry out her mad scheme to get to London right after the Battle of Concord, and never come back! Let her bleed, and it was a pity that the ice water in her veins wouldn't all run out and set poor Mr. Armitage free.

"This bottle is empty. Go and fetch me another."

The cook rose and ponderously, because of her swollen legs, left the room. She did not come back. If her mistress wanted another bottle, let her fetch it herself. Mistress Gatesby was tired and she was going to rest in the kitchen for a while before she went to her bed. There was some cold roast fowl, and she'd have a glass of ale with it, or maybe even two glasses. If she couldn't be at Tamara's wedding because Mistress Millicent had to have someone with her at all times, not because she'd been forbidden, as Millicent thought, she'd at least celebrate by herself.

"Your poor leg!" Mark protested.

"Bother my leg! It isn't my leg you're going to make love to." Tamara's arms held Mark tight, and her mouth was like fire under his.

"But I'll hurt you."

"You couldn't hurt me. Even if you do, I won't care. I've waited a long time, Mark, and I'm not going to wait any longer. This is my wedding night that I'd begun to think would never happen." Tamara drew Mark's mouth down on hers again, and Mark groaned. He'd married a wildcat, without a lick of sense in her head. Her leg . . .

He forgot her leg. The cry she gave as he entered her wasn't from pain in her leg. He tried to hold back, to be gentle, but she was writhing under him, sending his blood to boiling. Her head tossed on the pillows. She was a virgin and he'd never had a virgin before, he'd only had the girls who could be bought in the North End, and very few of them because their shoddiness had made him feel unclean. Not that Luke had lectured him on the subject. It had been Martha who'd made him feel that he was dirtying himself even though she had probably not known a thing about it. With Martha as a mother, other women had a hard time measuring up.

He had to stop, he couldn't go on inflicting such pain on the girl beneath him. She'd hate him. She wasn't very big and he was a big man, bigger even than his father. But when he attempted to withdraw, her arms tightened around him and her body arched to his even though tears were streaming down her face. She moved against him, and her mouth parted under his, and he was lost in her as he was lifted up into an oblivion of ecstasy.

They lay quiet at last, drained, spent, still pulsing with the wonder of it, and Tamara seemed to read his mind.

"Of course it hurt!" she said. "But what hurts more is thinking of all the time we wasted. But never mind. We'll make up for it. I'll make you make up for it. You owe it to me."

At The Temptation, Eli was getting tired. "Drink up," he told the few diehard guests who had not as yet realized that it was time that all honest folk should be in their beds. "Finish what you have and get on home."

It had been a long day. Patience had gone home some time ago, along with Tod and Annabelle, who was expecting again, and Charity and Ned had left with them. Except for the potboy he had hired a few weeks past, an urchin who vaguely reminded him of Tod at that age so that he had felt an impulse to get him off the streets, Eli was alone at last.

Jamie, the potboy, approached him with a folded

piece of paper in his hand, looking shamefaced and a little frightened. "I forgot to tell you because of all the excitement, but some sailor left this here earlier this afternoon while you were at the marrying, and told me to give it to you."

Eli turned it over in his hands. It was sealed with a fancy-looking crest, and Mistress Armitage's name was written on the outside. A sailor, Jamie had said. Eli frowned. It must be a letter from that Lillian who was a Lady now, but he was tired and he wanted nothing more than to go home and lay his head on his own pillow. He wouldn't admit it to Patience but he was getting too old for these shenanigans.

"Jamie, you know the Armitage house, don't you?"

" 'Course I do."

"Then be a good lad and take this here letter over there. Don't give it into anybody else's hand, mind."

Jamie was tired, too, but he set out clutching the letter in his grimed hand, further smudging its already badly smudged surface.

It took Mistress Gatesby a long time to answer the door. She had been enjoying her ale and the cold fowl and she resented being disturbed at such an hour. When Jamie saw her frowning face he didn't bother waiting around to see if she'd give him a little something for his trouble. It never entered his head that the cook wasn't the mistress of the house. Mistress Armitage was old, she had to be if her daughter had just gotten married, and the woman who had answered the door was old.

Millicent looked up, a frown of annoyance on her face, when Mistress Gatesby shuffled into the drawing room. "Here you are at last! Where have you been, you worthless woman? I don't need you now, I found a bottle of brandy in my husband's library."

"There's a letter for you, Mistress Armitage." The

cook handed it over, filled with curiosity about how a letter had happened to be delivered to her mistress, by such an unlikely messenger, at such a late hour. Mistress Gatesby should have been in her bed three hours gone, and she resented, deeply, the necessity to stay awake until Charity and Ned should return. She was an old woman and she needed her rest. She had served the Armitage family faithfully for more years than she cared to count, and she deserved better than this, the task of watching over a half-mad woman, when by rights she should have been pensioned off with enough to live on comfortably for the rest of her life. Either the wedding celebration was going to last until dawn, or Charity and Ned must have stopped in at Patience's house after they had left the party.

But maybe the letter would make her having had to stay up so late worth her while. Housebound as she was because of her infirmity, she lived for bits and pieces of gossip, anything that might enliven the monotony of her days. Not that any knowledge that came her way ever passed her lips, but having served the family for so long she considered that she had a right to know everything that concerned any one of them.

This time, however, she was fated for disappointment. Millicent accepted the soiled missive gingerly, her distaste for its smudged state evident until she saw the crest. Then she turned on Mistress Gatesby, her eyes flashing with all of her old imperiousness.

"You may leave, Mistress Gatesby. But don't go to bed. I may need you again. Mind you stay awake in case I ring for you."

Ring for her! Snorting, Mistress Gatesby left the room. As if she'd hear the bell, even if her mistress clanged it as if the house were on fire! Only the fact that there was plenty of ale left for her consumption brought her a degree of comfort. If she was to remain awake, without learning what the letter contained, then she'd at least remain awake in comfort.

Left alone, Millicent turned the letter over in her hands much as Eli had done, and then she broke the seal, her fingers trembling with eagerness. Had Sir Basil died at last, was Ned now the heir? Lillian had made no attempt to contact her since this ridiculous rebellion had started, and she could think of no other reason for her eldest daughter to write to her now. The letter had probably been months in the coming, passed from one hand to another in all the devious ways that people had to resort to to send and receive communications between England and the colonies.

A glance at the bottom line showed that the missive was indeed from Lillian. There was no mistaking the signature, written with the exaggerated flourishes she had affected since her husband had come into the title, although the body of the letter was scribbled in a cramped, erratic hand that betrayed the writer's impatience with studying penmanship, and some strong agitation as well.

Sir Basil was indeed dead. He had expired at last, countless years after his normal time should have come. And he had disinherited Ned as the son of a rebel, an enemy of the Crown.

The letter was filled with reproach. There was no use in trying to fight the will. There was no way to repair the damage wrought by Charles Armitage's treason against the King. Lillian would be obliged if her mother would refrain from attempting to get in touch with her, now or at any time in the future. Their own fortunes were at a low ebb, and having relatives in the colonies who were rebels did nothing to alleviate their situation. If this war ever ended, and when her father died, Lillian would be obliged if her mother would see to it that she received her share of the inheritance, but failing that, there was to be no more communication between them.

"It is hopeless," Lillian wrote. "My husband has made exhaustive inquiries and there is no way to reinstate Ned as my great-uncle's heir. You should have found a means to remain in London with Ned when you were here those several years ago. Now all is lost and my own expectations concerning Ned's goodwill are at naught. You have no one to blame but yourself for the ruin."

Millicent read the letter through laboriously. All the wine and brandy she had drunk that evening made the tiny, cramped handwriting blur and run together.

When she had come to the end for the second time the letter fell from her bloodless fingers to the floor. She looked down at it uncomprehendingly as a bright spot of blood stained it. Her fingers were still bleeding, and the handkerchief she had wrapped around them had loosened and fallen off.

She looked at the blood as it dripped, drop by drop, down onto the letter that spelled ruin to all her dreams. It was bright, glowing, spreading. The red seemed to spread through the room.

Like a sleepwalker, Millicent moved from the drawing room to her husband's library. There was a silver letter opener on the desk, a plain sort of ornament, the sort of thing that you'd expect Mr. Revere to make, without artistic worth but highly valued by Charles, who had the incomprehensible idea that its plainness of design enhanced its beauty.

She felt no pain as the sharp point dug at and then opened the vein in her left wrist. She stood there watching the blood spurt, and there was a half smile on her face. Charles' Turkey rug was being ruined, he'd never be able to look at it or at the letter opener again without a feeling of revulsion. He wouldn't enjoy sitting in this room again, not ever, with the memory of her dead body here to haunt him, to remind him of what he had done to her.

She was dizzy now, and she sat down on the carpet in front of the cold hearth. The front of her gown was stained, the stain spreading. So much blood, she hadn't supposed that there was that much blood in a human body.

That was her last coherent thought.

Charity knelt beside Millicent, the skirt of her dress turning crimson as she ripped a strip of cloth from her petticoat and bound up the ugly gash in Millicent's wrist as best she could. Standing over her, Ned's face was so white that she was afraid that he was going to faint.

"Ned, you must keep hold of yourself, I need you. You must go at once for Dr. Peabody, and then go to the Martins' house and tell Tamara and Mark to come at once."

There was no one else to send. Jonas was off fighting with the Army, as was Abel, the coachman, and Mistress Gatesby's legs would never carry her so far.

"Rouse Mistress Gatesby first, and then run as fast as you can. Tell Dr. Peabody that Mistress Armitage, that your mother, has met with an accident and suffered severe loss of blood."

She should have returned much earlier, but when Annabelle had developed those pains she had stayed with Patience and Martha at Eli's house to make sure that she wasn't going to lose the baby she was carrying. Annabelle was three months pregnant and the pains had been severe.

Together, the three women had gotten the suffering girl into bed and elevated her legs with pillows while

Ned had run for the doctor. Peabody had been attending another patient, called from the wedding celebration, much to his annoyance, because a foolish householder had stupidly stepped on a rake left lying tine-side up in his yard when he'd returned from another tavern the worse for drink, and had stepped on it. His heavy shoes had protected him from the deep puncture wounds that would have been an almost certain death from lockjaw, but the handle, flying up, had struck him a blow on his forehead that had laid him out and raised a lump that would be days going down, a mute and painful reminder not to leave rakes lying about if you were going to drink and walk.

So Ned had had to locate the doctor before he could fetch him to tend Annabelle, and still Charity had stayed on, wanting to be sure that there would not be a tragedy. Ned, the worse for the tippling he'd done, had fallen asleep in a chair in the parlor while he'd waited to escort Charity home, convinced that weddings weren't all they were cracked up to be if they made you feel as queasy as he felt.

It had taken Charity a few more minutes to rouse Ned enough to make sure he could walk, and his groans had been a good deal louder than Annabelle's stifled ones before the cramping had eased and she had fallen asleep, assured by Peabody that the danger had passed. Charity had sympathized with Ned but her main emotion had been one of profound relief that Annabelle was not going to lose this new infant. Not only would Annabelle's heart have been broken and Tod bitterly disappointed, but also it would have been one more blow to Charles Armitage, who had had enough grief already to last him a lifetime.

Charity's heart twisted whenever she thought of Charles, which was almost constantly. She loved him, and the fact that nothing, not even one more casual night together, could come of it did nothing to make her love waver. She had given him comfort once; now even that was denied her.

She waited now, her fingers on Millicent's pulse. It was so weak that she had little hope that Dr. Peabody could save her. A tragic end to a marriage that had been tragic from its inception, and there was nothing she could do to help. This time she could not even offer the solace of her body.

They'd left Tamara alone with her mother in the bedchamber where she had been carried. There was no hope. Millicent was dying. But her eyes had opened, and she seemed to be rational.

Tamara had to know. She could not live out the rest of her life without knowing. She leaned close to her mother. "Mother, did you know that George Hartgrave tried to kill me the last time he visited Grace Gammage? Tell me, did you know?"

It was cruel and she would probably hate herself for tormenting a dying woman, but still she had to know.

Millicent's eyes darkened, and an expression of pain flickered on her bloodless face.

"No, no." The words were so weak that Tamara had to lean even closer to hear them. "Not you, Tamara! It was Agnes he killed. I always suspected it. But not you! He wouldn't have, even he wouldn't have dared. You're my daughter, I wouldn't have allowed it, not even for him."

She hadn't known. There was the ring of truth in her voice, the look of truth in her fast-glazing eyes. Tamara's breath came in a long, gulping sigh that hurt her throat.

Peabody had come back into the room. "Come away, Tamara. There's nothing more you can do here."

This was her wedding night, Tamara thought dully as Mark's arms enclosed her. His touch broke her, and she wept, long and bitterly, while he held her close.

Thirty

They were going to fight at last, a real fight, maybe throw a spoke in General Clinton's wheel as he tried to get his Army and his supply trains to New York. Tim wished that they were going after the main Army, he was tired of this war, and he wanted to get it over with.

Sitting at Valley Forge all the whole freezing winter had been enough to drive a man crazy. Nothing to do but drill when the cold was enough to freeze a man's toes off, and hope that more supplies would get through. Clothing, anything to put on to fight the cold, something to eat, enough to eat for once so that your belly wouldn't go on rumbling after you'd eaten it.

But they were going to fight now, and it wasn't cold, not by a damned sight it wasn't, it was hot, hot enough to melt the meat right off your bones and to slick your hands with sweat so they could hardly hold onto the musket. Sweat ran down into your eyes so you couldn't see. Blasted New Jersey marshlands, how anybody could live hereabouts was more than Tim Martin could fathom.

He'd give his soul for a breath of clean, fresh, salt-tanged Massachusetts air, even if his mother would still wash his mouth out with her strongest lye soap for thinking it much less saying it. A man couldn't breathe this air, it was thick, thick and hot and wet so you strangled on it and when it got to your lungs it didn't do much good, you were still gasping like a fish out of water.

Whoever'd heard of a place called Monmouth Court House anyway? A hamlet somewhere in New Jersey, a speck on the map, someplace on the outskirts of hell because hell itself couldn't be much hotter than this place, or any steamier.

On the march from Valley Forge, men had dropped from heat exhaustion and some of them had died but Tim was still alive and so was John, right up there ahead of him, encouraging the falterers just like he'd encouraged men driven desperate by cold and hunger and boredom and the general hopelessness, all last winter. Tim, shamed by his older brother's steadfastness, had tried to do his share in keeping spirits up. His way had been taken out in clowning, in trying to raise a laugh, while John had talked to them as though he were their big brother as well as his, and put enough heart into some of them so that they didn't desert like so many had done, or just walk out when their enlistments were up.

Tim still wasn't sure whether the ones who'd walked out hadn't been the smart ones. At least they weren't in this hellhole, dying of the heat while they waited to be butchered by the Queen's Rangers, the crack outfit of the whole danged British Army.

But they were going to fight, and something would be decided one way or another, and that was better than doing nothing. He owed those red-coated bastards advancing on them something—a few musket balls for White Plains, for Valley Forge, for all the days and weeks and months of retreating, of going cold and hungry, and of sitting on his tail wondering what the hell he was doing here anyway if the general wasn't going to fight.

Crossing the Delaware River had been all right, Tim had been in on that the same as John, they'd at least given the lobsterbacks something to think about even if they had near froze doing it, instead of feasting on roast goose at home the way they should have been on Christmas. But Valley Forge hadn't been all right, and Tim was getting almighty sick of the Army.

Look at John up there ahead. John wasn't thinking thoughts like that. John was thinking that it was a blamed-fool mistake on the general's part to have put Charles Lee in command of this expedition to snip the tail off of Clinton's supply train. There wasn't a man around him who didn't think it was a mistake; there was one consolation, though, and it was a big one: Tony Wayne was here, too, and if anybody'd fight, he was the man.

"They're coming!"

It was the truth; they were coming. Cavalry, by God! They were coming at them with cavalry, and Tim felt bile rise in his throat. Getting run over by a dozen galloping, trampling horses, with their riders slashing at him with sabers, wasn't the most pleasant thought in the world.

No time to think about that now. They were here and Wayne was bellowing for them to use bayonets after they'd shot their balls. Tim aimed and fired, but he couldn't tell if he'd hit anything. The mist and the smoke from hundreds of muskets couldn't be seen through. The man beside him fell, his head severed by a swinging saber, and Tim wished that he had time to stop and vomit, but he didn't. Fighting for his life, there wasn't any time to be sick.

A man went down ahead of him, gutted by a bayonet that a Ranger whose horse had been shot from under him had grabbed from a fallen rebel. Tim was running forward at the time and he didn't have time to check his run and the man's guts were spilling out, wrapping around his own legs, his own hands, he was tangled in them. His attention was distracted for a split second as he saw a woman off to the left of him taking the place of a man who had fallen by the cannon he was tending, and crazily, her name popped into his mind, Mary Ludwig Hayes McCauley, one of the camp followers who'd come with her husband. Molly, the men called her.

He cursed mindlessly. What kind of a war was this, with women fighting alongside their men? It wasn't right. . . .

And then he saw who it was who was dumping his intestines all over him, and he began to scream.

"John, oh God, John, get up, John!"

John looked at him, his eyes already glazing. Tim held him in his arms, the blood and intestines all over him, and his screaming went on and on, endlessly, blotting out everything else in the world.

He was screaming again. He realized it, vaguely, and he didn't care, except that it hurt his throat.

They'd made him leave John where he'd fallen. They'd dragged him away, and he didn't even know if John had ever been buried or if he'd rotted there on the wet ground, trampled by horses, by men, into a thing unrecognizable as a human being before it rotted.

He'd heard that General Washington himself had galloped up, after that fool Lee had ordered a retreat, and turned the men and they'd gone on and made a victory of sorts out of what had been turning into a debacle. He'd heard that Mad Tony Wayne had wanted Lee strung up to the nearest tree, that Wayne had been livid, that Wayne would have shot Lee down himself if he hadn't been prevented but Tim didn't know if that were true or not. He couldn't even remember where he'd heard it, who had told him. It didn't matter anyway. When he got like this, when he'd had too much to drink and his mind could no longer hold his memories at bay, the only thing that mattered was that John was out there somewhere in that damned New Jersey swamp with his guts spilled out and his body trampled into the wet, teeming ground.

"Hush, Tim. It's all right. Let me take you home."

"Don't want to go home." Martha and Tam were at home, and Tam was seven months pregnant and when he got like this it upset them. He lifted his head from the table where it had fallen when he'd dozed off from too much rum, and realized that he was still at The Temptation. His bleary eyes made out that everyone else had gone and only Eli and Charity were there.

"Dang it, Charity, what're we goin' to do with him?" Eli wiped his sleeve across his forehead. It gave him the cold chills when Tim started in like this. Tim would come in and sit with the other men and he'd seem to be all right except that he was so quiet, he who'd never been quiet in his life. He'd drink too much even when they tried to persuade him that he'd had enough. If they refused to serve him he'd become abusive and sometimes even violent, and have to be held down until he either came to his senses, or passed out.

Eli didn't know which was worse: Tim trying to smash up everything in the place, or Tim drinking quietly, never saying a word, until he fell asleep and came out of it screaming. Likely if he didn't get over these spells he'd have to be locked up and that would just about kill Martha. It was bad enough she'd lost one son, without losing her youngest. Quiet, dependable John had gone down honorably; having a madman locked up where he couldn't harm himself or anyone else would be a deal worse. His heart ached for the Martins. His and Patience's Tod, with his peg leg, seemed like small potatoes compared to the things that had happened to Luke and Martha.

Charity had come back to The Temptation after Mistress Armitage had died, a suicide after reading that letter she'd gotten from Lillian over there in England. As disliked as Millicent had been, nearly the whole of Boston had turned out for her funeral, and not out of curiosity either, but out of respect for Charles Armitage.

But there was nothing more for Charity to do at the Armitage house now that Ned had taken it on himself to run off to the Army again. The lad had gone in the middle of the night, only this time it'd been in the summer, not in a blizzard, soon after Tim had been brought home with a saber slash across his forehead and another down his right side that had nearly done for him. One of those hell-spawned Queen's Rangers had got him while he'd been holding John's body in his arms and it was God's own mercy that he hadn't died along with John on the spot. Or was it? If Tim was going to be like this all the rest of his life maybe it would've been just as well if he'd died.

That was no way to think. Tim'd been almighty fond of John, and between seeing his brother die the way he had, and his own wounds, it was no wonder he went off the deep end sometimes. Anyway, he'd stopped his screaming now and Eli hoped he wouldn't start it up again so's they'd have to fetch Peabody to dose him with laudanum before they dared to take him on home. He was too much for Martha to handle when he was like this, even with Tamara's help, and the two women were alone again mostly because Mark had gone back to driving supply wagons for the Army and he didn't get home too often.

It was a good thing Tam had gotten pregnant before Mark had gone. If that young scamp Ned went and got hisself kilt in the war Charles would need more than the fine boy Annabelle had presented them with, and her mite of a girl, to make up for it. Spittin' image of Charles young Charles was, but it'ud be nice if Tam had a boy too. There was no such thing as too many boys in a family.

"Come along, Tim. I'll walk home with you." Charity put her hand on Tim's arm and helped him to his feet.

A lopsided grin twisted Tim's face. "Haven't you got that backward? I'll walk you home. It's dark enough so my face won't scare you."

"Tim, you stop that! You aren't the only man in the world with a scar. Besides, it's fading."

"Sure it is. By next Pope's Day I'll be able to march in the parade without a mask and they'll think I'm wearing one but maybe it won't be bad enough to scare the younger fellers into fits."

"You're alive. You still have most of your family. Nobody cares that your face is scarred."

"I suppose you'd marry me, looking like this." There was bitterness in Tim's voice, reflected in the twist of his mouth. Pretty little Naomi Fairchild, the girl he'd been walking out with ever since they'd been youngsters, had burst into tears and had hysterics the first time she'd seen Tim's face. Charity wished she could shake the girl's teeth loose. Even with the shortage of men now that so many of them were away with the Army, Naomi hadn't come to see Tim the second time, and it had cut him deep.

"Of course I would, if I wasn't years too old for you. I happen to like your face."

Eli cocked a worried eye at them as they started to leave The Temptation. "Sure you'll be all right?" he asked Tim.

"He'll be fine," Charity answered for him. "The fresh air will do him good." But once on the street, Tim held back, and there was enough light from the stars for Charity to see the stubborn look on his face.

"I don't want to go home. Mother wants to fuss over me but she won't let herself, and Tam tries to act like nothing's changed. They'll wonder if I've had too much to drink again but they won't ask."

"They'll be in bed. It's late."

"Mother'll wake up and get up to ask me if I want something to eat. It's her way of being tactful while she checks to see what condition I'm in."

"You don't eat enough. You're as thin as a rake."

"After Valley Forge, being thin's a habit." Once again, bitterness edged Tim's voice, although he was making an effort to treat it lightly.

Charity hesitated, and then made up her mind.

"Come along home with me, then. There's some cold ham." She still lived and slept at the Armitage house, even though she'd gone back to work at The Temptation. Now that Mistress Gatesby was having more and more trouble moving around, it was better to have someone there nights, and besides, Charles wanted Charity on the spot in case Ned were wounded again and carted home. It gave him peace of mind to know that Charity was in his house, ready and capable of handling any emergency.

"And rum?" Tim asked hopefully.

"Cider. But not too much, you don't want to drink yourself asleep again."

They walked in silence now, toward the Armitage house. Tim's hands were thrust into his pockets and his shoulders were slumped. Charity could feel his bitter loneliness like a palpable thing.

"I hear that you're working at the shipyard. Do you like the work?" She had to break the silence, get his mind off whatever brooding thoughts they were on.

"It's all right. Tam kept after Mr. Potts till he gave me a chance against his better judgment. He watches me like a hawk, just waiting for me to have a crazy spell. I think he's disappointed that it hasn't happened yet, at least during working hours."

"You're too suspicious of people. He's probably only watching to make sure you don't overdo. You don't have your full strength back yet."

"I'm crazy," Tim said. "Everybody knows it. I'm as mad as a hatter."

Charity put her hand on his arm. "Don't say that. It isn't true. You're young and strong and you'll get over having these attacks. You have to give it time."

"Will time bring John back? Will time put his insides back where they belong, pick up his trampled, rotted carcass from the mire, give him back to us?"

Charity's hand tightened on his arm and she urged him forward. His voice was rising and she was afraid he might go into one of his attacks right here on the street, and she couldn't let that happen. The watch might come along and he might end up locked in Boston's jail all night, a place Charity wouldn't wish on her worst enemy let alone a young man she was as fond of as she was of Tim.

Thank heavens, the house was directly in front of them now. There was no light showing, Mistress Gatesby would have gone to bed hours ago. It was a blessing that the housekeeper slept so soundly that she wouldn't hear Tim's ravings even if he went off the deep end again tonight in spite of everything she could do.

She took him into the library because that was the room where she herself felt most at home even though Millicent Armitage had killed herself there. The other rooms were too elegantly ornate and reminded her too sharply of the woman who had chosen their furnishings. But the library seemed to hold something of Charles' presence, a comforting feeling that she wouldn't have admitted to anyone except herself and God.

Tim slumped in Charles' favorite chair, his hands over his eyes to shield them from the candle Charity lighted and set on the mantel. He still hadn't stirred when she came back from the kitchen with a plate of bread and ham and a glass of cider.

Tim took his hand away from his eyes and when he saw the cider his mouth curved in a parody of a smile. "Charity, if I drank Eli's tavern dry it wouldn't do me any good." His face looked ashen in the light of the candle, and the scar on his forehead stood out in livid relief.

"Then eat."

He pushed the plate aside. Charity saw that his eyes were haunted with more than the memory of John's death. They were haunted with the terror of going mad.

Once before she had been confronted with a man who had been in the depth of despair. She had known what to do then, and had done it instinctively, and just as instinctively she knelt beside Tim's chair and put her arms around him and held him close.

He clung to her like a child, like a little boy might cling to his mother during a thunderstorm. "Hush, hush," Charity murmured, her lips on his forehead.

His arms were around her now, strong with intensity. "Charity, help me! For the love of God help me!" His hand went to her breast, fumbling, searching. He was like a man going down in the water for the third time, clinging to the only safety available.

"I'm ugly. I'm crazy and ugly, you wouldn't want me, no woman could want me." His voice was muffled but there was no mistaking its anguish.

She held him in her arms, stroking his hair back from his forehead, her fingers gentle on the scars. Tim was young, hardly more than a boy, and he was hurt, and he needed someone and she was the only one who could help him. He wouldn't go home while he was feeling like this, he always avoided going home when these black moods were on him.

She went on holding him, rocking him a little, crooning to him as if he were a little boy who had been hurt and needed his mother's comfort. When he was quieter, she urged him to his feet and led him, still gently, to the room she had occupied ever since she had come to stay in this house. She put him into her bed, and then she lay down beside him still fully clothed, and held him in her arms again until he relaxed and she felt the stiffness leave his body and his trembling abate.

She was startled when he kissed her, hungrily, eagerly, driven by the desperate need inside of him. Oh, God, what should she do? He wanted her, he needed her, and if she could give him ease and comfort by the simple gift of her body, would it be wrong to do it? But in spite of her yearning compassion for him she stiffened, remembering Charles and the night she'd given herself to him, freely, with her whole heart, and asking nothing in return.

He pushed her away from him with such sudden violence that it shocked her, and then he was on his feet. "No! I don't want your pity, I don't want any woman's pity! Thank you for trying to help me, but you can't, no one can!"

He'd rushed from the room and down the stairs before she could get on her own feet and catch up with him. "Stay here! Don't follow me, I'll be all right, I'm going home. Stay here, I say!"

She wanted to follow him, to make sure he got home all right, but she didn't dare. It would only make him feel that she thought he wasn't capable of taking care of himself.

She slept poorly, and wondered in the morning if she should stop in at the Martins' to make sure that Tim was all right before she went on to The Temptation.

On second thought she decided against it. Tim would be embarrassed to see her after last night, and he wouldn't want his mother and Tam to know that he'd had another of his bad times. Sighing, she looked in on Mistress Gatesby, who was just beginning to stir, built up the fire in the kitchen, and set water to boiling for their breakfast porridge and the herb tea that was what they drank these days. She didn't mind for herself, but it was a pity that Mistress Gatesby, at her age and poor health, could no longer have one of the greatest pleasures left to her, a cup of genuine tea.

The awkwardly moving woman noticed nothing unusual about her this morning, but rambled on in her garrulous way as she always did, wanting only to extract every crumb of gossip that might have come the younger woman's way at The Temptation. Charity obliged her, concealing her impatience. She always remembered to store away any tidbits that might interest the ailing woman.

The breakfast dishes washed and the house dusted, Charity left for The Temptation, still worried, unreasonably worried, she tried to tell herself, about Tim.

It was late afternoon before she learned that Tim had neither returned home that morning, nor shown up for his day's work at the shipyard. Patience had gone to visit Martha, and she came bustling in, fanning herself after her unusually rapid walk to her husband's tavern, to demand if Eli or Charity had any inkling of where Tim might be.

"Martha and Tam are practically beside themselves. Samuel Potts sent around to ask if Tim was ailing when he didn't show up this morning, and nobody can find hide nor hair of the boy. It's worrisome, having him missing, the state he's in."

Eli looked at Charity, and she flushed, but she met his eyes without flinching. "He stayed very late at the Armitage house. He wasn't feeling well, so I took him there rather than have Martha and Tam worried. But I have no idea where he might have gone after he left me."

If Eli suspected how late Tim had stayed with her, he gave no indication of it, and it would never have entered Patience's moral head that anything more than Charity had said might be involved.

"We haven't laid eyes on him today, Patience. I'll set the men who come in here to lookin' around, and you'd best stop in at Mr. Armitage's office and tell Tod. We'd better set wheels turnin' to find him, for Martha and Tam's peace of mind, but likely as not he's all right, just holed up somewhere with someone he knows."

"That's what I told Martha, but she's worried all the same and I can't blame her. It isn't like he's normal yet, he still has a long way to go. You'd better find him, Eli Bates, that's all I have to say!" Patience was so agitated that she drew herself a mug of cider and downed half of it before she realized what she was doing. "Ugh! How a body can drink this abomination is more than I can understand! I'd as lief drink vinegar!" With that, she was gone, on her way as fast as she could walk to tell Tod that Tim was nowhere to be found. Eli would try to find him, but Tod was smart, he'd be the one to figure out where the boy might have gotten to.

The next eight days were agonizing not only for Martha and Tamara, but for Charity as well. Had what she'd done had anything to do with Tim's disappearance? All of Boston had been combed, and no trace of him had been found. Had he disappeared because he was afraid that she'd make some claim on him, or because he was ashamed that she'd let him make love to her, thinking she'd done it out of pity?

But he'd know better than that, he must know better than that! Only with Tim's mind as twisted as it was from the experiences he'd gone through, how could she or anyone else be sure of what he might be thinking?

No one mentioned it, not even Eli, who was usually so outspoken, or Patience, who worried out loud, but Charity knew that all of them, and especially Martha and Tam, were afraid that Tim had done away with himself, thrown himself in the river or the harbor. But no body was washed up, no body was found either in the water or out of it. All they could do was to cling to the hope that if his body hadn't been found, he must still be alive.

It was on the morning of the ninth day that a man came into the tavern and asked for Charity. He was unshaven and his clothing was threadbare, and there was a filthy bandage around his right forearm. Half starved, too, from the way he eyed the food on another patron's plate and swallowed before he averted his eyes.

"Let me get you something to eat and drink, and then I'll look at your arm. It needs a clean bandage, at least."

"Thankee kindly, ma'am. I'll be obliged. I have something for you, a young feller asked me to bring it along since I was comin' this way anyways. Here it be."

It was a piece of paper, rumpled and smudged but still all in one piece. Charity had never seen Tim's handwriting but she had a sinking feeling in the pit of her stomach that it was from him, and the same feeling that it wasn't going to be good news.

Her fingers shook as she spread out the paper, blotted and spattered from having been written with a quill that needed sharpening. Her intuition had been right. Tim's name was scrawled at the bottom of the page.

"Dear Charity: I'm going back to the fighting. If I'm well enough to work in the shipyard I'm well enough to carry a musket, and I owe the redcoats something for John. Thank you for what you did for me, and for being so kind, but I'm no good for any woman and I never will be. Please tell my mother and Matt and Tam that I'm all right and if they don't see me when this war is over it'll be because I've headed on West. I can't face being a burden to them or to anyone, even you, so it's better that I don't ever come back to Boston where they'd feel obliged to look after me. Don't show anyone this letter, just tell them you heard that I've gone back to the fighting."

Silently, a lump in her throat, Charity handed the letter to Eli. He had to hold it at arm's length to make it out. At his age, his eyesight couldn't see things clearly at close range, but he could make out a leaf on a tree a quarter of a mile away.

"I'll be dad-burned! Back to the fightin'! It's what I was afeared of, Charity. You go ahead and burn up this letter. We'll tell Martha we heard it by word of mouth."

Quietly, without speaking, she carried the letter to

the kitchen and consigned it to the fire, and then waited for the stranger to finish wolfing down the huge plate of mutton and beans that Eli had placed in front of him, refusing payment. The man didn't have so much as a shilling in his pocket anyway, Charity could tell that without asking. When he'd sopped up the last trace of gravy with his bread, she took him to the kitchen and cleaned and rebandaged his arm. And before full noon he was gone, almost tearfully grateful because Eli had managed to find a ride for him on a farm cart as far as the farmer was going.

Charity didn't sleep again that night, but sat beside her window, open to the soft summer air, until nearly dawn. She'd prayed for Tim, and cried for him, and now there was nothing she could do but hope that his bitterness and near madness wouldn't make him hurl himself into the face of the enemy and throw his life away.

She knew that it was unlikely that she, or anyone else in Boston, would ever see him again, even if he managed to come out of the fighting alive. If she could have, she would have given her own life to help him, but now it was in the hands of God.

Charity looked up to see who had entered the tavern and her whole body stiffened and it took all her effort to keep her face calm, with no more than a welcoming smile.

"Mr. Armitage, when did you get into town?"

"Just now, Charity. I haven't even been home." The expression in his eyes told her that he had no desire to go home to his empty house. His wife dead, Annabelle and Tamara married and gone, Lillian in England, and Ned somewhere with Washington's Army.

I could have him again, Charity thought. I could take up where we left off, after that one time. There's no wife standing between us now. And we could go on like that for the rest of our lives, or until he finds another woman he wants to marry.

The thought was like a knife in her breast. She couldn't bear it if he found another woman, one of a station for him to marry, to introduce proudly as his wife, a woman who could give him more children that he could be proud of, not a tavern wench's children.

But what if he should fall in love with her, what if it should happen? What if he actually asked her to marry him?

She knew that it was impossible, more impossible for her than it would be for him. She was what she was, a tavern woman. A woman who had been used, ruined, before they had met, a woman who was so far beneath him that to marry him would be to do him an irreparable hurt.

His mistress, then. But here again she felt the knife in her heart. That would never be enough for her, and what if she bore him a child? Could she bear to bring a bastard into the world, even though she knew that Charles would see to its welfare? And even if she could bear it, could he? He wasn't the kind of man who sired bastards, it would hurt him more than it would hurt her.

"Lord, but I'm tired," Charles said. He sat down wearily and smiled at her, a smile that proved how tired he was, how lonesome, how vulnerable.

She made his flip and brought it to him without being asked. To her relief, Eli entered the tavern as she was serving him. She could leave now.

"I hope I'll see you again soon, Mr. Armitage. I'm going over to Martha's now," Charity said. "Did you know that Tim went back to the Army? Eli will tell you about it."

Eli stared after her as she left, but he didn't say

anything to keep her from leaving. He'd suspected, no, he'd known, for a long time, that Charity was in love with Charles Armitage, and Eli's heart was troubled for her. Shaking his head, he sat down opposite Charles while he nursed his flip, the empty feeling in the just-returned man alive and aching inside of him. The disappointment he felt because Charity had left as soon as he'd come in startled him, as though he had taken a hard, unexpected blow in the pit of his stomach.

"Eli, I'm getting old," Charles said.

Eli grunted. "Ain't we all. How's that boy of yours? You heard anything of him recent?"

"He's been made an orderly. I have an idea that he doesn't like it but I'm just as satisfied to have him out of the fighting as much as possible. I'd like to see him come back from this war alive."

"You ever hear any more of George Hartgrave?"

"Not a thing. I know he didn't die. Likely he's joined up with his regiment again, unless he's been killed for trying an ambush on someone else, and I haven't heard of any such incident."

"Small loss, if it happened." Eli grunted again. "When's that new grandchild of yours going to git hisself born?"

"Soon now, I believe. You seem very sure that it will be a boy."

"Tam wouldn't produce a girl first, not her! It'll be a boy." Eli was convinced of it, so much so that he drew himself a mug of cider to drink to it before he told Charles about Tim Martin having run off without telling anyone to join up again. The two friends, so different in station, sat drinking in companionable silence, neither of them mentioning how much they wished that Luke could be with them, because it wasn't necessary.

Thirty-one

Hiram Weatherby pushed his plate aside and propped his elbows on the farmhouse table and looked his brother-in-law straight in the eye. Hiram was a hard man, as tough as hickory, already on his third wife, his first two having died from "natural causes" brought on by overwork and constant childbearing. Not one of the children from those first two marriages had survived, but now Dorcas, a sturdy twenty-two-year old woman with a plain face and hands as big and capable as a man's, was expecting her first and it bade fair to be a healthy one and please God, a boy.

Three boys in the church yard, and four daughters, and all Hiram had to show for his years of labor was this farm and his sister's two children, whom he had taken in when Ann had died and Henry was off with the Army, and if anyone was to ask Hiram it was too bad that Henry hadn't stayed there because he was no farmer and never would be, any more than he was any good at anything except bragging about how he was going to get even with anyone who had ever done him dirt.

That and his exploits in the Army, but Hiram knew that Henry had walked off from Valley Forge as soon as his enlistment had been up and he'd spent his last weeks there in the stockade because he'd been caught pilfering food. It was Mark Martin who'd caught him at it, when he'd brought a supply wagon in clear at the end of the winter, his first trip since he'd been hurt at White Plains, and finally been strong enough to quit the shipyard and get back to work for the Army.

Henry's children didn't know it and Hiram wouldn't be the one to tell them, but Henry had been whipped for that bit of business; he still bore the marks of the stripes on his back. Henry wasn't one to make himself well liked and the man who'd been assigned to do the whipping had laid on heavy, breaking the skin in more than one place.

Henry's son now, he bade to turn out all right. He took after the Weatherby side of the family, Jacob did, and he'd make a farmer when he was full grown and Hiram was glad for his help. The girl, Ruth, was a spindly thing and not much for looks but she pulled her weight, such as it was, helping Dorcas with the salad garden and the churning, tending the fowl and the cows, and she was a good hand at the spinning wheel for all that she was as quiet and downtrodden-looking as her mother had been after Henry'd had her for a few years. Hiram didn't begrudge Ruth her keep any more than he begrudged Jacob, but Henry Atkins was another thing altogether. Henry Atkins, to put it bluntly, wasn't worth his salt.

Hiram had given him a fair trial. Kin was kin and you couldn't turn your brother-in-law away when he came back from the Army and had no place to go because his house had been sold out from under him for debt and he couldn't get work. But it hadn't worked out. Even Jacob and Ruth were ashamed of their father; Ruth looked ashamed when Henry reached for everything in sight on the table and ate as if he'd done a full day's work when he'd hardly turned a lick, and Jacob looked pained and Dorcas looked downright angry.

"The fact is that I can't use you any longer. There isn't enough work on this place to keep us all busy. You'd best get yourself back to Boston and see if you can't scare up some odd jobs there, enough to keep you, anyways. If you'd lay off the drink you'd have a better chance."

Henry glowered, his back up, the stubble on his face bristling with indignation as his face turned red with anger.

"What drink? It's damned little spirits I see around here, it's all I can do to talk you out of a mug of second-rate cider after a hard day's work in the fields! You've cheated me, Hiram, and you know it! Makin' me work for my keep and never a bit of hard cash to go with it, and now you talk of turnin' me out! There ain't any work in Boston and you know it, and there won't be till this war is over one way or the other. Nobody's buildin', nobody's got any money."

"You'll have to find something. I can't go on keeping you. The children now, they're all right. I'll go on keeping them as long as necessary. They're my sister's children and they'd be welcome here even if they weren't of an age to be useful. Likely Ruth'll be getting married one of these days, and Jacob pulls his weight."

Across the table, Dorcas looked spitefully satisfied. Henry knew that the bitch couldn't wait to get shut of him. Selfish, she was, right down to the core, wanted it all for herself and her own children. All that time he'd spent in the Army, fighting so's the British wouldn't overrun the country and take this farm away from Hiram, cut no ice with her. She just plain didn't like him, it was her doing that Hiram was telling him he had to go.

"Mr. Potts is looking for help," Dorcas said. There

was a smug look on her face. She knew perfectly well that Lemuel Potts wouldn't take him on, she was just rubbing salt in his wounds. "I heard it from Mistress Ormond only last week." She helped herself to another piece of apple pie, without offering him another. "There's work for them as don't mind working."

"Now you see here, I work! I work damned hard! All day in the fields, gettin' the hay in, that's hard work!"

"Jacob scythed twice as much as you did without raising a sweat," Hiram said flatly. "It's settled, Henry. I'm telling you to leave."

"Jacob, Ruth, you goin' to stand for this? You goin' to stand for your pa bein' put out?"

Jacob and Ruth kept their eyes on their plates and their mouths shut. They were against him too. It was their mother's doing, she'd turned them against him while they were still little, always complaining that there wasn't enough food in the house and insinuating that he spent too much time in the taverns.

A sniveling woman Ann had been, sniveling and sickly and no help to a man, and then she'd gone and died on him whilst he'd been away fighting. He'd come back to find his children with Hiram here instead of out working the way they should have been, to keep their house for him and make him comfortable. Instead of coming home to a happy, secure family he'd had to come begging, hat in hand, to Hiram, and it hadn't set well with him.

How much fighting had Hiram done? Stayed safe to home all these years because he'd hurt his leg at Breed's Hill and it was stiff and he claimed he couldn't march. Had the gall to claim that the Army needed the food he grew as much as it needed men.

A thought crossed his mind, a possible reprieve. "Jacob here's most of an age to join up with the Army.

How're you goin' to git along without me when he goes? Answer me that!"

"Jacob's only thirteen. It'll be a spell yet before he goes, and maybe the war'll be over by then. Ruth'll likely wed one of the Smith boys up North a ways, the middle one's got his eye on her and he'll be glad enough to come in here to live and help out until he can set up on his own."

"Another cripple! His leg's as bad as yours!"

"There isn't anything the matter with *your* legs and he'll still outwork you six to the dozen." Hiram was tired of this fruitless discussion. "So you can get on your two good legs first thing in the morning and take yourself away from here."

"Folks ain't goin' to take kindly to your puttin' me out!" The bluff was an empty one. Henry was licked and he knew it. It had been a sad day for him when he'd decided that Ann would make him a good match, coming from a substantial family and being pretty in a wishy-washy way. How was he to have known then that she hadn't inherited her father's and her brother's stamina, that she'd quit childbearing after only two children, the first a girl as piddling as she was and the boy not coming along until seven years later? There were half a dozen miscarriages in between, and Ann was forever sniveling and whining and nagging. No wonder he'd turned to drink for solace, any man would have, with the kind of luck Henry'd had.

"I can let you have a few shillings. It'll have to last you till you can find work," Hiram said, finality in his tone.

They didn't even say good-bye to him in the morning, neither Jacob nor Ruth. Jacob made himself scarce before daylight so he wouldn't have to face him, and Ruth's pale face was averted as she went upstairs to make the beds as soon as breakfast was over. Hiram handed Henry half a dozen paper notes, not worth the paper they were printed on likely, none of that scrip was, hard money was the only thing that'd buy anything but there wasn't any use asking for hard money because even if Hiram had any he wouldn't give it to him. Dorcas, busy at the fireplace, looked over her shoulder with that smug, satisfied expression on her face as Henry left. It made the bile rise in his throat.

"Don't go spending it all in the first tavern you come to," Hiram warned Henry as he shouldered his kerchief of possessions and stepped through the door. "There won't be any more where that came from."

"Bastard!"

Hiram's jaw clamped shut, and he didn't answer. He'd done his duty and more; no other man would have carried that worthless excuse for a man as long as he had. He turned back into the house and Dorcas straightened up from the fireplace, her pregnancy showing.

"Well, we're shut of him at last. Don't you go letting him come back, Hiram."

"I won't. You know something, Dorcas? When I think of how many good men have been killed in this war, and Henry came back without a scratch, it makes me sick."

"Jacob and Ruth are all right, though. They're good young'uns. I'll think of something special for supper tonight, they'll be feeling bad, ashamed of their father and all."

"No," Lemuel Potts said.

"But you need men. And I'm a danged good carpenter, you know that yourself." Coming to Potts had been a last resort, he'd known it wouldn't do any good, but now that he was here he might as well put up an argument.

"I don't care how good you are when you're sober. You aren't sober enough, often enough, to make it worth my while putting you on. Go look someplace else, or starve, it's all the same to me."

Henry squinted against the sun and anger ate in him like acid when he thought how he'd heard that Potts had taken on Tim Martin, and everybody knew, it was the talk of all this part of the colony, that Tim was as mad as a hatter, driven plumb crazy by seeing his brother killed the way he had. There it was again, there was always work for the Martins, but none for him. It had started way back when Peters had fired him and put Luke Martin in his place, he hadn't had a lick of decent luck since then. If it wasn't for Luke he'd have kept his job with Peters and still be welcome there. Those Martins had been the bane of his life and they were still going strong, getting all the breaks.

It was true that the middle boy had been killed at Monmouth, but Mark was all right now, driving wagons for the Army and married right into the damned aristocracy. He was only a carpenter and the son of a carpenter and he had wed that snippy one, that Tamara, had a baby boy and likely Armitage would set them up in style as soon as the war was over, if the rebels won.

Luke Martin and Charles Armitage and Eli Bates, Henry hated them all but he hated the Martins the most. He could still feel those stripes on his back that Mark had got him, still hear the angry shouts and the threats of the hungry men at Valley Forge when Mark'd caught him sneaking a little something from the supply wagon, just enough to keep life in his body. He wasn't the only one who'd cheated a little, he'd just had the bad luck to get caught and it was Mark who had caught him and he might've had enough human charity to overlook it but he hadn't. Those damn Martins—it was enough to make a man sick right through to his soul.

Henry said a word to Lemuel Potts that made Lemuel's face turn as red as a fresh-boiled lobster, and turned on his heel and left the shipyard. He spent the rest of the day in a tavern, and he was still there when he was asked to leave that night because the owner wanted to lock up and go home.

He spent the night curled up in a shed that a householder had neglected to lock, with only some old sacks for a bed and the drink roiling sourly in his stomach and making him sick but making him want another drink even more. He hated his brother-in-law and he hated Dorcas and he hated his children for turning against him, but the Martins and Charles Armitage were at the head of the list.

It was the worst luck in his life that he'd missed the chance to shoot Luke in the back whilst the fighting had been going on back there at White Plains. He'd almost got him but the man next to him had stumbled over a clump of grass and knocked into him and spoiled his aim. After that Luke'd been kept mostly at hauling, and so another chance hadn't presented itself. Now Luke was God knew where and no way to pay him back for all the hurt he'd done him.

No way, no way. Pay him back, pay him back. But how?

It came to him after he was sick. It messed up the sacks he was sleeping on but his excitement at the idea that had come to him made such a trifling thing of no importance. He only kicked the sacks aside and sat, chin propped on his bony knees, mulling over his plans, discarding this, replacing it with something better, until it all fell into place.

Luke Martin and Charles Armitage were going to suffer, and Mark, and the others through them. All of them tied in together, they were, Luke and Mark and the lawyer and Eli, and all of them were going to suffer and then he'd make tracks away from Boston and never come back.

He'd head South, where the land and the climate were softer and when his pockets were empty he wouldn't suffer so much having to sleep wherever he found himself, like tonight, without a roof. Likely he could find something to do on one of the plantations. They always needed overseers, a white man who knew how to keep niggers in line. He'd enjoy that. That black bastard of Armitage's had looked at him more than once as if he thought he was dirt. A nigger, daring to think a white man was dirt even if he didn't dare say it! He'd enjoy holding a whip and using it on black bastards like that. He'd show them that when he said jump, they'd better jump higher and farther than they'd ever jumped before.

The others first, though. Luke and Mark and Charles Armitage, and all of the rest of that tribe with them, were going to suffer, even Eli, because Eli belonged to that tribe now, through Armitage's blond girl marrying that little bastard Eli had picked up at a sale of paupers. They were going to suffer and they'd never get over it as long as they lived. First he had to come by a horse and wagon. . . .

"Henry Atkins is back in town," Patience Bates had told Martha and Tam that afternoon. If there was any news, Patience could be trusted to be the first to hear it and pass it along. "He went to the shipyard and asked for work. Hiram Weatherby must have finally had a stomachful of him and turned him out."

"Good for Mr. Weatherby, but bad for Boston," Martha had replied. "We don't need his kind around here. I feel sorry for his children, though. Tam, are you going to feed the baby before or after we eat?"

"After, Martha. He's sleeping like an angel." Tamara stood up from where she had been crouched beside the cradle admiring her son, who was without any doubt the most beautiful baby who had ever been born since the world began, with the exception only of Jesus.

At three months, the child already showed signs of becoming remarkably brilliant, as well as so handsome that Tam's heart caught every time she looked at him. She'd been afraid that she'd be bored, just staying at home and being a mother, but she had changed overnight from a forceful girl with a notion that women were the equals of men in any work the world would give them a chance to do, into a doting mother whose only thought was for her child. Martha, amused, knew that given a few more weeks, when the novelty had worn off, Tam would be champing at the bit again, hell-bent to get back to work at the shipyard to help get this war over with so that Mark and Luke could come home for good. But for now, she'd hardly let even Martha pick young Luke up to change his napkin.

"I wonder if it's true, the way Tod heard, that Henry Atkins actually tried to shoot Luke in the back at White Plains?" Patience mused, her face screwed up with worry.

"Knowing Henry, it probably is. But Luke can take care of himself, and you can be sure he'll keep a sharp eye out if he and Henry are ever in the same place again." Martha's voice was comfortable, showing nothing of the agitation she'd felt when she'd first heard the story. If anything had happened to Luke, she didn't know how she'd have been able to bear it. She'd go on, doing the best she could for those she had left, but the heart would have gone out of her and nothing would have ever been the same.

Where were Luke and Mark now? she wondered, forcing herself not to let the other two women know that she worried about them night and day. It hurt her, as it hurt Tam, that Mark couldn't be at home to watch the baby grow and change with every week that passed. He'd be walking in no time at all, and what if Mark wasn't home to see his first steps, to hear his first words? Drat the British! This war was raising hob with people's lives, and she wished that General Washington would find a way to lick the redcoats before her grandson graduated from Latin School and had to pick up a musket and go off to help his father and grandfather fight.

"Lemuel didn't take Atkins on, did he?" Tamara asked, giving the cradle one final, gentle rock.

"Sent him packing," Patience said with satisfaction. "I doubt that anybody else will give him work, either. It could be that we'll be lucky and he'll leave Boston again, looking for something to do on a farm."

"Amen to that," Martha said, her voice fervent. "Tam, come away from that baby and let him sleep in peace. You can set the table. Patience, you'll stay and eat with us, won't you?"

"I don't mind if I do." Patience still liked to give Tod and Annabelle all the privacy she could, and as Eli wouldn't be home for supper, he hardly ever was, because trade at The Temptation was so brisk, the invitation was welcome. Come peace, Tod and Annabelle would set up for themselves, and just as likely Mark and Luke would build them their house. Until then, she'd make herself as scarce as possible without neglecting her own grandchildren.

The three women, the two older ones and the girl, chattered and gossiped all through the meal, taking their time. With no menfolk to do for, any company was welcome, and Patience was a font of information about everything that went on in Boston. It was well after dark before Patience said good night to them and set off for her own home, and young Luke fed and sleeping again, Martha and Tamara sought their own beds.

Henry was in no hurry. He had to do it right because this time if he flubbed it up he'd never get another chance. He'd had a chance at Tamara once, and he'd flubbed it. He'd wished at the time that he'd at least raped her before he'd dumped her into the harbor, but now he was just as glad he'd neither raped her nor succeeded in drowning her. It would have been just Tamara then; now it would be both Tamara and the infant, Luke's grandson, Charles Armitage's daughter, and Mark's wife and son. He no longer hungered to kill Luke and Mark and Charles Armitage. Letting them live, to suffer for what he was going to do, to suffer for as long as they lived, was a far better revenge than death.

It had been three days since the idea had come to him of how he could avenge himself on the Martins and the lawyer for good and all. During those three days and nights Henry would have refrained from drinking even if he hadn't been so nearly out of money to buy it. He also refrained from showing himself anywhere he might be recognized, buying bread and cheese at a tavern he had never frequented before. It would suit him best if those who knew he'd been in Boston seeking work thought he'd left again.

But he wasn't idle during those three days. Taking care not to be seen by anyone who knew him, using the darkness of night as cover while he holed up in alleys during the day, he'd scouted the town, searching for a horse and cart that he could appropriate. It took him the first two nights to find what he was looking for, a stable that the householder didn't bother locking, and a cart left out in the open. It would teach the careless man a lesson, Henry thought, spitefully, when he found that his property was missing.

He almost came to grief before he'd accomplished this crucial stage of his mission. A neighbor's dog came sniffing and barking as he entered the back yard where the stable and the cart were kept, and he had to move fast to throttle the dog and then cut its throat before it roused the householder and the entire neighborhood.

The incident shook him, so that his hands shook as he hitched the horse to the cart, stopping every few seconds to put his hand over the old nag's muzzle so that it wouldn't whinny. Then there was the matter of the dog. He couldn't leave it out here in the open, for someone to stumble over the first thing in the morning and know that something was wrong. He had to pick it up and search for a clump of bushes thick enough to conceal it, and stumbling around with a dead dog in his arms, dripping blood all over him, wasn't exactly to his liking.

All the same, he was making progress, and no one had seen nor heard him. All these fools who looked down on him would have a surprise coming, when he'd accomplished what he'd set out to do. Then he'd abandon the cart and ride the horse, and he knew ways to go so's nobody would ever come up with him, and he'd be away free, his revenge accomplished, and they'd never see hide nor hair of him again.

It was still too early to carry out the last step of his mission. He wouldn't be able to leave Boston and cross the Neck until first light, or someone would be bound to challenge him. Once it was light, when a man had reason to be moving around, he wouldn't have any trouble. Most everyone knew him, they might not think much of him but they knew that he wasn't any Tory or traitor, and they'd let him pass across the Neck unmolested, probably sniggering behind their hands because he hadn't been able to find work and was heading on back to Hiram's farm to beg charity.

He was almighty dry. The tension of the last half hour had puckered up his mouth, and his throat felt like sandpaper. A thought came to him, and he grinned wolfishly. Leading the horse and cart, his hand over the animal's muzzle again, he left them in an alley near The Temptation. It took him another half hour to break into the place without making any noise and help himself to a jug of rum. There were other taverns he could have broken into but it was better this way. Eli'd have a dozen kinds of fits when he found out he'd been robbed, and that made his pleasure the greater. There wasn't any use in doing what he was going to do unless he was in a fit state to enjoy it, and he couldn't be in a fit state without something to warm his insides.

He had a few swallows while he waited until he judged it was time. He had to cut it pretty close to be safe.

It was as easy as falling off a log to get into the house, once he'd stashed the horse and cart in the nearest alley. All he had to do was stick his jackknife between the shutters of the back window and pry open the catch. It wasn't fixed up as tight as a fortress, the way some people kept their places. Luke and Martha figured that they had no enemies, and even the worst of the town's riffraff respected Luke enough so's they didn't go out to rob them. Luke, and Mark and the lawyer, and Eli as well. It was best to leave them alone lest they be caught up and it went the worse for them.

He didn't have to worry about the stairs creaking as he made his way up them to the upper floor. Luke Martin didn't build staircases that creaked. He didn't dare risk lighting a candle, but he had eyes like a cat. He could see perfectly well in the dark once they'd adjusted. He didn't stumble over any furniture or bump into any walls, to wake up the two women who were alone in the house with the baby.

Locating which bedroom was Martha's and which was Tamara's was easier than he'd hoped, because his ears, straining for the least sound, picked up the soft gurgling of a baby, that unmistakable sound that only an infant makes when it puts its curled fist to its mouth and sucks just before it wakes to announce that it's hungry. A glance through the doorway, the door ajar, confirmed what his ears had told him. There was a cradle close by the bed, and the slender mound under the light coverlet could only belong to Tamara.

He hesitated for only the fraction of an instant. The baby wouldn't begin to cry just yet. His own experience as a father told him that. It had used to drive him into a rage when he'd heard that sucking noise when Ruth was an infant, and knew that in a few minutes she'd begin to howl. Ann had never had enough milk, so Ruth had been perpetually hungry, that in itself had been enough to drive a man out of his house and into a tavern. A body ought to be able to have peace and quiet in his own home, not to have to listen to a brat squawl till it set his nerves to crawling.

As silently as a shadow, he found Martha's room, the mound in her bed rounder than in Tamara's. She stirred as he entered, but she never had time to wake up and cry out and alert the bitch in the other bedroom. One violent blow to the side of her head silenced her before she could utter a sound. By all rights he ought to finish her off too, but that would take time and if the baby woke up yelling, Tamara would wake up instantly, the way Ann had used to, and it was too risky. She might call out and ask Martha to bring a clean napkin or something, and come to investigate when there was no answer.

It didn't matter. He had nothing against Martha except that she was married to Luke, and she'd suffer too when she, and the whole tribe of them, found out what he'd done.

In another instant he was back in Tamara's room. He held the strip of cloth he'd brought along to use as a gag in his hands as he bent over her bed, and it was around her mouth before her eyes as much as flickered. The cord, then, to tie her hands and feet, and then he wrapped her, cocoon-fashion, in the top coverlet so tightly that she couldn't wriggle. He lifted her and slung her over his shoulder and scooped up the infant, keeping his hand over his mouth. It was only another moment before he had them both safe in the cart, with a strip of linen across the baby's mouth as well to keep him crying until they were well out of town. He'd take it off then, he didn't want the baby to die, not just yet. A good clout to the side of Tamara's head, and she'd lie quiet under the empty sacks in the bottom of the cart, the same sacks he'd slept on that first night in town, and nobody'd have an inkling she was there, or the brat either.

There was a place he knew, he'd reach it sometime in the morning, a heavily wooded place well off the traveled roads. He wanted full daylight for the things he was going to do to Tamara. He wanted to see her face while he did them to her. He'd strip her, and spread her, and take her, more than once, as many times as he could, and it had been a long time since he'd had a woman so he'd be able to do it three or four times. The rum in his brain gave him full confidence of that. And then he'd kill the child before her eyes, but he'd cut off its privates first. And then his knife would go to work on her. . . .

As he drove through the dawn, saliva dribbled from the corners of his mouth and his eyes glittered and the chuckles that came from his throat were no longer human. Henry Atkins was stark, raving mad.

Thirty-two

Ned Armitage was holding his tired horse to a slow trot when he passed the cart going in the opposite direction, away from Boston. Some farmer getting an early start home, after going in to trade, he expected, and likely his wife would have a few words to say to him for spending the night instead of getting on home yesterday.

His horse stumbled and Ned pulled it up and patted its neck. A glance at the sun, barely risen, told him that it was an ungodly time to arrive. He wouldn't want to disturb Mistress Gatesby at this early hour, it would probably frighten the poor, sick woman; the cook might have a heart attack if he went pounding at the door at this early hour, soon after dawn, provided she heard him at all, and that was doubtful.

He'd go to the Martins', he thought. None of them would be upset no matter how early the hour, and he hadn't seen Tam's baby yet, his own nephew. That made him an uncle, and his chest expanded. Uncle Ned! He could hardly wait to see Tam and the child. It was his driving need to see them that had kept him on the road all night, when any sensible man would have put up somewhere and gotten some rest.

How lucky could a man get, being sent with a message for his father, who was expected in Boston someday soon, the general hadn't known exactly when, so he'd sent Ned a day or two ahead to make sure he'd be there when Charles arrived. It amounted to leave of absence even if he was on official business, giving him a chance to see Tam and young Luke, and Annabelle and Tod and Martha and Eli and Patience, all the people he loved the most.

And then his father would come, and that would be the best of all. They'd talk as one man to another, as father to son, as friend to friend. He'd sit at The Temptation with his father and talk to Eli and the other men, he'd be one of them, his father's son, grown now and an Armitage. The lump in his throat was almost too big to swallow past.

He crossed the Neck, and soon he was in familiar streets, his horse's hoofs striking sparks from the cobbles. "It won't be long now, old boy," he encouraged the animal. He'd tether it where it could graze, and after he'd seen Tam and Martha and little Luke he'd go on home and give the poor beast a good rubdown and some oats if there were any in the stable, and then put it out to graze some more and fall into his own bed and sleep for hours, until his father got there. The hardest part about being in the Army was that there was never enough unbroken sleep.

It was still unreasonably early when Ned turned his horse into the Martins' yard and took it on out back where he could tether it in the grass. Then, on foot, he retraced his steps to the front and knocked on the door.

He waited, straining his ears, but there was no stirring, no voice raised in question from inside the house. He knocked again, frowning. It wasn't like either Tam or Martha to sleep so soundly. Maybe the baby had kept them awake last night and they were more tired than usual. A third knock, and still no response. You'd think that Tam at least would hear him. She'd always had ears like a wild animal, coming alert at the slightest sound. But that was when they'd been children. She was a grown woman now, a mother, not a child exceptionally close to nature anymore.

All the same, something inside him began to quiver. Something was wrong, he felt it deep in his gut. A soldier acquires that sense of danger, even when everything seems quiet and normal. If he doesn't, he doesn't live long.

The door was securely barred from the inside. He went around to the back, and found the kitchen door similarly barred.

The windows, then. He started from where he was, at the back door, and the first window he came to was open, the shutter swinging loose when he touched it.

He crawled through, no task at all for someone as agile as he was. The moment his feet touched the floor he called out. "Tam? Martha? Anyone? Where is everybody?"

There was no answer. It was eerie. He felt his scalp begin to crawl and a prickling sensation on the back of his neck. He went up the stairs fast, his heart pounding.

Tam's bed was empty, and so was the cradle that stood beside it. Thoroughly alarmed now, because the bed was rumpled, Tam had slept in it sometime last night, he bolted across to the room he knew Martha slept in. Was the baby sick, had she risen and taken him in to Martha? But in that case, why hadn't anyone answered him when he'd called, why wasn't there any movement or voices from Martha's room?

God in heaven, what had happened here? There

was blood on Martha's face, on her pillow, and her eyes were still glazed as she struggled to open them. And where was Tam, where was the baby?

"Martha, wake up! It's me, Ned! What's happened, where's Tam? Try to wake up!"

Martha moaned, not yet conscious. Ned stared at her helplessly. What should he do? She'd been hurt, badly hurt, and he had no experience with things like this, not when it was a woman, rather than a man injured on a battlefield.

How badly was she hurt? He had no way of knowing, and his stomach knotted as he saw how much blood there was. Her face itself was as white as the pillowcase on which her head lay. He didn't dare to touch her to try to rouse her, he didn't know how badly she was hurt and how much harm he might do. His feet turned him toward the stairs without any direction from his mind, and in another moment he was on his tired horse, whipping it toward Dr. Peabody's house.

It took several minutes for him to rouse the house. When he'd made himself understood, Peabody pulled his breeches on over his nightshirt and climbed up on Ned's horse behind him, his bag clutched in one hand while he hung onto Ned with the other arm.

"She's been struck. Hard enough to lay her out for several hours, I should say. But her pulse is strong. She's going to be all right, Ned. Martha, are you awake? Can you hear me? Do you know who did this to you, do you know what's happened to Tamara and the baby?"

Martha's eyes were open now, and she understood what was said, but she had no answers for them. She'd never seen her assailant. She was so agitated at learning that Tam and the baby were missing that Peabody had to dose her to make sure that she stayed quiet so that she could begin to recover.

"Who could have done it? And why? And where's my sister and the baby?" Ned kept demanding even though he knew that Peabody knew no more than he did.

"We have no way of knowing, lad. But I'll get the watch out, and the whole town if need be, to find out. This is worse than anything the British dreamed of doing. Whoever did it, I'll make one guarantee: He's crazy. Only a crazy man would attack Martha and make off with Tam and little Luke. You sit with Martha, there's nothing you can do that others can't do as well or better. I'll get things moving."

An hour later Eli walked into the house without knocking. He had his musket cradled in his good arm, and his face was grim. Patience was right behind him, come to stay with Martha.

"Come along, boy. Bring that horse of yours, but don't git on it yet. I think I've found something."

Together, Ned leading the horse, Eli led the way to an alley off a side street and pointed at the ground.

"Cart and horse. Tracks of a shoe with a patch on the left sole. Whoever was wearin' it was carryin' something heavy. The horse tracks show the right front foot toed in, won't be hard to pick up agin once we git out of town and you can bet your hope of salvation that whoever done it ain't still in town. All right, help me up on that critter now. He'll hev to carry double till we git out in open country, off the cobbles, then I'll git down and see what I kin see."

For a moment Ned was dumfounded, and then he remembered. Eli had always claimed to be a woods runner, an Indian fighter, he'd claimed that he was bald because he'd been scalped. Ned had never been sure he'd believed the half of what Eli claimed, but now Ned had a sure and absolute conviction that every word of it was true.

"Hadn't we better find the watch, get more help?"

"Not by a danged sight. They'd only git in the way, trample out all the signs I might find. Let the fools scour the town like they're doin'. Our man ain't there, and neither's Tam or little Luke, and you and me's goin' to git 'em."

Throat tight and aching, eyes smarting from lack of rest and sleep, his breath hurting with each one he drew, his dread weighing him down like the threat of damnation, Ned watched as Eli dismounted again after they had crossed the Neck. Eli got down stiffly; he was an old man and his joints weren't what they'd used to be. But once on the ground, he changed.

"There it be," he said. "Same toed-in tracks, right twixt the cart tracks. No, I ain't gittin' back on yet, boy. Hev to make sure it keeps goin' in the same direction."

Eli moved out in the bent-kneed lope of the woodsman, awkward-looking but one that covered ground at an amazing pace. He seemed tireless as he ranged ahead, and Ned, following with the horse, marveled when he stopped short and pointed off at a tangent.

"Done took the fork there. Well, hop down an' boost me up, boy."

"Why would he have taken Tam and the baby? He almost killed Martha. Why didn't he just kill them too?"

"You heared the doctor. The critter's plumb crazy. Mebby it's a good thing for Tam that he is. Mebby he ain't kilt her yet." Eli wasn't any too sure of that but the lad looked so forlorn that he had to say something to ease him even if it didn't turn out to be true.

As to who had done this thing, he had a pretty good idea but he didn't want to voice it to Ned. There was only one man who hated the Martins enough to have done this, and that was Henry Atkins. And Atkins had been in town a few days back, put off Hiram Weatherby's farm, and he'd been turned down at the shipyard, and God knew what insanity was festering in his rum-rotted brain. If it was Henry, and Eli couldn't figure how it could be anyone else, then God help Tam and young Luke if they couldn't get to them in time. The cart hadn't stopped since it had left Boston, that was a good sign. Maybe it hadn't stopped yet, and if it hadn't, then the chances were fair to middling that Tam and the baby were still alive.

They jogged on for a while in silence, each immersed in his own thoughts. Ned's were nearly all for Tam; outside of his father, she was the one he loved with a love that was like the need for nourishment and shelter. Since his earliest babyhood, Tam had always been there, his protector, his nurse, his mentor, his playmate. If she were dead, if the madman who had her had already killed her, Ned's life would seem empty no matter how many others tried to fill the space she had left.

Eli was thinking about Charles Armitage and Luke and Mark as much as he was about Tam. More than anything he'd ever wanted in the world, more than he'd wanted Patience even, he wanted to find that girl and her baby safe, and return them to Charles and Luke and Mark. It would about kill them, if they were dead. It had to be Atkins. Who else would have set out to destroy the whole family by taking Tam and little Luke and killing them? He'd have to kill them, he wouldn't dare to leave Tam alive to tell he'd done it.

To lose Tam and the baby, Charles Armitage's grandson, Luke's grandson, with no sense to it but the spite of a no-good sot; it was more than a man could understand, more than he ought to be called on to bear. It was true that the lawyer would still have Annabelle and her two youngsters, but Tam was the one he set such store by and always had.

As for Luke, he'd already lost one boy to the British, dead on the battlefield, and another half mad and God knew whether he was alive or dead by now. Hadn't anybody heard tidings of Tim since he'd taken off after the night he'd spent with Charity, except for that one letter saying he'd gone back to the fighting. Losing little Luke, and Tam, whom he'd always looked on as his own daughter, would just about take the spirit out of him.

"Haul up there, Ned," Eli said. Once again he clambered laboriously from the back of the tired, patient horse that stood with its head hanging. Eli's bones creaked these days, there was no two ways about it. Come winter, Patience'ud have to rub him good with goose grease or he might just freeze up and not be able to move at all.

He stooped over, casting this way and that, before he gave a grunt of satisfaction.

"Ground's most too hard to take a decent track. We ain't had a spit of rain worth mentioning for a month of Sundays. But here 'tis. He turned off the road here." Eli straightened up and squinted his faded eyes against the sunlight. "I couldn't say for sure, but I got me a notion he might of been headin' for them trees up yonder."

"I don't see any sign of a horse and cart." Ned's voice sounded like a croak. He'd been in the saddle for fourteen straight hours before he'd arrived in Boston, and now he was in the saddle again, without having eaten and, more important, without having quenched his thirst. His throat was so dry that it felt cracked.

"He may be crazy but he ain't crazy enough to leave them in plain sight. Nor so crazy he won't see us comin' if he's in there. Here's where we hev to use some strategy. Hoist me up."

Once aboard the horse again, Eli indicated that Ned should turn to the right and give the woods a wide berth. "Swing a good long ways around 'em. And don't go lookin' at 'em, neither. We got to make him think we're a-headin' somewheres else."

"But that will waste time!"

"An' if he sees us comin', he'll likely finish off Tam and the young'un right there." Eli's voice was flat. "Do as I say, dang it! Go a good long ways around to the right."

To Ned, time seemed to stretch into eternity as he obeyed Eli's order. It raked at his soul to put so much distance between them and those woods instead of lessening the distance till they could come right up on them with a rush. But instinct told him that Eli was right. The old woodsman knew what he was doing, and if they were too late it wouldn't be because they'd gone bursting right up to the place in plain sight, and panicked the kidnaping madman into killing Tam and little Luke.

As he rode, as the distance lengthened between him and the patch of woodland, memories of Tam seemed to float in front of the boy. Tam as she had been when he'd first been old enough to know her, all arms and legs, elbows and sharp knees that had jutted into him when she'd happened to knock him down during one of their games. Tam on the day when she had been caught swimming in the river with Mark and dragged home by Parson Eldridge with her dress unbuttoned in the back, her hair lank around her shoulders, blisters on her heels that had filled her eyes with tears that she had refused, out of pride, to shed.

Tam in London, keeping watch over him, keeping

those deviates at bay so they couldn't corner him and slobber over him and worse. Tam guarding their father when he'd been stabbed and had nearly died, and she had refused to leave him alone for a moment. Tam explaining, her face intense, how she had happened to lend her cloak to a runaway tavern girl, her voice, just as intense, begging Charles Armitage to go to the girl's rescue.

Tam in church, getting married, her face as shining as an angel's, her happiness emanating an aura that had filled Old North and rubbed off on everyone there. Tam, her face as white as bed linen, coming from the room where their mother had just died, but still with a look of relief, of inner peace, on her face that Ned still didn't understand. She had never explained and he had never asked her, sensing that it was something that she had no wish to talk about, even to him. If it had been something she wanted him to know she would have told him without being asked.

"All right, lad. We're well around now. Help me light down."

They tied the horse to a sapling, and the animal gave them a look filled with mournful reproach as they walked away from it.

"Down on your belly. Keep low, take advantage of every piece of cover there is. Don't go makin' that grass wave when you crawl through it, there ain't no wind! Keep down, dang it! Get your rump down! If that was Injuns in there you'd hev an arrow in it 'fore you knew what was happenin'!"

Their pace, as they crawled forward, was agonizingly slow, but Eli refused to allow more speed. "And now keep yer tarnation trap shut. We're gittin' close. We'll go in right there, where that oak's been split by lightnin'.

I'll go first and you follow after you see that I ain't been seen."

They crawled through low brush now, and Ned found himself tangled in a clump of poison oak. He didn't think about what he'd look like when it got to working on him, or how it would itch fit to drive him crazy, there was no time for that. He kept Eli in sight, and when the old man held up his hand he stopped, and then crawled forward again until he was abreast of him behind a fallen log.

It was a good thing that Eli's hand clamped over his mouth before he could let out the shout of rage that tore at his throat.

Tam was there, tied to a tree. There wasn't a stitch on her. The man circling her, stopping to put his hands on her, to fondle her breasts and twist them, to probe between her legs with rough, filthy fingers, was Henry Atkins.

Tamara's face was white, so white that for a few seconds Ned thought that she was already dead. And then her neck moved, and her head, as she snapped at her tormentor and her teeth sank into his arm.

"I'll kill you!" they heard her say, the words distinct and filled with fury. "There's no place on earth you'll be able to hide, Henry Atkins!"

"You won't have the chance, you spitfire bitch! I'm goin' to fix it so you won't be able to find anybody, once I get through with you, because you'll be deader than a doornail, you and your brat both. But first I'm going to have all the fun I want with you, and it's going to take a long time."

"You wouldn't dare! Do you think you can get away, if you do what you say you're going to do? Don't you know that Mark will hunt you down, even to the ends of the earth? And Luke, and my father! Let us go while you still have the chance, and maybe they'll let you live, even if it's in prison for the rest of your life. If you don't, you'll find yourself in hell before your time, provided the devil will have you!"

"They won't never find me. It's you they'll find, you and that Martin-Armitage brat. They'll see what I done to you and it'll eat at them like hating them and all your tribe's been eating at me all these years. They'll see what I done, and they'll know how you suffered, and how you died, you and your fine son!" Henry stopped nursing his arm and struck out at her. His hand crashed against the side of her face and made her head crack back against the tree trunk, half stunning her. "I'm tired of this part of the game, it's time for something more interesting!"

Even at that distance, Ned could see Tam's mouth curl. Only half conscious because of the blow, stripped, tied to a tree, helpless, she was going to go on fighting. Once Henry untied her, she'd turn into a wildcat that even a man as insane as Atkins would find it hard to control.

Atkins would be up against a force that he knew little or nothing about, a mother fighting not only for her own life, but even more for the life of her child. Even if they hadn't gotten here in time, he couldn't help but wonder if Tam wouldn't have managed to hurt or maim Henry Atkins enough so that she and the baby could escape.

He couldn't stand any more. Tam wasn't going to have to fight for her life and that of her child, because they had gotten here in time. In spite of Eli's restraining hand, he leaped to his feet and charged forward, a howl of rage bursting from his throat.

"Git out of the way, you young fool! Move to the

side!" Eli bellowed. Ned hardly realized that he had heard the words but he dodged to the left an instant before Eli's musket roared. Almost merging with the blast of gunpowder, there was the sound of Eli's cursing.

"Missed! Dad-blasted musket, I missed!"

Henry was off and running. Ned was after him without pausing in his own headlong rush. As he gained on the older man, Henry turned, his teeth bared, a knife in his hand. The knife gleamed in a shaft of sunlight as Henry lunged for him. Strangling, Ned threw himself forward, under the blade, and caught Atkins around the knees.

They rolled over and over on the ground, fighting for possession of the knife. Ned felt a burning in his arm, all along the length of it, as the blade found him and slashed. Then both of his hands were on Atkins' wrist and slowly, as if something had happened to time, as if a second, for some incomprehensible reason, now took an hour to pass; he forced Atkins' hand down, farther down, turned it.

Henry didn't look like a human being, there under him. His eyes were wild, insane, his stained teeth bared like an animal's, the grunts that came from his throat were like nothing Ned had ever heard before. The creature, he could scarcely be thought of as a man, fought like the maniac he was, with the strength of a maddened animal in a trap.

But Ned was young, and enormously big for his age. He was already as tall as Luke and in another year he'd be as big as Mark, taller than either of them and broader, and he had the strength that went with his size.

"Damn you!" Ned cursed, his voice hoarse. And the knife, driven by both of his knotted hands, drove deep into Henry's chest.

For one brief instant, before he died, Henry recognized the boy who had killed him. The lawyer's boy, Charles Armitage's boy, Tamara's brother. He opened his mouth to cry out his protest to heaven or hell, but the sound never reached his lips.

Spent, shaking, his throat burning with the bite of acid nausea, Ned struggled to his feet and had to cling to the nearest tree for support before he could make his legs bear his weight. He looked once at the man who lay at his feet, the eyes vacant now, staring at nothing, the stubbled jaw hanging slack.

Ned's feet would move, if he cursed at them hard enough. He had to get back there, back to see to Tam.

He could see her now. She had Eli's shirt on, and what in all tarnation was Eli doing, beating on the baby? He opened his mouth to tell him to stop, but before he had a chance to voice his protest he heard another protest, long and loud and wailing, filled with fury.

Eli looked up as Ned stumbled the last few feet toward him. "Little feller's all right, but I had to thump him some. He was mighty nigh smothered in that there blanket. All right, young'un, here's your ma."

Tam's knees went out from under her and she sat. Her arms opened to receive her baby, and right there, in front of them, she held him to her breast to still his anger and hunger. As they watched, before they thought to turn away, both Ned and Eli thought that they had never seen anything so beautiful.

Thirty-three

Bone-weary, but still so exhilarated by the final, almost unbelievable victory at Yorktown that they still weren't feeling the full effects of the exhaustion that the years of war had left in both mind and body, Charles Armitage looked at Ned and felt his heart swell with pride.

Charles himself had not been at Yorktown while the final, decisive struggle was going on, and he couldn't help but feel cheated. His role of relaying messages from one place to another had kept him from actual fighting during most of the war. He was intelligent enough to realize that without men like himself, and like Mr. Revere and many others, the war might not have been won at all, but still he wished that he had been allowed to give better account of himself.

But here beside him was Ned, who'd done his share and more than his share. If Charles personally hadn't accounted for any enemy soldiers, Ned had accounted for enough of them to share with him, and some left over. Ned had been here, at the finish. He'd been with Washington while the general had marched one way and then another, keeping the British guessing, never letting them know where he was going to strike, and all the time making for Yorktown to put an end to it.

Charles had known, or rather made an educated guess, what the general was up to, but Ned, nor probably any of the men who'd followed where he led, had not. Washington was as adept at keeping his own council as he was at strategy.

There had been times, many of them, during these past grim years, when the general had refused to let any other man have access to all the reports for fear that the colonials would lose heart and surrender, convinced that their cause was lost. He'd kept it all to himself, borne the full burden of it single-handed. Charles doubted that even those men who knew him best would appreciate the man's greatness during his lifetime. His admiration for the man who had brought them through to this final victory knew no bounds. He was a giant among men, and the lawyer was not referring to his great size, but to the great mind and the determination that had won through against all odds.

And here with Charles, reunited at last, hopefully never to be parted again as they had been so often during the long years of war, was his son. Tall, broad of shoulder, his open face alight with integrity and purpose, Ned was a lad any man could be proud of. He'd been in the forefront of those who had taken the first British redoubt that had stood in the way of building the second siege line. He'd acquitted himself well, he'd taken his turn at pick and shovel like the others, digging those lines under heavy fire in the black of night. His hands still bore the callouses to show for it, badges of honor. Looking at his own hands, Charles wished that he could say as much.

He remembered, as though it had been only days ago, the night Ned had run away in a full-fledged blizzard because he'd been ashamed to face the man he'd learned was not his father. He'd gone after him and brought him back, and somehow made him understand that it didn't matter. Charles had been repaid for it many times over, because it was Ned who had killed Henry Atkins, Ned who had helped track down the madman and then killed him when Atkins had kidnaped Tam and little Luke with the intention of mutilating and murdering them in revenge for his fancied wrongs.

Not that the boy took much credit for what he had done. His relating of the event to Charles had been factual, playing down his own part while he gave Eli all the credit for the actual tracking, making Tam and the baby's rescue possible. But the fact remained that Eli's musket had misfired and Ned had been the one who was fast enough and strong enough to bring Atkins down.

Atkins! Charles had seldom wished for any man's death, but he could find no drop of pity for this man who had caused him, and Luke Martin, so much trouble ever since Luke had arrived in Boston and Luke and Charles had become friends.

They were resting around a campfire, surrounded by hundreds of other men as weary and elated as they were. The talk was all of how Cornwallis had refused to surrender his sword to General Washington. The doughty British general had gone into a fit of the sulks and refused to play the game according to the rules, and turned the honor of accepting defeat over to General Charles O'Hara. Even at that, O'Hara had tried at first to surrender his sword to Rochambeau, so as not to give Washington the satisfaction of accepting it, but Rochambeau had soon set him straight as to who was in command.

They were still laughing, slapping their knees and

wiping tears of mirth from their eyes, at the general's repaying of Cornwallis' compliments by passing O'Hara on to General Lincoln. It was Lincoln who accepted the sword and handed it back to O'Hara, as a gentleman should. Didn't want to go on dirtying his hands on it, was the sly consensus of opinion, as laughter still pealed out at this umpteenth telling and retelling, a subject that those who had been present would never weary of for as long as they lived.

"Father, there's Tim!" Ned got to his feet, his face filled with excitement. "See, just there, to the right!"

As tired as he was, Charles also came to his feet. "Go and bring him to me," he ordered. "Luke's been frantic all this time, wondering whether he was dead or alive."

"Right. I knew I'd seen him, during the siege, I was almost certain of it, but I never could work my way close enough to him to be positive. We'll all go home together. This'll make it up to Luke for having that wagon turn over on him and put him out of action before the surrender! Tim, over here!" Ned started forward, and Tim looked in their direction, startled, and then started to edge his way back into the men who surrounded him, intent on losing himself in the crowd.

Ned was off like a shot, elbowing and shoving his way through. His hand came down on Tim's shoulder in a grip like a vise.

"Tim, what in all get-out ails you? Father wants to speak to you, come along now. Why have you been avoiding me all this time? You must have known I was here! This is a great bit of luck, finding you so we can all go home together!"

"I'm not going home, Ned." His face pale, his body more gaunt than Ned had ever seen it, Tim shook his head and met the younger lad's eyes without flinching.

"There's nothing for me there. Just leave me be. You can tell my mother and father that I'm all right, but don't try to talk me into going back because you'll just be wasting your breath."

Seeing the two deep in some kind of an argument, Charles worked his way toward them until he came up with them just in time to hear Tim's last few words.

"What's all this, Tim? Not go back? Of course you're going back. Anything else in unthinkable! Don't you realize how worried Luke and Martha have been? I won't ask your reasons for disappearing the way you did, but now that the war is over, certainly you'll go home, just like the rest of us."

"No." Tim's face was set and pale so that the scar on his forehead stood out in the light from the campfires. "I have other plans."

"Other plans?" Charles' brow furrowed, and Ned looked astonished. What other plans could possibly be as important as going home, home to stay, after all these years of hunger and exhaustion, of despair and defeat, of the fear, unspoken but all the more fearsome for that, that they might never see their homes or their loved ones again?

Something strange was happening to Tim, he seemed to change, to grow in stature, even as they looked at him. His shoulders were straighter, his head held higher, and there was a light of fanaticism in his eyes.

"I'm heading West," Tim said. "There's a man I met, a preaching man. He made me see that being scarred doesn't matter, not being scarred on my face or even worse scarred inside of me. He made me see that God has a plan for me: He talked to me, talked to me for hours, when he saw how it was with me. He's a traveling man of God, he goes to all the outlying farms and towns, way beyond regular churches and preachers, and brings them the word of God. He said I could join up with him, he gave me his intinerary, I'll come up with him sooner or later. He said he'll teach me, make a preaching man of me so that we can reach twice as many folks as he could alone. We might even go amongst the Indians and bring them enlightenment. . . ."

Ned's mouth dropped open. He's got religion, he thought, dumfounded. Tim's got religion, he's caught the fever, and nothing's going to hold him back.

"But you could go home for a while, before you set out to find this preacher. It would mean so much to your family," Charles argued.

Tim's eyes were alight with a force that sent shivers up and down Ned's spine. Indians, he'd said! Preaching to white folks was one thing. Although Ned himself wasn't inclined that way, he could understand how a man might feel called to go and preach, especially someone like Tim, who'd come as near to giving up all hope as anyone he'd ever known. But how could any man teach Indians about the love of Jesus, and make them listen? Still, from looking at Tim now, with his eyes shining like that and that eerie light on his face, he supposed that if any man could do it, Tim could.

"No, Mr. Armitage. I'm sorry, but I'll have to be heading West. I'm fixing to pull out tonight, so's Preacher Elmwood won't get too far ahead of me."

Charles' face filled with concern. "But you can't do that. You haven't been mustered out of the Army. It would be desertion."

"I'm in another army now, Mr. Armitage. An army that outranks this one. I'm leaving tonight." There was solid conviction in Tim's voice, and a determination that would admit to no obstacles.

"Tim, listen to me. If you have to follow this Preacher Elmwood, then you know that you'll go with your family's blessing and mine. But not this way, not without being mustered out, and seeing your family first."

"I reckon you'll speak a word for me, seeing that you're here." Tim's eyes were steady. "They'll listen to you, the officers will, when you tell them how it is."

Charles rubbed his fingers across the dull ache between his eyes. "I expect I will," he said, resigned. He only hoped that they'd listen to him as reasonably as Tim was convinced that they would. He'd have to tell them that Tim wasn't like ordinary men, that there'd be no holding him back and no telling what might happen if they tried to restrain him. He expected, come to think of it, that they already knew that. No man, not even a superior officer, could look at Tim the way he was now and think that he was like ordinary men. Likely they'd be just as glad to be shut of him, put him down as insane or some other such nonsense. Tim wasn't insane. He was inspired.

Defeated, Charles held out his hand. "I'll wish you luck, then. And I'll relay your message to your family. Is there anyone else to whom you'd like to send a message?"

Tim hesitated, and then nodded. "Tell Charity that I thank her. Tell her she'll be in my prayers."

Charity? What on earth did Tim mean by that? Charles looked at him waiting for some explanation, but none was forthcoming. With his last words, Tim turned and melted into the crowd, and Charles and Ned both knew that they wouldn't see him again unless and until he ever decided to come home.

Luke shifted his weight to ease himself on the hard bench, and drew aimless circles on the table with his mug of cider. His ribs still bothered him a little, even though

Peabody had taken the bandages off a couple of weeks ago.

"Bones achin'?" Eli asked him.

"Some. Nothing to complain about. What gets me hot under the collar is that I had to let that wagon roll over on me just when we were getting toward the end, and miss the best battle of the whole war."

Eli's eyebrows shot up. "What's good about any battle? A lot of shootin' and killin', and maybe you on the receivin' end!"

"It was the last battle, that's what was good about it. And I had to miss it. Mark, too. He's still fit to be tied."

"Seems to me Mark ought to count his blessin's. Men got kilt in that there battle, and he mighta been one of 'em and never got home to Tam and that fine grandson of yours, to say nothin' of never havin' seen the new young'un. Victory! What a name to hang onto an innocent baby! I know why Tam done it, of course. She was bound and determined that we was goin' to win, and it was a way of provin' her faith. But she mighta compromised for Victoria, now mightn't she? Patience's fair to have convulsions about it. She keeps sayin' what if we lost, and that poor child would of had to go all through her whole life with strangers thinkin' she was named to celebrate the British victory over us!"

"With a general like Mr. Washington, how could we have lost? Calm down, Eli. Likely everybody'll call the baby Vicky anyway, and think her name's Victoria. As pretty as she is, the image of her mother, it hardly matters what she's called."

The door of The Temptation opened, and Ned Armitage came in. He moved with confidence as he crossed the room and sat down with Luke and Eli. Lord, what a big lad he was, Luke thought. He looked a full-grown man, except for that young, open face, filled with an eagerness that generally wears off with time unless a man's luckier than most.

"Have you heard the talk of making General Washington King?" Ned asked, accepting the mug of cider that Patience brought him at Eli's signal. Patience's face expressed disapproval of Ned's partaking of cider along with the grown men, and Eli's scowl didn't keep her from voicing her opinion.

"Hadn't you ought to be home, Ned, or visiting Martha and Mark and Tam, instead of wasting your time in a tavern, at your age?"

"Go away, woman. Scat and leave us men be," Eli snapped at her. "If'n he was old enough to fight he's old enough to drink."

"I just came from seeing Tam and the children." Ned's smile forgave Patience for insinuating that he was still a boy rather than a man. "I wanted to talk to Luke and Eli a little. I'm all for the general being made King. He'd be the best King the world ever had."

"King!" Cider splattered across the table as Eli choked and spluttered, his face a study in indignation. "What in tarnation you talkin' about, boy?" That remark of Ned's relegated him to boyhood again, no man grown would have had such a harebrained opinion, much less voiced it. "We don't want no more Kings, not even if it's the gen'ral. No sir-ee, this here country's had enough of Kings!"

"But you'll be loyal to him, if he is made King?" Ned looked worried at Eli's outburst, as though he envisioned the old man being arrested as a traitor.

Eli's face blackened, but then it cleared. He thumped his mug down on the table with such force that the remainder of the cider in it slopped out.

"The gen'ral ain't goin' to be no King. He knows

better'n that. He knows we don't hold with Kings, and no more does he. He won't accept the offer, that's all. He can be head of the country for all the rest of his life for all of me, God knows he's earned the right, but he won't be no King."

A laugh from the doorway made them look up from where they'd been so engrossed in Eli's tirade that they hadn't noticed that Charles Armitage had entered the tavern only moments behind Ned.

"I'm inclined to agree with you, Eli. I'm sure that General Washington will decline the honor. Nevertheless, it's almost certain that he'll be our head of state for some time to come. The people aren't in the mood to accept anyone else."

The people. How good that sounded, what a ring it had to it! Here in this new country, what the people wanted was what they would get. Eli was right, they'd had enough of Kings. A people free in their own right, never to bend knee before King or Parliament again, but to make their own laws, to send men from their own districts to represent them in the Congress, to vote them out again if they turned out not to be to their liking after all.

It would take time to get things straightened around and functioning smoothly, and there would inevitably be quarrels and dissension, but in the end a new kind of nation would emerge, a banner of freedom for all of mankind to wonder at.

Charles joined them at the table, and Luke felt a great contentment that filled him more satisfyingly than food had ever filled a hungry man. These were his friends, tried and proven over the years. He still had Martha, in spite of the blow that Henry Atkins had inflicted on her the night he'd taken Tam and little Luke. She'd come out of it with nothing worse than a throbbing headache and a raging anger at the man who had dared to invade her home and try to harm her family. If Eli and Ned hadn't caught up with Atkins in time, Luke didn't doubt that Martha herself would have hunted him down no matter where he tried to hide.

Mark was fine, already making plans for expanding their business, for building a separate house for himself and Tam and the children. If it weren't for Tim, chasing off into the wilderness God only knew where, he'd be satisfied that he was luckier than the general run of humans on this earth. Nothing could bring John back, but John had died as he would have wanted to die, doing his duty as he saw it, knowing that no man could do more.

At least Tim was alive, and according to what Charles and Ned had told him, he was happy. Luke reckoned that when a man got religion, nothing else could satisfy him, and things being what they were, maybe it was a good thing. For Tim to be happy, to find his own fulfillment, was all that mattered. Eli said that the Indians, if that was where he'd end up, preaching to the savages, would set store by a man like Tim, that they'd consider his near-mad zeal and the scars he bore as marks of honor, deeming that he'd been touched by the spirits and must be accorded protection and respect. And maybe, when he'd gotten the first raging fever of it out of his system, he'd come back and pay them a visit, if only to make sure of their own salvation.

Charles was immersed in his own thoughts. All the long journey home, he'd looked forward to this night when he'd be reunited with his friends, but even more, he ached to see Charity. He'd had to see Tam and little

Luke and his newest grandchild first, and Annabelle and her two children, but now he was here, but Charity was nowhere to be seen.

"I'm sorry, Luke. I didn't hear what you just said." Startled, Charles came back to the present and realized that he had not only not heard what Luke had said, but also that he hadn't noticed that Ned had left them.

Eli grinned. "Your youngster's gone chasin' off after a girl, I wouldn't doubt. He had that look about him."

"I was only wondering if you ever heard anything more of George Hartgrave," Luke said. "It doesn't seem right that he should have got off scot-free after he tried to kill you."

"Hartgrave? He's back in England. He was wounded and invalided home. My sources of information told me that he's married to a dowager of uncertain age who keeps strict control over her purse strings and even stricter control over her husband. He was pretty well crippled, but he's still a damnably good-looking man, and the lady was glad to take over his support for the reflected glory of snaring a man younger than she is and one so charming, a real social asset."

"Wouldn't wish a life like that on a dog," Eli grunted. "But then, I wouldn't go insultin' any dog by comparin' it to Hartgrave. Any self-respectin' dog'ud likely bite me in the seat of my britches and I wouldn't blame it. It beats me how a man like that ever sired a boy as fine as Ned."

"One rotten apple doesn't necessarily spoil the barrel, provided it's removed in time," Charles told his friends. "Hartgrave came from good stock. The trouble was that he was so handsome that not only his mother but also every other woman he came into contact with spoiled him unmercifully. His aunts, his grandmothers while they lived, and when he became old enough to go out into society, those same kinds of doting women led him into thinking that the world owed him whatever he wanted simply for the taking. His father tried to keep him in hand but he was busy struggling to keep his estate in some kind of order. He wasn't a good businessman and he suffered reverses, and so he knew little about what his son was up to in London."

"Could happen to any man, I reckon, not bein' able to keep his boy in line. I've heard tell of such," Eli commented.

"And then, although Ned resembles George in his physical appearance, he also resembles Millicent's father, and he was as fine a man as they come. Sir Basil just goes to prove how different branches of the same tree can be. I believe it's partly a matter of necessity. As the younger son, Millicent's father had to make his own way while Sir Basil lived in the lap of luxury from an early age, with no restraining hand on the reins."

"Making his own way never hurt a man." Luke nodded. "At least it never hurt me, that I can see."

"I'm afraid that Ned will have to pretty much make his own way as well." Charles also nodded. "None of us came out of this war rich. But he has ability, and ambition, and hopefully he'll marry a girl who will be a help to him, not some flighty young miss who thinks of nothing but fashion and society."

It was true that none of them had come out of the war rich. Luke's carpentry business had come to a standstill, Eli had been hard put to keep his tavern open, and Charles himself had depleted his fortune by giving all he could scrape up to aid the war effort. But now that the war was over they could start rebuilding, and if they had enough fortitude and confidence none of them would suffer unduly. Their newly won freedom from British rule would more than make up for the lack of luxuries while they set about recouping.

Charles' own losses cut deep, and he wasn't thinking of money or material possessions. Jonas was gone, his life laid down for his fellow man at a minor battle that people scarcely remembered anymore. He had not gone out in a blaze of glory any more than John Martin had, but the black man, like John, had simply and gladly given all he had to give. Charles missed him so much that it didn't bear thinking about.

There were no live-in daughters and grandchildren to fill Charles' house. A house without a mistress was a house without a soul, Charles thought. Charity had given the house life and warmth while she had lived there, but now she, too, was gone. Mistress Gatesby had told him that she'd packed up her few belongings and moved out, to take a room with Widow Morgan, when she'd known that he and Ned would be home soon. She still looked in on Mistress Gatesby, and she'd arranged, with Tam's help, for a fifteen-year-old girl to stay with her and do the housework. Seeing the round, stolid face of the girl Emily, instead of Charity's, had given Charles a jolt that he still hadn't recovered from.

All the long way back, Charles had dreamed of seeing Charity again. The years of war, of horror and destruction, had driven home to him the need a man has for a woman, a good woman who loved and cherished him, who would always be there to give him comfort and support and the loving companionship that was, when all was said and done, the only thing that made life worth living.

Was he too old to take another wife? Would he be doing Charity an injustice if he asked her to marry him? He had no conceit, but he was realistic enough to know that he could have his choice of a good many women, all of them, in society's priggish opinion, more suitable to his estate in life than Charity. But he didn't want another woman, he wanted Charity. If he couldn't have her, he'd spend the rest of his life alone.

Charity! Why had she simply moved out of his house, why had she neglected to come in to work at The Temptation this evening? He hadn't seen her since he'd gotten back late this afternoon. Did she have some inkling of how he felt, was she avoiding him because she didn't want to hurt him by refusing him? He was too old for her, he was a fool even to consider asking her to be his wife, but his yearning, his soul-aching need for her, drove him until he could think of nothing else.

"Eli, did Charity give you any reason for moving out of my house?" He had to know, although he had to force himself to ask the question. "Has she by any chance met some man she likes, is she thinking of marrying?"

"Nope. Reckon she figured it wouldn't be proper for her to go on living in your house once you were home. You know how folks talk. Scandalmongers, the lot of 'em!" Eli's voice was filled with disgust. "Not that she'd a cared for herself, it was you she was thinkin' of."

"You're sure there's no one else?"

"Dad-blast it, how can any man be sure about a woman? If you want to know, whyn't you go ask her?"

Charles stood up. "That's the best piece of advice anyone had ever given me," he said. Eli and Luke watched him leave, each thinking their own thoughts. If Charles Armitage wasn't a man eaten up by love, they had another thing coming. Of course Charity would have some notion that she wasn't good enough for him, but if Charles couldn't talk her out of that then he wasn't enough of a lawyer so they'd trust him with any case of theirs.

Charles knew where the Widow Morgan lived, in a neat clapboard house with a tiny scrap of lawn in front, enclosed by a picket fence that she paid a boy to paint for her every spring. It was a longish walk from The Temptation, and with every step of the way Charles steeled himself to ask Charity straight out if she'd have him as her husband. All she could do was say either yes or no, and if it was no, then he'd lost nothing through the asking. But if she said yes . . .

She had to say yes. Her saying yes was the most important thing in the world, it relegated everything else into insignificance.

The widow was flustered to see the lawyer, Mr. Armitage, on her doorstep, and her hand went to her cap to make sure it was on straight.

"Charity? Yes, she's here. It's a mercy you came this evening if you want to see her, because she's taking the stage tomorrow, she's going to New York Town."

The blood left Charles' lips, turning them white. Charity leaving Boston, without a word to him or even to Eli? He knew that she hadn't told the tavernkeeper of her plans, or Eli would have told him. All Charles could think, in his stunned surprise, was that Eli had been mistaken, that there was another man, one she was going to meet and marry.

His impression of the widow's parlor was blurred, of no importance in spite of its immaculate neatness. He felt suddenly like a stripling, wanting to turn tail and run before he faced the first girl he had ever asked to walk out with him. He was on a fool's errand, he'd only hurt himself and cause Charity embarrassment when she had to tell him that she didn't love or want him, that there was someone else.

But he was too good a lawyer to concede a case before the last shred of evidence was in, and so he waited, his hands clasped behind him to keep them from shaking and betraying his agitation. Then he heard light, quick footsteps on the stairs, and Charity came into the room, Charity just as he had remembered her, her hair caught back in a loose knot at the back of her neck, her face not beautiful but something better than beautiful, with an inner strength and light that made men think her the loveliest woman in the world.

"Mr. Armitage! Is something wrong, is Ned sick, or one of the girls, or the children?"

Charles brushed her question aside and drove in for the attack. "What's all this about you going to New York?"

Charity's face paled, but her eyes were steady as they met his. "I thought it best, Mr. Armitage. I can find work there."

"Then there isn't a man involved?"

"No, there isn't."

"Then, in the name of God, will you tell me why you're going? Leaving your friends, leaving everyone who loves you, everyone I thought you loved and would be loyal to for as long as you live?"

"I don't have to answer that." Charity struggled to retain her composure, to hang onto her pride.

"Yes, you do. I demand an answer, I have the right to an answer. Charity, don't you know that I love you? Didn't you know that I'd ask you to marry me, as soon as I came back?"

"Charles, don't!" Charity's voice broke, and then steadied again. "Yes, I knew, or at least I was afraid that it might happen. And that's why I'm leaving, because it's impossible, you could never marry me, a tavern woman, it wouldn't do at all."

"You're talking nonsense. This is America, Charity, there are no classes here, we just fought a long and bloody war to abolish all that. A tavern woman! That name applied to you makes being a tavern woman the proudest thing any woman could aspire to be! The only question that signifies is whether or not you love me, whether or not you think that I could make you happy."

"You know what I was." Charity's face was very white now, her eyes almost black with agony. "You know that I was used, that other men had me, before. . . ."

"And through no fault of your own, and you had the courage to escape from that, you risked being captured and punished as a runaway bondswoman. And your life has been without blemish ever since, you've proved, countless times over, that you are what you are, a woman of character, of integrity, with more to give than any other woman I've ever known. You're the only woman in the world who could make me a suitable wife, and I mean to have you unless you're disgusted by me, unless you find me too old, the idea of marrying me repulsive to you."

Charity shook her head, her eyes blinded by tears. "You know that isn't true! But it isn't just my past, the things I couldn't help happening to me. There's something else, something that happened while you were away. Tim . . ."

A vague recollection came back to Charles, of the moments when he'd tried to persuade Tim Martin to return home with him after the victory at Yorktown. "Tell Charity that I thank her," Tim had said. He'd had no idea then what the boy had meant, but now . . .

"I almost gave myself to Tim." Charity said it flatly. "I might have, I think I would have, if he hadn't refused to have me, thinking I was doing it out of pity.

We were afraid for him, all of us, afraid he'd go mad and destroy himself. I felt I had to help him, if I could. The fact that I didn't, and that he disappeared the next day and went back to the Army, has nothing to do with it. I still might have, Charles, if he'd wanted me, even though I loved you and no one else. I never dreamed you'd actually want me to marry you, and he needed someone so desperately!"

Charles caught her in his arms. Her words tore at him, but he knew they meant nothing at all. Give herself? Hadn't she done that same thing, for him, one night when he too had been at the end of his endurance, when he'd despaired that life would ever be worth living again? That was what Charity was all about, giving of herself, with no thought for herself but only for the one who needed her. It had nothing to do with being a loose woman, or with sin. There would never be another Tim in her life, once they were married. He knew that as firmly as he knew that he and she had been destined for each other.

"No, Charles, please don't, I can't bear it. . . ."

Charles kissed her words away, kissed her with a rising tide of passion that threatened to break its bonds, and finally managed to tear his mouth away from hers. How sweet her lips were, as sweet as honey, as warm as the glow in her eyes that he felt he could drown in.

He touched the streaks of wetness from her tears, her cheeks soft and satiny under his fingers. "Don't cry," he said. "It's all right now, everything is all right, we're together."

"But I love you so much. I'd have died if I'd had to leave you. I know now that I would have died."

"I know." He couldn't help it, he had to hold her close again, kiss her again, and this time it was almost their undoing. "Charity, I love you. Nothing else matters, nothing else can ever matter. If God is willing, we'll never be apart again."

He broke off, laughing a little. "Except until we're married, of course. I have to go now, but only until tomorrow. I can't trust myself, I've been away from you for too long, I've needed you too much."

"Yes, go. Go now, quickly!" Charity's voice was a gasp. "I'll be waiting, in the morning." She'd wait forever, she'd wait until the sun dimmed and the world froze over, but she wouldn't have to, she only had to wait until morning, and she'd be with him again. And again, and again, until they would be together for all of eternity and never have to say good-bye again.

It was late when Charles returned to The Temptation. No one was there except Luke and Eli. Eli had sent Patience home, with his pot boy Jamie escorting her, an hour ago.

"I was afraid you'd be closed. I only stopped by in case you were still here, to tell you the news."

"News?" Eli looked innocent. "What could have happened tonight, late as it is?"

"Charity and I are going to be married. It will be as soon as it can be arranged."

"Well, now, ain't that somethin'!"

Luke's mouth had been twitching, and now he broke into loud laughter, unable to contain himself any longer. "Eli's been checking his stock ever since you left, and making lists, to see if he has enough for a rip-snorting celebration after the wedding! I guess your news wasn't news to him, Mr. Armitage. He was bound it was going to turn out like this."

"Set," Eli invited. "I'll fetch you a flip. It ain't

so late that we can't chew the fat for a while, just like old times."

Sighing a sigh of heartfelt contentment, Charles sat down and accepted the flip, savoring it as he hadn't savored a drink for as long as he could remember. Eli was right, it was just like old times, only infinitely, indescribably better, because the old would merge with the new, which would be better than anything Charles had ever dared to dream of.